# A Christmas Gift

JENNIFER FAYE

ANNIE CLAYDON

FIONA McARTHUR

MILLS & BOON

First Published in Great Britain 2022
By Mills & Boon, an imprint of HarperCollins*Publishers* Ltd
1 London Bridge Street, London, SE1 9GF

www.harpercollins.co.uk

HarperCollins*Publishers*
1st Floor, Watermarque Building,
Ringsend Road, Dublin 4, Ireland

A CHRISTMAS GIFT © 2022 Enterprises ULC.

*Her Festive Baby Bombshell* © 2016 Jennifer F. Stroka
*Firefighter's Christmas Baby* © 2018 Annie Claydon
*Midwife's Mistletoe Baby* © 2014 Fiona McArthur

ISBN: 978-0-263-31804-3

# HER FESTIVE BABY BOMBSHELL

**JENNIFER FAYE**

For Nancy F.
To a wonderful lady that I'm honoured to know.
Thanks so much for the encouragement.

# PROLOGUE

*Lockwood International Offices, New York City*

"WHAT ARE YOU doing here?" a rich, deep voice called out from the shadows of the executive suite.

Holly Abrams froze. The breath caught in her throat. The pounding of her heart echoed in her ears. She searched the darkness for the mysterious man.

And then he stepped into the light. She immediately recognized him. It was the CEO of Lockwood International, Finn Lockwood. The air whooshed from her lungs.

This wasn't the first time their paths had crossed, but they weren't by any stretch of the imagination what you would consider friends. And he didn't sound the least bit happy to see her, but then again, why should he?

When her gaze met his, her palms grew damp. "Hi." Why did her voice have to be so soft—so seductive? She swallowed hard.

"Isn't it a bit late for you to be working?"

Overtime was nothing new to Holly. After a failed engagement, she'd sworn off men and instead focused all of her energy on her career. When she was working, she felt confident and driven.

"I...uh, have these papers for you." She held out the large manila envelope to him. "I was told you wanted this contract right away." When he went to retrieve the envelope, their fingers brushed. A jolt of awareness arched between them. The sensation zinged up her arm and settled in her chest.

"Thank you." As the seconds ticked by, he asked, "Is there something else you need?"

Need? Her gaze dipped to his lips—his very kissable lips.

She remembered their last meeting in the elevator. They'd been alone when she'd dropped a slip of paper. They'd simultaneously bent over to retrieve it, bringing their faces so close. When they'd straightened, he'd stared at her as though seeing her as a woman instead of as a paralegal in Lockwood's legal department. She knew when a man was interested in her, but when the elevator dinged and the doors slid open, the moment had passed. It had left her wondering if it'd been a product of wishful thinking on her part.

And now, before she made a further fool of herself, she needed to make a speedy exit. "I'll just let you deal with that." She turned to retrace her footsteps back to the elevator when she remembered her manners. She glanced over her shoulder. "Good night."

"Wait."

With her back to him, she inwardly groaned. Her gaze moved to the elevator at the end of the hallway. Her escape was so close and yet so far away. Suppressing a resigned sigh, she turned.

"Come with me." Without waiting for her response, he strode into his office.

What in the world did he want with her? Her black peep-toe platform pumps echoed as she crossed the marble floor. She couldn't tell which was louder, the *click-click* of her heels or the *thump-thump* of her heart. Most people didn't make her nervous, but Mr. Lockwood was the exception.

When Holly entered the spacious office, she had to admit she was awed. While he read over the document, she took in her surroundings. Behind Mr. Lockwood's desk stood a wall of windows. Being so high up, it provided the most amazing view of Manhattan. She longed to rush over and stare out at the bustling city, but she didn't dare.

The sound of a desk drawer opening distracted her. Mr. Lockwood appeared to be searching for something. While he was preoccupied, she continued her visual tour of his office. It reminded her of a museum with its impressive sculptures as well as a baseball collection ensconced in glass cases. But the bookcases spanning an entire wall were what drew her in.

She struggled not to gape at the large collection of books. He liked to read. They had that in common. She wanted to slip across the room and examine the titles, but when she glanced over at Mr. Lockwood, he pointed to one of the two chairs in front of his desk. Without a word, she complied.

"What do you think of the office?"

"It's very nice." She indicated the floor-to-ceiling bookcases. "Have you read them all?"

"I have. And what about you? Do you like to read?"

"Oh, yes." She laced her fingers together to keep from fidgeting with the hem of her skirt. "I read every chance I get."

"Is that why you're not downstairs at the company's fiftieth anniversary celebration? Would you prefer to be at home reading?"

Was this some sort of test? She hesitated. Was there a right and a wrong answer? Her clasped hands tightened as his gaze probed her. Could he tell how nervous his presence made her?

"I missed the party because I needed to finish the contract." She indicated the document on his desk. "I was just going to leave it for you before I headed home." She wasn't the only one not attending the party. What was his excuse for skipping his own celebration? "I figured you'd be at the party."

"I already made a brief appearance. No one will let their guard down around the boss so I made a quick exit, letting everyone get back to having a good time."

She could totally understand people being nervous around him. He was an intense man, who insisted on only the best from his employees. "That can't be much fun for you."

He shrugged. "I'm fine with it."

She looked at him in a new light, realizing for the first time that the privilege of working up here in this ivory tower was also a sentence of isolation. "It doesn't seem right that you're working instead of celebrating your family's accomplishments."

He shook his head. "This is the way it must be."

Well, now, that was an odd comment. It was on the tip of her tongue to question him about it, but she thought better of it. She had a feeling his pleasantness had its limitations.

Quietness settled over the room as Mr. Lockwood scanned the twenty-one-page document. Holly struggled to sit still—waiting and wondering why he wanted her to remain there. Her index finger repeatedly smoothed over the chipped nail polish on her thumb.

There was something about this man that turned her into a mass of jittery nerves. But what? It wasn't his billions or his power. It was something more intrinsic, but she couldn't quite put her finger on it.

"This exhibit isn't right." He gestured to a page in the contract. "Do you have your source material?"

"Not on me. But I double-checked everything." In actuality, she'd quadruple-checked the figures, but she didn't want to sound like she'd been trying too hard to impress him.

His brows drew together into a formidable line. "You had to have made a mistake. This doesn't make sense."

"Prove it." The words slipped past her lips before she could stop them.

Mr. Lockwood's eyes widened as though unaccustomed to being challenged. She continued to hold his gaze. She wasn't going to back down—not when the one thing she greatly valued was in question—her reputation.

"These exhibits are skewed. I'm positive of it." His eyes darkened. "I'll log in to the system and then you can show me where you pulled your numbers."

For the next hour they worked side by side, going over the figures in the exhibits. In the end the contract was wrong, but to Holly's relief, it hadn't been her fault. The numbers on one of the source files had been transposed. After printing a revised copy, Finn signed it. Holly used his personal assistant's scanner to email the contract to the designated party.

"Thanks for the assistance." Finn slipped the hard copy back into the envelope. "Sorry to take up so much of your evening and for causing you to miss dinner." He glanced at his Rolex. "We'll have to remedy that."

"That's okay. It's not a big deal."

"I insist on dinner." He stood and then moved around the desk. "You did me a big favor tonight by helping with the contract." His gaze dipped to her lips before quickly returning to her face. The corners of his mouth lifted into a sexy smile. "And I'd like to show you how thankful I am for the help with meeting that deadline."

Oh, he definitely had more than dinner on his mind. The thought sent a new wave of nervous tremors through her stomach. She glanced away. Her initial inclination was to turn him down. Her experience with men was less than impressive. But did that mean she had to live in solitude?

What was wrong with a little company? A little laughter and perhaps flirting? And maybe a little more. Her gaze met his once more. It'd all be fine as long as neither of them had any expectations. After all, it wasn't like it would ever happen again.

"Dinner sounds good."

"Great." He made a brief phone call and then turned to her. "It's all arranged. I'll just drop this envelope on Clara's desk and then we'll be off."

A little voice inside Holly said to be cautious. Finn Lockwood wasn't just any man and she knew nothing of his world. But another part of her was drawn to him like a moth to a flame—and boy, was he hot.

The sizzling tension smoldered between them as they quietly rode down in the elevator. When they stepped into the parking garage beneath the building there was a sleek black town car waiting for them. A driver immediately alighted and opened the door for them.

Holly climbed in first, followed by Finn. When he joined her, his muscular leg brushed against hers. Her stomach shivered with excitement. When their hands came to rest side by side on the leather seat, neither pulled away. It felt as though the interior of the car was statically charged. Every nerve ending tingled with anticipation.

As the car eased into the Friday evening traffic, she glanced over at Finn. She was surprised to find him staring back at her. Her heart *thump-thumped*, loud and fast.

"Where to, sir?" the driver asked.

"The penthouse." Finn's darkened gaze returned to Holly. "I thought we would dine in. Unless, of course, you have something else in mind."

She had something on her mind, but it wasn't food. Perhaps she had been spending too much time working these days because there had to be a reasonable explanation for her lack of common sense. Because all she could think about was how much she longed to press her lips to his.

# CHAPTER ONE

*Seven weeks later...*

*BAH, HUMBUG...*

Finn Lockwood didn't care if the saying was cliché. It was how he felt. Even though this was the first week after Thanksgiving, the holiday festivities were in full swing. He wanted no part of having a holly jolly Christmas. Even though he'd turned off the speakers in his office, the music still crept down the hallway, taunting him with its joyous melody.

He did his utmost to block out the mocking words. Instead, he focused on the stack of papers awaiting his signature. He was so close to being out of here—out of the office—out of New York City.

"I just love this." His longtime assistant, Clara, strode into his office with a hefty stack of papers.

"Love what? The endless phone calls and this mess of paperwork?"

"Um, no." Color filled her cheeks as she placed the papers on his desk. "I meant this song, 'Home for the Holidays.' It puts me in a warm fuzzy mood."

His pen hovered over the document as he paused to listen. The sentimental words about home and family stabbed at his scarred heart. "To each his own."

She swept her dark bobbed hair behind her ear. "Although it never feels like the holiday season until that first snowflake falls. Don't you think so?"

He frowned at her. "How long have you known me?"

"Almost eight years."

"And by now I'd have thought you'd realize I don't do holidays."

"I… I just keep hoping—"

"Don't. It's not going to happen." An awkward silence ensued as he glanced over a disbursement and then signed it.

"Oh. I almost forgot. These came for you." She handed over two tickets for the Mistletoe Ball.

He accepted the tickets. Without bothering to look at them, he slipped them in a side desk drawer with other tickets from years gone by. When he glanced back at his assistant, unspoken questions reflected in her eyes. "What?"

Clara hesitated, fidgeting with the pen in her hand. "Why do you order tickets every year but then never use them?"

"Don't you think it's a worthy cause?" When Clara nodded, he continued. "I want to do my part." His voice grew husky with emotion. "If everyone does their part, maybe they'll find a cure for leukemia. The damn disease steals lives far too soon." His hand tightened around the pen. "It leaves nothing but devastation in its wake."

Clara's eyes widened. "I… I agree. I, um, just can't afford the tickets."

Finn realized he'd said too much. No one knew he was the sole sponsor of the ball and that was the way he intended for it to remain. But he just couldn't attend—couldn't face the guilt. If it wasn't for him and his actions, his mother and father would still be alive. They'd be attending the ball each year just like they'd always done in years past.

Finn pulled open the desk drawer and removed the tickets. "Here. Take them. It'd be better if they were used rather than sitting around gathering dust."

Her gaze moved from the tickets to him. "But I couldn't. You should give them to someone else."

When she rattled off the names of people who headed up his various divisions and departments, he said, "I want you to have them."

"Thank you." She accepted the tickets with a hesitant smile.

"Now back to business. I hope this is the last of what I need to sign because we have a trip to prepare for."

"A trip? When?"

"Tomorrow morning." This wasn't the first time he'd sprung a spur-of-the-moment trip on her. "And I'll need you there—"

"But…" Clara worried her bottom lip.

"But what? Surely you can reschedule anything on my calendar for some time after the first of the year."

"It's not that."

Color stained her cheeks as she glanced down at the tickets. She remained quiet, which was so unlike her. Something was definitely amiss and he didn't like it, not one little bit. They were set to leave in the morning for his private island in the Caribbean for a secret business meeting. When it concluded, Clara would return to New York while he remained in the sun and sand until after the New Year—when life returned to normal and people were no longer gushing with the holiday spirit.

Clara's continued silence worried him. He leaned back in his chair, taking in the worry lines bracketing her eyes. "What's the problem?"

"I got engaged last night." She held up her hand. A sparkly diamond now resided on her ring finger.

"Congratulations."

"Thank you."

"I'm sure you'll have lots of planning to do after our trip—"

"Well, um…that's the thing." Her gaze dipped again. "We're eloping this weekend."

"What?" She couldn't be serious. He had everything worked out. His business associates were meeting them on his private island in two days. "You can't back out on me now."

"I'm really sorry. But Steve, my fiancé, he, um…surprised me with tickets to fly to Vegas."

Finn resisted rolling his eyes. *Could things get any worse?* His plans had already hit a major snag, prompting this emergency meeting, and now his trusted employee was running off to Vegas to get hitched by some Elvis impersonator. *This is just great!*

"You can't bail on me." He raked his fingers through his hair. "I need your assistance for this meeting. It's important."

"Oh. Um…" She wrung her hands together.

He caught the shimmer of unshed tears in Clara's eyes. This was not good—not good at all. He was so used to having Clara at his beck and call that he hadn't anticipated this scenario. He hated being put in this position—choosing between his work and his associate's happiness. There had to be a compromise.

After a bit of thought, he conceded. "If you can find a suitable replacement, you can have the time off. But it'll have to be done pronto. My meeting can't be delayed."

Clara's eyes widened. "I'll get right on it. I'll have someone by this afternoon."

She turned and rushed out the door, leaving him alone to scowl about his plans being upended. Normally he'd have insisted on being involved in the selection of a temporary PA, but these weren't normal circumstances. His private jet was already being fueled up for tomorrow's flight.

He tapped his pen repeatedly on the desk. Why did Clara have to pick now to elope? Not that he wasn't happy for her. He was. He just wasn't happy about the surprise. Okay, so he didn't like surprises and certainly not when they caused his plans to go awry.

Just like his evening with Holly. Talk about everything going sideways—in a mind-blowing way. It'd been weeks since they'd been together and he still couldn't get her out of his system. Though they'd agreed there would be no repeat of the amazing evening, he regretted letting her go more than he thought possible.

* * *

What had she been thinking?

Holly Abrams stood alone in the elevator at Lockwood International. She pressed the button for the top floor—Finn's floor. The last time she'd visited the executive suite things had spiraled totally out of control. One moment they were talking work and the next she'd been in Finn's luxury penthouse. The memory made her stomach dip.

There'd been candles, delicious food, sparkling wine and honeyed compliments. It'd been quite a heady combination. And when at last he'd pressed his lips to hers, she'd have sworn she'd fallen head over heels in love with him. It was though this thing had been building between them since they first met. Love at first sight?

She didn't believe in it. This thing, it had to be infatuation—a great big case of it. And even though they'd mutually agreed to go their separate ways, her oasis at the office had turned stressful with reminders of Finn at every turn.

The elevator dinged and the door slid open. She stepped out. Taking a deep, steadying breath, she started down the hallway toward Clara's desk—toward Finn's office. However, Clara wasn't at her desk. Holly's gaze moved to Finn's closed door. She had a moment of déjà vu and her heart raced.

The door swung open. Who was it? Finn?

And then Clara stepped into the hallway. Holly sighed. She dismissed the disappointment that assailed her as Clara headed toward her.

The young woman's eyes reflected an inner turmoil. "There you are. Thank goodness you came."

"What's the matter?"

"Everything."

"Whoa. It can't be that bad."

"You're right." The frown on Clara's face said otherwise. "I… I need to ask you for a huge favor. And I'll totally understand if you can't do it. I just don't know anyone else who can help. And this just has to work out—"

"Slow down. Tell me what it is." Holly thought of Clara as a friend ever since they met on the charity committee. The woman was always generous in word and deed.

"My boyfriend proposed last night." A smile lifted her lips as she held up her left hand.

"Wow! Congratulations! I'm so happy for you." She gave Clara a brief hug.

Clara pulled back. "Thank you. It really was a surprise. We've been together for over five years now. I'd pretty much given up on him ever proposing. Anyway the plan is we catch a plane tomorrow and elope in Vegas followed by a honeymoon in Napa Valley. I can't postpone it. I don't want him changing his mind."

"Don't worry. Everything will work out." She was happy that Clara was finally getting her happily-ever-after. Holly didn't see such a rosy future for herself, but it didn't mean she didn't believe it could happen for others. "What can I do to help?"

"I know this is a lot to ask, but I need you to fill in for me while I'm off on my honeymoon."

"What?" Clara wanted her to be Finn's assistant? No. Impossible. Finn would never agree. She must have misunderstood. "You want me to be Mr. Lockwood's assistant?"

Clara nodded. "It won't be for long."

Her friend had absolutely no idea what she was asking of her. None whatsoever. She'd given Finn her word that she'd stay clear of him just as he'd agreed to do the same for her.

Now it appeared she had to make a very difficult choice—keep her word to Finn or keep her friendship with Clara. Holly's stomach plummeted into her Louis Vuittons. She desperately wanted to do both.

But that wasn't possible.

# CHAPTER TWO

*THERE HAD TO be a way out.*

But how? Holly couldn't bear to hurt Clara's feelings. But Holly acting as Finn's assistant for even the briefest time would be at the very least awkward. It'd raise too many memories—memories best left alone.

How did she explain that this arrangement would never work? No one knew about that special evening she'd spent with Finn. And it had to remain that way.

Holly smoothed a nonexistent wrinkle from her skirt. "I can't just move up here. What about my work in the legal department?"

Clara sent her a pleading look with her eyes. "If that's all you're worried about, I worked it out with your boss. You are temporarily transferred here. But don't worry. Working for Mr. Lockwood comes with benefits."

She'd already sampled Mr. Lockwood's benefits and they were unforgettable, but she was certain that was not what Clara meant. "Did you talk this over with F...ah, Mr. Lockwood?"

Clara's eyes momentarily widened at Holly's slip of the tongue. "I did and he's on board."

He was? Really? She was running out of excuses about why this wouldn't work. But maybe this was the break she was looking for. If Finn was open to taking her on as his assistant, would it be such a stretch to think he'd consider giving her a personal referral?

It was time she left Lockwood International. And like a sign, there was an opening at another *Fortune 500* company for an assistant to the lead counsel. She'd heard about the position through a friend of a friend. But the attorney was older and wanted someone closer to his age with top qualifications.

The cards were stacked against Holly as she was in her twenties and her experience was so-so, depending on what the position required. But it would be a big boost for her and it would make it possible for her mother to make her time off permanent.

Holly had come up with one thing that just might make gaining the new position a real possibility, a letter of recommendation from Finn—a well-respected businessman. Although she hadn't quite figured out how to approach him. But then again, it appeared he'd taken that problem out of her hands.

After all, she'd only have to be his PA for one week and then he'd be on his annual holiday. She'd have the office to herself. In the meantime, it wasn't like they were going to be working in the same office. He'd be down the hall behind a closed door and she'd be out here. If he could make it work, then so could she.

"I'll do it."

Clara's face lit up like a Christmas tree. "I was hoping you'd say that. I can spend the rest of today going over current projects with you, but first let's go get you introduced to Mr. Lockwood."

On wooden legs, Holly followed Clara down the hallway. Her morning coffee sloshed in her stomach, making her nauseated. *Keep it together. Just act professional.*

Clara knocked on the door and then entered. Holly followed her inside. Her heart picked up its pace as her gaze eagerly sought him out. His hair appeared freshly trimmed. And the blue button-up accentuated his broad, muscular shoulders. Holly swallowed hard.

He glanced up from his computer monitor. Was that surprise reflected in his blue-gray eyes? It couldn't be. He'd approved this scenario. In a blink, the look was gone.

"Mr. Lockwood, I'd like to introduce Holly Abrams." Clara's voice drew Holly from her thoughts. "She's from the legal department."

"We've met." His gaze moved between the two women. "The question is what's she doing in my office?"

Clara sent him a nervous smile. "She's agreed to step up and fill in for me while I'm away on my honeymoon. Her boss in legal gave nothing but rave reviews about her."

"I see." Finn's gaze moved to Holly.

What was she missing here? Hadn't Clara said Finn had approved of this temporary assignment? She forced a smile to her lips as his intense gaze held her captive. Her heart continued to race and her palms grew damp. She should say something, but the jumbled words in her mind refused to form a cohesive sentence.

Clara spoke, breaking the mounting silence. "She'll do a really good job for you."

"I don't know about this." Finn leaned back in the black leather chair. "Why don't you give us a moment to talk?" Clara made a discreet exit. It wasn't until the door snicked shut that Finn spoke again with a serious, no-nonsense tone. "Okay, we're alone now. Please explain to me what happened to our agreement to keep clear of each other."

"Clara said that she okayed this with you. I figured if you were big enough to deal with this awkward situation for Clara's sake then so was I. After all, Clara would do most anything for anyone. And it is her wedding—"

"Enough. I get the point. But this—" he gestured back and forth between them "—it won't work."

"That's fine with me. Do you have someone else who can fill in?"

Finn cleared his throat. "No, I don't."

Holly clasped her hands together to keep from fidgeting and straightened her shoulders. "I know that we've never worked together, but I think I can do the job."

Finn leaned back in his chair and crossed his arms. "Tell me why I should give you a chance."

Holly swallowed hard, not expecting to have to interview for the position, but when she recalled the desperation in her friend's voice, she knew she couldn't let Clara down. "I'm a hard worker. I'm the first through the door in the morning and I'm the last out in the evening."

"Are you sure that's a good thing? Perhaps you just don't get your work done in a timely manner."

Her gaze narrowed. Why exactly was he giving her such a hard time? A smart retort teetered on the tip of her tongue, but she choked it back, refusing to let him provoke her. "No. I like to be punctual. I like to have the coffee brewing and a chance to take off my coat before the phone starts ringing. And I don't rush out the door at the end of the day simply because I can't. I usually have a task or two dropped on my desk by my boss as he's leaving."

Finn nodded as though her answer pleased him. "And you think you're up to the challenges of being my PA?"

"I do."

"You do realize that what happened between us is in the past. It will have no bearing on our working relationship."

"I wouldn't have it any other way."

"Good."

"Does that mean I have the position?" The breath caught in her throat as she waited for his answer.

Seconds ticked by and still he said nothing. What in the world? She thought of all the things she could say to him to sell herself, but she didn't want to look desperate because she wasn't. Oh, maybe she was just a bit. She had a plan and he played a pivotal role.

"Okay. You've convinced me. We'll do this."

The breath rushed from Holly's straining lungs. "Thank you. I'll go catch up on everything I need to know from Clara."

"Holly, remember this is strictly work."

Like she could or would forget. "I understand, Mr. Lockwood."

He frowned. "I don't think we have to be that formal. Finn will do."

"Yes, sir...erm...Finn."

This was it, she was in. She should be inwardly cheering or smiling or something. And yet she stood there transfixed by the man who danced through her dreams each night and left her longing for a glance of him each day. The truth was that she didn't know how to react. It was one of those good news–bad news scenarios.

The best thing she could do was leave. The sooner, the better. She turned for the door.

"Holly, there's one more thing." He waited until she turned around before continuing. "Make sure you aren't late tomorrow morning. Takeoff is at six a.m. sharp."

"Takeoff?"

Finn's brows scrunched together. "Clara didn't tell you?"

"Tell me what?"

"We're leaving first thing in the morning for the Caribbean. I have an extremely important meeting there."

This was not what she'd been expecting at all. How was she supposed to fly to a sunny destination spot with the sexiest guy alive—a man who could heat her blood with just a look? She inwardly groaned. She was in so much trouble here.

Not only was she nervous about being around him—about remembering their first night together in vivid detail—but she was also a nervous flier, as in white-knuckling it through turbulence. Exactly how long was a flight from New York City to the Caribbean?

No matter what, she wasn't about to back out of this arrangement. There was too much riding on it—too many people counting on her. Her mother's pale face flashed in her mind. After her mother's recent stroke, the doctor had warned that with her other medical conditions, if she didn't slow down, her health would be put at greater risk. Holly needed to do whatever she could to further her career in order to support her and her mother.

"Holly? Will that be a problem?"

His voice drew her from her frantic thoughts. "I didn't know. Where will we be staying?"

"On my private island."

Oh, boy! One private island. One sexy guy. And a whole lot of chemistry. What could possibly go wrong with this scenario?

# CHAPTER THREE

TWENTY-TWO MINUTES LATE, Holly rushed through the airport early the next morning. Her suitcase *clunk-clunked* as it rolled over the tiled floor.

She hadn't meant to stay up late the night before, talking on the phone, but it'd been a long time since she'd heard her mother so exuberant. Apparently the Sunshine State agreed with her, especially the strolls along the beach while Holly's aunt was off at her waitressing job.

When her mother mentioned returning to New York, Holly readily assured her there was no rush. At the same time, she'd made a mental note to send her aunt some more money to cover her mother's living expenses. Holly proceeded to fill her mother in on the business trip, citing her absence as another reason for her mother to remain in Florida. Her mother actually sounded relieved, confirming Holly's belief that she needed to do everything to ensure her mother didn't have to worry about money. And that hinged on impressing Finn.

But this morning, if anything could have gone wrong, it had. As late as she was, Finn would think she was incompetent or worse that she'd changed her mind and backed out without a word. And because she'd been so rattled yesterday, she'd forgotten to get his cell number.

When she finally reached the prearranged meeting spot, Finn stood there, frowning. She was breathless and feeling totally out of sorts.

His piercing gaze met hers. "I didn't think you were going to show up."

She attempted to catch her breath. "There was an accident."

Immediately his anger morphed into concern. "Are you okay?"

"It wasn't me. It was the vehicle two cars up from my cab." In that moment the horrific events played in her mind. "One second we're moving along the highway and the next a little sports car attempts to cut off a souped-up pickup truck with large knobby tires. The car swerved wildly across the lanes as tires screeched and the driver tried to regain control, but the car lifted and flipped a couple of times." Tears welled up in her eyes. "I never witnessed something so horrific. I... I don't think the driver made it."

Finn reached out to her and pulled her close. Her cheek rested against his shoulder. "Thank God you're safe."

Her emotions bubbled to the surface. The worry. The fear. The shock. She wasn't sure how much time had passed as Finn continued to hold her. Horrific scenes of the accident played in her mind, one after the other. She knew she shouldn't seek comfort in his arms. Although it was innocent enough, it wasn't part of their agreement. And yet, she didn't move.

It was only when she started to gather herself that she noticed the spicy scent of his cologne. It would be so easy to forget about their agreement and turn in his arms, claiming his very kissable lips. Every cell in her body longed to do just that. Just once more.

But she couldn't. Once would not be enough. Frustration balled up inside her. Besides, he was just being nice— a gentleman. She refused to throw herself at him and ruin everything. After all, she was out to prove to him that she was an invaluable asset in the office.

With great regret, she extricated herself from his arms, already missing the warmth of his touch. "I must be such a mess." She swiped her hands over her cheeks. "Sorry about that. I... I'm usually—"

"No apologies necessary." He waved away her words. "I'm just relieved you're safe."

The sincerity in his words had her glancing up at him. In that moment he'd reverted back to Finn Lockwood, the friendly man who'd taken her to his penthouse to thank her for her help with the contract. The man who'd spent the evening wining and dining her with some pasta he'd whipped up himself. The same man who'd entertained her with tales of hilarious fiascos at the office. The man who'd swept her off her feet.

"What are you thinking?"

His voice drew her from her thoughts. Not about to tell him the truth, she said, "That we should get moving. I've already put you behind schedule."

"You're right." He gestured for her to walk ahead of him.

Her insides shivered with nervous tension. She couldn't tell if it was from being held in Finn's arms or the thought of soaring through the air in his jet. Maybe she should mention her fear of flying to Finn. Then again, they'd already shared more than enough for now. She would just lose herself in her work. If all went well, he'd never even know of her phobia of heights.

What had he been thinking?

Finn sat across the aisle from Holly on his private jet. They were in midflight and Holly had been surprisingly quiet. It suited him just fine. He was preparing for his upcoming meeting, or he had been until thoughts of Holly infiltrated his mind. Truth be told, he hadn't been able to let go of the memories of their night together. She was amazing and so easy to be with. Most people wouldn't find that to be a problem, but he did.

He refused to let someone get close to him—he would do nothing but lead them to unhappiness. Because that was what happened to the people he cared about—he let them down. And Holly was too nice to get caught up with the likes of him.

The onboard phone buzzed. Finn took the call from the pilot. After a brief conversation, he turned to Holly, who had her window shade drawn. He presumed it was to cut down on the glare on her digital tablet. He, on the other hand, enjoyed being able to look out at the world around them. However, the overcast day hampered much of his view. "That was the captain. He said we should buckle our seat belts as we're about to hit some rough weather."

Without argument or for that matter a word, Holly did as he asked. She then returned her attention to the tablet as though she hadn't heard him. What in the world had her so absorbed?

He gave a shake of his head and turned back to his laptop. He'd been working on an agenda for his upcoming meeting, but he'd totally lost track of his line of thought. He started reading the last couple of bullet points when his attention meandered back to Holly.

Giving up on his attempt to work, Finn closed his laptop. He glanced over at her, which was a mistake. He was immediately drawn in by her natural beauty. He loved that she didn't wear heavy makeup, only a little bit to accent her own unique qualities.

There was just something so different about Holly, but he couldn't quite put his finger on exactly what made her so much more appealing than the other women who had passed through his life. Maybe it was that she was content with her life—not looking to him for a leg up in her career. Or maybe it was that she treated him like everybody else instead of trying to cater to him. Whatever it was, he was intrigued by her.

Realizing he was staring, he cleared his throat. "What are you reading?"

She glanced up as though completely lost in thought. "What did you say?"

He smiled, liking the sheepish look on her face and the touch of pink in her cheeks. "I was wondering what had you so deep in thought."

She glanced down at her tablet and then back at him. "Um, nothing."

"Must be something to have you so preoccupied."

"Just some work."

"Work? I don't recall giving you anything to do on the way to the island."

She worried her bottom lip. "I was doing a little research."

"Do tell. I'm thoroughly intrigued."

She set aside her tablet. "I downloaded some background on the businessmen that you'll be meeting with."

"Really? I thought you'd prefer to read a book."

"I like to be prepared. Clara gave me their names. I hope you don't mind."

"What else did she tell you about the meeting?"

"Nothing except that it is extremely important and top secret."

He smiled, liking that Clara had emphasized discretion. Of course, Holly would learn all about his plans soon enough. "Let me know if you uncover anything noteworthy."

"I will." She once more picked up her tablet.

Why was she working so hard on this? Surely she wasn't this thorough normally. There had to be something driving her. Was she afraid of disappointing him?

Or more likely, she was doing whatever she could to ignore him.

Just then the plane started to vibrate. Finn glanced over at Holly and noticed that she had the armrests in a death grip. "Don't worry. It's just some turbulence."

She looked at him, her eyes as big as saucers. "Maybe we should land until it passes over."

"You don't fly much, do you?"

She shook her head. "Never had much reason. Anyplace I've ever wanted to go I can get to by train or car."

"Well, relax. Turbulence is common. It's nothing to worry about."

"Easy for you to say," she said in a huff.

He suppressed a chuckle. She did have spirit. Maybe that was what he liked so much about her. Otherwise, why would he have agreed to this completely unorthodox arrangement?

Perhaps if he could get her talking, she'd temporarily forget about the turbulence. "Where are these places you visit by car or train?"

She glanced at him with an *Are you serious*? look. He continued staring at her, prompting her to talk.

"I… I don't go away often."

"But when you do travel, where do you go?"

"The ocean."

It wasn't much, but it was a start. "Which beach is your favorite?"

"Ocean City and…" The plane shook again. Her fingers tightened on the armrests. Her knuckles were white.

"I must admit I've never been to Ocean City. Is there much to do there?" When she didn't respond, he said, "Holly?"

"Um, yes. Ah, there's plenty to do along the boardwalk. But I like to take a book and sit on the beach."

"What do you read?"

"Mysteries. Some thrillers."

He continued talking books and authors with her. He found that she was truly passionate about books. As she talked about a series of suspense novels she was in the process of reading, his attention was drawn to her lips—her tempting lips. It'd be so easy to forget the reason for this trip and the fact she was helping him out.

What would she say if he were to take her in his arms and press his lips to hers?

His phone buzzed again. After a brief conversation with the pilot, he turned to Holly. "The pilot believes we're past the bad weather. You can relax. It should be smooth flying from here on out."

The tension visibly drained from her as her shoulders relaxed and her hands released the armrests. "That's good news. I guess I'm not a very good flyer."

"Oh, trust me, you're doing fine. I've experienced worse. Much worse." He inwardly shuddered, recalling a couple of experiences while flying commercial airlines.

His attention returned to his laptop. He was surprised the break had him feeling refreshed. His fingers flew over the keyboard. Some time had passed when he grew thirsty.

He got up from his seat. "Can I get you something to drink?"

"That sounds good. But I can get it."

She stood up and followed him to the front of the plane where there was a small kitchenette. "I'm surprised you don't have any staff on board."

"Staff? For just me?" He shook his head. "I don't need anyone standing around, waiting for something to do. Besides, I appreciate the time alone."

"Oh."

"Sorry. I didn't mean that the way it sounded. I'm happy having you along."

"You are?" Her eyes widened. And was that a smile playing at the corners of her lips?

"I am. You're doing me a big favor. This meeting can't be rescheduled. It's time sensitive. And I didn't want to ruin Clara's wedding."

"Seems it all worked out."

He arched a brow. "Did it? Are you really okay with being here?"

"I—"

The plane violently shuddered. Then the plane dipped. A gasp tore from Holly's lips. Her body swayed forward. He sprang into action, catching her.

"It'll be okay."

The fear in her eyes said she didn't believe him.

As the pilot guided the plane through a particularly rough patch of airspace, Finn held on to Holly, who in turn held on to him. This was the exact thing he'd told himself that wouldn't occur on this trip, but fate seemed to have other plans.

He looked down at her as she lifted her chin. Their gazes met and held. Even when the plane leveled out, he continued to hold her. The emotions reflected in her eyes were intense. Or was he reading what he wanted to see in them?

He did know one thing—having her this close was doing all sorts of crazy things to his body. He caught a whiff of her soft floral scent and inhaled deeper. The pleasing scent swept him back to that not-so-long-ago night. Maybe playing it safe was overrated.

The plane started to vibrate again. Her wide-eyed gaze reflected fear. He knew how to distract her. His head dipped. His lips swooped in, claiming hers. She didn't move at first as though surprised by his actions. But in seconds her lips moved beneath his.

Holly was amazing. He'd never met a woman who intrigued him both mentally and physically. Her lips parted and his tongue slipped inside. She tasted of mint with a hint of chocolate. A moan swelled in his throat.

His thoughts turned toward the big bed in the back of the plane. Should he even entertain such an idea? But with the heat of their kiss, it wasn't out of bounds. All he had to do was scoop her up in his arms. It wasn't like it'd be their first time. Or even their second.

There was a sound. But he brushed it off, not wanting

anything to ruin this moment. And yet there it was again. He concentrated for a second and realized it was the private line from the cockpit.

With great regret, he pulled back. "I better get that. It's the pilot."

Her lips were rosy and slightly swollen. And her eyes were slightly dilated. He'd never seen a more tempting sight. And yet his mind told him the interruption was exactly what they needed. It would give them time to come to their senses.

# CHAPTER FOUR

"This is your place?"

Holly exited the helicopter that had transported them from the airstrip on the big island to Finn's private island. The landing zone sat atop a hill. It was the only place on the small island cleared of greenery except for the white sandy beach.

Finn moved to her side. "Do you like it?"

"I do. I've only ever seen places like this on television or on the internet. I never imagined I would one day step foot in paradise."

"Paradise?"

"Yes. You don't think so?"

"I never really thought about it." He rolled her suitcase to the edge of the helipad. "I'm afraid we have to walk to the house. It isn't far."

"No worries. This jaunt is nothing compared to the hour I spend each day at the gym sweating my butt off." She pressed her lips together, realizing she'd probably shared more than he ever wanted to know about her.

When she reached for her suitcase, their fingers brushed. He looked at her. "I can take it."

She wasn't about to be treated like a helpless woman. She'd been standing on her own two feet since she was ten and her father had walked out on her and her mother. Someone had to pick up the slack. At that point in time, her mother hadn't been in any condition.

Holly's grip tightened around the handle. "I can manage."

"You do know it'll have to be carried over the rough terrain."

"Understood. I'll count it as exercise on my calorie counter."

He shook his head as he stepped back. "By the way,

there's a gym at the house. Please feel free to use it. I certainly don't make it there nearly enough."

"Thanks. I just might take you up on the offer." When he gestured for her to go ahead of him, she said, "I'd rather follow while I get my bearings."

With a shrug, he set off down the stone path surrounded by lush green foliage.

Her gaze followed him and he set a steady pace.

But it wasn't the beautiful setting that held her attention—it was Finn. His shoulders were broad and muscled, while his waist was trim without an ounce of flub. And his backside, well, it was toned. A perfect package.

"See anything in particular you like?"

Heat rushed to her cheeks. Had he just busted her checking him out? Her gaze lifted and she was relieved to see that he was still facing straight ahead. "Lots. You're so lucky to live here."

"Only part-time. When you're done working, please feel free to use all of the facilities including the pool."

He didn't have to give her any more encouragement. She had every intention of checking it all out since she would never be back here again. "I do have to admit that this does feel strange."

"How so?"

"Leaving the snow and Christmas decorations in New York and landing here where there's nothing but a warm breeze and sunshine. Do you decorate a palm tree instead of a pine tree for Christmas?"

He stopped walking and turned to her. "I don't do either. I thought Clara might have mentioned it."

"She didn't say a word."

"Long story short, I don't like Christmas." He turned and continued along the path to the house.

He didn't like Christmas? She really wanted to hear the long version of that story. Was he a real-life Grinch? Impossible. He was friendly—when he wanted to be. Social—again, when he wanted to be. So why did he hate Christmas?

Wait. Who hated Christmas? It was full of heartwarming, sentimental moments. Twinkle lights. Snowflakes. Presents. Shopping. Definitely lots of shopping. And the most delicious food.

Whatever. His reasons for not enjoying the holiday were his problem. They were certainly none of her business. But that wasn't enough to suppress her curiosity.

"Why don't you like Christmas?" she blurted out.

He stopped. His shoulders straightened. When he turned, his forehead was creased with lines and his brows were drawn together. "Does everyone have to enjoy the holidays?"

She shrugged. "I suppose not. But I'm sure they all have a reason. I was just curious about yours."

"And if I don't want to share?"

"It's your right. I just thought after we talked on the plane that we were at the stage where we shared things with each other."

"You mean you equate our talk of books to digging into my life and finding out how my mind ticks? No." He shook his head. "My personal life is off limits." His tone lacked its earlier warmness. In fact, it was distinctly cold and rumbled with agitation. "You might research prospective business associates, but I'd appreciate it if you wouldn't put my life under your microscope."

*What is he afraid I'll find?*

She gave herself a mental shake. He was right. She was treading on a subject that was none of her business. His dislike of Christmas had nothing to do with her presence on—what was the name of this island? She scanned her mind, but she didn't recall him ever mentioning it.

"What did you say the name of this island is?"

"I didn't."

Surely this wasn't another one of those subjects that was off limits. Even she couldn't be that unlucky.

As though reading her mind, he said, "It's called Lockwood Isle."

Not exactly original, but fitting. "Your own island nation."

He shrugged. "Something like that. It's a place to get away from everything."

Her phone buzzed with a new email. "Not exactly everything. I see there's internet access."

"As much as I'd like to totally escape, I do have an international company to run. I can't cut myself off completely."

Holly was relieved to know that she could keep in contact with her mother. Even though she'd made financial arrangements with her aunt for her mother to make her very first visit to Florida, she still wanted to talk with her daily. Holly needed the reassurance that there weren't any setbacks with her health.

Her gaze strayed back to her host. She might not have to worry too much about her mother right now, but she did have to worry about Finn. That kiss on the plane, it couldn't happen again. He wasn't looking for anything serious and neither was she. Her focus had to be on getting his recommendation for the new job.

Finn stopped walking. "Here we are."

She glanced up at the white house with aqua shutters. The home was raised up on what looked like stilts. Each post was thick like an enormous tree trunk. It certainly looked sturdy enough.

Still staring at the impressive structure, she asked, "Why is the house on pylons? Are there a lot of storms?"

"No. But some of them bring in a high storm surge. I like to be prepared."

She had a feeling it wasn't just storms he liked to be prepared for. He struck her as the type of man who carefully plotted out not only his business but also his whole life, avoiding as many storms as possible.

"Will this do?"

Later that afternoon Finn glanced up from his desk in his study to find Holly standing there in a white sundress, holding a file folder. The bodice hugged her generous curves and tied around her neck, leaving just enough of her cleavage to tempt and tease. He swallowed hard. He should tell her to change clothes because there was no way he could conduct business with her looking so desirable.

Instead, he said, "Thank you." He accepted the file. "By the way, don't forget to pack lots of sunscreen."

"Pack? I never unpacked." Her eyes filled with confusion. "We're leaving?"

"Yes. Tomorrow morning we're setting sail on my yacht."

"Yacht?"

"Did I forget to mention it?" When she nodded, he added, "We'll be cruising around the islands for a couple of days until my business is concluded."

"Sounds great." Her voice lacked conviction.

"Have you been sailing before?"

She hesitated. "No."

Why exactly had he brought her along on this trip? Oh, yes, because her credentials were excellent. But that was when she was in a skyscraper in New York City. She didn't seem to fare so well outside her element. But it was too late to change course now. He just had to hope for the best— definitely not his idea of a good strategy, but the only one he had at this particular moment.

"Don't worry." He hoped to ease the worry lines now marring her face. "The yacht is spacious. You'll have your own stateroom." He took a moment to clarify the importance of the meeting. "I have worked for a number of months to bring these very influential men together. Discretion is of the utmost importance."

She nodded. "I understand. I've worked in your legal department for the past five years. Everything that passed over my desk was confidential. You can count on me."

He knew that. It was one of the reasons he'd agreed to this arrangement. Now, if he could just keep his mind from straying back to her luscious lips. His gaze zeroed in on them. They were painted up in a deep wine color. It was different from her usual earthy tones. But it was a good look on her.

He forced his mind back to business. "Did you reply to all of the outstanding emails?"

"I just finished them. The personal ones I've forwarded to your account as directed. I thought you might have some last-minute items you need completed before the meeting."

She was good. Really good. Normally that would be awesome, but when he was trying to keep her busy to avoid temptation, he wished she wasn't quite so competent.

"Have you returned all of the phone calls?"

She nodded. "I even called my mother."

"Your mother?"

"I just wanted to let her know that we arrived safely. She's actually off on her own holiday."

Was Holly attempting to make small talk? Boy, was he out of practice. He wasn't even sure how to respond. "That's good." He was better off sticking to business. "It sounds like you have everything under control. You can take the rest of the day off. We'll head out this evening as soon as all of our guests have arrived. Why don't you take a book and relax by the pool until then."

"I didn't bring a book. I didn't see a need since I planned to be working."

"But not from the time you woke up until you went to bed."

"You mean like you're doing?"

He glanced down at the papers littering his desk. "Guilty

as charged. But you don't want to end up like me. You're young and have so much to look forward to."

"You make it sound like you're old and your life is almost over."

"My life is Lockwood International. It's the reason I get out of bed in the morning."

"I'm sorry."

"Sorry? Sorry for what?"

"That you think that's all you have to live for."

"It's the way it has to be."

The pity reflected in her eyes had him recoiling. He didn't deserve pity or sympathy. She had no idea about his life—none whatsoever. Not even the press knew the entire truth.

Living and breathing everything about Lockwood International was his punishment. He'd lived while the rest of his family had perished. It was what his aunt had told him quite frequently when he rebelled about doing his schoolwork or having to stay in boarding schools. She told him he had no room to complain. He had lived while the others had died a painful death, and then she'd glare at him like it was all his fault. And for the most part, she was right.

Holly moved to the window. "Have you looked around this place? It's amazing. When's the last time you enjoyed it?"

"I don't have time for fun."

"Everyone needs to loosen up now and then. You don't want your guests showing up and finding that scowl on your face, do you?"

What scowl? He resisted the urge to run his hands over his face.

"I don't scowl." Her eyes widened at the grouchy tone of his voice. What was it about this woman that got under his skin? "I just need to stay on track and focus."

"Then I won't distract you any longer." She turned to the door.

She'd only tried to get him to relax, and yet he'd made her feel awkward. "Holly, wait." When she hesitated, he added, "I've been working so hard to pretend nothing happened between us that I've made matters worse. That was never my intention."

She turned. "Is it that hard to forget?"

"You know it is." His mind spiraled back to the kiss they'd shared on the plane. "But we can't go back there. It was a mistake the first time. And now that the fate of this project rests on how well you and I work together, we can't get distracted."

"I understand. I'll let you get back to work."

After Holly was gone, his concentration was severely lacking. He kept going over their conversation. Was his mood really that transparent? Usually business provided him solace from all that he'd done wrong in life and all that his life was lacking, but he couldn't find that escape anymore. He wondered if he'd done things differently, how his life would have turned out.

His chair scraped over the floor as he got to his feet. There was no point in staring blindly at the monitor. He wasn't going to get any more work done—at least not now. Maybe Holly was right. He should take a break. A run along the beach would be nice.

After changing his clothes, Finn stepped onto the patio. The splash of water drew his attention. He came to a complete halt as he watched Holly swim the length of the pool. He'd had no idea that she had taken him up on his suggestion that she go for a swim. He quietly watched, impressed with the ease of her strokes as she crossed the pool.

If he was smart, he'd head back inside before she noticed him. But his feet wouldn't cooperate. Sometimes being smart was overrated.

When she reached the edge of the pool, she stopped and

straightened. That was when he noticed her barely there turquoise bikini. The breath caught in his throat.

"Oh, hi." Droplets of water shimmered on her body as she smiled up at him. "Did you change your mind about unwinding?"

He struggled to keep his gaze on her face instead of admiring the way her swimsuit accented her curves. He made a point now of meeting her gaze. "I was going to take a run on the beach."

"In this heat?" When he shrugged, she added, "You'd be better off waiting until later when it cools down."

She was right, but he couldn't bring himself to admit it. "I'll be fine."

"Why don't you come swimming instead? The water is perfect."

He moved to the edge of the pool and crouched down. He dipped his hand in the water. She was right. The water was not too cold and not too warm. "I don't want to bother you."

"You won't be. The pool is plenty big for the both of us."

He had his doubts about the pool being big enough for him to keep his hands to himself. And with Holly in that swimsuit, he'd be so tempted to forget that they'd come to the island to work.

Finn raked his fingers through his hair. "I don't know. I really should be working."

"Your problem is that you think about work too much."

And then without warning, she swiped her arm along the top of the water, sending a small wave in his direction. By the time he figured out what she was up to, he was doused in water.

"Hey!" He stood upright and swiped the water from his face. "What was that all about?"

Her eyes twinkled with mischievousness. "Now you don't have an excuse not to join me."

Why was he letting his worries get the best of him and

missing out on this rare opportunity to have some fun? After all, it was just a swim.

"Okay. You win." He stripped off his T-shirt and tossed it on one of the lounge chairs.

He dove into the pool, enjoying the feel of the cool water against his heated body. He swam the length of the pool before returning to Holly. She was still smiling as she floated in the water.

"Not too bad for an old man—"

"Old man. I'll show you who's old. Let's race."

She eyed him up but didn't say a word.

"What's the matter?" he asked. "Afraid of the challenge."

"No. I'm just wondering if an old man like you can keep up with me."

"Seriously? You have to race me now."

She flashed him a teasing grin. "First one back gets their wish."

Without waiting for him, she took off. He smiled and shook his head. And then he set off in her wake. His muscles knew the motions by heart. He'd swam this pool countless times over the years, but this time was different. This time he wasn't alone.

He pushed himself harder. He reached the end of the pool and turned. He wanted to win. Not because he wanted to be the best. And not because he couldn't be a good loser. No. He wanted to win because the winner could name their wish.

And his wish—

His hand struck the end of the pool. His head bobbed above the water. A second later Holly joined him.

"About time you got here," he teased.

She sent him a cheesy grin before sending another splash of water in his direction. He backed away, avoiding most of the spray.

Holly was about to swim away when he said, "Not so fast. I won."

"And?"

"And I get my wish." He moved closer to her.

She didn't back away. It was as though she knew what he wanted. Was he that obvious?

Her voice grew softer. "And what did you have in mind?"

His gaze dipped to her lips. It seemed like forever since he last felt her kiss. There was something about her that got into his veins and made him crave her with every fiber of his being.

His gaze rose and met hers. His heart hammered against his ribs. Was she as turned on as he was? There was only one way to find out.

He reached out to her. Her skin was covered with goose bumps. He knew how to warm her up. His fingers slid over her narrow waist.

He'd never wanted anyone as much as Holly. And she was the last person he should desire. She was a serious kind of girl—the kind who didn't get around.

She was the type of woman you married.

The thought struck him like a lightning rod. As though she'd also had a moment of clarity, they both pulled back. Talk about an awkward moment.

"I…ah, should get back to work." Holly headed for the pool steps.

It was best that he didn't follow her, not right now. "I'll be in shortly. I think I'll swim a few more laps."

Finn groaned before setting off beneath the cool water, hoping to work Holly out of his system. He was beginning to wonder if that was even possible. He kicked harder and faster.

The one thing he knew was that he wasn't falling for Holly. No way. He didn't have room in his life for that major complication.

# CHAPTER FIVE

*ONE POUNDING HEART pressed to the other. Heated gazes locked. Lips a breath apart.*

Holly gave herself a mental jerk. Not even a night's sleep had lessened the intensity of that moment in the pool with Finn. Oh, how she'd wanted to feel his touch again.

But then she'd spotted the passion in his eyes. One kiss wouldn't have been enough—for either of them. The acknowledgment of just how deep this attraction ran had startled her. She'd pulled back at the same time as Finn.

Now aboard Finn's luxury yacht, the *Rose Marie*, Holly took a seat off to the side of the room as the meeting commenced. With a handful of notable and influential businessmen in attendance, she couldn't let herself dwell on the almost-kiss. As each man took a seat at the long teakwood table, she quietly observed. Her job was to step in only when needed. Other than that, she was to remain virtually invisible on the sidelines.

*So this is the hush-hush, wink-wink meeting.*

A small smile pulled at Holly's lips as she glanced around the room. Finn sat at the head of the table in a white polo shirt and khaki shorts. A very different appearance from what she was accustomed to seeing on those rare times when she caught a glimpse of him at the office.

On either side of the table sat four men. Mr. Wallace, Mr. Santos, Mr. McMurray and Mr. Caruso. All influential men in their own rights—from toys to office supplies, electronics and snack foods. No wonder there were bodyguards littering the upper deck.

"Welcome." Finn began the meeting. "I've invited you all here in hopes that we will be able to rescue Project Santa."

He'd given her the information about this holiday project just before the meeting. He made it perfectly clear that it was not to be leaked to anyone for any reason. What took place on this boat was to remain top secret for now.

Talk about surprised.

Holly stared at Finn as though seeing him for the first time. He was a man known for his shrewd business dealings, not his philanthropy. And here she thought this meeting was about conquering the world—about a major corporate take-over. She couldn't have been more wrong.

Finn and his cohorts were planning a way to bring Christmas to many underprivileged children. If it worked, it would be the beginning of an ongoing project aimed at putting food and educational materials in the hands of children.

Holly was truly in awe of Finn. He was such a contradiction at times. He worked long, hard hours, but he didn't expect his employees to do the same. He didn't celebrate Christmas, yet he planned Project Santa. At the office, he was all about profits and yet here he was planning to donate a portion of those profits to people in need.

For a man who hated Christmas, he certainly was doing a fine job of filling the boots of Santa this year. And she was more than willing to help him pull off this Christmas miracle. Although it was odd to have all of this talk about Christmas and presents surrounded by sunshine and the blue waters of the Caribbean.

Holly redirected her attention to the meeting, taking notes on her laptop and pulling up information as needed. She was tasked with running interference when tempers soared. Each of these men were billionaires and used to getting their own way, so compromise was not something they entertained often.

Some wanted to switch the Project Santa packaging to gift bags to cut costs. Others wanted to make the content more meaningful—something that wouldn't just entertain but help the recipient.

"Gentlemen." Finn's face was creased with stress lines. "This was all decided long ago. It's too late to change our plans. The gift boxes are strategically packed according to the location of each child."

Mr. McMurray leaned forward. "And how do we know these packages will get to the children?"

"Yeah, I've heard that a lot of these outreach programs are fronts for scams." Mr. Caruso, a gray-haired man, crossed his arms. "What if they steal them?"

"I hear your concerns. That's why some of my best Lockwood employees will escort each shipment to their destination. They are each tasked with making sure the packages get to their intended targets."

There was a murmur of voices. Holly noticed that Finn wasn't happy with the distractions, but he patiently let the men voice their concerns before they moved on to the reason for this meeting.

"Gentlemen, we need to address the problem we have with the lack of transportation now that Fred has suddenly pulled out."

Thanks to her research, Holly knew Fred Silver owned a delivery company that spanned the globe. As she listened to the men, she learned a federal raid on a number of Fred's distribution centers put his whole company in peril. It seemed Fred didn't have enough controls in place and the cartel got a foothold in his distribution routes. What a mess.

"Without Fred, I don't see how it's possible to complete Project Santa." Mr. Wallace shook his bald head in defeat.

"I agree." Mr. McMurray leaned back in his chair. "It's already December. It's too late to fix this."

The other men nodded in agreement.

Mr. Caruso stared at Finn. "But we still have all of the

books, toys and whatnot already allocated to this project. What do we do with it all?"

The men started talking at once. Voices were raised as each tried to talk over the other. Holly found it amusing that these men, who were well-respected in their own worlds, had a tough time playing nice with their peers. Each thought they had the right answer. And none wanted to stop and consider the other's perspective.

"Gentlemen!" Finn leaned forward, resting his elbows on the table. A hush fell over the room. "I think we need some coffee."

Finn glanced at Holly, prompting her into motion. She moved to grab the coffeepot with one hand and in the other she picked up a tray of pastries. As she headed for the table, each man settled back in their chair as though gathering their thoughts.

Holly pasted on her best and brightest smile. "Mr. Wallace, can I get you some coffee?"

The deep-set frown melted from the man's face and in its place was the beginning of a smile. "Why, yes, coffee sounds good."

She turned the coffee cup upright on the saucer and started to fill it. "I think what you all have come together to do is amazing. Project Santa will give hope to so many children." And then she had an idea. "And it will be such great publicity for your companies."

"Publicity." Mr. Wallace shook his head. "There's to be no publicity. Is that what Finn told you?"

"No, he didn't. I just presumed—obviously incorrectly." She was utterly confused. She'd missed something along the way. "Why then are all of you working so hard on this project when you each have global companies to tend to?"

They leaned back in their chairs as though contemplating her question. That was exactly what she was hoping would happen—that they'd remember why they were here and not give up. In the meantime, she served coffee for everyone.

"Finn should have told you." Mr. Santos reached for the creamer in the center of the table. "We each have so much that we wanted to do something to help those who have had a rough start in life. And with this being the season of giving, Finn came up with this idea. If we can make it work, it might be the beginning of something bigger."

"That sounds fantastic." Holly smiled, hoping to project her enthusiasm. "Too bad you can't make it work—you know, now that Mr. Silver isn't able to participate. I'm sure it's too big of a problem for you men to work around at this late date. Those poor children."

She turned to Finn, whose eyes widened. Oh, no. Had she gone too far? She'd merely wanted to remind these powerful men that they'd overcome greater obstacles in order to make their respective companies household names. If they really put their heads together and pulled in their resources, she was certain they could overcome this issue.

"She's right." Finn's voice commanded everyone's attention. "We can't stop now."

Tensions quickly rose as each powerful man became vocal about their approach to overcome these last hurdles and make the project a go. But this time they were pausing to hear each other out. And at times, building on each other's ideas.

Finn mouthed, "Thank you."

It wasn't exactly the use of her mind that she'd prefer, but the more she heard about this project, the more she believed in it—the more she believed in Finn. He was nothing like his ruthless businessman persona that was portrayed by the press. Why didn't he show the world this gentle, caring side of himself?

After spending hours to resolve the transportation problem with Project Santa, they were still no closer than they had been that morning.

Finn had just showered and changed into slacks and a dress shirt before meeting up with his associates for a card game. This trip wasn't all business. He'd learned long ago that keeping his allies happy was just as important as presenting them with a profitable deal.

He'd just stepped out of his cabin and glanced up to find Holly coming toward him. Her hair was wet and combed back. She looked refreshed and very tempting. His gaze dipped, finding she was wearing a white bikini. She must have been unwinding in the hot tub. He swallowed hard. *Look away. Concentrate on her face.*

Finn met her amused gaze. "Thank you."

"For what?" She adjusted a white towel around her slender waist.

His mouth grew dry. "For your help at the meeting. You were a big help getting everyone to work together."

"I'm glad I could help."

And then realizing they were talking in the hallway where anyone might overhear, he opened his cabin door. "But the distribution is more than we can overcome at this late date."

Holly didn't move. "Actually, I have some thoughts about your problem with the distribution. I don't think it's insurmountable."

He worried that she was a bit too confident. This was a national endeavor—coast to coast. But he had to admit he was intrigued. "Why don't you step in here a moment?"

Her hesitant gaze moved from him to the interior of his stateroom and then back to him. "I really shouldn't. I'm still wet."

"I promise I won't keep you for long. In fact, I'm due at a card game in a couple of minutes."

She noticeably relaxed. Without another word, she passed by him and entered the room. His heart thumped as he contemplated reaching out and pulling her close. What was it about her that had such a hold over him?

She turned as he pushed the door closed. She averted her gaze as her hands wrung together. Was she aware of the energy arching between them? Could she feel his draw to her? Was she as uncertain as he was about what to do about it?

"I don't think I told you, but your boat is amazing." She looked everywhere but at him. "I had no idea they were so elaborate."

"I'm glad you like your accommodations. I take it you enjoy sailing more than you do flying?"

"Definitely. I don't have to worry about falling out of the sky and—"

"No, you don't," he said, not wanting her to finish that graphic image. "If there's anything you want but can't find, just let me know."

"You know if you keep this up, you'll ruin your image."

"My image?"

At last, her gaze met his. "The one of you being a heartless corporate raider."

He pressed a hand to his chest. "I'm wounded. Do you really believe those nasty rumors?"

"Not anymore. I've seen the part you hide from the outside world." Her voice took on a sultry tone as her gaze dipped to his mouth. "Why do you do that?"

He swallowed hard, losing track of the conversation. "Do what?"

"Hide behind your villainous persona when in reality you're not like that at all."

His gaze shifted to her rosy lips. "How am I?"

"You're tough and hard on the outside, but inside…" She stepped closer, pressing a hand to his chest. "In there where it matters, you have a big heart."

"No one ever said that before."

Her hand remained on his chest as though branding him as hers and hers alone. "They just don't know you like I do."

His heart pounded against his ribs. "And do you like what you've gotten to know?"

"Most definitely."

His hand covered hers. "You do know if you don't leave right now that I'm not responsible for what happens next."

"But what about your guests?"

"They're involved in a card game."

"Oh, yes, the card game. You don't want to miss it."

By now she had to be able to feel the rapid beating of his heart. "I don't think they'll miss me."

"Are you sure?"

He nodded, not caring if they did. There was nowhere else he wanted to be at this moment. "Are you sure about this? You and me?"

"I'm sure that I want you to kiss me."

"Holly, I'm serious."

"I am, too. You do still want me, don't you?"

He groaned. "You know that I do."

His hands wrapped around her shapely hips and pulled her to him. In the process her towel came undone, pooling at her feet. He continued to stare into her eyes, watching to see if she'd change her mind, but he only found raw desire reflected in them.

She lifted up on her tiptoes and he didn't waste a moment claiming her lips. He was beginning to think he'd never tire of kissing her. The thought should worry him, but right now he had other things on his mind—things that were drowning out any common sense.

As their kiss deepened, so did his desires. Once was definitely not enough with Holly. Her beauty started on the inside and worked its way out. If he were to ever entertain the idea of getting serious with someone, it would be her.

Her fingers slid up his neck and combed through his hair. Her curves leaned into him, causing a moan to form in the back of his throat. Perhaps they could be friends with benefits. There wouldn't be any harm in that, would there?

He clearly recalled when things ended between them that Holly had said she didn't want anything serious. In fact, she was the first one to say there couldn't be anything more between them. For a moment he'd been floored and then relieved.

Now as her lips moved passionately over his, he wondered what he'd been thinking by letting her walk away. They had so much to offer each other with no strings attached.

But first he had to be sure Holly was still on board with the idea. He just couldn't have her expecting some sort of commitment from him because in the end, he'd wind up letting her down.

He grudgingly pulled back. Cupping her face in his hands, he gazed deep into her eyes. "Holly, are you sure about this?"

She nodded.

"Even though it'll never lead to anything serious?"

Again she nodded. "I told you I don't do serious."

A smile tugged at his lips. How could someone be as perfect as her? The thought got shoved to the back of his mind as she reached up and pulled his head down to meet her lips. This was going to be a night neither of them would forget—

*Knock-knock.*

"Hey, Finn, you coming?" Mr. Caruso's jovial voice came through the door. "Everyone's anxious to get the game started."

Holly and Finn jumped apart as though they were teenagers having been caught making out beneath the bleachers. She looked at the door and then him. Her lips lifted into a smile before she started to laugh. Finn frowned at her. She pressed a hand to her lips, stifling the stream of giggles.

"I'll be right with you." Finn ran a hand over his mouth,

making sure there were no lingering signs of lip gloss. And then he finger-combed his hair.

Holly gestured that she would wait in the bathroom. He expelled a sigh of relief. He really didn't want to have to explain what she was doing in his room scantily dressed in that tempting bikini.

With Holly out of sight and his clothes straightened, he opened the door. "Sorry I'm running late. I had something come up at the last minute. You know how it is."

The man clapped him on the shoulder. "You work too hard. Come on. The guys are waiting."

"I don't think so. I really need to finish this—"

"Work can wait, your guests can't." Mr. Caruso reached out, grabbed his arm and pulled him into the hallway. "After all, you're the host."

Finn glanced back in his suite longingly, knowing the exquisite night he'd be missing. Playing cards had never looked so dull and tedious before.

"You coming?"

With a sigh, Finn pulled the door shut. "Sure. The work can wait till later."

"Try the morning. I have a feeling this game is going to last most of the night. Should we invite your assistant?"

"I passed her in the hallway earlier. Holly—um, Ms. Abrams called it a night already."

"That's too bad. I like her."

He liked her, too—perhaps far more than was wise. Or perhaps he was blowing everything out of proportion since it'd been a while since he'd been dating. In fact, he hadn't dated anyone since his evening with Holly. No other woman had even tempted him after her. He wasn't sure what to make of that.

# CHAPTER SIX

THE NEXT MORNING Holly awoke late. But she didn't feel too guilty. It was work that had her burning the midnight oil—not Finn.

She ran her fingers over her lips, recalling Finn's kiss before he'd left her for the card game. If there hadn't been a knock at his door, she knew where things would have led. Part of her knew it was for the best, but another part ached for the missed opportunity.

What was wrong with her? Why couldn't she be immune to his charms? It was like once his lips touched hers any logic disengaged and her impulses took over. She wondered if he had this effect over all women or just her.

She knew this thing between them couldn't go anywhere. Her experience with men should be proof enough. First, her father walked out on her and her mother. And then while she was earning her paralegal degree, she'd met Josh. He was good-looking and charming. Deciding all men couldn't be like her father, she let herself fall for him.

Holly felt ill as the memories washed over her. Everything between her and Josh had been great for a while. In fact, it was the happiest she'd ever been. And then she'd learned Josh had a gambling problem that led to him stealing from her—the person he was supposed to love. She'd arranged to get him help and he'd sworn he would complete the twelve-step program.

She'd wanted to believe him, but after what her father had done to her mother, Holly had to be sure. And that was when she'd caught Josh in a web of lies with another woman. Holly's stomach soured at the memory.

The depth of his betrayal had cut her deep. After Josh,

she'd sworn off relationships. Her independence gave her a much-needed sense of security. And with her full attention focused on her work, she didn't have time to be lonely. Guys just weren't worth the heartache. And she'd stuck by her pledge until now. Finn had her questioning everything—

*Knock-knock-knock.*

She had a feeling there'd only be one person who'd come calling at her door this early in the morning. Still, she asked, "Who is it?"

"It's me." The voice was very distinct. "Finn."

"Hang on." She scrambled out of bed and rushed to grab her robe. It was then that she noticed her stomach didn't feel right. It was way more than being upset about the unpleasant memories. She took a calming breath, willing the queasiness away.

She moved to the door and pulled it open. Finn stood there freshly showered and shaved, looking like he was ready to tackle the world. "Good morning."

His gaze narrowed in on her. "Everything okay?"

She ran a hand over her hair. "Sorry. I slept in." Her stomach lurched. She pressed a hand to her midsection, willing it to stop. "I'll, ah, take a quick shower and be right with you."

"You know, you don't look so good."

Right then her stomach totally revolted. She dashed to the bathroom. Thankfully her cabin wasn't that big. She was quite certain she wouldn't have made it another step. She dropped to her knees, sick as a dog. What in the world? She hadn't even eaten that morning.

Once her stomach calmed, she heard the sink turn on. Finn? He was here? He'd witnessed her at her worst. She would have groaned, but she feared doing anything that might upset her stomach again.

"Here. Take this." He handed her a cold cloth.

"You shouldn't be here."

"And leave you alone when you obviously don't feel well?"

No matter what she said, he wasn't leaving. And at that moment she didn't have the energy to argue. Once she'd cleaned up, she walked back to the bedroom. Her stomach wasn't totally right, but it did feel somewhat better.

"I'm sorry about that." Her gaze didn't fully meet his. "You...you were quite the gentleman. Thank you."

"Do you know what's bothering you? Is it something you ate?"

"I think it's seasickness."

"I'm sure it doesn't help that we hit some rough water this morning. Are you sure that's all it is?"

She nodded, certain it had to be the constant roll of the boat.

"You should lie down."

"I don't have time."

"Sure you do." He guided her back to the king-size bed. "Stay here. I'll be right back."

She did as he asked, hoping she'd soon feel like herself. He disappeared out the door like a man on a mission. As she lay there, her mind strayed to her plan for Project Santa. Perhaps she should run it by Finn first. She didn't want to do anything to embarrass either of them in front of those powerful men.

A few minutes later Finn came rushing back into the room. "How are you feeling now?"

"Better." It wasn't a lie.

"I grabbed some ginger ale and toast. Hopefully you'll be able to keep that down. And I grabbed some medicine for the motion sickness."

"Thank you." She sat up in bed and accepted the glass of soda. She tentatively took a sip, not sure what to expect when it hit her stomach. Thankfully, it remained calm.

"I also talked with the captain and he's set course for what he hopes is smoother water."

Finn was changing his trip just for her? She didn't know what to think, except that Finn was a lot more Santa-like than Grinchy.

She took another drink of the soda. So far, so good. Anxious to get on with her day, she got to her feet. She glanced over to find Finn staring at her. "What?"

"The look on your face. Something is bothering you. Is it your stomach again?"

She shook her head. "I told you I'm feeling better."

He sighed. "You're sure? You're not just telling me this to get rid of me?"

"I'm certain. I'll just get showered and be up to the meeting soon."

"I could use your help, but I don't want you pushing yourself." His gaze searched her face and then he moved to the door. "I should be going."

"Finn?"

"Yes."

"There is something I wanted to talk to you about."

His brow arched. "Is it about your health?"

"No. It's nothing like that. It's just an idea I wanted to run past you."

He glanced at his Rolex. "I'd be happy to hear you out, but not right now. I'm late." He opened the door. "I'll see you on deck." He rushed out the door.

"But—"

The door closed. Her words had been cut off. A frown pulled at her lips. She knew how to help him with Project Santa if he'd just slow down and listen to her. She refused to give up now. There had to be a way to get his attention.

Had he made a mistake?

Finn sat uncomfortably at the end of the table, knowing

if they didn't come up with a reasonable resolution to their transportation problem today that they would have to cut their losses and scrap the idea of Project Santa. The thought deeply troubled him.

He glanced at his watch for the third time in ten minutes. Where was Holly? Had she been struck with another bout of sickness?

"Listen, I know we need a solution regarding transportation, but all of my rigs are booked from now until Christmas, delivering our toys to stores." Mr. Wallace tapped his pen on the blank legal pad. "Besides, this wasn't my part of the arrangement. It's not my fault Fred wasn't on top of his business dealings and got in bed with the cartel."

Mr. Caruso sighed. "I couldn't possibly reroute all of my snack food shipments. It'd be a logistic disaster. And it would only cover the east coast. What about the children west of the Mississippi?"

All eyes turned to Mr. Santos. The guy shook his head. "I'm in the same boat. My network is on the east coast. And I have no transportation."

That left one man who hadn't spoken up, Mr. McMurray. He cleared his throat, visibly uncomfortable being in the hot seat. "And what makes you all think I can pull this off when none of you can?"

Immediately everyone spoke at once, defending why they couldn't take over the shipping part of the plan. Finn sat back quietly wondering why he ever thought they'd be able to pull off such a big project. It dashed his hopes for future projects of this scale.

At that moment Holly walked into the room. A hush fell over the men and Finn knew why. She looked like a knockout. She wore an aqua, sleeveless sundress. Her golden-brown hair had been piled on top of her head while corkscrew curls framed her face. She wore a little makeup, but definitely on the conservative side. If he hadn't known that she was feeling under the weather earlier, he wouldn't have been able to guess it by looking at her.

"Good morning, gentlemen. I'm sorry to be late. But I promise I was hard at work."

The tension around the table evaporated, replaced with smiles and warm greetings. Finn shook his head in disbelief. Who'd have thought a bunch of workaholics could be so easily swayed by a pretty face and long, toned legs?

"Don't let me interrupt your discussion." Holly moved to the chair she'd sat in the day before.

Mr. Wallace grunted. "You didn't interrupt much. Everyone was just making excuses about why they couldn't take on the shipping portion of Project Santa. We could use a fresh perspective. Do you have any thoughts on the matter?"

"Actually, I do. First, I want to say I'm very impressed with the endeavor you all are undertaking." She made a point of making eye contact with each man. "And if you would indulge me, I might have a suggestion about the transportation problem."

"Holly." The room grew silent. Finn had to give her a chance to gracefully bow out. "Perhaps I didn't make clear the enormity of this project. The gifts will need to be delivered from coast to coast in every town or city where our companies have a presence."

She nodded as her steady gaze met his. "I understood." She leveled her shoulders. "From what I understand, you have a master list of names and locations for the gifts. You also have all of the items sorted and boxed. All you're lacking is a delivery system."

Finn noticed a couple of the men had started to fidget with their cell phones. They didn't have faith in Holly's ability to overcome such a large obstacle. He had to admit he didn't know what she could do that they hadn't already considered.

"That would be correct." Finn really wanted to know where she was headed. He didn't like surprises. "We have a sorting facility in St. Louis. From there the packages need to be distributed to numerous cities."

"And if I understand correctly, you were planning to do this by way of long-haul trucks."

"Yes, until Fred's company was seized by the government. There's no way he'll be able to unravel that ugly mess in time to help us. So do you have a lead on some other trucking firm?"

She shook her head. "My idea is a little different. I started to think about all of the modes of transport. And then I started to think about who I knew in the transportation industry. And I realized my neighbor in New York is a pilot."

Finn cleared his throat. "So you're suggesting we have your friend fly all of the packages around the country."

She frowned at him. "Of course not. That wouldn't be possible considering there are thousands of packages."

"Then I'm not following what you're telling us."

"My friend is a pilot, but he's just one of many. When he's not flying commercially, he takes part in a national flying club." She glanced around the table and when no one said anything, she explained further. "This flying club has hundreds of members around the country. If we were to enlist their help, we could get the packages to their destinations."

"I don't know." Finn had to think this over. The men started chatting amongst themselves. Finn glanced up to find Holly with a determined look on her face. When she opened her mouth to elaborate, no one noticed.

Finn cleared his throat and then said loudly, "Gentlemen, shall we let Ms. Abrams finish her presentation?"

When silence fell over the room, Holly continued. "I've already put feelers out to see if there would be an interest in helping such a worthy cause, and I have close to a hundred pilots willing to fly the packages."

Finn rubbed his chin. "You trust these people? And they're going to do it out of the goodness of their hearts?"

"Yes, I trust them. And aren't you all doing this project out of the goodness of your hearts?"

One by one the men's heads nodded except Finn's. He didn't have faith in her plan. There were just too many moving parts. But he would give her credit for thinking outside the box. He was lucky to have her on staff at Lockwood.

Not about to discuss the pros and cons of her plan in front of her, Finn said, "Thank you for your input. We greatly appreciate your efforts. We'll need a little bit to discuss it. In the meantime, you could—"

"But don't you want to hear the rest of my plan?" Holly sent a pleading stare his way.

How could he say no when she turned those big brown eyes his way? He felt his resolve melting.

"Let her finish," Wallace chimed in.

The other men agreed.

Finn nodded at her to proceed.

"Getting the presents from the distribution center to the airstrip will take more transportation."

He was almost afraid to ask. "And what did you have in mind?"

"We'll go public and ask for volunteers."

"More volunteers?" He shook his head. "I don't think so."

"Listen, I know you were hoping to operate under the radar. And I know none of you are in this for the publicity, but if you would reconsider, this project might be bigger and better than before."

He wanted to put a stop to this, but he knew what it was like to be a child with no Christmas presents. Although his lack of presents had nothing to do with his parents' financial standing, it still hurt. He didn't want that to happen to other children, not if he could make a difference.

But he refused to put out a public plea asking for help. He didn't do it for the Mistletoe Ball, which meant so much to him—a continuation of his mother's work and a way to support the foundation seeking a cure to the horrible disease that stole his brother's life. Besides, he was the very last person in the country whom people would want to help. After all of the companies that he'd bought up and spun off into separate entities, causing job consolidation and ultimately downsizing, he was certain people would go out of their way to make sure he failed. He couldn't let that happen with Project Santa.

Finn met her gaze. "I'm not going to make this a publicity campaign."

"But at least hear me out."

He didn't want to. His gut told him she was about to give them a unique but tempting solution to their problem—but it would come at a steep price.

"Go ahead." Wallace spoke up. "Tell us how you would recruit these people?"

"We could start a media page on MyFace." She paused and looked around the table. "Do you know about the social networking service?"

They all nodded.

"Good. Well, it's hugely popular. With a page set up on it specifically for Project Santa, we can post updates and anything else. It even allows for spreadsheets and files. So there can be an official sign-up sheet. Or if you are worried about privacy, I could set up an online form that dumps into a private spreadsheet. In fact, last night when I couldn't sleep I started work on the graphics for the media page."

Caruso smiled at her. "You're a real go-getter. I can see why Finn scooped you up. You must make his life so easy at the office."

"Actually, he and I, well, we don't normally work together."

"Really?" Caruso turned to Finn. "What's wrong with you? How could you let this bright young lady get away from you?"

Finn kept a stony expression, not wanting any of them to get a hint that there was far more to this relationship than either of them was letting on. "I already had a fully capable assistant by the time Holly was hired. She normally works in the legal department, but with my assistant eloping, Holly agreed to fill in."

"And she's done an excellent job with her research." Caruso turned a smile to Holly.

"Yes, she has," Mr. McMurray agreed. "It isn't exactly the most straightforward option, but it definitely deserves further investigation."

Finn was proud that she'd taken the initiative, but he was not expecting the next words out of his mouth. "And we need to give her presentation some serious consideration."

"Agreed." The word echoed around the table.

Holly's hesitant smile broadened into a full-fledged smile that lit up her eyes. "Thank you all for listening to me." Her cloaked gaze met Finn's. "I have work to do. I'll be in my cabin should you need me."

# CHAPTER SEVEN

WHAT HAD SHE been thinking?

Holly paced in her cabin, going over the meeting in her mind—more specifically the deepening frown on Finn's face as she'd presented her idea to distribute the gifts. Why had she even bothered? It wasn't like it was part of her job duties—far from it. But there was something about Project Santa that drew her in. She'd wanted to help.

And now she'd made a mess of things. Having Finn upset with her would not help her get the personal recommendation she needed to land the new job and get her the big pay increase she needed to secure her mother's early retirement.

She should have kept the ideas to herself. When would she ever learn? When it came to Finn, she found herself acting first and thinking later. Just like that kiss in his cabin. If they hadn't been interrupted, she knew there would have been no stopping them. Her logic and sanity had gotten lost in the steamy heat of the moment.

Going forward, she would be the perfect employee and that included keeping her hands to herself. She glanced down, realizing she'd been wringing her hands together. She groaned.

She knew Finn was going to shoot down her proposal. His disapproval had been written all over his face. She didn't understand his reaction. It wasn't like he had a better suggestion. No matter what Finn said, she still believed in her grass-roots approach.

*Knock-knock.*

For a moment she considered ignoring it. She wasn't in any state of mind to deal with Finn. She didn't think it was possible to paste on a smile right now and act like the perfect, obedient assistant. And that would be detrimental to her ultimate goal—leaving Lockwood—leaving Finn.

*Knock-knock.*

"Holly, I know you're in there. We need to talk." Finn's tone was cool and restrained.

She hesitated. He was obviously not happy with her. And on this yacht, even though it was quite spacious, she wouldn't be able to avoid him for long. So she might as well get it over with.

She took a calming breath, choking down her frustration. On wooden legs, she moved toward the door. Her stomach felt as though a rock had settled in the bottom of it. *You can do this.*

She swung the door open. "Can I do something for you?"

"Yes. I need an explanation of what happened at the meeting." He strode past her and stopped in the middle of the room.

Was it that he didn't like her idea? Or was he upset that it had been her idea and not his? She'd heard rumors that he was a bit of a control freak.

She swallowed hard. "I presented an idea I thought would save Project Santa. What else is there to explain?"

"When did you have time to come up with this idea?"

"Last night when you were playing cards."

His gaze narrowed in on her. "You should have brought it to my attention before making the presentation." His voice rumbled as he spoke. "We should have gone over it together. I'm not accustomed to having employees take the lead on one of my projects without consulting me."

Seriously? This was the thanks she got for going above and beyond her job duties—not to mention sacrificing her sleep—all in order to help him. Maybe it was her lack of sleep or her growing hunger, but she wasn't going to stand by quietly while he railed against her efforts to help.

She straightened her shoulders and lifted her chin. "I'll

have you know that I tried to tell you about my idea this morning, but you didn't have time to listen. And something tells me that isn't what has you riled up. So what is it?"

His heated gaze met hers. "I knew this was going to be a mistake—"

"What? My plan?"

"No. Your idea has some merit. I meant us trying to work together."

"Well, don't blame me. It wasn't my idea."

He sighed. "True enough."

"Wait. Did you say my plan has merit?"

"I did, but I don't think it's feasible."

Her body stiffened as her back teeth ground together. Really? That was what he was going with? Feasible?

She pressed her lips together, holding back her frustration. After all, he was the boss—even if he was being a jerk at the moment.

"I know you're not happy about this decision, but it's a lot to ask of so many pilots, and what happens if they back out at the last minute? It would be a disaster." He glanced down at his deck shoes. "I hope you'll understand. This is just the way it has to be."

"I don't understand." The cork came off her patience and out spewed her frustration and outrage. "I have given you a cost-effective, not to mention a timely solution, to your problem and yet you find every reason it won't work. If you didn't want to go through with Project Santa, why did you start it in the first place?"

"That's not what I said." He pressed his lips into a firm line as his hand came to rest on his trim waist. When she refused to glance away—to back down, he straightened his shoulders as though ready to do battle in the boardroom. "Okay. Your idea could work, but how do you plan on getting the message out to the people about Project Santa and the MyFace page?"

"We'll need a spokesperson."

"Where will you get that?"

She stared pointedly at him. "I'm looking at him."

"Me?"

"Yes, you."

"No way."

"Why not? All you have to do is a few promo spots to secure the public's assistance. What's the problem?"

His heated gaze met hers. "Why are you pushing this?"

She implored him with her eyes to truly hear her. "Do you realize the number of children you could help with your generous gifts?" When he refused to engage, she continued. "It would give them hope for the future. It might influence the path they follow in life." And then for good measure she added, "And without your cooperation, they'll never have that chance."

"That's not fair. You can't heap all of that guilt on me."

"Who else should I blame?"

A muscle flexed in his jaw. "You know, I didn't come here to fight with you."

"Then why are you here?"

A tense moment passed before he spoke again. "I wanted to tell you how impressed everyone was with your presentation."

"Everyone but you." The words slipped past her lips before she could stop them.

"Holly, that's not true." He raked his fingers through his hair, scattering it. "You don't know how hard this is for me."

"Then why don't you tell me?"

Conflict reflected in his eyes as though he was warring with himself. "I don't want to talk about it."

"Maybe you should. Sometimes getting it all out there helps." She walked over to the couch and had a seat. She patted the cushion next to her. "It might not seem like it at this particular time, but I am a good listener."

His gaze moved from her to the couch. She didn't think

he would do it—trust her with his deeply held secret. But if it stood in the way of his helping with the publicity for Project Santa, then they needed to sort it out.

When he returned his eyes to hers, it was as though she was looking at a haunted person. She hadn't even heard his story yet and still her heart swelled with sympathy for him. Whatever it was, it was big.

"Christmas wasn't always good at our house." His voice held a broken tone to it. "I mean it was when I was little, but not later." He expelled a deep breath.

"I'm sorry for pushing you. I shouldn't have done it—"

"Don't apologize. I understand why you want Project Santa to succeed. And I want the same thing."

"Then trust me. A little publicity is all we need to gain the public's assistance."

"But it has to be without me. Trust me. I'm not the right person to be the face of a charitable event."

"I disagree."

"That's because you don't know me." Pain reflected in his eyes. "Appearances can be deceiving. I'm not the man everyone thinks I am. I'm a fraud."

"A fraud?" She instinctively moved away. "If you aren't Finn Lockwood, who are you?"

"Relax. I'm Finn Lockwood. I'm just not supposed to be the CEO of Lockwood International. I got the job by default."

She was confused. "Who is supposed to be the CEO?"

"My brother."

"Oh." She still didn't understand. "He didn't want the job?"

"He wanted it but he died."

"I'm sorry." She slipped her hand in his. "Sometimes when I have an idea, I don't back off when I should."

For a while, they just sat there in silence. Hand in hand, Holly once again rested her head on Finn's shoulder as though it was natural for them to be snuggled together. Her heart ached for all he'd endured. She felt awful that she'd pushed him to the point where he felt he had to pull the scabs off those old scars.

"You didn't do anything wrong." Finn pulled away and got to his feet. "I should be going. I just wanted you to understand why I can't be the spokesman for Project Santa."

She rolled his words around in her mind, creating a whole new set of questions. She worried her bottom lip. After everything that had been said, she realized that it was best to keep her questions to herself. Enough had been said for one evening.

Finn placed a finger beneath her chin and lifted until they were eye to eye. "What is it?"

She glanced away. "It's nothing."

"Oh, no, you don't get off that easy. What are you thinking?"

She shook her head, refusing to say anything to upset him further. She was certain if she thought about it a bit longer, she'd be able to connect the dots. It was just that right now it was all a bit fuzzy. "It's not important."

"I'm not leaving here until you talk to me. Whatever it is, I promise not to get upset with you. Because that's what you're worried about, isn't it?"

She took a deep breath, trying to figure out how to word this without aggravating him further. "I'm sure it's my fault for not understanding. If I just think it over some more, it'll probably make perfect sense."

He moved his hand from her face and took her hands in his. "Holly, you're rambling. Just spit it out."

She glanced down at their clasped hands. "It's just that I don't understand why the way you became CEO would keep you from getting personally involved with the publicity for Project Santa."

He frowned. See, she knew she should have kept her questions to herself. Clearly she hadn't been listening to him as closely as she'd thought. She prepared herself to feel silly for missing something obvious.

"I don't deserve to take credit for the project. I don't deserve people thinking I'm some sort of great guy."

Really? That was what he thought? "Of course you do. This project was your brainchild. You're the one who brought all of those businessmen together to orchestrate such a generous act. There aren't many people in this world who could have done something like this."

"I'm not a good guy. I've done things—things I'm not proud of."

"We all have. You're being too hard on yourself."

He shook his head. "I wish that was the case. Besides, I'm not even supposed to be doing any of this. This company was supposed to be handed down to Derek, not me. I'm the spare heir. Anything I do is because of my brother's death. I don't deserve any pats on the back or praise."

What in the world had happened to him? Was this some sort of survivor's guilt? That had to be it. She had no idea what it must be like to step into not one but two pairs of shoes—his father's and his brother's.

"I disagree with you."

Finn's brows drew together. "You don't get it. If it weren't for my brother dying, I wouldn't be here."

"Where would you be?"

He shrugged. "I'm not sure. After my brother died, I gave up those dreams and embraced my inevitable role as the leader of Lockwood."

"Did you want to be a policeman or a soldier?" When he shook his head, she asked, "What did you dream of doing with your life?"

"I thought about going into medicine."

"You wanted to be a doctor?"

"I wanted something behind the scenes. I was thinking about medical research. My mother was always going on about how much money her charity work raised to find cures for diseases, but it was never enough. I excelled in math and science—I thought I could make a difference."

"But don't you see? You are making a difference. You gave up your dreams in order to take over the family business, but you've made a point of funding and planning charitable causes. You are a hero, no matter what you tell yourself."

His mouth opened and then he wordlessly closed it. She could tell he was stuck for words. Was it so hard for him to imagine himself as a good guy?

She squeezed his hand. "This is your chance to live up to your dreams."

"How do you get that?"

"You can make a difference to all of those children. You can give them the Christmas you missed out on. Maybe you'll give them a chance to dream of their future. Or at the very least, give them a reason to smile."

His eyes gleamed as though he liked the idea, but then he shook his head. "I'm not hero material." And then his eyes lit up. "But you are. You could be the face of Project Santa."

"Me?" She shook her head. "No one knows me. I won't garner the attention that Finn Lockwood will." Feeling as though she was finally getting through to him, she said, "Please, Finn, trust me. This will all work out. I know you aren't comfortable with the arrangement, but do it for the kids. Be their hero."

There was hesitation written all over his face. "There's no other way?"

"None that I can think of."

The silence stretched on as though Finn was truly rolling around the idea. The longer it took, the more optimistic she became.

His gaze met hers. "Okay. Let's do this."

"Really?" She couldn't quite believe her ears. "You mean it?"

He nodded his head. "As long as the promo is minimized."

"It will be. Trust me."

He didn't look so confident, but in time he'd see that her plan would work. And then a bunch of children wouldn't feel forgotten on Christmas morning. Knowing she'd had a small part in giving them some holiday cheer would make this the best Christmas ever.

"What are you smiling about?"

She was smiling? Yes, she supposed she was. Right now she felt on top of the world. Now that she'd proven her worth to Finn, she thought of asking him for that recommendation letter, but then she decided not to ruin the moment.

"I'm just happy to be part of this meaningful project."

"So where do we begin?" Finn sent her an expectant look.

In that moment all of her excitement and anticipation knotted up with nerves. She'd talked a good game but now it was time to put it all into action. Her stomach churned. She willed it to settle—not that it had any intention of listening to her.

When she didn't say a word, Finn spoke up. "Where do we start?"

The *we* in his question struck her. They were now a team. Not allowing herself to dwell on this new bond, she asked, "What about your guests? Shouldn't you be with them?"

"McMurray said he wasn't feeling so good and went to lie down. The other guys are taking in some sun and playing cards. So I'm all yours."

She eyed him up, surprised by his roll-up-his-sleeves-and-dive-in attitude. "The first place we start is on MyFace and work on recruiting additional pilots. Do you have a My-Face account?"

"No. I'll get my laptop." He got to his feet and headed for the door. He paused in the doorway and turned back to her. "On second thought, why don't you bring your laptop and work in my suite? It's a lot bigger."

Holly paused. The last time she'd been in his room, work had been the very last thing on either of their minds. The memory of him pulling her close, of his lips moving hungrily over hers, sent her heart pounding. She vividly remembered how he'd awakened her long-neglected body. Their arms had been entangled. Their breath had intermingled. And any rational thoughts had fled the room.

"I know what you're thinking."

Heat flared in her cheeks. *Are my thoughts that transparent?*

"But don't worry, it won't happen again. You have my word."

*Maybe I can trust you, but it's me that I'm worried about.*

# CHAPTER EIGHT

SHE AMAZED HIM.

Finn awoke the next morning thinking of Holly. They'd worked together until late the night before. She had truly impressed him—which wasn't an easy feat. To top it off, she was efficient and organized. He knew she was good at her job, but he had no idea just how talented she was until last night.

They'd taken a long break for dinner with his associates. They updated them on all they'd accomplished and what Holly hoped to achieve over the next few days. The men promised to do their part to ensure the success of Project Santa, including putting out a call for volunteers to their employees and their families.

And to Finn's shock the two men who weren't active on social media were open to having Holly assist them with setting up a personal MyFace account. Everyone wanted to do their part to promote the project so that it was a success.

Finn slipped out of bed and quietly padded to the shower. With Project Santa underway, he had to concentrate on to-day's business agenda. He had a business venture that he wanted to entice these men to invest in. And thanks to Holly, everyone appeared to be in fine spirits. He hoped to capitalize on it.

Today he'd switched from his dress shorts and polos to slacks and a dress shirt. He couldn't help it. When he wanted to take charge of a business meeting, he wanted to look the part, too. He supposed that was something his father had taught him. Though his father had spiraled out of control after his brother's death, before that he was a pretty good

guy, just a bit driven. He supposed his father was no more
a workaholic than himself.

Finn straightened the collar of his light blue shirt with
vertical white stripes sans the tie. Then he turned up the
cuffs. After placing his Rolex on his wrist, he was ready
to get down to business. Now he just needed Holly to take
some notes.

He headed down the passageway to her cabin and
knocked. There was no answer.

"Holly, are you in there?"

*Knock-knock.*

"Holly?"

That was strange. When they'd parted for the evening,
they'd agreed to get together first thing in the morning to
go over today's agenda. And then he recalled her picking
her way through her dinner. Maybe he should be sure she
was okay.

He tried the doorknob. It wasn't locked. He opened it a
crack. "Holly, I'm coming in."

No response.

He hesitantly opened the door, not sure what he expected
to find. He breathed easier when he found her bed empty.
Before he could react, the bathroom door swung open and
she came rushing out.

Dressed in a short pink nightie, she was a bit hunched
over. Her arm was clutched over her stomach.

"Holly?"

She jumped. Her head swung around to face him. The
color leached from her face. He wasn't sure if the lack of
coloring was the result of his startling her or if it was because she didn't feel well.

"What are you doing here?"

"Sorry. I didn't mean to startle you. I…uh, well, we were
supposed to meet up this morning. And when you didn't an-

swer the door, I got worried. I came in to make sure you're all right."

Holly glanced down at herself as though realizing her lack of clothing. She moved to the bed and slid under the sheets. "I'm fine."

"You don't look fine."

"Well, thanks. You sure know how to make a girl feel better." She frowned at him.

"That's not what I meant. I...uh, just meant you don't look like yourself. What can I get for you?"

"Nothing."

"Are you sure? Maybe some eggs?" Was it possible that her pale face just turned a ghastly shade of green? She vehemently shook her head. Okay. Definitely no eggs. "How about toast?"

Again she shook her head. "No food. Not now."

"Are you sick?"

"No." Her answer came too quickly.

"Something is wrong or you wouldn't be curled up in bed."

"It's just the sway of the yacht. I'm not used to it."

He planted his hands on his waist. He supposed that was a reasonable explanation. "You aren't the only one with a bout of motion sickness. McMurray still isn't well. I guess my sailing expedition wasn't such a good idea."

"It was a great idea. And I'll be up on deck shortly."

"Take the morning off and rest—"

"No. I'm already feeling better. Just give me a bit to get ready."

"Why must you always be so stubborn?"

She sent him a scowl. "I'm not stubborn. It isn't like you know me that well."

"Since we started working together, I've learned a lot about you."

"Like what?"

He sighed but then decided to be truthful with her. "I know that you're honest. You're a hard worker. And you go above and beyond what is asked of you in order to do a good job."

A smile bloomed on her still-pale face. "Anything else?"

"I know you can be passionate—about causes you believe in. And sometimes you push too hard if you think it will help someone else."

She eyed him up. "You really believe all of that nice stuff about me? You're not saying it because you feel sorry for me, are you?"

Was she hunting for more compliments? He searched her eyes and found a gleam of uncertainty. He had to wonder, if only to himself, how someone so talented and sure of herself when it came to business could be so insecure behind closed doors.

"Yes, I meant everything I said. You're very talented."

Holly worried her bottom lip. When his gaze met hers, she glanced away. What did she have on her mind? Something told him whatever it was he wasn't going to like it. But they might as well get it over with.

"What else do you have on your mind?"

She blinked as though considering her options. Then she sat up straight, letting the sheet pool around her waist. He inwardly groaned as her nightie was not exactly conservative, and that was not something he needed to be contemplating at this moment.

*Stay focused on the conversation! Don't let your eyes dip. Focus on her face.*

Holly lifted her chin. "I would like to know if you'd write me a personal recommendation."

"Recommendation? For what?"

She visibly swallowed. The muscles in her slender neck worked in unison. "I have an inside source who says a prime opportunity is about to open up and I'd like to apply for the position."

"No problem. Just tell me what department it is and I'll make it happen. But I thought you liked working in the legal department."

"I did—I mean I do. But you don't understand. This job isn't within Lockwood."

He had to admit that he hadn't seen that one coming. And for a man that prided himself on being able to plan ahead, this was a bit much to swallow. "But I don't understand. You like your job, so this has to be about us."

Her slender shoulders rose and fell. "It's too complicated for me to stay on at Lockwood."

"You mean the kiss the other evening, don't you?"

Her gaze didn't quite meet his. "It would just be easier if I were to work elsewhere."

"When would you be taking this new position?"

"At the beginning of the year. So you don't have to worry about Project Santa. It will be completed before I leave and I'll be out of Lockwood before you return to New York."

"Sounds awfully convenient." His voice took on a disgruntled tone.

He didn't like the thought of Holly going to such lengths to keep her path from crossing his. Up until this trip, they'd done so well avoiding each other at the office. He had to admit a few times he'd hoped to bump into her in a hallway or the elevator, but that had never happened.

Holly was smart for wanting to get away from him. When his ex-fiancée hadn't been able to deal with his moods and distance, she'd left. He'd never blamed her. It was what he'd deserved. He should be relieved that Holly wanted to move on, but he couldn't work up the emotion.

He told himself that he didn't want to see her go because she was a good worker. She was smart and a go-getter. She wasn't afraid to think outside the box. His company needed more innovative people like her.

Holly smoothed the cream-colored sheet as though sorting her thoughts. "Listen, I know this comes as a surprise, but I really do think it would be for the best. It isn't like either one of us wants a serious relationship. You have your company to focus on."

"And what do you have?" He knew there was more to this request than she was saying, perhaps something even beyond what was going on between the two of them. Because if her reasons extended beyond the attraction between them, then he could fix it and she would stay, he hoped.

"I have my work, and this new position will help me to grow and to take on greater responsibility."

"And you can't do that at Lockwood?"

She shrugged, letting him know that she'd already dismissed that option.

Without Holly to liven things up, he would return to a downright boring existence. Before he handed over the golden ticket to another position, he needed more time to think this over. Surely there had to be a way to persuade her into staying.

"You've caught me off guard. Can I have some time to think over your request?"

"Of course. But don't take too long. Once word gets out about the opening, the candidates will flood the office with résumés."

He could see she'd given this a lot of thought and her mind was made up. "Just tell me one thing and be honest. Is this because you're trying to get away from me?"

Her gaze met his. "Maybe. Partly. But it's an amazing opportunity and I don't want to miss out on it."

"Would you be willing to tell me what the position is?"

"That would be telling you two things and you said you'd only ask one thing."

"And so I did." He sighed. "This isn't over."

"I didn't think that it was."

"I'll go get you some ginger ale and crackers."

"You don't have to do that. You have a business meeting to attend."

"Not before I see that you're cared for."

And with that he made a hasty exit from the cabin, still digesting the news. It left an uneasy feeling in his gut. And this was why he never got involved with employees of Lockwood. It made things sticky and awkward, not to mention he couldn't afford to lose such talent.

# CHAPTER NINE

IT WAS SO good to be back on solid ground.

The next morning Holly stood on the balcony of Finn's beach house that was more like a mansion. He'd just escorted his last guest to the helipad. Their sailing trip had been cut short due to the rough waters. She thought for sure Finn would be upset, but he took it all in stride.

She shouldn't be standing here. There was work to be done on Project Santa—work that could be done from anywhere in the world, including New York.

The sound of footsteps caused her to turn around. Finn stopped at the edge of the deck. He didn't smile and the look in his eyes was unreadable.

"Did everyone get off okay?"

"They did."

The silence between them dragged on. Finn obviously had something on his mind. Maybe this was her chance to broach the subject of her leaving.

She turned to him.

"I was thinking I should get to work. You know, there's no reason I can't complete Project Santa in New York. I can make my travel arrangements and be out of your way shortly."

"You're not in my way." His voice dropped to a serious tone. "Have I somehow made you feel unwelcome?"

"Well, no, but I just thought that, ah, well, there's no point in me staying on the island. That is, unless you still need my assistance."

"You're right." His voice was calm and even. "Any work from here on out can be done via phone or the internet."

His sudden agreement stung. She knew she should be relieved, but she was conflicted. His eagerness to see her gone almost felt as though she was being dismissed—as though she hadn't quite measured up as his PA. Was that what he was thinking? Or had he merely grown tired of her like the other men in her life had done?

"I'll pack my bags and leave tomorrow."

She moved swiftly from the large deck and into the cool interior of the house. The sooner she got off this island, the better. She'd forget about Finn and how every time she was around him she wanted to follow up their kiss with another and another.

A new job was just what she needed. It'd give her the time and space to get over this silly crush she had on Finn. Because that was all it was, a crush. Nothing more.

So much for Holly's departure and having his life return to normal.

She was sick again.

Finn paced back and forth in his study.

He didn't care what Holly said, it obviously wasn't seasickness any longer. Her illness could be anything, including something serious. He hadn't gotten a bit of work done all morning. At least nothing worthwhile. And now that lunch was over and Holly hadn't shown up, he wasn't sure what to do. He'd never been in a position of worrying about someone else.

When his brother had been sick, it had been his parents who'd done most of the worrying and the caretaking. And then there had been his great-aunt who'd taken him in after his parents' deaths, but she was made of hearty stock or so she'd liked to tell him. She'd barely been sick a day while he'd known her. Even on the few times she'd gotten the sniffles, she carried on, doing what needed to be done until her final breath.

But he couldn't ignore how poorly Holly looked. And

her appetite at best was iffy. Then a thought came to him. He'd take a tray of food to her room. There had to be something she could eat.

When he entered the kitchen, Maria, his cook/housekeeper, glanced up from where she was pulling spices to prepare the evening dinner. "Can I get you something?"

Finn shook his head. "Don't let me bother you. I'm just going to put together a tray to take to Miss Abrams."

"I can do it for you."

"I've got it." There was a firm tone to his voice, more so than he'd intended. He just needed to do this on his own. "Sorry. I'm just a little worried."

Maria nodded as in understanding before turning back to her work.

Finn raided the fridge, settling on sandwich makings. It was what he ate late at night. And then he thought of something that Holly might enjoy. It was something his aunt swore by. Tea. "Maria, do we have some tea around here?"

The older woman smiled and nodded as though at last happy to be able to do something to help.

Between the two of them, they put together an extensive tray of food plus spearmint tea. And just to be on the safe side, he added a glass of ginger ale and crackers. As an afterthought, he snagged one of the pink rosebuds from the bouquet on the dining room table, slipped it into a bud vase and added it to the full tray. Hopefully this would cheer Holly up.

He strode down the hallway, up the steps and down another hallway until he stopped in front of her door. He tapped his knuckles on the door.

"Holly, it's me."

Within seconds, she pulled open the door. Her hair was mussed up and there was a sleepy look on her face. Her gaze lowered to the tray. "What's all of this?"

"It's for you. I noticed you missed lunch. I thought this might tide you over until dinner."

"Till dinner? I think that amount of food could last me for the next couple of days."

He glanced down at the sandwich. "I wasn't sure what meat and cheese you prefer so I added a little of everything. I figured you could just take off what you don't like."

"And the chips, fruit, vegetables and dip. Is there anything you forgot?"

He glanced over the tray and then a thought came to him. "I forgot to add some soup. Would you like some?"

"I think I'll get by with what you brought me."

A smile lifted her lips, easing the tired, stressed lines on her face. His gaze moved past her and trailed around the room, surprised to find that her laptop was closed. And then he spied the bed with the wrinkled comforter and the indent on the pillow. She'd been lying down.

"I'll put it over here." He moved toward the desk in the corner of her room. When she didn't follow him, he turned back to her. There were shadows under her eyes and her face was void of color. "Holly—"

She ran out of the room. She sent the bathroom door slamming shut.

That was it. He was done waiting for this bug or whatever was ailing her to pass. He pulled his cell phone from his pocket and requested that the chopper transport them to the big island where there would be medical help.

He didn't care how much she protested, this simply couldn't go on. There was something seriously wrong here. And he was worried—really worried.


"Finn, don't forget your promise."

"I won't." He stared straight ahead as he searched for a parking spot on the big island.

Before they flew here, Holly had extracted a promise from him. If she agreed to this totally unnecessary doctor's appointment, he would help her catch the next flight home.

She was certain whatever was plaguing her was no more than a flu bug. No big deal. She had no idea why Finn was so concerned.

Being an hour early for her appointment, Holly took advantage of the opportunity to meander through the colorful shops and the intriguing stands along the street. And in the end, it was a productive visit as she bought a few gifts.

When it was time to head to the clinic, Holly pleaded that it wasn't necessary. She was feeling better, but Finn insisted, reminding her that they had an agreement. And so they did. It also meant that she was almost homeward bound...just as soon as this appointment was concluded. She'd even packed her bag and brought it with her.

In the doctor's office Holly completed the paperwork and then they took her vital statistics. An older doctor examined her. He did a lot of hemming and hawing, but he gave her no insight into what those sounds meant. When she pointedly asked him what was wrong with her, he told her that he'd need to order a couple of tests.

*Tests? That doesn't sound good.*

She was feeling better. That had to be a good sign. But why was the doctor being so closemouthed? Although she recalled when her mother had suffered a stroke, trying to get information out of doctors was nearly impossible until they were ready to speak to you.

So she waited, but not alone. With her exam over, she invited Finn back to the room so he could hear with his own ears that she was fine. She was certain the doctor was only being cautious.

In the bright light, she noticed that Finn didn't look quite like himself. "Are you feeling all right?"

His gaze met hers. "I'm fine. It's you we should worry about."

She studied him a bit more. His face was pale and his eyes were dull. There was definitely something wrong with him.

"Oh, no, have I made you sick, too?"

He waved away her worry. "I'm like my great-aunt. I don't get sick."

"I don't believe you."

Finn's jaw tensed and a muscle in his cheek twitched, but he didn't argue with her. Okay, so maybe she was pushing it a bit. Doctor's offices made her uptight.

"I'm sorry," she said. "I didn't mean anything by that. I guess I don't do well with doctors."

The lines on Finn's handsome face smoothed out. "Why? What happened?"

She shrugged. "You don't want to hear about it."

"Sure, I do. That is, if you'll tell me."

Oh, well, what else did they have to do while waiting for the test results? There weren't even any glossy magazines in the small room. So while she sat on the exam table, Finn took a seat on the only chair in the room.

"It was a couple of days after you and I, you know, after—"

"The night we spent together?"

She nodded. "Yes, that. Well, I got a call from my mother's work. They were taking my mother to the hospital." She paused, recalling that frantic phone call when life as she knew it had come to a sudden standstill. "I'd never been so scared. I didn't know what was going on. I just knew an ambulance had been called for my mother. That's never a good sign."

"I'm sorry. I didn't know. I… I would have done something."

She glanced at him. "There was nothing for you to do. Remember, we agreed to stay clear of each other."

"Even so, I would have been there for you, if you'd have called me."

Holly shook her head. "I was fine. But thanks."

"I'm sure you had the rest of your family and friends to keep you company."

Holly shrugged. "I was fine."

He arched a brow. "When you said that the first time, I didn't believe you. And I don't believe it this time, either."

"Okay. I wasn't fine. I was scared to death. Is that what you want to hear?"

"No, it isn't what I want to hear. But I'm glad you're finally being honest with me."

Her gaze met his. "Why? It isn't like there's anything between us. At least, not anymore."

"Is that the truth? Or are you trying to convince yourself that you don't feel anything for me?"

She inwardly groaned. Why did everything have to be so complicated where Finn was concerned? Why couldn't things be simple, like her life had been before she'd walked into his office all those weeks ago?

# CHAPTER TEN

NOW, WHY HAD he gone and asked her if she had feelings for him?

Finn leaned his head back and sighed. It wasn't like he wanted to pick up where they'd left off. It didn't matter that they had chemistry and lots of it. In time, he'd forget about her sweet kisses and gentle caresses. He had to—she was better off without him.

He'd tried having a real relationship once. Talk about a mess. He wasn't going to repeat that mistake. Not that Holly was anything like Meryl. Not at all.

"Holly—"

The exam room door swung open. The doctor strode in and closed the door behind him. He lowered his reading glasses to the bridge of his nose. His dark head bent over a piece of paper. When he glanced up, his gaze immediately landed on Finn.

"Oh, hello." The doctor's puzzled gaze moved to Holly.

"It's okay. You can talk in front of him."

The doctor hesitated.

Holly sent the doctor a reassuring smile. "Finn's the one who insisted on bringing me here, and I just want to show him that he was overreacting."

"If you're sure."

She smiled and nodded.

"Okay then. I have the results back. It's what I initially suspected. You have morning sickness."

"Morning sickness? You mean I'm pregnant?" Holly vocalized Finn's stunned thoughts.

The doctor's bushy brows drew together. "I thought you knew."

Holly turned to Finn, the color in her face leaching away,

but no words crossed her lips. That was okay because for once, Finn couldn't think of anything to say, at least nothing that would make much sense.

*A baby. We're having a baby.*

Disbelief. Surprise. Excitement. Anger. It all balled together and washed over Finn.

Holly stared at him as though expecting him to say something, anything. But he didn't dare. Not yet. Not until he had his emotions under control. One wrong word and he wouldn't be able to rebound from it. And to be honest, he was stuck on six little—life-changing—words.

*I'm going to be a father. I'm going to be a father.*

Holly turned her attention back to the doctor. "You're sure? About the baby, that is."

The doctor's gaze moved to Finn and then back to her. The question was in his eyes, but he didn't vocalize it.

"Yes, he's the father."

Finn realized this was another of those moments where he should speak, but his mind drew a blank. It was though there was this pink-and-blue neon sign flashing in his mind that said *baby*.

"I'm one hundred percent certain you're pregnant." The doctor's forehead scrunched up. "I take it you have your doubts."

"Well, I, um—" she glanced at Finn before turning back to the doctor "—had my period since we were together. Granted it was light."

"Recently?"

"The week before last."

"Was there any cramping associated with it?"

She shook her head. "None that I recall."

"A little spotting is not uncommon. Have you had any spotting since then?"

"No. I'm just really tired. Are…are you sure everything is okay with the baby?"

"I'll be honest, you're still in your first trimester, which means the risk of miscarriage is higher. But I didn't tell you that to worry you. I just want you to realize that taking care of yourself is of the utmost importance."

"The baby." Her heart was racing so fast. "It's okay, right?"

"At this point, yes. I've arranged for a sonogram." He moved to the counter to retrieve a stack of literature. "You might like to read over these. They're about prenatal care and what to expect over the next several months. I'll be back."

Finn paced. Neither spoke as they each tried to grasp the news. Seconds turned to minutes. At last, Finn sank into the chair, feeling emotionally wiped out. His gaze moved to Holly but she appeared engrossed in a baby magazine the doctor had given her.

*Where was the doctor? Had he forgotten them?*

As though Finn's thoughts had summoned the man, the door swung open. A nurse walked in. Her eyes widened at the sight of Finn.

The nurse handed Holly a pink gown. "The straps go in the front." Then the nurse turned to him. "You might want to wait outside."

"I think you're right." That was it. Finn was out of there. He had no idea what was involved with a sonogram, but he'd give Holly her privacy.

When he reached the waiting room, he was tempted to keep going. In here he felt as though he couldn't quite catch his breath. Outside, in the fresh air, he would be able to breathe again. But he didn't want to move that far from Holly. What if she needed him?

And so he remained in the waiting room. He picked up a baby magazine, glanced at the cover and put it back down. He picked up another magazine, but it was for women. He put it down, too.

The door he'd just exited opened. A different nurse poked her head out. "Mr. Lockwood."

He approached her, not having a clue what she wanted. "I'm Mr. Lockwood."

"If you would come with me, sir." She led him back to Holly's exam room.

When he stood in the doorway, he found Holly lying on the exam table with a large sheet draped over her legs. He did not want to be here. He shouldn't be here.

Holly held her hand out to him. "Come see our baby."

He did want to see the baby. It would make it real for him. He moved to Holly's side, all the while keeping his gaze straight ahead, focused on the monitor. He slipped his hand in hers, finding her fingers cold. He assumed it was nerves. He sandwiched her hand between both of his, hoping to warm her up a little.

In no time at all, there was a fuzzy image on the monitor. Finn watched intently, trying to make out his child. And then it was there. It didn't look much like a baby at this point, but the doctor pointed out the head and spine.

"Wait a second, I need to check one more thing."

The doctor made an adjustment. Holly's fingers tightened their hold on Finn. Her worried gaze met his. Was there something wrong with their child?

Finn fervently hoped not. He just didn't think he could go through all his parents had endured with his brother. It was an experience he'd never forget.

"Okay." The doctor's voice rose. "Here we go. Just as I suspected."

Finn couldn't be left in the dark. He had to know what they were facing. "What's the matter?"

The doctor smiled up at him. "Nothing at all. You are having twins."

"Twins!" Holly said it at the same time as Finn.

"Yes, see here." The doctor showed them both babies.

It was the most amazing thing Finn had ever witnessed in his life. Twins. Who'd have thought? His vision started to blur, causing him to blink repeatedly. He was going to be a father—twice over.

He glanced down at Holly. A tear streamed down her cheek. His gut clenched. Was that a sign of joy or unhappiness? It was hard for him to tell. And then she turned and smiled at him. He released the pent-up breath in his lungs.

Holly squeezed his hand. "Did you see that? Those are our babies."

"I saw."

The doctor cleared his throat. "Well, you'll want to see your OB/GYN as soon as possible. But in the meantime, you need some rest and lots of fluids."

"Rest?"

"Yes and fluids. You have to be careful not to become dehydrated with the morning sickness."

"Okay. Whatever you say. I still can't believe I missed all of the signs."

"You aren't the first. Some women are in labor before they realize they are pregnant. These things happen."

Finn followed the doctor into the hallway while Holly got dressed. When they reentered the room, Holly looked different. Was it possible there was a bit of a glow about her? Or was he imagining things?

The doctor went over some suggestions on how to minimize her morning sickness and gave her a bottle of prenatal vitamins to get her started. "If you have any problems while you're in the islands, feel free to come back. I'm always here."

"I was planning to fly to New York today or tomorrow. Would that be all right?"

"I'd like to see you rested and hydrated before you travel. Get your morning sickness under control first."

Finn could feel everyone's attention turning his way, but he continued to study the random pattern of the floor tiles. He had nothing to contribute to this conversation, not at this point. This sudden turn of events was something he'd never envisioned.

The door opened and closed.

"Finn, are you okay?"

He glanced up, finding that he was alone with Holly. "Okay? No."

Her lips formed an O. "Can I say or do anything?"

He shook his head. He should be the one reassuring her, letting her know this was all going to be all right, but he couldn't lie to her. He had no idea how any of this was going to be all right. He was the last person in the world who should be a father. In fact, up until this point, he'd intended to leave all of his estate to designated charities.

But now, wow, everything had just changed. He raked his fingers through his hair. He had to rethink everything.

*Pull it together. She's expecting me to say something.*

He lifted his head and met her worried gaze that shimmered with unshed tears. That was the last thing he'd expected. Holly was always so strong and sure of what she wanted. Her tears socked him in the gut, jarring him back to reality. She was just as scared as he was, if not more so.

Oh, boy, were his children in big trouble here. Neither Holly nor himself was prepared to be a parent. They had so much to learn and so little time.

Finn stood. "Let's go back to the island."

Her worried gaze met his. "But what about New York?"

"You heard the doctor. You need to rest first." He held his hand out to her.

She hesitated but then grasped his hand.

He didn't know what the future held, but for now they were in it together. For better. Or for worse.

# CHAPTER ELEVEN

WHAT WERE THEY supposed to do now?

A few days after returning from their trip to the big island, Holly was starting to feel better. The suggestions the doctor had given her for morning sickness were helping. And she'd been monitoring her fluid intake.

She was still trying to come to terms with the fact that she was pregnant. There was no question in her mind about keeping the babies, but that was the only thing she knew for sure.

Maria and Emilio had been called away from the island. This meant Holly and Finn had the entire island to themselves. In another time, that might have been exciting, even romantic, but right now, they had serious matters on their minds.

She paced back and forth in the study. Where would she live? How would she manage a job, helping out her mother and being a mom all on her own? And where did this leave her and Finn?

The questions continued to whirl around in her mind. She would figure it out—she had to—because she wasn't going to fall back on Finn. She'd counted on two men in her life and they'd both failed her. She knew better this time around. She could only count on herself.

Deciding she wasn't going to get any more work done, she headed for the kitchen. She needed something to do with her hands and she had an urge for something sweet.

As she searched the cabinets, looking for something to appease her craving, her thoughts turned to Finn. He'd barely spoken to her since they left the doctor's office. The occasional nod or grunt was about as much as she got out of him.

She couldn't blame him. It was a lot to adjust to. Her mind was still spinning. Her hand ran over her abdomen.

*A baby. No, two babies. Inside her. Wow!*

"How are you feeling?" Finn asked.

Four whole words strung together. She would take that as a positive sign. "Better."

"And the babies?"

"Are perfectly fine." She bent over to retrieve a cookie sheet from the cabinet.

"I can get that for you." Finn rushed around the counter with his hands outstretched.

"I can manage." She glared at him until he retreated to the other side of the counter.

She placed the cookie sheet on the counter before turning on the oven. "Did you need something?"

"You're planning to bake? Now?"

"Sure. Why not? I have a craving."

"Isn't it a little early for those?"

She sighed. Why did he have to pick now of all times to get chatty? She just wanted to eat some sugary goodness in peace. "Not that kind of craving."

"Then what kind?"

What was up with him? He'd never been so curious about her dietary habits before. Or maybe he was just attempting to be friendly and she was being supersensitive. She choked down her agitation, planning to give him the benefit of the doubt.

"These are cravings that I get when I'm stressed out." She pulled open the door on the stainless-steel fridge and withdrew a roll of premade cookie dough. "Do you want some cookies?"

"If you're stressed about Project Santa—?"

"It's not that!"

His eyes widened. "Oh. I see."

This was another opening for him to discuss the big pink

or perhaps blue elephant in the room. And yet, he said nothing. Her gaze met his and he glanced away. Was this his way of telling her that he wasn't interested in being a father?

She placed the package of cookie dough on the counter before moving to the oven to adjust the temperature. Next, she needed a cutting board. There had to be one around here somewhere. The kitchen was equipped with absolutely everything. At last, she spotted a small pineapple-shaped board propped against the stone backsplash.

With the cutting board and a knife in hand, she moved back to the counter. "I'll have some reindeer cookies ready in no time. I thought about some hot chocolate with the little marshmallows, but it's a little warm around here for that."

"Thanks. But I'll pass on the cookies. I have some emails I need to get to. By the way, do you have a copy of the Cutter contract?"

"I do. It's in my room. Just let me finish putting these cookies on the tray." She put a dozen on the tray and slipped it in the oven. "Okay. There." She turned back to him. "Stay here and I'll be right back."

She rushed to her spacious guest room that overlooked the ocean. It was a spectacular view. She was tempted to take a dip in the sea or at the very least walk along the beach, letting her feet get wet. Maybe she'd do it later, after she was done working for the day.

Turning away from the window, her gaze strayed over the colorful packages she'd brought back from the big island. She'd splurged a bit, buying a little something for everyone, including her half-sisters, Suzie and Kristi.

Holly worried her bottom lip. She always tried so hard to find something that would impress them and each year, she'd failed. Thankfully she'd bought the gifts before her doctor's appointment because afterward she hadn't been in a holly-jolly spirit. The bikinis, sunglasses, flip-flops and a cover-up with the name of the island were placed in yellow tissue-paper-lined shopping bags. The girls would be all set for summer. About the same time she was giving birth.

With a sigh, Holly continued her hunt for the contract. On top of the dresser, she found the file folder. She pulled it out from beneath a stack of papers and an expandable folder when the back of her hand struck the lamp. Before she could stop it, the lamp toppled over.

Holly gasped as it landed on the floor and shattered, sending shards of glass all over the room. As she knelt down to clean up the mess, she muttered to herself. It was then that she heard rapid footsteps in the hallway.

"What happened?" Finn's voice carried a note of concern. "Are you okay?"

"I am. But the same can't be said for the lamp."

"I'm not worried about it." His concerned gaze met hers.

"I'll have this cleaned up in no time. Your contract is on the edge of the dresser."

When he stepped forward, she thought it was to retrieve the contract. However, the next thing she knew, he knelt down beside her.

"What are you doing?" she asked, not quite believing her eyes.

"Helping you."

"I don't need your help—"

"Well, you better get used to it because I plan to help with these babies."

It wasn't a question. It was an emphatic statement.

Her stomach churned. She was losing her control—her independence. She was about to lose her sense of security because her life would no longer be her own—Finn and the babies would now be a part of it—forever.

Holly sucked in a deep breath, hoping it'd slow the rapid pounding of her heart.

"Did you cut yourself on the broken glass?" Finn glanced down at her hands.

"I'm fine." She got to her feet, needing some distance from him. And then she smelled something. She sniffed again. "Oh, no! The cookies."

She rushed to the kitchen and swung the oven door open. The Christmas cookies were all brown and burnt. With Finn hovering about, she'd forgotten to turn on the timer. She groaned aloud, not caring if he heard her or not.

She turned to the garbage and dumped the cookies in it. Her gaze blurred. The memory of Finn's words and the knowledge that life would never be the same made her feel off-kilter and scared. What were they supposed to do now?

# CHAPTER TWELVE

HE HAD TO do something, but what?

The next evening, Finn did his best to concentrate on the details of a potential acquisition for Lockwood. Try as he might, his thoughts kept straying back to Holly and the babies. This was the time when his family would be invaluable. A deep sadness came over him, realizing that his children would never know his parents or his brother, Derek. In that moment he knew that it would be his responsibility to tell his children about their past—about their grandparents and uncle. Finn didn't take the notion lightly.

He glanced across the study to where Holly was sitting on the couch, working on her laptop. She'd been feeling better, which was a relief. Whatever the doctor had told her to do was helping. Now they could focus on the future.

His gaze moved to the windows behind her. The day was gray and glum just like his mood. He knew what needed to be done. They needed to get married.

He'd wrestled with the thought for days now. And it was the only solution that made sense. Although, he wasn't ready to get down on one knee and lay his heart on the line. Just the thought of loving someone else and losing them made his blood run cold. No, it was best their marriage was based on something more reliable—common goals.

The welfare of their children would be the tie that bound them. Finn's chest tightened when he realized that he knew less than nothing about babies. He would need help and lots of it. That was where Holly came in. He needed her guidance if he wanted to be the perfect parent—or as close to it as possible. Without her, he wouldn't even know where to start.

He assured himself that it would all work out. After all,

Holly was the mother to the Lockwood heirs. Their fates had been sealed as soon as she became pregnant. They would have to marry. And he would do his utmost to keep his family safe.

Holly leaned back. "I'm almost finished with the last details for Project Santa. I've reviewed the list of volunteers, state by state and city by city. I've been trying to determine whether there are enough volunteers to transport the gifts from the airports to the designated outreach centers."

Finn welcomed the distraction. "And what have you determined?"

"I think we need a few more drivers. I've already posted a request on MyFace. I'll wait and see what the response is before I take further steps."

"Good. It sounds like you have everything under control."

The fact that they worked well together was another thing they could build on. It would give their marriage a firm foundation. Because he just couldn't open his heart—he couldn't take that risk again.

A gust of wind made a shutter on the house rattle, jarring Finn from his thoughts. It was really picking up out there. So much for the sunshine in paradise. It looked like they'd soon be in for some rain.

"Finn, we need to talk." The banging continued, causing Holly to glance around. "What was that pounding sound?"

"I think it's a shutter that needs tightening."

Holly closed her laptop and set it aside. She got to her feet and moved to the window as though to inspect the problem. "Do you have a screwdriver and a ladder?"

"Yes, but why?"

"I'll go fix it."

"You?"

She frowned at him. "Yes, me. If you haven't noticed, I'm not one to sit around helplessly and wait for some guy to come take care of me."

"But you're pregnant and have doctor's orders to rest. You shouldn't be climbing on ladders. I'll take care of it later."

She sighed loudly. "I've been following his orders and I'm feeling much better. But if you insist, I'll leave the house repairs to you. Besides, there's something else we need to discuss."

"Is there another problem with Project Santa?"

"No. It's not that." She averted her gaze. "Remember how I asked you for a letter of recommendation?"

Why would she bring that up now? Surely she wasn't still considering it. Everything had changed what with the babies and all. "I remember."

Her gaze lifted to meet his. "Have you made a decision?"

"I didn't think it was still an issue."

"Why not?"

"Because you won't be leaving Lockwood, unless of course you want to stay home with the babies, which I'd totally understand. They are certainly going to be a handful and then some."

"Why do you think I won't leave to take that new job?"

Finn sent her a very puzzled look. "Because you're carrying the Lockwood heirs. And soon we'll be married—"

"Married?" Holly took a step back.

What was Finn talking about? They weren't getting married. Not now. Not ever.

"Of course. It's the next logical step—"

"No." She shook her head as her heart raced and her hands grew clammy. "It isn't logical and it certainly isn't my next step. You never even asked me, not that I want you to or anything."

"I thought it was implied."

"Implied? Maybe in your mind, but certainly not in mine. I'm not marrying you. I'm not going to marry anyone."

"Of course you are." His voice rumbled with irritation.

"This isn't the Stone Age. A woman can be pregnant without a husband. There are plenty of loving, single mothers in this world. Take a look around your office building. You'll find quite a few. But you won't find me there after the first of the year."

Had she really just said that? Oh, my. She'd gotten a little ahead of herself. What if he turned his back and walked away without giving her the recommendation? And she didn't have the job. It was still iffy at best. And without her position at Lockwood to fall back on, how would she support herself much less the babies and her mother?

"You're really serious about leaving, aren't you?"

She nodded, afraid to open her mouth again and make the situation worse.

"Do you really dislike me that much?"

"No! Not at all." In fact, it was quite the opposite.

She worried the inside of her lower lip as she glanced toward the window. The wind had picked up, whipping the fronds of the palm trees to and fro. She did not want to answer this question. Not at all.

"Holly?" Finn got to his feet and came to stand in front of her. "Why are you doing this? Why are you trying to drive us apart?"

"You…you're making this sound personal and it isn't." Heat rushed up her neck and made her face feel as though she'd been lying in the sun all day with no sunscreen.

"It is personal. It couldn't be more personal."

"No, it isn't. It's not like you and I, like we're involved."

"I don't know your definition of involved, but I don't think it gets much more involved than you carrying my babies."

"Finn, we both agreed after that night together that we wouldn't have anything to do with each other. We mutually decided that going our separate ways was for the best—for both of us."

"That was before."

"The pregnancy is a complication. I'll admit that. But we can work out an arrangement with the babies. We don't have to live out of each other's back pockets."

"I don't want to live in your back pocket. I want to provide a home for my children and their mother—"

"I don't need you to take care of me or the babies. I can manage on my own."

"But the point is you don't have to. I'm here to help. We can help each other."

She shook her head. "A marriage of convenience won't work."

"Sure it will, if we want it to."

Holly crossed her arms. "Why are you so certain you're right? It's not like we're in love. This thing between us will never last."

"And maybe you're wrong. Maybe the fact that we aren't in love is the reason that it will work. There won't be any unreasonable expectations. No emotional roller coaster."

"And that sounds good to you?"

He shrugged. "Do you have a better suggestion?"

"Yes. I think some space will be best for everyone."

"I don't agree. What would be best is if we became a family—a family that shares the same home as our children."

"And what happens—" She stopped herself just in time. She was going to utter, *What happens when you get bored*? Would he trade her in for a younger model? But she wasn't going there. It didn't matter because what Finn was proposing wasn't possible.

His gaze probed her. "Finish that statement."

"It's nothing."

"It was definitely something. And I want to know what it is." He moved closer to her.

His nearness sent her heart racing. It was hard to keep

her mind on the conversation. No man had a right to be so sexy. If only real life was like the movies and came with happily-ever-afters.

"Holly?"

"I honestly can't remember what I was going to say. But it's time I go back to New York."

Finn's eyes momentarily widened in surprise "What about the project?"

"The event is ready to go."

"You just said you had a problem with transportation."

"That…that's minor. I can deal with it from anywhere."

His gaze narrowed. "You're serious, aren't you?"

She settled her hands on her hips. "I am. You don't need me here. You can email me or phone, but you no longer need my presence here."

"Is there anything I can say to change your mind?"

There were so many things she wanted him to say. But she feared they were both too damaged—too cynical about life to be able to create a happily-ever-after.

And instead of trying and failing—of taking what they have and making it contentious, she'd rather part as friends. It'd be best for everyone, including the babies.

But finding herself a bit emotional, she didn't trust her voice. Instead, she averted her gaze and shook her head.

Finn sighed. "Fine. I'll call for the chopper."

"Really?" He was just going to let her walk out the door? It seemed too easy.

"It's what you want, isn't it?" He retrieved the phone.

"Yes, it is." She turned away and walked to the French doors. They were usually standing open, letting in the fresh air and sunshine, but not today. She stared off into the distant gray sky. Dark clouds scudded across it as rain began to fall.

She couldn't believe he was just going to let her walk away. A man who liked to control everything in his life surely couldn't live with just handing over his children with no strings attached.

In the background, she could hear the murmur of Finn's voice. He'd lowered it, but not before she caught the rumble in it. He wasn't happy—not at all. Well, that made two of them. But they'd have to make the best of the situation.

Her hand moved to her abdomen. It wouldn't be long now before she really started to show. She didn't even want to guess how big she'd get carrying not one but two babies. She had no doubt her figure would never be quite the same. But it would be worth it.

To be honest, she'd never thought of having children before. After her family had been ripped apart, she told herself she wasn't getting married or having children. She'd assured herself that life would be so much simpler when she only had herself to worry about.

Now she had two little ones counting on her to make all of the right decisions.

She turned, finding Finn with his back to her as he leaned against the desk. He certainly was different from Josh. Where Josh was a real charmer, Finn only gave a compliment when he truly meant it. Where Josh ran at the first sign of trouble, Finn was willing to stand by her. So why couldn't she give him a chance to prove that he truly was an exception?

He certainly was the most handsome man she'd laid her eyes on. Her gaze lingered on his golden hair that always seemed to be a bit scattered and made her long to run her fingers through it. And then there were his broad shoulders—shoulders that looked as though they could carry the weight of the world on them. She wondered how heavy a load he carried around.

Something told her he'd seen far too much in his young life. And she didn't want to add to his burden. That was never her intention. With time, she hoped he'd understand that she never meant to hurt him by turning down his suggestion of marriage.

Finn hung up the phone and turned to her. "We can't leave."

Surely she hadn't heard him correctly. "What do you mean we can't leave?"

"There's a storm moving in and with these high winds it's too dangerous to take up the chopper." His gaze met hers. "I'm sorry. I know how much you wanted off the island."

"So what are you saying? That we're stranded here?"

"Yes." He didn't look any happier about it than she did.

"What are we going to do?"

"You're going to wait here." He turned toward the door. "With Emilio and Maria away, I've got a lot of work to do before the storm. I won't get it all done tonight, but I can at least start."

"Wait for me. I want to help."

She rushed after him. There was no way she was planning to stand around and have him do all of the work. She knew her way around a toolbox and power tools. She could pull her own weight.

Hopefully this storm would pass by the island, leaving them unscathed. And then she'd be on her way home. She wasn't sure how much longer she could keep her common sense while around Finn.

Her gaze trailed down over Finn from his muscled arms to his trim waist and his firm backside. The blood heated in her veins. Enjoying each other's company didn't mean they had to make a formal commitment, right?

Wait. No. No. She couldn't let her desires override her logic. She jerked her gaze away from Finn. It had to be the pregnancy hormones that had her thinking these truly outlandish thoughts.

She was immune to Finn—about as immune as a bee to a field of wildflowers. She was in big trouble.

# CHAPTER THIRTEEN

WHY WAS SHE fighting him?

The next day, Finn sighed as he stared blindly out the glass doors. No matter what he said to Holly, there was no reasoning with her. She was determined to have these babies on her own.

He knew that she wouldn't keep him from seeing them, but he also knew that visitation every other weekend was not enough. He would be a stranger to his own children—his only family. His hands clenched. That couldn't happen.

He'd never thought he'd be a part of a family again. And though he had worries about how well he'd measure up as a husband and father, he'd couldn't walk away. Why couldn't Holly understand that?

He didn't know how or when, but somehow he'd convince her that they were better parents together than apart. If only he knew how to get his point across to her—

The lights flickered, halting his thoughts. The power went completely out, shrouding the house in long shadows. After a night and day of rain, it had stopped, but the winds were starting to pick up again. And then the lights came back on.

Finn didn't like the looks of things outside—not one little bit. Normally there weren't big weather events at this time of the year, but every once in a while a late-season storm would make its way across the Atlantic. This just happened to be one of those times.

Finn rinsed a dinner plate and placed it in the dishwasher. Yes, to Holly's amazement, he did know his way around the kitchen. He was a man who preferred his privacy and he didn't have a regular household staff in New York, just a maid who came in a couple of times a week.

But here on the island, it was different. Maria and Emilio had a small house off in the distance. They lived here year-round. Maria looked after the house while Emilio took care of the grounds. They were as close to family as Finn had—until now.

He ran the dishcloth over the granite countertop before placing it next to the sink. Everything was clean and in its place. He wondered what Holly was up to. She'd been particularly quiet throughout dinner. He made his way to the study.

Though she wouldn't admit it, he could tell the storm had her on edge. He was concerned, too. The tide was much higher than normal and the wind was wicked. But this house had been built to withstand some of the harshest weather. They'd be safe here.

Now if only he could comfort Holly, but she resisted any attempt he made to get closer. He wondered what had happened for her to hide behind a defensive wall. It had to be something pretty bad. If only he could get her to open up to him.

He was in the hallway outside the study when the lights flickered and went out. This time they didn't come back on. He needed to check on Holly before he ventured outside to fire up the emergency generator.

He stepped into the study that was now long with shadows. He squinted, looking for her. "Holly, where are you?"

She stood up from behind one of the couches. "Over here."

"What in the world are you doing?"

"Looking for candles in this cabinet."

"There are no candles in here. I have some in the kitchen."

She followed him to the supply of candles. There were also flashlights and lanterns in the pantry. It was fully stocked in case of an emergency.

"Do you think we'll really need all of this?" She fingered

the packages of beef jerky and various other prepackaged foods.

"I hope not. The last I checked the weather radio, the storm was supposed to go south of us."

"And I think it's calming down outside. That has to be a good sign, doesn't it?"

When he glanced over at the hopefulness in her eyes, he didn't want to disappoint her. He wanted to be able to reassure her that everything would be fine, but something told him she'd already been lied to enough in her life. So he decided to change the subject.

He picked up a lantern. "I think this might be easier than the candles."

"Really?"

Was that a pout on her face? She wanted the candlelight? Was it possible there was a romantic side to her hidden somewhere beneath her practicality and cynicism?

Deciding it wouldn't hurt to indulge her, he retrieved some large candle jars. "Is this what you had in mind?"

She nodded. "But we won't need them, will we?"

Finn glanced outside. It was much darker than it normally would be at this time of the day. "Come on. I have a safe place for us to wait out the storm."

She didn't question him but rather she quietly followed him to the center of the house. He opened the door to a small room with reinforced walls and no windows.

"What is this?"

"A safe room. I know it's not very big, but trust me, it'll do the job. I had it specifically put in the house for this very reason." With a flashlight in hand, he started lighting the candles. "There. That's all of them." A loud bang echoed through the house. "Now, I'll go work on the generator."

Holly reached out, grasping his arm. "Please don't go outside."

"But I need to—"

"Stay safe. We've got everything we need right here."

"Holly, don't worry. This isn't my first storm."

"But it's mine. Promise me you won't go outside."

He stared into her big brown eyes and saw the fear reflected in them. It tore at his heart. He pulled her close until her cheek rested against his shoulder.

"Everything will be fine."

She pulled back in order to gaze into his eyes. "Promise me you won't go outside."

He couldn't deny her this. "Yes, I promise."

This time she squeezed him tight as though in relief.

Seconds later, Finn pulled away. "I think we'll need some more candles and I want to do one more walk through the house to make sure it's secure. I'll be back."

"I can come with you."

"No. Stay here and get comfortable. I'll be right back. I promise." He started for the door.

"Finn?"

He paused, hearing the fear in her voice. "Do you need something else?"

"Um, no. Just be careful."

"I will." Was it possible that through all of her defensiveness and need to assert her independence that she cared for him? The thought warmed a spot in his chest. But he didn't have time to dwell on this revelation. The winds were starting to howl.

He hurried back to the kitchen where he'd purposely forgotten the weather radio. He wanted to listen to it without Holly around. He didn't know much about pregnant women, but he knew enough to know stress would not be good for her.

The radio crackled. He adjusted it so he could make out most of the words. The eye of the storm had shifted. It was headed closer to them. And the winds were intensifying to hurricane strength. Finn's hands clenched tightly.

This was all his fault. He should have paid more attention to the weather instead of getting distracted with the babies and his plans for the future. Now, instead of worrying about what he'd be like as a father, he had to hope he'd get that chance. He knew how bad the tropical storms could get. He'd ridden one out in this very house a few years back. It was an experience he'd been hoping not to repeat.

With a sigh, he turned off the radio. He made the rounds. The house was as secure as he could make it. With the radio, satellite phone and a crate of candles and more water, he headed back to Holly.

"How is everything?" Her voice held a distinct thread of worry.

He closed the door and turned around to find a cozy setting awaiting him. There were blankets heaped on the floor and pillows lining the wall. With the soft glow of the candles, it swept him back in time—back to when his big brother was still alive. They were forever building blanket forts to their mother's frustration.

The memory of his mother and brother saddened him. Finn tried his best not to dwell on their absence from his life, but every now and then there would be a moment when a memory would drive home the fact that he was now all alone in this world.

"Finn, what is it?" Holly got to her feet and moved to him.

It wasn't until she pressed a hand to his arm that he was jarred from his thoughts. "Um, nothing. Everything is secure. It's started to rain."

"The storm's not going to miss us, is it?"

"I'm afraid not. But we'll be fine."

"With the door closed, it's amazing how quiet it is in here. I could almost pretend there isn't a big storm brewing outside."

He didn't want to keep talking about the weather. He didn't want her asking more questions, because the last thing he wanted to do was scare her with the word *hurricane*. After all, it wasn't even one yet, but there was a strong potential.

"I see you made the room comfortable."

She glanced around. "I hope you like it."

"I do." There was one thing about this arrangement—she couldn't get away from him. He had a feeling by the time the sun rose, things between them would be drastically different.

This was not working.

Holly wiggled around, trying to get comfortable. It wasn't the cushions so much as hearing the creaking of the house and wondering what was going on outside. Finn hadn't wanted to tell her so she hadn't pushed, but her best guess was that they were going to experience a hurricane. The thought sent a chill racing down her spine.

"Is something wrong?"

"Um, nothing."

She glanced across the short space to find Finn's handsome face illuminated in the candlelight. Why exactly had she insisted on the candles? Was she hoping there would be a bit of romance? Of course not. The soft light was comforting, was all.

His head lifted and his gaze met hers. "Do you need more cushions? Or a blanket?"

"Really, I'm fine." There was another loud creak of the house. "I... I'm just wondering what's going on outside. Should we go check?"

"No." His answer was fast and short. "I mean there could be broken glass and it's dark out there. We'll deal with it in the morning."

She swallowed hard. "You really think the windows have been blown out?"

"The shutters will protect them. Hopefully the house is holding its own."

"Maybe you should turn on the radio." Whatever the

weather people said couldn't be worse than what her imagination had conjured up.

"You know what I'd really like to do?" He didn't wait for her to respond. "How about we get to know each other better?"

"And how do you propose we do that?"

"How about a game of twenty questions? You can ask me anything you want and I have to be absolutely honest. In return, I get to ask you twenty questions and you have to be honest."

She wasn't so sure honesty right now would be such a good idea, especially if he asked if she cared about him. "I… I don't know."

"Oh, come on. Surely you have questions."

She did. She had lots of them, but she wasn't so sure she wanted to answer his in return. She didn't open up with many people. She told herself it was because she was introverted, but sometimes she wondered if it was more than that.

On this particular night everything felt surreal. Perhaps she could act outside her norm. "Okay, as long as I go first."

"Go for it. But remember you only get twenty questions so make them good ones."

# CHAPTER FOURTEEN

HOLLY DIDN'T HAVE to think hard to come up with her first question. "Why did you look like you'd seen a ghost when you stepped in here?"

There was a pause as though Finn was figuring out how to answer her question. Was he thinking up a vague answer or would he really open up and give her a glimpse of the man beneath the business suits and intimidating reputation?

He glanced off into the shadows. "When I walked in here I was reminded of a time—long ago. My brother and I used to build blanket forts when we were kids. Especially in the winter when it was too cold or wet to go outside. My mother wasn't fond of them because we'd strip our beds."

Holly smiled, liking that he had a normal childhood with happy memories. She wondered why he kept them hidden. In all the time she'd been around him, she could count on one hand the number of times he spoke of his family. But she didn't say a word because she didn't want to interrupt him—she found herself wanting to learn everything she could about him.

"I remember there was this one Christmas where we'd built our biggest fort. But it was dark in there and my brother wanted to teach me to play cards. My mother would have been horrified that her proper young men were playing cards—it made it all the more fun. We tried a flashlight but it didn't have enough light. So my brother got an idea of where to get some lights."

Holly could tell by the gleam in Finn's eyes that mischief had been afoot. He and his brother must have been a handful. Would her twins be just as ornery? Her hand moved to her stomach. She had a feeling they would be and that she'd love every minute of it. She might even join them in their fort.

"While my parents were out at the Mistletoe Ball and the sitter was watching a movie in the family room, we took a string of white lights off the Christmas tree."

Holly gasped. "You didn't."

Finn nodded. "My brother assured me it was just one strand. There were plenty of other lights on the tree. After all, it was a big tree. So we strung the lights back and forth inside our fort. It gave it a nice glow, enough so that we could see the cards. There was just one problem."

"You got caught?"

He shook his head. "Not at first. The problem was my brother for all of his boasting had no clue how to play cards. So we ended up playing Go Fish."

Holly couldn't help but laugh, imagining those two little boys. "I bet you kept your parents on their toes."

"I suppose we did—for a while anyway." The smile slipped from his face and she wanted to put it back there. He was so handsome when he smiled.

"So what happened with the lights?"

"Well, when my parents got home, my mother called us down to the living room. It seems my father tried to fix the lights that were out on the lower part of the tree, but he soon found they were missing. My mother wanted to know if we knew anything about it. I looked at my brother and he looked at me. Then we both shrugged. We tried to assure her the tree looked good, but she wasn't buying any of it. My mother didn't have to look very long to find the lights. As I recall, we were grounded for a week. My father had the task of putting the lights back on the tree with all of the ornaments and ribbon still on it. He was not happy at all."

"I wouldn't think he would be."

"Okay. So now it's my turn. Let's see. Where did you grow up?"

She gave him a funny look. "Seriously, that's what you want to know?"

He shrugged. "Sure. Why not?"

"I grew up in Queens. A long way from your Upper East Side home."

"Not that far."

"Maybe not by train but it is by lifestyle." When Finn glanced away, she realized how that sounded. She just wasn't good at thinking about her family and the way things used to be so she always searched for a diversion.

"It's my turn." She thought for a moment and then asked, "Okay, what's your favorite color?"

He sent her a look of disbelief. "Are you serious?"

"Sure. Why wouldn't I be?"

"It's just that I thought these were questions to get to know each other. I don't know how my favorite color has much to do with anything."

"I'll tell you once you spit it out."

He sighed. "Green. Hunter green. Now why was that so important to you?"

"Are you sure it isn't money green?" He rolled his eyes and smiled at her before she continued. "It's important to me because I need a color to paint the babies' bedroom."

"Oh. I hadn't thought of that. Then I get to ask you what your favorite color is."

"Purple. A deep purple."

"Sounds like our children are going to have interesting bedrooms with purple and green walls."

Holly paused and thought about it for a minute. "I think we can make it work."

"Are you serious?"

"Very. Think about green foliage with purple skies. A palm tree with a monkey or two or three. And perhaps a bunch of bananas here and there for a splash of yellow."

His eyes widened. "How did you do that?"

"Do what?"

"Come up with that mural off the top of your head?"

She shrugged. "I don't know. It just sounded fun and like something our children might enjoy."

"I think you're right. I'll have the painters get started on it right away."

"Whoa! Slow down. I don't even know where we'll be living by the time these babies are born." When the smile slipped from his face, she knew it was time for a new question. "Why do you always leave New York at Christmastime? No, scratch that. I know that answer. I guess my real question is why do you hate Christmas?"

He frowned. "So now you're going for the really hard questions, huh? No, what's your middle name? Or what's your favorite food?"

She shrugged. "I just can't imagine hating Christmas. It's the season of hope."

There was a faraway look in his eyes. "My mother, she used to love it, too. She would deck out our house the day after Thanksgiving. It was a tradition. And it wasn't just her. The whole family took part, pulling the boxes of decorations out of the attic while Christmas carols played in the background. After we hung the outside lights, my mother would whip up hot chocolate with those little marshmallows."

"So you don't like it anymore because it reminds you of her?"

Finn frowned. "You don't get to ask another question yet. Besides, I wasn't finished with my answer."

"Oh. Sorry."

"Now that my family isn't around, I don't see any point in celebrating. I'll never get any of those moments back. When I'm here, I don't have to be surrounded by those memories or be reminded of what I lost."

There was more to that story, but she had to figure out the right question to get him to open up more. But how deep would he let her dig into his life? She had no idea. But if she didn't try to break through some of the protective layers that he had surrounding him, how in the world would they ever coparent? How would she ever be able to answer her children's questions about their father?

She didn't want to just ignore her kids' inquiries like her mother had done with her. Initially when her father had left, she'd been so confused. She thought it was something she'd done or not done. She didn't understand because to her naive thinking, things had been good. Then one day he packed his bags and walked out the door. Her mother refused to fill in the missing pieces. It was really hard for a ten-year-old to understand how her family had splintered apart overnight.

Finn cleared his throat. "Okay, next question. Do your parents still live in Queens?"

"Yes, however right now my mother's visiting my aunt in Florida. And my father moved to Brooklyn."

Finn's brow arched. "So they're divorced?"

"You already had your question, now it's my turn." Finn frowned but signaled with his hand for her to proceed, so she continued. "What happened to your brother?"

Finn's hands flexed. "He died."

She knew there had to be so much more to it. But she didn't push. If Finn was going to let down his guard, it had to be his choice, and pushing him would only keep him on the defensive.

And so she quietly waited. Either he expanded on his answer or he asked her another question. She would make peace with whatever he decided.

"My brother was the star of the family. He got top marks in school. He was on every sports team. And he shadowed my father on the weekends at the office. He was like my father in so many ways."

"And what about you?"

"I was a couple of years younger. I wasn't the Lockwood heir and so my father didn't have much time for me. I got the occasional clap on the back for my top marks, but then my father would turn his attention to my brother. For the most part, it didn't bother me. It was easier being forgotten than being expected to be perfect. My brother didn't have it easy. The pressure my father put on him to excel at everything was enormous."

Holly didn't care what Finn said, to be forgotten by a parent or easily dismissed hurt deeply. She knew all about it when her father left them to start his own family with his mistress, now wife number two.

But this wasn't her story, it was Finn's. And she knew it didn't have a happy ending, but she didn't know the details. Perhaps if she'd dug deeper on the internet, she might have learned how Finn's family splintered apart, but she'd rather hear it all from him.

"Everything was fine until my brother's grades started to fall and he began making mistakes on the football field. My father was irate. He blamed it on my brother being a teenager and being distracted by girls. My brother didn't even have a girlfriend at that point. He was too shy around them."

Holly tried to decide if that was true of Finn, as well. Somehow she had a hard time imagining this larger-than-life man being shy. Perhaps he could be purposely distant, but she couldn't imagine him being nervous around a woman.

"My brother, he started to tire easily. It progressed to the point where my mother took him to the doctor. It all snowballed from there. Tests and treatments became the sole focus of the whole house. Christmas that year was forgotten."

"How about you?" He didn't say it, but she got the feeling with so much on the line that Finn got lost in the shuffle.

He frowned at her, but it was the pain in his eyes that dug at her. "I didn't have any right to feel forgotten. My brother was fighting for his life."

She lowered her voice. "But it had to be tough for you with everyone running around looking after your brother. No one would blame you for feeling forgotten."

"I would blame me. I was selfish." His voice was gravelly with emotion. "And I had no right—no right to want presents on Christmas—no right to grow angry with my parents for not having time for me."

Her heart ached for him. "Of course you would want Christmas with all of its trimmings. Your life was spinning out of control and you wanted to cling to what you knew—what would make your life feel normal again."

"Aren't you listening? My brother was dying and I was sitting around feeling sorry for myself because I couldn't have some stupid toys under the Christmas tree. What kind of a person does that make me?"

"A real flesh-and-blood person who isn't perfect. But here's a news flash for you. None of us are—perfect that is. We just have to make the best of what we've been given."

He shook his head, blinking repeatedly. "I'm worse than most. I'm selfish and thoughtless. *Uncaring* is the word my mother threw at me." He swiped at his eyes. "And she was right. My brother deserved a better sibling than I'd turned out to be."

Holly placed her hand atop his before lacing their fingers together. A tingling sensation rushed from their clasped hands, up her arm and settled in her chest. It gave her the strength she needed to keep going—to keep trying to help this man who was in such pain.

"Did you ever think that you were just a kid in a truly horrific situation? Your big brother—the person you looked up to—your best friend—was sick, dying and there was nothing you could do for him. That's a lot to deal with as an adult, but as a child you must have felt utterly helpless. Not knowing what to do with the onslaught of emotions, you pushed them aside. Your brother's situation was totally out of your control. Instead you focused on trying to take control of your life."

Finn's wounded gaze searched hers. "You're just saying that to make me feel better."

"I'm saying it because it's what I believe." She freed her hand from his in order to gently caress his jaw. "Finn, you're a good man with a big heart—"

"I'm not. I'm selfish."

"Is that what your mother told you?"

"No." His head lowered. There was a slight pause as though he was lost in his own memories. "It's what my father told me."

"He was wrong." She placed a fingertip beneath Finn's chin and lifted until they were eye to eye. "He was very wrong. You have the biggest, most generous heart of anyone I know."

"Obviously you don't know me very well." His voice was barely more than a whisper.

"Look at how much you do for others. The Santa Project is a prime example. And you're a generous boss with an amazing benefits package for your employees—"

"That isn't what I meant. My father...he told me that I should have been the one in the hospital bed, not my brother." Holly gasped. Finn kept talking as though oblivious to her shocked reaction. "He was right. My brother was the golden boy. He was everything my parents could want. Derek and I were quite different."

Tears slipped down her cheeks. It was horrific that his father would spew such mean and hurtful things, but the fact that Finn believed them and still did to this day tore her up inside. How in the world did she make him see what a difference he continued to make in others' lives?

And then a thought occurred to her. She pulled his hand over to her slightly rounded abdomen. "This is the reason you're still here. You have a future. You have two little ones coming into this world that you can lavish with love and let them know how important each of them are to you. You can make sure they know that you don't have a favorite because they are equally important in your heart."

"What…what if I end up like my father and hurt our children?"

"You won't. The fact you're so worried about it proves my point."

His gaze searched hers. "Do you really believe that? You think I can be a good father?"

"I do." Her voice held a note of conviction. "Just follow your heart. It's a good, strong heart. It won't lead you astray."

"No one ever said anything like this to me. I… I just hope I don't let you down."

"You won't. I have faith in you."

His gaze dipped to her lips. She could read his thoughts and she wanted him too. Not waiting for him, she leaned forward, pressing her lips to his.

At first, he didn't move. Was he that surprised by her action? Didn't he know how much she wanted him? Needed him?

As his lips slowly moved beneath hers, she'd never felt so close to anyone in her life. It was though his words had touched her heart. He'd opened up and let her in. That was a beginning.

Her hands wound around his neck. He tasted sweet like the fresh batch of Christmas cookies that she'd left on a plate in the kitchen. She was definitely going to have to make more of those.

As their kiss deepened, her fingers combed through his hair. A moan rose in the back of her throat. She'd never been kissed so thoroughly. Her whole body tingled clear down to her toes.

Right now though, she didn't want anything but his arms around her as they sank down into the nest of blankets and pillows. While the storm raged outside, desire raged inside her.

# CHAPTER FIFTEEN

IT COULD BE BETTER.

But it could have been so much worse.

The next morning, Finn returned to the safe room after a preliminary survey of the storm damage. He glanced down at the cocoon of blankets and pillows to find Holly awake and getting to her feet. With her hair slightly mussed up and her lips still rosy from a night of kissing, she'd never looked more beautiful.

She blushed. "What are you looking at?" She ran a hand over her hair. "I must be a mess."

"No. Actually you look amazing."

"You're just saying that because you want something from me."

He hadn't said it for any reason other than he meant it. However, now that she'd planted the idea into his head, perhaps now was as good a time as any to tell her what he had on his mind. He'd stared into the dark long after she'd fallen asleep the night before. He'd thought long and hard about where they went from here.

But now as she smiled up at him, his attention strayed to her soft, plump lips. "You're right, there is something I want." He reached out and pulled her close. "This."

Without giving her a chance to react, he leaned in and pressed his lips to hers. Her kisses were sweet as nectar and he knew he'd never ever tire of them. He pulled her closer, deepening the kiss. He needed to make sure that last night hadn't just been a figment of his imagination.

And now he had his proof. The chemistry between them was most definitely real. It was all the more reason to follow through with his plan—his duty.

When at last he let her go, she smiled up at him. "What was that about?"

"Just making sure you aren't a dream."

"I'm most definitely real and so was that storm last night. So, um, how bad is the damage?" She turned and started to collect the blankets.

"There's a lot of debris on the beach. It'll take a while until this place looks like it once did, but other than a few minor things, the house held its own."

"That's wonderful. How long until we have power?"

"I'm hoping not long. I plan to work on that first." They were getting off topic.

"Before I let you go, I do believe we got distracted last night before I could ask my next question."

"Hmm… I don't recall this." She sent him a teasing smile.

"Convenient memory is more like it."

"Okay. What's your question?"

Now that it was time to put his marriage plan in action, he had doubts—lots of them. What if she wanted more than he could offer? What if she wanted a traditional marriage with promises of love?

"Finn? What is it?"

"Will you marry me?"

Surprise reflected in her eyes. "We already had this conversation. It won't work."

"Just hear me out. It won't be a traditional marriage, but that doesn't mean we can't make it work. After all, we're friends—or I'd like to think we are." She nodded in agreement and he continued. "And we know we're good together in other areas."

Pink tinged her cheeks. "So this would be like a business arrangement?"

"Not exactly. It'll be what we make of it. So what do you say?"

She returned to folding a blanket. "We don't have to be

married to be a family. I still believe we'll all be happier if you have your life and I have my own."

A frown pulled at his lips. This wasn't the way it had played out in his imagination. In his mind, she'd jumped at the offer. If she was waiting for something more—something heartfelt—she'd be waiting a very long time.

There had to be a way to turn this around. The stakes were much too high for him to fold his hand and walk away. He needed to be close to his children—

"Stop." Her voice interrupted the flow of his thoughts.

"Stop what?"

"Wondering how you can get me to say yes. You can't. I told you before that I didn't want to get married. That hasn't changed."

But the part she'd forgotten was that he was a man used to getting his way. When he set his sights on something, nothing stood in his way. He would overcome her hesitation about them becoming a full-fledged family, no matter what it took.

He wanted to be a full-time father to his kids and do all the things his father had been too busy to do with him. He would make time for both of his children. He wouldn't demean one while building up the other. Or at least he would try his darnedest to be a fair and loving parent.

And that was where Holly came into the plan. She would be there to watch over things—to keep the peace and harmony in the family. He knew already that she wouldn't hesitate to call him out on the carpet if he started to mess up where the kids were concerned.

He needed that reassurance—Holly's guidance. There was no way that he was going to let her go. But could he give her his heart?

Everyone he'd ever loved or thought that he'd loved, he'd lost. He couldn't go through that again. He couldn't have Holly walk out on him. It was best that they go into this marriage as friends with benefits as well as parents to their twins. Emotions were overrated.

The storm had made a real mess of things.

And Holly found herself thankful for the distraction. She moved around the living room where one of the floor-to-ceiling window panes had been broken when a shutter had been torn off its hinge. There was a mess of shattered glass everywhere.

So while Finn worked on restoring the power to the house, she worked on making the living room inhabitable again. But as the winds whipped through the room, she knew that as soon as Finn was free, she needed his help to put plywood over the window. But for now she was happy for the solitude.

If she didn't know better, she'd swear she dreamed up that marriage proposal. Finn Lockwood proposed to little old her. She smiled. He had no idea how tempted she was to accept his proposal. She'd always envied her friends getting married...until a few years down the road when some of them were going through a nasty divorce.

No, she couldn't—she wouldn't set herself up to get hurt. And now it wasn't just her but her kids that would be hurt when the marriage fell apart. She was right in turning him down. She just had to stick to her resolve. Everyone would be better off because of it.

So then why didn't she feel good about her decision? Why did she feel as though she'd turned down the best offer in her entire life?

It wasn't like she was madly in love with him. Was she?

Oh, no. It was true.

She loved Finn Lockwood.

When exactly had that happened?

She wasn't quite sure.

Though the knowledge frightened her, she couldn't deny it. What did she do now?

"Holly?"

She jumped. Her other hand, holding some of the broken glass, automatically clenched. Pain sliced through her fingers and she gasped. She released her grip, letting the glass fall back to the hardwood floor.

Finn rushed to her side. "I'm sorry. I didn't mean to startle you." He gently took her hand in his to examine it. "You've cut yourself. Let's get you out of here."

"I… I'll be fine."

"We'll see about that." He led her to the bathroom and stuck her hand under the faucet. "What were you doing in there?"

"Cleaning up. What did you think?"

"You should have waited. I would have done it. Or I would have flown in a cleaning crew. But I never expected you to do it, not in your condition."

"My condition? You make it sound like I've got some sort of disease instead of being pregnant with two beautiful babies."

"That wasn't my intent."

She knew that. She was just being touchy because… because he'd gotten past all of her defenses. He'd gotten her to fall in love with him and she'd never felt more vulnerable.

"What had you so distracted when I walked in?" Finn's gaze met hers as he dabbed a soapy washcloth to her fingers and palm.

"It was nothing." Nothing that she was ready to share. Once she did, he'd reason away her hesitation to get further involved with him.

"It had to be something if it had you so distracted that you didn't even hear me enter the room. Were you reconsidering my proposal?"

He couldn't keep proposing to her. It was dangerous. One of these days he might catch her in a weak moment and she might say yes. It might have a happy beginning but it was the ending that worried her.

She knew how to put an end to it. She caught and held his gaze. Her heart *thump-thumped* as she swallowed hard, working up the courage to get the words out. "Do you love me?"

His mouth opened, but just as quickly he pressed his lips together. He didn't love her. Her heart pinched. In that moment she realized that she'd wanted him to say yes. She wanted him to say that he was absolutely crazy in love with her. Inwardly, she groaned. What was happening to her? She was the skeptic—the person who didn't believe in happily-ever-afters.

"We don't have to love each other to make a good marriage." He reached out to her, gripping her elbows and pulling her to him. "This will work. Trust me."

She wanted to say that she couldn't marry someone who didn't love her, but she didn't trust herself mentioning the L-word. "I do trust you. But we're better off as friends."

He sighed. "What I need is a wife and a mother for my children."

"You know what they say, two out of three isn't bad."

His brows scrunched together as though not following her comment.

She gazed into his eyes, trying to ignore the pain she saw reflected there. "We're friends or at least I'd like to think we are." He nodded in agreement and she continued. "And I'm the mother of your children. That's two things. But I just can't be your wife. I won't agree to something that in the end will hurt everyone. You've already experienced more than enough pain in your life. I won't add to it. Someday you'll find the right woman."

"What if I'm looking at her?"

She glanced away. "Now that the storm's over, I think I should get back to New York."

Finn dabbed antibiotic cream on her nicks and cuts before adding a couple of bandages. Without another word, he started cleaning up the mess in the bathroom. Fine. If he wanted to act this way, so could she.

She walked away, but inside her heart felt as though it'd been broken in two. Why did life have to be so difficult? Her vision blurred with unshed tears, but she blinked them away.

If only she could be like other people and believe in the impossible, then she could jump into his arms—she could be content with the present and not worry about the future.

# CHAPTER SIXTEEN

Two BUSY DAYS had now passed since the tropical storm. Finn had done everything in his power to put the house back to normal. The physical labor had been exactly what he needed to work out his frustrations.

Toward the end of the day, Emilio phoned to say that the storm was between them and he couldn't get a flight out of Florida yet. Finn told him not to worry, he had everything under control and that Emilio should enjoy his new grandchild.

"Do you want some more to eat?" Holly's voice drew him from his thoughts.

Finn glanced down at his empty dinner plate. She'd made spaghetti and meatballs. He'd had some jar sauce and frozen meatballs on hand. He didn't always want someone to cook for him—sometimes he liked the solitude. So he made sure to keep simple things on hand that he could make for himself.

"Thanks. It was good but I'm full."

"There's a lot of leftovers. I guess I'm not so good with portions. I'll put them in the fridge in case you get hungry later. I know how hard you worked today. I'm sorry I wasn't any help."

"You have those babies to care for now. Besides, you cooked. That was a huge help."

She sent him a look that said she didn't believe him, but she wasn't going to argue. "I'll just clean this up."

He got to his feet. "Let me help."

She shook her head. "You rest. I've got this."

"But I want to help. And I'd like to make a pot of coffee. Do you want some?"

"I can't have any now that I'm pregnant."

"That's right. I forgot. But don't worry. I plan to do lots of reading. I'll catch on to all of this pregnancy stuff. Well, come on. The kitchen isn't going to clean itself."

When he entered the kitchen, he smiled. For a woman who was utterly organized in the office, he never expected her skills in the kitchen to be so, um, chaotic.

Normally such a mess would have put him on edge, but this one had the opposite effect on him. He found himself relaxing a bit knowing she was human with flaws and all. Maybe she wouldn't expect him to be the perfect dad. Maybe she would be understanding about his shortcomings.

Holly insisted on cleaning off the dishes while he placed them in the dishwasher. In the background, the coffeemaker hissed and sputtered. They worked in silence. Together they had everything cleaned up in no time.

"There. That's it." Holly closed the fridge with the leftovers safely inside.

After filling a coffee mug, he turned to Holly. "Come with me. I think we need to talk some more."

She crossed her arms. "If this is about your marriage proposal, there's nothing left to say except when can I catch a flight back to New York?"

He'd already anticipated this and had a solution. "Talk with me while I drink my coffee and then I'll go check on the helipad."

"Do you think it's damaged?"

Luckily the helicopter had been on the big island for routine maintenance when the storm struck. It was unharmed. However, with so many other things that had snagged his immediate concern, he hadn't checked on the helipad. Anything could have happened during that storm, but his gut was telling him that if the house was in pretty good condition then the helipad wouldn't be so bad off.

"Don't worry. The storm wasn't nearly as bad as it could have been."

The worry lines marring Holly's face eased a bit. With a cup of coffee in one hand and a glass of water in the other for her, he followed Holly to his office. Luckily the windows had held in here.

"Why don't we sit on the couch?"

While she took a seat, he dimmed the lights and turned on some sexy jazz music. Cozy and relaxing. He liked it this way. And then he sat down next to Holly.

Her gaze narrowed in on him. "What are you up to?"

He held up his palms. "Nothing. I swear. This is how I like to unwind in the evenings."

The look in her eyes said that she didn't believe him.

"Listen, I'll sit on this end of the couch and you can stay at the other end. Will that work?"

She nodded. "I don't know why you'd have to unwind on a beautiful island like this—well, it's normally beautiful. Will you be able to get it back to normal?"

She was avoiding talking about them and their future. It was as though she was hoping he'd forget what he wanted to talk to her about. That was never going to happen.

Still needing time to figure out exactly how to handle this very sensitive situation, he'd come up with a way to give them both some time. "I have a proposition for you—"

"If this is about getting married—"

"Just hear me out." When she remained silent, he turned on the couch so that he could look at her. "Can I be honest with you?"

"Of course. I'd hope you wouldn't even have to ask the question. I'd like to think that you're always honest—but I know that isn't true for most people." Her voice trailed off as she glanced down at her clenched hands.

She'd been betrayed? Anger pumped through his veins. Was it some guy that she'd loved? How could anyone lie to her and hurt her so deeply? The thought was inconceivable until he realized how he'd unintentionally hurt those that were closest to him. And he realized that if he wasn't careful and kept her at a safe distance that he would most likely hurt her, too. The fire and rage went out of him.

Still, he had to know what had cost Holly her ability to trust in others. "What happened?"

Her gaze lifted to meet his. "What makes you think something happened?"

"I think it's obvious. I shared my past with you. It's your turn. What's your story?"

She sighed. "It's boring and will probably sound silly to you because it's nothing as horrific as what you went through with your brother."

"I'll be the judge of that. But if it hurt you, I highly doubt that it's silly. Far from it."

Her eyes widened. "You're really interested, aren't you?"

"Of course I am. Everything about you interests me."

Her cheeks grew rosy as she glanced away. "My early childhood was happy and for all I knew, normal. My father worked—a lot. But my mother was there. We did all sorts of things together from baking to shopping to going to the park. I didn't have any complaints. Well, I did want a little brother or sister, but my mother always had an excuse of why it was best with just the three of us. I never did figure out if she truly wanted another baby and couldn't get pregnant or if she knew in her gut that her marriage was in trouble and didn't want to put another child in the middle of it."

"Or maybe she was just very happy with the child she already had." He hoped that was the right thing to say. He wasn't experienced with comforting words.

"Anyway when I was ten, my father stopped coming home. At first, my mother brushed off my questions, telling me that he was on an extended business trip. But at night, when she thought I was sleeping, I could hear her crying in her room. I knew something was seriously wrong. I started to wonder if my father had died. So I asked her and that's when she broke down and told me that he left us to start a new family. Then he appeared one day and, with barely a word, he packed his things and left."

"I'm so sorry." Finn moved closer to Holly. Not knowing what words to say at this point, he reached out, taking her hand into his own.

"My mother, she didn't cope well with my father being gone. She slipped into depression to the point where I got myself up and dressed in the morning for school. I cooked and cleaned up what I could. I even read to my mother, like she used to do with me when I was little. I needed her to get better, because I needed her since I didn't have anyone else."

"That must have been so hard for you. Your father...was he around at all?"

Holly shook her head. "I didn't know it then, but later I learned my stepmother was already pregnant with Suzie. My father had moved on without even waiting for the divorce. He had a new family and he'd forgotten about us...about me."

Finn's body tensed. He knew what it was like to be forgotten by a parent. But at least his parents had a really good excuse, at first it was because his brother was sick and then they'd been lost in their own grief. But Holly's father, he didn't have that excuse. Finn disliked the man intensely and he hadn't even met him.

"When the divorce was finalized, my father got visitation. Every other weekend, I went to stay with him and his new family. Every time my parents came face-to-face it was like a world war had erupted. My mother would grouch to me about my father and in turn, my father would bad-mouth my mother. It was awful." She visibly shuddered. "No child should ever be a pawn between their parents."

"I agree." Finn hoped that was the right thing to say. Just for good measure, he squeezed Holly's hand, hoping she'd know that he really did care even if he didn't have all of the right words.

"I don't want any of that for our children. I don't want them to be pawns between us."

"They won't. I swear it. No matter what happens between us, we'll put the kids first. We both learned that lesson first-hand. But will you do something for me?"

"What's that?"

His heart pounded in his chest. He didn't know what he'd do if she turned him down. "Would you give us a chance?"

Her fine brows gathered. "What sort of chance?"

That was the catch. He wasn't quite sure what he was asking of her—or of himself. Returning to New York with the holiday season in full swing twisted his insides into a knot. The reminders of what he'd lost would be everywhere. But it was where Holly and the babies would be.

He stared deep into her eyes. His heart pounded. And yet within her gaze, he found the strength he needed to make this offer—a chance to build the family his children deserved.

He swallowed hard. "I'd like to see where this thing between us leads. Give me until the New Year—you know, with us working closely together. That will give Clara time for an extended honeymoon and to settle into married life. And we'll have time to let down our guards and really get to know each other."

"I thought that's what we've been doing."

"But as fast as you let down one wall, I feel like you're building another one."

She worried her bottom lip. "Perhaps you're right. It's been a very long time since I've been able to count on someone. It might take me a bit of time to get it right." She eyed him up. "But I have something I need you to do in return."

"Name it."

"Be honest with me. Even if you don't think that I'll like it, just tell me. I couldn't stand to be blindsided like my mother. And there was a guy I got serious with while I was getting my degree. Long story short, he lied to me about his gambling addiction and then he stole from me to cover his debts."

"Wow. You haven't had it easy."

She shrugged. "Let's just say I have my reasons to be cautious."

"I promise I won't lie to you." She meant too much to him to hurt her. "Now, I need to go check on the helipad."

"What about the recommendation?" When he sent her a puzzled look, she added, "You know, for that other job?"

"You still want to leave? Even though we agreed to see where this leads us?"

"What if it leads nowhere? It'll be best if you don't have to see me every day."

His back teeth ground together. Just the thought of her no longer being in his life tied his insides up in a knot. For so long, he'd sentenced himself to a solitary life. And now he couldn't imagine his life without Holly in it.

"Let's not worry about the future. We can take this one day at a time." It was about all he could manage at this point.

"It's a deal." And then she did something he hadn't expected. She held her hand out to him to shake on it.

It was as though she was making this arrangement something much more distant and methodical than what he had in mind. He slipped his hand into hers. As her fingertips grazed over his palm, the most delicious sensations pulsed up his arm, reminding him that they'd passed the business associates part of their relationship a long time ago.

He needed to give Holly something else to think about. Without giving himself the time to think of all the reasons that his next actions were a bad idea, he tightened his fingers around her hand and pulled her to him.

Her eyes widened as he lowered his head and caught her

lips with his own—her sweet, sweet lips. He didn't care how many times he kissed her, it wouldn't be enough.

And then not wanting to give her a reason to hide behind another defensive wall, he pulled away. Her eyes had darkened. Was that confusion? No. What he was seeing reflected in her eyes was desire. A smile tugged at his lips. His work was done here.

He got to his feet. "I'll go check on the helipad."

With a flashlight in hand, he made his way along the path to the helipad. He had no idea what to expect when he got there. If it was clear, there was no reason Holly couldn't leave in the morning. The thought gutted him.

He'd just reached the head of the path when the rays of his flashlight skimmed over the helipad. As though fate was on his side, there were a couple of downed trees, making the landing zone inaccessible. But luckily it didn't appear they'd done any permanent damage—at least nothing to make the helipad inoperable.

It was much too dark now, but in the morning he'd have to get the chain saw out here. He imagined it'd be at least a couple of days to get this stuff cleared. It was time that he could use to sort things out with Holly.

# CHAPTER SEVENTEEN

A PAIN TORE through Holly's side.

The plates holding cold-cut sandwiches clattered onto the table. Holly pressed a hand to her waistline, willing the throbbing to subside. She rubbed the area, surprised by how much she was actually showing. But with twins on board, she figured that was to be expected. Thankfully when they'd visited the big island, she'd picked up some new, roomy clothes. They were all she wore now.

The discomfort ebbed away. Everything would be okay. It had to be. She was in the house alone. Finn had gone to the helipad first thing that morning to clear the debris. He didn't say exactly how bad it was, but she had a feeling he had a lot of work ahead of him if it was anything like the beach area.

She'd offered to help, but he'd stubbornly refused. So she set about cleaning the patio and washing it down so that it was usable again. All in all, they'd fared really well.

In a minute or so the discomfort passed. Realizing she might have overreacted, she shrugged it off and moved to the deck. She loved that Finn had installed a large bell. It could be rung in the case of an emergency or to call people for lunch, as she was about to do.

She wrapped her fingers around the weathered rope and pulled. The bell rang out.

*Clang-clang. Clang-clang.*

"Lunch!" She didn't know if he'd hear her, but hopefully he'd heard the bell.

She turned back to go inside the house to finish setting the table for lunch. She smiled, wondering if this was what it felt like to be a part of a couple. She knew they weren't a real couple, but they were working together. And she was happy—truly happy for the first time in a long while. She glanced around the island. Wouldn't it be nice to stay here until the babies were born?

A dreamy sigh escaped her lips. If only that could happen, but the realistic part of her knew it wasn't a possibility. Soon enough this fantasy would be over and she'd be back in New York, settling into a new job and trying to figure out how to juggle a job and newborns.

*One day at a time. I have months until these little ones make their grand entrance.*

At last, having the table set, she heard footsteps outside. Finn had heard her. Her heart beat a little faster, knowing she'd get to spend some time with him. Sure it was lunch, but he'd been gone all morning. She'd started to miss him.

*Quit being ridiculous. You're acting like a teenager with a huge crush.*

*No. It's even worse. I'm a grown woman who is falling more in love with my babies' daddy with each passing day.*

"I heard the bell. Is it time to eat?" He hustled through the doorway in his stocking feet. "I'm starved."

She glanced up to find Finn standing there in nothing but his jeans and socks. She had no idea what had happened to his shirt, but she heartily approved of his attire. Her gaze zeroed in on the tanned muscles of his shoulders and then slid down to his well-defined pecs and six-pack abs. Wow! She swallowed hard. Who knew hard work could look so good on a man?

His eyes twinkled when he smiled. "Is something wrong?"

*Wrong? Absolutely nothing. Nothing at all.*

"Um…no. I… I made up some sandwiches." Her face felt as though it was on fire. "The food, it's on the table. If you want to clean up a bit, we can eat." Realizing that she hadn't put out any refreshments, she asked, "What would you like to drink?"

"Water is good. Ice cold."

It did sound particularly good at the moment. "You got it."

She rushed around, getting a couple of big glasses and filling them with ice. Right about now she just wanted to climb in the freezer to cool off. It wasn't like he was the first guy she'd seen with his shirt off. Why in the world was she overreacting?

*Get a grip, Holly.*

She placed the glasses on the table and then decided something was missing. But what? She glanced around the kitchen, looking for something to dress up the table and then she spotted the colorful blooms she'd picked that morning. They were in a small vase on the counter. Their orange, yellow and pink petals would add a nice splash to the white tablecloth.

A pain shot through her left side again. Immediately her hand pressed to her side as she gripped the back of a chair with her other hand.

"What's the matter?" Finn's concerned voice filled the room, followed by his rapid footsteps.

She didn't want to worry him. "It's nothing."

"It's something. Tell me."

"It's the second time I've had a pain in my side."

"Pain?" His arm wrapped around her as he helped her sit down. "Is it the babies?"

"I... I don't know." She looked up at him, hoping to see reassurance in his eyes. Instead his worry reflected back at her. "It's gone now."

"You're sure?"

She nodded. "Let's eat."

"I think you need to see a doctor. The sooner, the better." He pulled out his cell phone. "In fact, I'm going to call the doctor now."

"What? But you can't. Honest, it's gone."

"I'll feel better once I hear it from someone who has experience in these matters."

A short time later, after Finn had gotten through to the doctor who'd examined her on the big island, Finn had relinquished the phone to Holly. She'd answered the doctor's questions and then breathed a sigh of relief.

When she returned the phone to Finn, his brow was knit into a worried line. She was touched that he cared so much. It just made her care about him all the more.

"Well, what did he say?"

"That without any other symptoms it sounds like growing pains. But it was hard for him to diagnose me over the phone. The only reason he did was because I told him we were stranded on the island due to the storm."

The stiff line of Finn's shoulders eased. "He doesn't think it's anything urgent?"

She shrugged. "He said I needed to make an appointment and see my OB/GYN as soon as possible just to be sure."

"Then that's what we'll do. We'll be out of here by this evening."

"What? But we can't. What about the trees and stuff at the helipad?"

"I just got the motivation I need to clear it. So you call your doctor and see if they can squeeze you in for tomorrow, and I'll call my pilot and have him fuel up the jet. We'll leave tonight."

"But you don't have to go. I know you don't want to be in New York for the holidays."

"That was before."

"Before what?"

"You know."

Her gaze narrowed in on him. "No, I don't know. Tell me."

"Before you and me...before the babies. We agreed we

were going to give this thing a go and this is me doing my part. You haven't changed your mind, have you?"

He cared enough to spend the holidays with her in the city. Her heart leaped for joy. Okay, so she shouldn't get too excited. She knew in the long run the odds were against them, but Christmas was the season of hope.

Things were looking up.

Finn stared out the back of the limo as they inched their way through the snarled Manhattan traffic. He could at last breathe a lot easier now. The babies and their mother were healthy. It was indeed growing pains. The doctor told them to expect more along the way.

Signs of Christmas were everywhere from the decorated storefronts to the large ornaments hung from the lampposts. As he stared out the window, he saw Santa ringing a bell next to his red kettle. It made Finn wish that he was back on the island. And then, without a word, Holly slipped her hand in his. Then again, this wasn't so bad.

She leaned over and softly said, "Relax. You might even find you like the holiday."

"Maybe you're right." He had his doubts, but he didn't want to give her any reason to back out of their arrangement. He only had until the first of the year to convince her that they were better off together than apart.

"We turned the wrong way. This is the opposite direction of my apartment." Obvious concern laced Holly's words. "Hey!" She waved, trying to gain the driver's attention. "We need to turn around."

"No, we don't," Finn said calmly. "It's okay, Ron. I've got this."

"You've got what?" She frowned at him.

"I've instructed Ron to drive us back to my penthouse—"

"What? No. I need to go home."

"Not yet. You heard the doctor. You have a high-risk pregnancy and your blood pressure is elevated—"

"Only slightly."

"She said not to overdo it. And from what you've told me, your apartment is a fifth-floor walk-up with no elevator."

"It… It's not that much. I'm used to it."

He wasn't going to change his mind about this arrangement. It was what was best for her and the babies. "And then there's the fact that your mother is out of town. There's no one around if you have any complications."

"I won't have any." Her hand moved to rest protectively over her slightly rounded midsection. "Nothing is going to happen."

"I sincerely hope you're right, but is it worth the risk? If you're wrong—"

"I won't be. But…your idea might not be so bad. As long as you understand that it's only temporary. Until my next appointment."

Which was at the beginning of the new year—not far off. "We'll see what the doctor says then. Now will you relax?"

"As long as you understand that this arrangement doesn't change anything between us—I'm still not accepting your proposal."

He wanted to tell her that she was wrong, but he couldn't. Maybe he was asking too much of her—of himself. He couldn't promise her forever.

An ache started deep in his chest.

What if he made her unhappy?

Maybe he was being selfish instead of doing what was best for Holly.

# CHAPTER EIGHTEEN

IT DIDN'T FEEL like Christmas.

Holly strolled into the living room of Finn's penthouse. There was absolutely nothing that resembled Christmas anywhere. She knew he avoided the holiday because of the bad memories it held for him, but she wondered if it would be possible to create some new holiday memories.

She'd been here for two days and, so far, Finn had bent over backward to make her at home. He'd set her up in his study to monitor the final stages of Project Santa. And so far they'd only encountered minor glitches. It was nothing that couldn't be overcome with a bit of ingenuity.

That morning when she'd offered to go into the office, Finn had waved her off, telling her to stay here. Meanwhile, he'd gone to the office to pick up some papers. He'd said he'd be back in a couple of hours, but that was before lunch. And now it was after quitting time and he still wasn't back.

Perhaps this was the best opportunity for her to take care of something that had been weighing on her mind. She retraced her steps to the study where she'd left her phone. She had Finn's number on it because he refused to leave until he had entered it in her phone with orders for her to call if she needed anything at all.

Certain in her plan, she selected his number and listened to the phone ring. Once. That's all it rang before Finn answered. "Holly, what's the matter?"

"Does something have to be the matter?"

"No. I just… Oh, never mind, what did you need?"

"I wanted you to know that I'm going out. There's something I need to take care of."

"I'm almost home. Can I pick something up for you?"

"It's more like I have to drop off something."

"Tonight?" His voice sounded off.

"Yes, tonight."

"I just heard the weather report and they're calling for snow. A lot of it."

Holly glanced toward the window. "It's not snowing yet. I won't be gone long. I'll most likely be home before it starts."

"Holly, put it off—"

"No. I need to do this." She'd been thinking about it all day. Once the visit with her family was over, she could relax. It'd definitely help lower her blood pressure.

Finn expelled a heavy sigh. "If you aren't going to change your mind, at least let me drive you."

He had no idea what this trip entailed. To say her family dynamics were complicated was an understatement. It was best Finn stay home. "Thanks. But I'm sure you have other things to do—"

"Nothing as important as you."

The breath caught in her throat. Had he really just said that? Was she truly important to him? And then she realized he probably meant because she was carrying his babies. Because she'd asked him straight up if he loved her and he hadn't been able to say the words.

"Holly? Are you still there?"

"Um, yes."

"Good. I'm just pulling into the garage now. I'll be up in a minute. Just be ready to go."

She disconnected the call and moved to her spacious bedroom to retrieve the Christmas packages and her coat. Her stomach churned. Once this was done, she could relax. In and out quickly.

She'd just carried the packages to the foyer when Finn let himself in the door. She glanced up at him. "You know I can take a cab."

"I told you if you're going out tonight, I'm going with you."

"You don't even know where I'm going."

"Good point. What's our destination?"

"My father's house. I want to give my sisters the Christmas presents I bought while we were in the Caribbean."

He scooped up the packages before opening the door for her. "So we've progressed to the point where I get to meet the family." Finn sent her a teasing smile. "I don't know. Do you think I'll pass the father inspection?"

She stopped at the elevator and pressed the button before turning back to him. "I don't think you have a thing to worry about."

His smile broadened. "That's nice to know."

"Don't get any ideas. In fact, you can wait in the car. I won't be long."

"Are you sure you want to take the presents now? I mean Christmas isn't until the weekend after next."

"I don't spend Christmas with them. I usually spend it with my mother. But after talking with my mother and aunt, I decided to give them something extra special for Christmas—a cruise." It would definitely put a dent in her savings, but it was worth it. This was her mother's dream vacation.

"That was very generous of you."

Holly's voice lowered. "They deserve it."

"And what about you?" When she sent him a puzzled look, he added, "You deserve a special Christmas, too. What would you like Santa to bring you?"

"I... I don't know. I hadn't thought about it."

The elevator door slid open. Finn waited until Holly stepped inside before he followed. "You know without your mother around, perhaps you could spend the time with your father."

She shook her head. "I don't think that would be a good idea."

Finn had no idea about her family. Thankfully she'd thought to tell him to stay in the car. She didn't want to make an awkward situation even more so.

Something was amiss, but what?

Was she really that uncomfortable with him meeting her family? Or was it something else? Finn glanced over at Holly just before he pulled out from a stop sign. The wipers swished back and forth, knocking off the gently falling snow.

The sky was dark now and all Finn wanted to do was turn around. He wasn't worried about himself. He never let the weather stop him from being wherever he was needed. But it was different now that he had Holly next to him and those precious babies. He worried about the roads becoming slick.

"We're almost there." Holly's voice drew him from his thoughts.

It was the first thing she'd said in blocks. In fact, she hadn't volunteered any details about her family. Why was that?

As he proceeded through the next intersection, Holly pointed to a modest two-story white house with a well-kept yard that was now coated with snow. "There it is."

He pulled over to the curb and turned off his wipers. "You've been awfully quiet. Is everything all right?"

"Sure. Why wouldn't it be?"

"You haven't said a word the whole way here unless it was to give me directions."

"Oh. Sorry. I must be tired."

"Sounds like a good reason to head back to the penthouse and deal with this another day."

"No." She released the seat belt. "We're here now. And I want to get this over with."

"Okay. It's up to you."

When he released his seat belt and opened the door, she asked, "What are you doing?"

"Getting the packages from the trunk."

She really didn't want him to meet her family. Why was she so worried? He didn't think he made that bad of a first impression. In fact, when he tried he could be pretty charming. And if they were going to be a family, which they were because of the babies, he needed to meet her father. He was certain he could make a good impression and alleviate Holly's worries.

With the packages in hand, he closed the trunk and started up the walk. Every step was muffled by the thin layer of snow.

"Where do you think you're going?" Holly remained next to the car.

He turned back and noticed the way the big flakes coated the top of her head like a halo. "I presume we're taking the presents to the door and not leaving them in the front yard."

"There's no *we* about it."

"Listen, Holly, you've got to trust me. This will all work out."

"You're right. It will. You're going to wait in the car." Her tone brooked no room for a rebuttal.

Just then there was a noise behind him. "Who's there?" called out a male voice. "Holly, is that you?"

She glared at Finn before her face morphed into a smile. "Yes, Dad. It's me."

"Well, are you coming in?"

Obediently she started up the walk. When she got to Finn's side, she leaned closer and whispered, "Just let me do the talking."

Boy, she was really worried about having him around her family. "Trust me."

He wasn't sure if she'd heard his softly spoken words as

she continued up the walk. He followed behind her, wondering what to expect.

They stopped on the stoop. Her father was still blocking the doorway. The man's hair was dark with silver in the temples. He wore dark jeans and a sweatshirt with the Jets logo across the front. Finn made a mental note of it. If all else failed, maybe he could engage the man in football talk—even though he was more of a hockey fan.

"Who's at the door?" a female voice called out.

"It's Holly and some guy."

"Well, invite them in." And then a slender woman with long, bleached-blond hair appeared next to Holly's father. The woman elbowed her husband aside. "Don't mind him. Come in out of the cold."

Once they were all standing just inside the door, Finn could feel the stress coming off Holly in waves. What was up with that? Was she embarrassed of him? That would be a first. Most women liked to show him off to their friends. As for meeting a date's family, he avoided that at all costs. But Holly was different.

"Here, let me take your coats." Holly's stepmother didn't smile as she held out her hand. She kept giving Finn a look as though she should know him but couldn't quite place his face.

"That's okay." Holly didn't make any move to get comfortable. "We can't stay. I… I brought some gifts for the girls."

"Suzie! Kristi! Holly's here with gifts."

"I hope they like them. I saw them while I was out of town and thought of them."

"I'm sure they will." But there was no conviction in the woman's voice. "You can afford to go on vacation?"

Holly's face paled. "It was a business trip."

"Oh."

Her father retreated into the living room, which was off

to the right of the doorway. A staircase stood in front of them with a hallway trailing along the left side of it. And to the far left was a formal dining room. The house wasn't big, but it held a look of perfection—as though everything was in its place. There was nothing warm and welcoming about the house.

Finn wanted to say something to break up the awkward silence, but he wasn't sure what to say. Was it always this strained? If so, he understood why Holly wouldn't want to spend much time here.

"Who's your friend?" Her stepmother's gaze settled fully on him.

"Oh. This is Finn. He's my—"

"Boyfriend. It's nice to meet you." He held out his hand to the woman.

"I'm Helen." She flashed him a big, toothy smile as she accepted his handshake. "I feel like I should know you. Have we met before?"

"No."

"Are you sure?" She still held on to his hand.

He gently extracted his hand while returning her smile. "I'm certain of it. I wouldn't have forgotten meeting someone as lovely as you."

Her painted cheeks puffed up. "Well, I'm glad we've had a chance to meet. Isn't that right, Fred?" And then at last noticing that her husband had settled in the living room with a newspaper, she raised her voice. "Fred, you're ignoring our guests."

The man glanced over the top of his reading glasses. "You seem to be doing fine on your own."

"Don't I always?" the woman muttered under her breath. "Lately that man is hardly home. All he does is work." She moved to the bottom of the steps and craned her chin upward. "Suzie! Kristi! Get down here now!"

Doors slammed almost simultaneously. There was a rush

of footsteps as they crossed the landing and then stomped down the stairs.

"What do you want? I'm busy doing my nails." A teenage girl with hair similar to her mother's frowned.

"And I'm on the phone." The other teenager had dark hair with pink highlights.

"I know you're both busy, but I thought you'd want to know that your sister is here."

Both girls glanced toward the door. But they were staring—at him.

Both girls' eyes grew round. "Hey, you're Finn Lockwood." They continued down the steps and approached him. "What are you doing here?"

His stomach churned as they both batted their eyes at him and flashed him smiles.

"He's your sister's boyfriend."

Surprise lit up both sets of eyes. "You're dating her?"

He nodded. "I am. Your sister is amazing."

"I brought you some gifts." Holly stepped next to Finn. "I found them when I was in the Caribbean and I thought you would like them."

Each girl accepted a brightly wrapped package.

"What do you say?" prompted their mother.

"Thank you," they muttered to Holly.

"I'm Suzie," said the blonde.

"And I'm Kristi."

Helen stepped between her daughters. "Why don't you come in the living room and we can talk?"

"We really can't stay." Holly glanced at him with uncertainty in her eyes.

He smiled at her. "Holly's right. We have other obligations tonight, but she was anxious for me to meet you all."

"How did she bag you?" Suzie's brows drew together. "You're a billionaire and she's nothing."

Ouch! Finn's gaze went to the stepmother, but Helen

glanced away as though she hadn't heard a word. That was impossible because Suzie's voice was loud and quite clear.

His gaze settled back on Suzie. "Holly is amazing. She is quite talented. And she spearheaded the Project Santa initiative."

"The what?"

"It's nothing," Holly intervened. "We really should go."

Finn took Holly's hand in his. "We have a couple of minutes and they haven't opened their gifts yet."

Both girls glanced down as though they'd forgotten about the Christmas presents. They each pulled off the ribbons first and then tore through the wrapping paper. They lifted the lids and rooted through the bikinis and cover up as well as sunglasses and a small purse.

Kristi glanced up. "Does this mean you got us tickets to the Caribbean? My friends are going to be so jealous. I'll have to go to the tanning salon first. Otherwise I'll look like a snowman in a bikini."

Suzie's face lit up. "This will be great. I can't wait to get out of school."

"Oh, girls, we'll have to make sure you have everything you need. I'll need to go to the tanning salon, too."

"You?" The girls both turned to their mother.

"This is our gift, not yours," Suzie said bluntly. "You aren't invited."

"But—"

"Um, there is no trip," Holly said.

"No trip?" All heads turned to Holly. "You mean all you got us was some bikinis that we can't even use because if you hadn't noticed, it's snowing outside—"

"Suzie, that's enough. I'm sure your sister has something else in mind." Her stepmother sent her an expectant look.

Wow! This family was unbelievable. If Finn had his choice between having no family and this family, he'd be much happier on his own. He glanced around to find out why Holly's father hadn't interceded on his daughter's be-half, but the man couldn't be bothered to stop reading his paper long enough.

Finn inwardly seethed. As much as he'd like to let loose on these people and tell them exactly what he thought of them and their lack of manners, he had to think of Holly. For whatever reason, they meant enough to her to buy them gifts and come here to put up with their rudeness. Therefore, he had to respect her feelings because it certainly appeared that no one else would.

"There is one other thing." Finn looked at Holly, willing her to trust him with his eyes as he gave her hand a couple of quick squeezes. "Do you want me to tell them?"

"Um…uh, sure."

"You know how Holly is, never wanting to brag. But she used her connections and secured tickets to the Mistletoe Ball for the whole family."

For once, all three females were left speechless. Good. That was what he wanted.

"You did that? But how?" Her stepmother's eyes reflected her utter surprise. "Those tickets cost a fortune and I heard they sold out back in October."

Holly's face drained of color. "Well, the truth is—"

"She has an inside source that she promised not to re-veal to anyone," Finn said. "They'll be waiting for the four of you at the door of the museum."

The girls squealed with delight as Helen yelled in to her husband to tell him about the tickets to the ball. If a man could look utterly unimpressed, it was Holly's father. And through it all, Finn noticed that not one person thanked Holly. It was though they felt entitled to the tickets. A groan of frustration grew down deep in his throat. A glance at Holly's pale face had him swallowing down his outrage and disgust.

He made a point of checking his Rolex. "And now, we really must be going."

As they let themselves out the front door, the girls were talking over top of each other about dresses, shoes, haircuts and manicures. And he had never been so happy to leave anywhere in his entire life. Once outside, Finn felt as though he could breathe. He was no longer being smothered with fake pleasantries and outright nastiness.

# CHAPTER NINETEEN

Big fluffy snowflakes fell around them, adding a gentle softness to the world and smoothing out the rough edges. Finn continued to hold Holly's hand, enjoying the connection. When they reached the car, he used his free hand to open the door.

She paused.

"Holly?"

When she looked up at him, tears shimmered in her eyes. The words lodged in his throat. There was nothing in this world that he could say to lessen the pain for her.

Instead of speaking, he leaned forward and pressed his lips to hers. With the car door ajar between them, he couldn't pull her close like he wanted. Instead he had to be content with this simple but heartfelt gesture.

With great regret he pulled back. "You better get in. The snow is picking up."

She nodded and then did as he said.

Once they were on the now snow-covered road, Finn guided the car slowly along the streets. He should have been more insistent about putting off this visit, not that Holly would have listened to him. When she set her mind on something, there was no stopping her. Although after meeting her family, he could understand why she'd want to get that visit out of the way.

As the snow fell, covering up the markings on the street, his body tensed. This must have been how it'd been the night his parents died. The thought sent a chill through his body.

"Are you cold?" Holly asked.

"What?"

"I just saw you shiver. I'll turn up the fan. Hopefully the heat will kick in soon." After she adjusted the temperature

controls, she leaned back in her seat. "What were you thinking by offering up those tickets to the ball? I don't have any
connections."

"But I do. So don't worry." He didn't want to carry on a
conversation now.

"You…you shouldn't have done it. It's too much."

"Sure, I should have." Not taking his eyes off the road,
he reached out to her. His hand landed on her thigh and he
squeezed. "I wanted to do it for you. I know how much your
family means to you."

"They shouldn't, though. I know they don't treat me…like
family. I just wish—oh, I don't know what I wish."

"It's done now so stop worrying." He returned his hand
to the steering wheel.

"That's easy for you to say. You're not related to them."

"But they are related to you and the babies. Therefore,
they are now part of my life." He could feel her eyeing him
up. Had that been too strong? He didn't think so. Even if
he never won over her heart, they would all still be one
mixed-up sort of family.

"You do know what this means, don't you?"

His fingers tightened on the steering wheel, not liking
the sound of her voice. "What?"

"That you and I must go to the ball now. And it's a well-
known fact that you make a point of never attending the ball."

"For you, I'll make an exception." The snow came down
heavier, making his every muscle tense. "Don't worry. It'll
all work out."

"I'll pay you back."

Just then the tires started to slide. His heart lurched. *No!
No! No!*

Holly reached out, placing a hand on his thigh. Her fingers tightened, but she didn't say a word.

When the tires caught on the asphalt, Finn expelled a
pent-up breath. This was his fault. He promised to take care

of his family and protect them like he hadn't been able to do with his parents and brother. And already he was failing.

Finn swallowed hard. "If you want to pay me back, the next time I tell you that we should stay in because of the weather, just listen to me."

She didn't say anything for a moment. And then ever so softly, she said, "I'm sorry. I didn't think it'd get this bad."

His fingers tightened on the steering wheel as he lowered his speed even more, wishing that they were closer to his building.

*Just a little farther. Everything will be all right. It has to be.*

His gut twisted into a knot. It was going to take him a long time to unwind after this. The snow kept falling, making visibility minimal at best. The wipers cleared the windshield in time for more snow to cover it.

His thoughts turned back to Holly. The truth was that no matter how much he'd fought it in the beginning, he'd fallen for Holly, hook, line and sinker. He couldn't bear to lose her or the babies. From now on, when they went out, he'd plan ahead. He'd be cautious. He'd do anything it took to keep them safe.

From here on out, they were a team. He had Holly's back. And he already knew that she had his—the success of Project Santa was evidence of it. Now he just had to concentrate on the roadway and make sure they didn't end up skidding into a ditch or worse.

*What an utter disaster.*

Back at the penthouse, Holly didn't know what to say to Finn. He'd been so quiet in the car. He must be upset that she let him walk into such a strained situation and then for him to feel obligated to come up with those tickets to the ball. They cost a small fortune. She didn't know how she'd ever repay him.

Now she was having second thoughts about telling Finn that they had to go to the ball. She didn't know how she'd explain it to her family, but she'd come up with a reason for their absence. Besides, it wasn't like she even had a dress, and the ball was just days away.

When she stepped into the living room, she found Finn had on the Rangers and Penguins hockey game. That was good. After the cleanup on the island, the work at the office and then meeting her family, he deserved some downtime.

She sat down on the couch near him. "I hope you don't mind that I ordered pizza for dinner."

"That's fine." His voice was soft as though he was lost in thought.

"Tomorrow I'll work on getting some food in the fridge."

He didn't say anything.

She glanced up at the large-screen television. She had to be honest, she didn't know anything about hockey or for that matter any other sport, but she might need to if these babies were anything like their father.

"Who's winning?"

He didn't say anything.

What was wrong with him? Was he mad at her? She hoped not. Maybe he was just absorbed by the game. "Who's winning?"

"What?"

"The score. What is it?"

"I don't know."

He didn't know? Wasn't he watching the game? But as she glanced at him, she noticed he was staring out the window at the snowy night. Okay, something was wrong and she couldn't just let it fester. If he had changed his mind about her staying here, she wanted to know up front. She realized she came with a lot of baggage and if he wanted out, she couldn't blame him.

She placed a hand on his arm. "Finn, talk to me."

He glanced at her. "What do you want to talk about?"

"Whatever's bothering you?"

"Nothing's bothering me." He glanced away.

"You might have been able to tell me that a while back, but now that I know you, I don't believe you. Something has been bothering you since we left my father's. It's my family, isn't it?"

"What? No. Of course not."

"Listen, I know those tickets are going to cost a fortune. I will pay you back."

"No, you won't. They are my gift. And so is your dress and whatever else you need for the ball."

"But I couldn't accept all of that. It… It's too much."

"The ball was my idea, not yours, so no arguments. Tomorrow we'll go to this boutique I know of that should have something for you to wear. If not, we'll keep looking."

"I don't know what to say."

"Good. Don't say anything. I just want you to enjoy yourself."

"But how am I supposed to after tonight? I'm really sorry about my family. It's complicated with them. I was less than cordial to my stepmother when she married my father. I blamed her for breaking up my parents' marriage since he had an ongoing affair with her for a couple of years before he left my mother."

Finn's gaze met hers. "And your mother didn't know?"

Holly shrugged. "She says she didn't, but I don't know how she couldn't know. He was gone all the time. But maybe it was a case of *she didn't want to know so she didn't look*."

"Sometimes we protect ourselves by only seeing as much as we can handle."

"Maybe you're right. But I think my mother's happy now. I just want to keep her that way, because she did her best to be there for me and now it's my turn to be there for her."

"And you will be. I see how you stick by those you love."

"You mean how I still go to my father's house even though I'll never be one of them?"

"I didn't mean that."

"It's okay. I realize this, but as much as they can grate on my nerves, I also know that for better or worse, they are my family. I just insist on taking them in small doses. And I'm so sorry I let you walk into that—I should have made it clearer to you—"

"It's okay, Holly. You didn't do anything wrong."

"But you didn't talk on the way home."

"That had nothing to do with your family and everything to do with me and my poor judgment. I'm forever putting those I care about at risk."

Wait. Where did that come from? "I don't understand. You didn't put me at risk."

"Yes, I did. And it can't happen again. We shouldn't have been out on the roads tonight. We could have…"

"Could have what? Talk to me."

He sighed. "Maybe if I tell you, you'll understand why I don't deserve to be happy."

"Of course you do." She took his hand and pressed it to her slightly rounded abdomen. "And these babies are proof of it."

"You might change your mind after I tell you this."

"I highly doubt it, but I'm listening."

"It had been a snowy February night a year after my brother died. I'd been invited to my best friend's birthday party, but I wasn't going. I was jealous of my friend because my Christmas had come and gone without lights and a tree. I'd been given a couple of gift cards, more as an afterthought."

Holly settled closer to him. She rested her head on his shoulder as she slipped her hand in his. She didn't know where he was going with this story, but wherever it led, she'd be there with him.

"My birthday had been in January—my thirteenth birthday—I was so excited to be a teenager. You know how kids are, always in a rush to grow up. But my parents hadn't done anything for it. There was no surprise party—no friends invited over—just a store-bought cake that didn't even have my name on it. I was given one birthday gift. There were apologies and promises to make it up to me."

Her heart ached for him. She moved her other hand over and rested it on his arm.

"When the phone rang to find out why I wasn't at my friend's party, my mother insisted I go and take a gift. Our parents were close friends, so when I again refused to go, my mother took back the one birthday gift that I'd received but refused to open. She insisted on delivering it to the party, but the snow was mounting outside and she was afraid to drive. My father reluctantly agreed to drive, but not before calling me a selfish brat and ordering me to my room."

Finn inhaled a ragged breath as he squeezed her hand. She couldn't imagine how much he'd lived through as a child. The death of his brother had spun the whole family out of control. No wonder he was such a hands-on leader. He knew the devastating consequences of losing control.

Finn's voice grew softer. "They only had a few blocks to drive, but the roads were icy. They had to cross a major roadway. My father had been going too fast. When he slowed down for the red light, he hit a patch of ice and slid into the intersection…into the path of two oncoming vehicles."

"Oh, Finn. Is that what happened tonight? You were reliving your parents' accident?"

He nodded. "Don't you see? If I had gone to that party, I would have been there before the snow. My parents would have never been out on the road. And tonight if I had paid attention to the forecast, I would have known about the storm rolling in."

"No matter how much you want to, you can't control the future. You had no idea then or now about what was going to happen. You can't hold yourself responsible."

"But you and those babies are my responsibility. If anything had happened to you, I wouldn't have known what to do with myself."

"You'd lean on your friends."

He shook his head. "I don't have friends. I have associates at best."

"Maybe if you let down your guard, you'd find out those people really do like you for you and not for what you can do for them." Her mind started to weave a plan to show Finn that he didn't need to be all alone in this world.

"I don't know. I've kept to myself so long. I wouldn't know how to change—how to let people in."

"I bet it's easier than you're thinking. Look how quickly we became friends."

"Is that what we are?" His gaze delved deep into her as though he could see straight through to the secrets lurking within her heart. "Are we just friends?"

Her heart *thump-thumped*. They were so much more than friends, but her voice failed her. Maybe words weren't necessary. In this moment actions would speak so much louder.

Need thrummed in her veins. She needed to let go of her insecurities. She needed to feel connected to him—to feel the love and happiness he brought to her life. She needed all of Finn with a force that almost scared her.

He filled in those cracks and crevices in her heart, making it whole. And not even her father's indifference tonight, her stepmother's coldness or her stepsisters' rudeness could touch her now. In this moment the only person that mattered was the man holding her close.

So while the snow fell outside, Holly melted into Finn's arms. She couldn't think of any other place she'd rather be and no one else she'd rather be with on this cold, blustery night.

# CHAPTER TWENTY

THIS WAS IT.

Holly stared at her reflection in the mirror. The blue spar-kly gown clung to her figure—showing the beginning of her baby bump. She frowned. What had she been thinking? Perhaps she should have selected something loose that hid her figure. But Finn had insisted this dress was his favor-ite. She turned this way and that way in front of the mirror. And truth be told, she did like it—a lot.

She took a calming breath. She was nervous about her first public outing on the arm of New York's most eligible bachelor. A smile pulled at her lips as she thought of Finn. He'd been so kind and generous supplying her family with tickets to the ball, and now she had a surprise for him.

It'd taken a bit of secrecy and a lot of help, but she'd pulled together an evening that Finn would not soon forget. To put the plan into action, she'd needed to get rid of him for just a bit. Unable to come up with a better excuse, she'd pleaded that her prenatal vitamin prescription needed refilling. To her surprise he'd jumped at the opportunity to go to the store. She might have worried about his eagerness to leave if her mind wasn't already on the details of her surprise. She liked to think of it as Project Finn.

She smoothed a hand over her up-do hairstyle. It was se-cured by an army of hairpins. Nothing could move it now. She then swiped a wand of pink gloss over her lips. She felt like she was forgetting something, but she couldn't figure out what it might be.

The doorbell rang. It was time for the evening's festivi-ties to begin. She rushed to the door and flung it open to find Clara standing there on the arm of her new husband. They were each holding a large shopping bag.

"Hi." Holly's gaze moved to Clara's husband. "I'm Holly. It's so nice to meet you."

"I'm Steve." He shook her hand. "Clara had a lot to say about you and Finn—all good. I swear."

Holly couldn't blame Clara. From the outside, she and Finn appeared to be an overnight romance. No one knew that it started a few months ago.

Then remembering her manners, she moved aside. "Please come inside. I sent Finn out on an errand. Hopefully he won't be back for a little bit. Is everything going according to plan?"

Clara nodded. "It is. Are you sure about this?"

"Yes." Her response sounded more certain than she felt at the moment. "This is my Christmas present to Finn."

"I didn't know he did Christmas presents."

"He doesn't, but that's all going to change now."

"Isn't this place amazing?" Clara glanced all around. "I'm always in awe of it every time I stop by with some papers for him. And as expected, there's not a single Christmas decoration in sight." Clara sent Holly a hesitant look. "Do you really think this is going to work?"

"As long as you have the ornaments in those bags, we're only missing the tree."

"Don't worry. I called on my way over and the tree is on its way."

"Oh, good. Thank you so much. I couldn't have done this without you. But no worries. If it doesn't go the way I planned, you're safe. I'll take full responsibility."

Holly thought of mentioning the baby news. She was getting anxious to tell people, but she didn't know how Finn would feel about her telling his PA without him. So she remained quiet—for now.

After pointing out where she thought a Christmas tree

would look best, Holly asked, "Where's everyone else? I was hoping they'd be here before he gets back."

As if on cue, the doorbell rang again.

"That must be them. I'll get it." Clara rushed over and swung open the door. "I was starting to wonder what happened to you guys."

A string of people came through the door carrying a Christmas tree and packages. Some people Holly recognized from the office and others were new to her. They were all invited to Finn's penthouse before attending the Mistletoe Ball. In all, there was close to a dozen people in the penthouse. Clara made sure to introduce Holly to all of them. Everyone was smiling and talking as they set to work decking Finn's halls with strands of twinkle light, garland and mistletoe.

Holly couldn't help but wonder what Finn would make of this impromptu Christmas party.

As though Clara could read her mind, she leaned in close. "Don't worry. He'll like this. Thanks to you, he's a changed man."

Holly wasn't so sure, but she hoped Clara was right. Instead of worrying, she joined the others as they trimmed the tree.

How long does it take to fill a prescription?

Finn rocked back on his heels, tired of standing in one spot. He checked his watch for the tenth time in ten minutes. There was plenty of time before they had to leave for the ball. Not that he wanted to go, but once he'd invited Holly's family there was no backing out.

He made a point of never going to the ball. Publicly, he distanced himself as much as he could from the event. He liked to think of himself as the man behind the magic curtain. He never felt worthy to take any of the credit for the prestigious event. He carried so much guilt around with him—always feeling like a poor replacement for his family.

But Holly was changing his outlook on life. Maybe she had a point—maybe punishing himself wasn't helping anyone.

He strolled through the aisles of the pharmacy. When he got to the baby aisle, he stopped. He gazed at the shelves crowded with formula, toys and diapers. All of this was needed for a baby? Oh, boy! He had no idea what most of the gizmos even did.

Then the image of the twins filled his mind. His fingers traced over a pacifier. He finally acknowledged to himself that he had to let go of the ghosts that haunted him if he had any hopes of embracing the future. Because deep down he wanted Holly and those babies more than anything in the world.

In no time, he was headed back to the penthouse with two pacifiers tucked in his inner jacket pocket and roses in his hand. He knew what he needed to do now. He needed to tell Holly how much he loved her and their babies—how he couldn't live without them.

But when he swung open the penthouse door, he came to a complete standstill. There were people everywhere. In front of the window now stood a Christmas tree. It was like he'd stepped into Santa's hideaway at the North Pole.

Where had all of these people come from? He studied their faces. Most were his coworkers. The unfamiliar faces he assumed were significant others. But where was Holly?

He closed the door and stepped farther into the room. People turned and smiled. Men shook his hand and women told him what a lovely home he had. He welcomed them and gave the appropriate responses all the while wondering what in the world they were doing there.

And then a hand touched his shoulder. He turned, finding Clara standing there, smiling at him. If this was her idea, they were going to have a long talk—a very long talk.

"Oh, I know who those are for. Nice touch." Clara sent him a smile of approval.

"What?"

She pointed to his hand.

Glancing down at the bouquet of red roses he'd picked up on his way home, he decided to give them to Holly later—when it was just the two of them. He moved off to the side and laid them on a shelf.

Finding Clara still close at hand, he turned back to her. "Looks like I arrived in time for the party."

"What do you think? Holly went all out planning this get-together."

Holly? She did this? "But why? I don't understand."

Clara shrugged. "Holly didn't tell me what prompted this little party. Maybe she just thought it would be a nice gesture before the ball. All I know is that she asked me to pull together all of your close friends."

Close friends? He turned to his PA and arched a brow. "And now you take directions from Holly?"

"Seemed like the right thing to do. After all, I'm all for helping the course of true love."

He turned away, afraid Clara would read too much in his eyes. True love? Were his feelings that obvious?

"Just be good to her. She's a special person." And with that, Clara went to mingle with the others.

His close friends? He glanced around the room. Yes, he knew many of these people. They'd been the ones to help him when he'd been old enough to step into his father's role as CEO. He'd had lunch or dinner with all of them at one point or another. He'd even discussed sports and family with them. He'd never thought it was any more than them being polite and doing what was expected, but maybe he hadn't been willing to admit that those connections had meant so much more.

Finn recalled the other night when he'd been snuggled with Holly on the couch. They'd been discussing friends and he'd said he didn't have any. Was this Holly's way of showing him that he wasn't alone in this world? That if he let down his guard, this could be his?

"Finn, there you are." Holly rushed up to him. "I have some explaining to do."

"I think I understand."

Her beautiful eyes widened. "You do?"

He nodded before he leaned down. With his mouth near hers, he whispered, "Thank you."

And then with all of his—their—friends around, he kissed her. And it wasn't just a peck. No, this was a passionate kiss and he didn't care who witnessed it. He was in love.

# CHAPTER TWENTY-ONE

HOLLY COULDN'T STOP SMILING.

A 1950s big-band tune echoed through the enormous lobby of the Metropolitan Museum. It was Holly's first visit and she was awed by the amazing architecture, not to mention the famous faces in attendance, from professional athletes to movie stars. It was a Who's Who of New York.

It also didn't hurt that she was in the arms of the most handsome man. Holly lifted her chin in order to look up at Finn. This evening was the beginning of big things to come—she was certain of it.

Finn's gaze caught hers. "Are you having fun?"

"The time of my life. But you shouldn't be spending all of your time with me. There are a lot of people who want to speak with you, including the paparazzi out in front of the museum."

"The reporters always have questions."

"Did you even listen to any of them?"

"No. I don't want anyone or anything to ruin this evening."

"You don't understand. It's good news. In fact, it's great news. Project Santa was such a success that it garnered national attention. The website is getting hit after hit and tons of heartfelt thank-yous from project coordinators, outreach workers and parents. There have even been phone calls from other companies wanting to participate next year. Just think of all the children and families that could be helped."

Finn smiled. "And it's all thanks to you."

"Me?" She shook her head. "It was your idea."

"But it was your ingenuity that saved the project. You took a project that started as a corporate endeavor and put it in the hands of the employees and the community. To me, that's the true meaning of Christmas—people helping people."

His words touched her deeply. "Thank you. I really connected with the project and the people behind the scenes."

"And that's why I think you should take it over permanently. Just let me know what you need."

Holly stopped dancing. "Seriously?"

"I've never been more serious."

This was the most fulfilling job she'd ever had. She didn't have to think it over. She knew this was her calling. Not caring that they were in the middle of the dance floor, she lifted on her toes and kissed him.

When they made it to the edge of the dance floor, Finn was drawn away from her by a group of men needing his opinion on something. Holly smiled, enjoying watching Finn animated and outgoing.

Out of excuses, Holly made her way to her family. It was time she said hello. She made small talk with her stepmother and sisters, but her father was nowhere to be seen. As usual, they quickly ran out of things to say to each other and Holly made her departure.

On the other side of the dance floor, Holly spotted her father dancing too close with a young lady. He was chatting her up while the young woman smiled broadly. Then her father leaned closer, whispering in the woman's ear. The woman blushed.

The whole scene sickened Holly—reminding her of all the reasons she'd sworn off men. They just couldn't be trusted and it apparently didn't get better with age.

Her stepmother was in for a painful reality check when she found out that she'd been traded in for a younger model just like her father had done to Holly's mother. The thought didn't make Holly happy. It made her very sad because she knew all too well the pain her half-sisters were about to experience.

Deciding she wasn't in any frame of mind to make friendly chitchat, she veered toward a quiet corner. She needed to gather herself. And then a beautiful woman stepped in her path. Holly didn't recognize her, but apparently the woman knew her.

"Hi, Holly. I've been meaning to get a moment to speak with you." The polished woman in a red sparkly dress held out a manicured hand.

"Hi." Holly shook her hand, all the while experiencing a strange sensation that she should know this woman.

Her confusion must have registered on her face because the woman said, "I'm sorry. I should have introduced myself. I'm Meryl."

Surely she couldn't be Finn's ex, could she? But there was no way Holly was going to ask that question. If she was wrong, it would be humiliating. And if she was right, well, awkwardness would ensue.

"If you're wondering, yes, I am that Meryl. But don't worry, Finn and I were over ages ago. I saw you earlier, dancing with him. I've never seen him look so happy. I'm guessing you're the one to do that for him. He's a very lucky man."

At last, the shock subsided and Holly found her voice. "It's really nice to meet you. Finn has nothing but good things to say about you."

Meryl's eyes lit up. "That's good to know. I think he's pretty great, too."

Really? Finn had given her the impression that hard feelings lingered. Her gaze scanned the crowd for the man they had in common, but she didn't see him anywhere.

"Ah, I see I caught you by surprise." The woman's voice was gentle and friendly. "You thought there would be lots of hard feelings, but there aren't. I assure you. Finn is a very generous and kind man. He just doesn't give himself enough credit."

"I agree with you."

Holly wanted desperately to dislike this woman, but she couldn't. Meryl seemed so genuine—so down to earth. There was a kindness that reflected in her eyes. Why exactly had Finn let her get away?

"And the fact that you were able to get him to attend his very own ball is a big credit to you."

"His ball?"

The woman's eyes widened in surprise. "I'm sorry. I said too much."

"No, you didn't." Holly needed to know what was going on. "Why did you call this Finn's ball? As far as I know, he's never even attended before this year."

"I thought he would have told you, especially since he just told me that he intends to marry you."

"He told you that?"

The woman nodded as her brows scrunched together. "Anyway, I do the leg work for the ball, but he's the drive behind it. It's not made public but the ball is done in memory of Finn's mother and brother. He says that he remains in the background underwriting all of the associated expenses because he's made a number of unpopular business deals as far as the press is concerned, but I think it's something else."

The thought that this woman had insights into Finn that Holly lacked bothered her. "What do you think his reasons are?"

"I think the ball reminds him of his family and for whatever reason, he carries a truckload of guilt that he survived and they didn't."

And that was where Holly was able to fill in the missing pieces, but she kept what Finn had told her about his past to herself. She knew all about his survivor's guilt. And now she realized how much it'd cost him to come here tonight.

*But what other secrets was he keeping from me?* Tears stung the backs of her eyes. *Stupid hormones.* "There appears to be a lot I have to learn about Finn."

"I'm not surprised he didn't mention it. Finn doesn't open up easily."

Just to those that are closest to him. Holly finished Meryl's statement. After all of their talk about being open and honest with each other, he let her come here not knowing the facts. He'd lied to her by omission. Now she wondered what else he was keeping from her.

"I… I should be going." Holly was anxious to be alone with her thoughts.

"Well, there I go putting my foot in my mouth. Sorry about that. Sometimes when I'm nervous I talk too much."

"It's okay. I've really enjoyed talking with you."

Meryl's eyes lit up as a smile returned to her face. "I'm really glad we met. I think we might just end up friends, of course if you're willing."

"I'd like that."

But as they parted company, Holly didn't think their friendship would ever have a chance to flourish. She doubted they'd ever run into each other again.

She turned to come face-to-face with her father. He was the very last person she wanted to speak to that evening. "Excuse me."

Her father stepped in front of her. "Not so fast. I did a little research into that boyfriend of yours. And I think I should get to know him better."

Not a chance. Her father caused enough destruction wherever he went. She wasn't going to give him a chance to hurt Finn.

Holly pointed a finger at her father. "You stay away from him."

Her father's eyes widened with surprise. "But it's a father's place to make sure the guy is worthy of his daughter."

She clenched her hands. "And you would be an expert on character and integrity?"

"What's that supposed to mean?"

"I saw you—everybody saw you flirting with that young woman who's what? My age? How could you?"

"I didn't mean for it to happen."

"You never do."

Her father at least had the decency to grow red-faced. "You don't understand—"

"You're right. I don't. I have to go."

She rushed past her father. Suddenly the walls felt as though they were closing in on her and it was hard to breathe. She knew not to trust men. Her father had taught her that at an early age. And he'd reinforced that lesson tonight.

What made her think that Finn would be different? No, he wasn't a womanizer, but he was a man. And he only trusted her so far. Without complete trust, they had nothing.

Except the babies, which she'd never keep from him. But they didn't have to be together to coparent. Because she refused to end up like her mother and blindsided by a man.

The fairy tale was over.

It was time she got on with her life—without Finn.

She headed for the door, needing fresh air.

*What in the world?*

Finn had caught glimpses of Holly and Meryl with their heads together. His gut had churned. *Nothing good will come of that.*

He tried to get away from a couple of gentlemen, but they were his partners in an upcoming deal and he didn't want to offend them. But for every excuse he came up with to make his exit, they came up with a new aspect of their pending deal that needed further attention.

He should have forewarned Holly that Meryl would be here. But honestly, it slipped his mind. Between the news of the babies and then Holly's surprise holiday gathering at the penthouse, his thoughts were not his own these days.

He breathed easier when the women parted. But the next time he spotted Holly, she was having a conversation with her father and if the hand gestures and the distinct frown were anything to go by, it wasn't going well.

"Gentlemen, these are all great points. And I look forward to discussing them in great detail, but I promised my date I wouldn't work tonight."

The men admitted that they'd made similar promises to their wives. They agreed to meet again after the first of the year. With a shake of hands, they parted.

Finn turned around in time to witness Holly heading for the door. He took off after her, brushing off people with a smile and promising to catch up with them soon. It wasn't in him to be outright rude, but his sixth sense was telling him Holly's fast exit was not good—not good at all.

He rushed past the security guards posted at the entrance of the museum, past the impressive columns, and started down the flight of steps. Snow was starting to fall and Holly didn't have a coat. What was she thinking?

When he stepped on the sidewalk, his foot slipped on a patch of ice. He quickly caught his balance. He glanced to the left and then right. Which way had she gone?

And then he saw the shadow of a person. Was that her? He drew closer and realized the person was sitting on the sidewalk. His heart clenched. He took off at a sprint.

When he reached Holly's side, he knelt down. "Holly, are you all right?"

She looked up at him with a tear trailing down her cheek. "No. I'm not."

"Should I call an ambulance?"

"No." She sniffled. "I just need a hand up. I… I slipped on some ice."

"Are you sure it's okay if you stand? I mean, what about the babies?"

"Just give me your hand." He did as she asked.

Once she was on her feet, she ran her hands over her bare arms. He noticed the goose bumps, which prompted him to slip off his jacket and place it over her shoulders. "Thank you. But you need it."

"Keep it. I'm fine." He had so much adrenaline flooding through his system at that particular moment that he really didn't notice the cold.

"Do you want to go back inside?"

She lifted the skirt of her gown. "I don't think so. My heel broke."

He glanced down, finding her standing on one foot as the other heel had broken and slipped off her foot. Without a word, he retrieved the heel and handed to her. Then he scooped her up in his arms.

"Put me down! What are you doing?"

"Taking you home."

"Finn, stop. We need to talk."

"You're right. We do. But not out here in the cold."

# CHAPTER TWENTY-TWO

SO MUCH FOR making a seamless exit.

Holly sat on the couch in Finn's penthouse feeling ridiculous for falling on the ice and breaking her shoe. The lights on the Christmas tree twinkled as though mocking her with their festiveness. She glanced away.

She'd trusted Finn and yet things about him and his past kept blindsiding her. How was she ever supposed to trust him? How was she supposed to believe he'd never hurt her?

Falling in love and trusting another human was like a free fall and trusting that your parachute would open. Holly wasn't sure she had the guts to free-fall. Her thoughts strayed back to her father. She inwardly shuddered, remembering him flirting with that young woman, and then he didn't even deny he was having an affair with her. Her mother had trusted him and then her stepmother. It was to their utter detriment.

Finn rushed back in the room with a damp cloth. "Here. Let me have your hand."

She held her injured hand out to him. He didn't say anything as he gently cleaned her scrapes and then applied some medicated cream before wrapping a bit of gauze around it.

"Did you hurt anything else?"

"Besides my pride? No."

"I wish you'd have talked to me before you took off. Anything could have happened to you—"

"If you hadn't noticed, I'm a grown woman. I can take care of myself."

He arched a brow at her outburst.

"Hey, anyone can slip on ice," he said calmly. "I just wish

you'd have talked to me. Why did you leave? Was it Meryl? Did she say something to upset you?"

"No. Actually she didn't. Not directly."

"What is that supposed to mean?"

"Why didn't you tell me she would be there? That you still interact with her?"

He shrugged and glanced away. "I don't know. I didn't think of it."

"Really? Is that the same reason you didn't tell me you're the mastermind behind the Mistletoe Ball? That without you, there wouldn't be a ball?"

"I guess I should have said something. I didn't think it was a big deal. I wasn't keeping it a secret from you, but I've been distracted. If you haven't noticed, we're having twins."

"What else haven't you told me?" Her fears and insecurities came rushing to the surface. "What else don't I know about you that's going to blindside me?"

His facial features hardened. "I'm sure there's lots you don't know about me, just like there's a lot I don't know about you." When she refused to back down, he added, "Do you want me to start with kindergarten or will a detailed report about my last five years do?"

She glared at him for being sarcastic. Then she realized she deserved it. She was overreacting. She'd let her family dig into her insecurities and her imagination had done the rest.

"You know what? Never mind." Finn got up from the couch. "If you don't trust me, this is never going to work. Just forget this—forget us. I was wrong to think it could work."

Her heart ached as she watched him walk out of the room. She didn't even know the person she'd become. It was like she was once again that insecure little girl who realized her father had lied to her—learning that her father had secretly exchanged his current family for a new one. And now her father was about to do it again.

But Finn hadn't done that. He hadn't done anything but be sweet and kind. Granted, he might not be totally forthcoming at times, but it wasn't because he was out to deceive her or hurt her. She couldn't punish him for the wrongs her father had done to her over the years.

If she was ever going to trust a man with her heart—it would be Finn. Because in truth she did love him. She'd fallen for him that first night when he'd invited her here to his penthouse. He'd been charming and entertaining.

Now, when it looked like she was going to have it all—the perfect guy, the amazing babies and a happily-ever-after—she was pulling away. In the light of day, the depth of her love for Finn scared her silly. Her instinct was to back away fast—just like she was doing now. And if she wasn't careful, she'd lose it all. If she hadn't already.

Still wearing Finn's jacket, she wrapped her arms around herself. She inhaled the lingering scent of his spicy cologne mingled with his unique male scent. Her eyes drifted closed.

There had to be a way to salvage things. Maybe she could plead a case of pregnancy hormones. Nah. She had to be honest with him about her fears and hope he'd be willing to work through them with her.

It was then she noticed something poking her. There was something in his inner jacket pocket. She reached inside and pulled out not one but two packages of pacifiers. One was pink and one was blue. Happy tears blurred her eyes as she realized just how invested Finn was in their expanding family. She had to talk to him—to apologize.

She swiped at her eyes and got to her feet, heading for the kitchen.

# CHAPTER TWENTY-THREE

WHAT WAS HE DOING?

Finn chastised himself for losing his cool with Holly. Every time she questioned him, she poked at his insecurities about being a proper husband and father. He had so many doubts about doing a good job. He didn't even know what being a husband and father entailed. All he knew was that he wanted to do his best by his family.

And he wasn't a quitter. He fought for the things he believed in. Sometimes he fought too long for his own good. But this was his family—there was no retreating. He would somehow prove to Holly—and most of all to himself—that he could be there for her and the babies through the good and the bad.

Certain in what he needed to do, he turned on his heels and headed back to the living room, hoping Holly hadn't made a quick exit. If she had, it wouldn't deter him. He would find her. He would tell her that he loved her. Because that was what it all boiled down to. He was a man who was head over heels in love with the mother of his children.

When he entered the living room, he nearly collided with Holly. He put his hands on her shoulders to steady her. "Where are you going in such a rush?"

"To find you. There's something I need to say."

"There's something I need to say to you, too."

At the same time, they said, "I'm sorry."

Finn had to be sure he heard her correctly. "Really?"

She nodded before she lifted up on her tiptoes and with her hands on either side of his face, she pulled him down to her. The kiss wasn't light or hesitant. Instead her kiss was heated and demanding. Need thrummed in his veins. He never wanted to let her go.

It'd be oh, so easy to dispense with words. His hands wrapped around her waist, pulling her soft curves to his hard planes. A moan grew in the back of his throat and he didn't fight it. Holly had to know all of the crazy things she did to his body, to his mind, to his heart.

But he wanted—no, he needed to clear the air between them. Christmas was in the air and it was the time for setting aside the past and making a new start. That was exactly what he wanted to do with Holly.

It took every fiber of his being to pull away from her embrace. Her beautiful eyes blinked and stared at him in confusion. It'd be so easy to pull her close again and pick up where they'd left off.

*No, Finn. Do the responsible thing. Make this right for both of you.*

"Come sit down so we can talk." He led her to the couch.

"Talk? Now?"

"Trust me. It's important."

"As long as I go first," she said. "After all, I started this whole thing."

"Deal."

She inhaled a deep breath and then blew it out. She told him about running into her family and how her father's actions and her stepsisters' words had ripped the scabs off her insecurities. "I know that's not a good excuse, but it's the truth. I've spent most of my life swearing that I would never end up like my mother—that I'd never blindly trust a man."

"And then you ran into my ex and found out I'd left out some important details about my life."

Holly shrugged and glanced away. "I just let it all get to me." She lifted her chin until her gaze met his. "I know you're not my father. You are absolutely nothing like him. I trust you."

"You do?"

She nodded. "I can't promise that every once in a while my insecurities won't get the best of me, but I promise to work on them."

"I love you, Holly."

Her eyes grew shiny with unshed tears. "I love you, too."

He cleared his throat, hoping his voice wouldn't fail him before he got it all out. "I would never intentionally hurt you or our children. You and those babies mean everything to me. I'm really excited to be a father."

"I noticed." She reached in his jacket pocket and pulled out the pacifiers. "I found these. And they're so sweet. Our babies' first gifts."

"You like them?"

She nodded. "How could I have ever doubted you?"

"I promise you here and now that I'll work on being more forthcoming. I've spent so many years keeping things bottled up inside me that I might slip up now and then. Will you stick by me while I work on this partnership thing?"

She nodded. "As long as you'll stick by me while I learn to let go of the past."

"It's a deal." Then recalling the flowers, he jumped to his feet. "I have something for you." He moved to the bookcase and retrieved the flowers. "I got these for you when I went to the pharmacy earlier." He held them out to her.

She accepted the bouquet and sniffed them. "They're beautiful."

This was his chance to make this Christmas unforgettable. He took her hand in his and gazed up into her wide-open eyes. "Holly, the most important thing you need to know about me is that I love you. And I love those babies you're carrying. I want to be the best husband and father, if you'll let me. Will you marry me?"

A tear splashed onto her cheek. She moved his hand to

her slightly rounded abdomen. "We love you, too. And yes. Yes! Yes! I'll marry you."

His heart filled with love—the likes he'd never known. And it was all Holly's doing. She'd opened his eyes and his heart not only to the spirit of the season, but also to the possibilities of the future.

He leaned forward, pressing his lips to hers.

This was the best Christmas ever.

# EPILOGUE

THERE—THAT SHOULD do it.

Finn stepped back from the twelve-foot Christmas tree that stood prominently in front of the bay windows of his new house—correction, *their* house...as in his and Holly's home. This was the very first Christmas tree that he'd decorated since he was a child. Surprisingly it didn't hurt nearly as much as he'd thought. The memories of his brother and parents were always there, lingering around the edges, but now he was busy making new memories with Holly and their twins, Derek, in honor of his brother, and Maggie, in honor of his mother.

"How's it going?" Holly ventured into the room carrying a twin in each arm.

"I just finished putting on the lights. And how about you? Is Project Santa a go?"

Holly's face lit up. "Yes. And this year will be even bigger than last year, which means we're able to help even more children."

"I knew you were the right person to put in charge."

Maggie let out a cry. Holly bounced her on her hip. "Sounds like someone is hungry."

"Did I hear someone cry out for food?" Holly's mother strolled into the room, making a beeline for Maggie.

Finn glanced over at his mother-in-law, Sandy, who now lived in a mother-in-law apartment on the other side of their pool. When Holly had suggested her mother move in, he had to admit that he'd been quite resistant to the idea. But when Holly really wanted something, he found himself unable to say no.

In the end, he and Sandy hit it off. The woman was a lot

more laid-back than he'd ever imagined. And she doted over her grandchildren, which won her a gold star. And with the help of a nanny and a housekeeper, they were one big, happy family—unless of course the twins were hungry or teething.

"I can do it, Mom," Holly insisted, hanging on to the baby.

"Nonsense. I wasn't doing anything important." Sandy glanced over at the tree. "And from the looks of things in here, your husband could use some help."

Holly smiled. "I think you're right." She handed over the fussing baby. "Thanks. I'll be in shortly."

"Don't hurry. I've got this." Sandy started toward the kitchen. "Isn't that right, Maggie? We're buddies."

Holly stepped up beside Finn. "Are you sure you bought enough lights to cover all of the tree?"

"Yes. I'll show you." He bent over and plugged them in.

His wife arched a brow at him as though she knew something that he didn't. This was never a good sign.

"You should have tested them before putting them on the tree."

"What?" He turned around to find the top and middle of the tree all lit up, but the bottom section was dark. But how could that be? "I swear I tested them before I strung them."

Holly moved up next to him and handed over Derek. "Maybe it's just payback."

He glanced at his wife, trying to figure out what payback she was referring to. And then he recalled that last Christmas he'd shared the story of how he and his brother had swiped a strand of lights from the Christmas tree in order to light up their blanket fort.

A smile pulled at Finn's lips at the memory. It was the first time he'd been able to look back on his past and smile. That was all thanks to Holly. Her gift to him last year was giving his life back to him. Instead of walking around a shell of a man, he was taking advantage of every breath he had on this earth.

"Perhaps you're right. Maybe Derek's playing tricks on me."

"Did you hear that?" Holly leaned forward and tickled their son's tummy, making him giggle and coo. "Are you playing tricks on your daddy?"

Finn knew she was adding a bit of levity to the moment to keep things from getting too serious. Finn liked the thought that his brother might be looking down over them and smiling. Right here and now the past and the present came together, making Finn feel complete.

"Would you do that?" Finn placed his finger in his son's hand. "Would you steal the lights from the Christmas tree to make a fort?"

"Don't give him ideas," Holly lightly scolded. "I have a feeling your son will get into enough trouble of his own without any help from you."

"I think you might be right."

"And if he has a little brother, we'll really have our hands full."

This was the first time Holly had ever mentioned having another baby. It was usually him going on about expanding their family because to his surprise and delight, he loved being a dad. He'd even considered quitting the day job to be a full-time parent until Holly put her foot down and told him that someone had to keep the family business going to hand down to their children. But he no longer worked from morning till late at night. He took vacations and weekends. He had other priorities now.

"I think it'd be great to have another baby. Just let me know when you want my assistance. I'm all yours."

"Oh, you've done plenty already."

"Hey, what's that supposed to mean?" Derek wiggled in his arms. "Oh, you mean the twins? What can I say? When I do something I go all out."

"Well, let's just hope this time around I'm not carrying

twins or you might just be staying home to take care of all of them while I run the office."

Surely he'd misunderstood her. She couldn't be—could she? "Are…are you pregnant?"

She turned to him and with tears of joy in her eyes, she nodded. "Merry Christmas."

Finn whooped with joy before leaning forward and planting a kiss on his wife's lips. He'd never been so happy in his life. In fact, he never knew it was possible to be this happy.

"You give the best Christmas presents ever, Mrs. Lockwood."

"Well, Mr. Lockwood, you inspire me." She smiled up at him. "I love you."

"I love you the mostest."

\* \* \* \* \*

# FIREFIGHTER'S
# CHRISTMAS BABY

**ANNIE CLAYDON**

To Sareeta.
With grateful thanks for steering me through
my last four books with such grace and aplomb.

# CHAPTER ONE

AFTER TWO WEEKS of feeling the sun on his skin, and not having to bother with a razor, Ben Matthews had cut himself shaving. His uniform had felt unfamiliar and a little too crisp when he'd put it on this morning, but it was good to be back in a routine. The thing about holidays was that they gave him far too much time to think, and he was ready to get back to work now.

'Good holiday?' The fire station commander smiled across his desk, and Ben nodded.

'Has anything been happening here that I should know about?'

'I imagine you've already read the station reports?' Ben nodded in response. 'The only other thing is our visitor this morning.'

'Yes?' As the watch manager, Ben always liked to have a little warning if an inspection was taking place, but he had no concerns. It was a matter of both principle and pride that he and his crew were constantly ready for anything.

'She's a photographer. This is just a preliminary visit, she'll be back again in a month to take photographs over Christmas. It's partly her own project, to widen her portfolio, but we have an option to use any of the photographs she takes in our publicity campaigns and there's also going to be a calendar, which we'll be issuing at the end of next year.'

This all seemed very rushed. Ben wished he'd known about it when it had been in the planning stage, rather than being presented with a fait accompli. 'And this has all been agreed?'

'There wasn't much time to set it up. Ms Walsh specifically requested that she take the photographs over Christmas to add authenticity to the calendar shots. She's hoping to include some off-duty moments.'

Ben frowned. The only calendar he'd seen that had featured firefighters had involved underwear and Santa hats. And that was just the men...

'This is going to be...done sensitively, I imagine?'

'Of course. It's a bit of fun but there's a serious message, too. We want to raise public awareness about what we do, as well as raise money.'

'Right.' Ben was all for the serious message. Just as long as this photographer understood that too. 'The crew knows about this?'

'Yes, they're all for it. Ms Walsh came in last week with her portfolio and showed us some of her work. I thought it was excellent, and there was some disappointment amongst the other crews when she chose to shadow Blue Watch.'

This photographer seemed to be calling all the shots. Not with *his* crew...

'And you've given her a free hand?'

The station commander smiled. 'I haven't imposed any restrictions on her, if that's what you mean. I know I can count on you to ensure the smooth running of the operation.'

'In that case...' Ben needed to get back to his crew. Now. Before this photographer started to think she *did* have a free hand and anyone persuaded anyone else that taking their shirts off was a good idea. 'I'll be getting on if there's nothing else.'

'No, nothing else.' The station commander picked up a file from his desk, and Ben rose, heading for the door.

Ben opened the door of the ready room and found it empty. Of course it was. Gleaming red and chrome was sure to appeal as the backdrop for the calendar photographs. Walking downstairs into the garage, he heard voices and laughter.

'No, I don't think that's going to work.' A woman's voice, clear and brimming with humour. 'I'm after something a bit more spontaneous...'

*'Spontaneous, my eye.'* Ben muttered the words to himself, marching through the narrow gap between the two fire engines and almost bumping into a woman who was standing by the front one of them.

At least she was good at getting out of the way. That was exactly the kind of aptitude she'd need. Ben caught a trace of her scent before she stepped quickly to one side and he came face to face with Eve and Pete, in full protective gear, standing beside the chrome fender, both with fixed smiles on their faces. That looked absolutely fine to him but, then, he wasn't in the business of art photography.

'Okay...let's break it up.' It seemed that the rest of the crew had decided that the taking of a few photographs required them to stand around watching. 'Give us a minute, will you?'

'Good to see you back, boss.' Eve grinned at him, taking her helmet off and unbuttoning her jacket. Ben heard the click of a camera shutter beside him and turned to the woman standing next to him as the crew dispersed quickly.

'Hi. I'm Callie Walsh.' She was holding the camera loosely in one hand, the other stretched out towards him. 'You must be Ben Matthews.'

'Yes.' Ben shook her hand briskly, omitting to say that

he was pleased to meet her. 'The station commander told me you'd be here.'

She nodded, looking up at him. She had green eyes, the kind that seemed wholly dedicated to making a man stare into them, and the prettiest face he'd seen in a long while. The softness stopped there. Her short, corn-blonde hair was streaked with highlights and slicked back from her face. Spray-on jeans, a fitted leather jacket with more zips than seemed entirely necessary, and a look of determination on her face gave the overall impression of a woman who knew how to steamroller her way over pretty much anything.

Instinctively, Ben stepped back, leaning against the chrome on the front of the fire engine. When she raised her camera, pointing the bulky lens in his direction, he frowned.

'Before you take any more photographs, I think there are a few ground rules we need to have in place.'

'Of course.' Her face was impassive, and Ben wondered what she was thinking. That didn't matter. It didn't matter what he thought either. What mattered was the well-being and effectiveness of his crew.

'This is a working fire station…'

'I understand that. I know how to keep out of the way.'

That had only been his first concern. There were many more. 'As Watch Manager I'm responsible for the safety of everyone connected with Blue Watch…' His gaze drifted to the high heels of her boots. What she was wearing didn't come close to practical, if she was reckoning on venturing anywhere other than the ready room.

She seemed to read his thoughts. 'I'm hoping to just get everyone used to the idea of me being here today. I won't be accompanying you to any calls…'

'You won't be doing anything, at any time, unless I allow it.'

Perhaps he should qualify that. She could do whatever

she liked, as long as she didn't mess with him or his crew. Callie was regarding him thoughtfully, as if she was assessing her next move.

'I can handle myself in emergency situations and I know how to follow operational and safety guidelines.' She unzipped her jacket, pulling a sheet of folded paper from an inside pocket. 'You probably haven't had a chance to look at my CV yet, but when you do you'll see that I'm a paramedic.'

If she'd been trying to surprise him, she'd pulled off a master stroke. When he took the paper, it seemed warm to the touch. Ben put that down to his imagination, rather than the heat of her body.

'When did you change jobs?' He unfolded the paper, scanning it.

'I didn't. I did an evening course in photography when I was at school and found that I can take a decent portrait. The income from that helped put me through my training as a paramedic, but now I want to extend my range a little. I think my first-hand experience of working with the emergency services gives me something unique to bring to this project.'

It was either a canny career move or some kind of personal crusade. It was difficult to tell what sparked the passion that shone in her eyes, and it really wasn't Ben's job to decide. All he needed to concern himself with was the practicalities, not whatever made Callie Walsh tick.

'All the same, I'd like to have first sight of all the photographs you take…'

Callie shook her head. 'That's not the way I work.'

'It's the way *I* intend to work.'

The edges of her mouth curved slightly, as if she already had her answer ready and had been waiting for the right time to slap him down.

'Then you'll have to adapt. I decide which of my photographs goes forward, and they go to the individuals concerned first, so they can review them and choose whether they want to sign a release. After that they go to the station commander. It's all agreed and I'm sure he'll show them to you if you ask nicely.'

Ben ignored the jibe. The procedure sounded reasonable enough but he would have no hesitation in circumnavigating it if he saw any threat to the welfare of the firefighters on his watch.

'All right. But if I feel that any of the photographs are inappropriate, I won't hesitate to block them.'

She folded her arms. 'You want to give me some artistic direction? What do you mean by "inappropriate"?'

He shouldn't feel embarrassed about this, even if her green eyes did seem to rob him of his capacity to stay dispassionate. It was simply an observation.

'I won't have any of my crew treated as…eye candy.'

Ben had expected she might protest. But her gaze travelled from his face, looking him up and down slowly. He tried to suppress the shiver that ran up his spine.

'You think you'd be good eye candy?'

Ben had a healthy regard for disdain, particularly when it emanated from a beautiful woman. It was almost refreshing.

'No, that's just my point.'

'Good. We're in agreement, then. Anything else?' Callie smiled. Her face became softer when she did that, and the temptation to enjoy this confrontation became almost overwhelming.

'Don't leave any of your equipment around. I don't want anyone tripping over anything.'

'I'm looking for spontaneity, not posed shots, and my camera is all I need. I never leave it around.'

'Okay. And if the alarm sounds, I need you out of the way. Quickly.'

'Understood. I'll flatten myself against the nearest wall.' Her gaze met his, and the thought of crowding her against a wall and kissing her burst into Ben's head. Maybe he'd muss her hair a little first and find out whether the soft centre that her lustrous eyes hinted at really did exist.

He dismissed the idea. If the alarm sounded, that would be the last thing he should be thinking about. And if it didn't then it was still the last thing he should be thinking about.

'That's great. Thank you.'

'My pleasure. May I get on and take a few shots now?'

'Yes, please do.' Ben turned, and walked away from her.

Maybe…

There was no maybe about it. Callie took his breath away. He'd aired his concerns less tactfully than usual because her mesmerising gaze had the power to make him forget all his reservations about her presence here. Even now, he was so preoccupied by the temptation to look back and catch another glimpse of her that he almost forgot he'd intended to go back his office and found himself heading on autopilot towards the ready room.

He didn't need this kind of complication. He'd been burned once, and if he allowed himself to be burned again, that would be entirely his fault. This was a professional relationship, and that was where it began and ended.

Callie watched his back as he walked away. Gorgeous. One hundred percent, knee-shakingly gorgeous. Dark, brooding looks, golden skin and bright blue eyes that the camera was sure to fall in love with. It was a shame about the attitude.

But he'd only said the things she'd known already. Stay out of the way. Treat the people she photographed with respect. Maybe he'd loosen up a bit when he saw that she knew how to handle herself.

Callie almost hoped that he wouldn't. If this guy ever

actually got around to smiling at her, she'd be tempted to throw herself at him. If she wanted to avoid all the woman-traps that her mother had fallen into over the years, it would be a great deal easier if Ben Matthews didn't smile. Ever.

Ben had watched her all morning, and had hardly got a thing done. His crew, on the other hand, had been subtly persuaded to get on with their jobs, while Callie observed. She asked questions, laughed at everyone's jokes, and made a few self-deprecating ones of her own. It was all designed to put them at their ease, wipe the fixed smiles from their faces and get them to act naturally.

He saw her quietly lining up a few shots from the corner of the garage, and Ben had puzzled over why she should want them. Then the alarm sounded and she was suddenly back in that spot. He realised that it was the optimum out-of-the-way location to catch the movement of men and women, and then the noisy rush as the fire engine started up and swept out of the garage. She was good.

Maybe the professional thing to do was to try giving her the benefit of the doubt. He'd assumed that Callie was all about the cliché, but everything she'd done so far told him that she was all about the reality. Ben waited for a lull in the morning's activity and saw her heading for the ready room. He followed her, pouring himself a cup of coffee.

'Would you like one?' He gestured towards his own cup and Callie shot him a suspicious look. He probably deserved that.

'No, thanks. A glass of water...' She pursed her lips and something in her eyes told him that one of the quiet, dry jokes he'd heard her share with the crew was coming. 'If you trust me not to throw it all over you, that is.'

'You're thinking about it?'

'I'm told that wet fireman shots are very popular.' She smiled suddenly, and Ben reconsidered the dilemma that had been bugging him all morning. The best thing about Callie wasn't the way she moved, or her long legs, or even her bright green eyes. It was her smile.

'I guess I deserve that.'

'I guess you do.'

The sound of ice breaking crackled in his ears as he filled a glass from the water dispenser. Ben walked over to the table, leaving an empty seat between his and hers when he sat down.

Callie was watching him thoughtfully. 'Your concerns are reasonable. Everyone wonders what a photographer is going to make of them, and one of the issues that was raised when I visited last week was that I didn't glamorise your work.'

Ben had missed that. Maybe that was why his crew all seemed so relaxed around her. She'd already talked about the kind of photos she intended to take, and they knew what he hadn't stopped to find out. Perhaps he should try asking questions before he jumped to conclusions.

'Why did you choose Blue Watch?'

'Because you're the only ones on duty over the whole of the Christmas period.'

Of course. Ben felt suddenly foolish.

'If there's anything else you want to ask me…' Her gaze dropped from his face suddenly and she started to fiddle with her camera.

There was something. 'You say you're just an observer. But you frame your shots. I saw you scoping out the best place to stand when the alarm rang.'

This time she thought about her answer. 'Sometimes you have to be in the right place to see things clearly.'

Callie reached for the tablet on the table in front of her. Switching it on, she flipped through the photographs. 'What do you think of this one? Is it an accurate representation?'

Ben caught his breath. It wasn't just a photograph of a

fire engine leaving the station, she'd caught the movement and urgency, hinting somehow at the noise and the touch of adrenaline that accompanied it. Ben hadn't thought that would be possible unless you'd lived those moments.

'That's really good.' *Really good* didn't sum it up. But, then, he was no art critic. 'I'd say it was accurate.'

'Thanks.' She stood up suddenly. 'I'd better get on.'

Ben watched her walk away from him. Perhaps *that* was the attraction. A beautiful woman who could walk away without looking back.

But maybe that was just the last eighteen months talking. He and Isabel had never really been right for each other, but he'd been intoxicated by her soft beauty. When he'd realised that it wasn't going to work between them, he'd tried to break things off gently, but Isabel wouldn't have it. Texts, phone calls. Looking out of his window to see her car parked outside at all hours of the day or night. And then the *real* craziness had started…

That was over now, and he didn't want to think about it. He wasn't particularly proud of the way he'd handled things and Isabel hadn't contacted him in months. A woman walking away from him was just that—not some sign that there was someone out there who could make him feel the things that had come so easily before he'd met Isabel.

He studiously ignored Callie for the rest of the day. She was making a good job of keeping out of the way, and that suited Ben just fine.

# CHAPTER TWO

'THE PHOTOGRAPHS ARE IN, BOSS.' Ben found Eve hovering at the door of his office.

'Photographs?' He wondered whether his expression of surprise cut any ice. He'd been thinking about Callie a lot more than was strictly necessary over the last two weeks.

Eve rolled her eyes. 'There's a parcel on your desk. It came by courier.'

'Okay, thanks.' It seemed that Eve wasn't going to leave him alone to open it. 'Let's take a look then.'

Eve followed him into his office, looking over his shoulder as Ben carefully ran a knife around the tape that bound the box on his desk. Inside was a brief letter from Callie, stating that she'd enclosed a few photographs for review. And underneath that a stack of sealed manila envelopes, each of which carried a name and a *Private and Confidential* sticker.

'Where are mine…?'

'Hold on a minute.' Ben sorted through the envelopes, handing over the one that bore Eve's name.

'You can show them to me…if you want to.'

Eve was the one member of his crew that he wanted most to protect. Ben hadn't been there when she'd sustained the burns on her shoulder, but he'd been told how much courage she'd shown that day. And he'd seen the pain in her face when he'd visited her at the hospital. Eve had cried, just the once, saying that the burns were so ugly, and when she'd finally returned to work, Ben had noticed that she never wore anything that exposed her upper arms, even on the hottest day.

'I might…' Eve sat down on the chair next to his desk, running her finger under the seal of the envelope and taking the A4 photographs out. She flipped through them carefully and Ben saw her cheeks burn red. Then a tear rolled down her cheek.

If Callie had upset Eve in any way, if she'd made her feel anything less than beautiful, she wouldn't be coming back here. No more photographs, no more talking to his crew to gain their trust.

'What's up, Eve?' He tried to banish the anger from his voice, speaking as gently and quietly as he could. Eve tipped her face up towards him and suddenly smiled.

'Look at me, boss.'

As she handed the photos over, her hand shook. Ben took them, forcing himself to look.

There was one of Eve running, buttoning up her jacket as she went. Another of her climbing into the cabin of the fire engine. Eve's frame seemed somehow diminutive next to her crewmates, but she was clearly one of a team and the angle from which the photographs had been shot showed her ahead of the men, not following on behind.

'These are… Do you like them?' Maybe Eve saw something in them that he didn't.

'Yes, I like them. I *really* like them.'

'Me too.' Ben looked at the next photograph, and saw what had prompted Eve's tears.

'Callie took this at your home?'

'Yes, we made an arrangement for her to come and see me. What…do you think?' Eve wiped the tears from her face with her sleeve.

She was sitting on the floor with her four-year-old son in her lap. Isaac was clutching a toy fire engine and Eve's

dark hair was styled softly around her face. She was wearing a sleeveless summer dress that showed the scars on
her shoulder.

'I think… It's a lovely photograph of you and Isaac.'
Ben decided to concentrate on the mother and son aspect,
and the love that shone in Eve's face.

'It is, isn't it? I didn't think…' Eve shrugged.

'Didn't think what?' Ben was still ready to spring to
Eve's defence, but perhaps he didn't need to. Maybe she
saw what he did, and that was what her tears were all
about.

'I didn't think I'd ever wear that dress again. Callie and
I talked about it for a while, she said that we could stop
if I felt uncomfortable and that these photos were just for
me, not anyone else.'

'You should be proud of yourself, Eve.' Somehow Callie
had captured everything in the image. Eve's love for her
son, her strength and her vulnerability. The scars looked
like badges of courage and they brought a lump to Ben's
throat.

'Yes.' Eve took the photographs back, hugging them to
her chest as if they were something precious. 'I'm going
to show the guys.'

Ben put his own envelope to one side, slightly surprised
that there was one, and stacked the rest back into the box.
'Will you take these out with you? Make sure everyone
gets just their own envelope.'

'Yep.' Eve paused, grinning. 'So you're not going to
show me yours?'

His could hardly be as moving, or mean so much. He
tore at the envelope, taking out the glossy prints.

'Go on. Take a look.' He handed them straight over to
Eve. He didn't much want to look himself, and find out
how Callie saw him.

'Nice… Very action hero.' Eve laid the first photo down
on his desk and Ben saw himself caught in the act of load-

ing equipment onto the fire engine. A second showed him climbing into the cabin.

There was one more to go. And Eve was grinning suddenly.

'Wow, boss. Never knew you were a pin-up.'

'Neither did I.' Ben reached for the photograph, snatching it from her.

Oh. He remembered that now. He'd been sitting in the ready room, after returning from the fire they'd been called to that afternoon. Watching as Callie had talked to a couple of the other firefighters. Suddenly she'd turned and pointed the camera at him.

Perhaps it was Ben's imagination, but he thought he saw the subtle winding-down process after a call where there had been no casualties and the fire had been successfully contained. And there was something else. His eyes looked almost startlingly blue under tousled hair that was still wet from the shower.

'Do I really look like that?' For the first time in his life it occurred to Ben that he looked handsome.

'Yeah, on a good day. Sometimes you look a bit rough…' Eve laughed at his protests, narrowing her eyes to squint at the photograph. 'Maybe she's turned up the blue tones a bit. She explained to me how you do that. She said that she could turn down the red of my scars a bit but when we'd talked about it I decided that she shouldn't. All or nothing, eh?'

'Good decision. You can be very proud of your photos, Eve.' Ben looked at his own photograph again. None of the other blues seemed to be so prominent. Maybe it was a trick of the light…

He decided not to think about it. Gathering up the photographs, he put them back into the envelope and threw it back into the box.

'Here. If anyone wants to see these, you can show them.' He led by example. If anyone on the crew wanted to see what Callie had made of him, they could have a good laugh over it.

'Right, boss. Thanks.' Eve put her envelope in the box with his and shot him a grin before she left him alone.

What Callie had made of him. It was a thought that wouldn't go away, because the photograph had hinted at the smouldering heat that invaded his thoughts whenever he looked at her.

He shook the thoughts from his head. Christmas was only a week away and Callie would be back to take the photos for the calendar. He would be sure to thank her for her sensitivity with Eve and then he'd keep his distance. Ben didn't trust himself to do anything else.

Callie had stared at Ben's photograph for a long time before deciding to include it in his envelope. Perhaps it looked a like a come-on, betraying the way she saw him a little too clearly. But it was really just the way that the lens saw him. The camera was indifferent to him and incapable of lying. That image was all about Ben and nothing about her.

Her friends would have taken one look at the picture and told her that capturing Ben's smile for real should be her number one priority over Christmas. But anyone who seriously thought she'd take that advice didn't know much about her. Callie was all about avoiding risk.

It was one of the reasons she'd wanted this job so much. She'd wanted to understand what made the firefighters tick, what allowed them to do a dangerous job and then go home to their families afterwards. She'd been too young to understand when her father had failed to come home from work one day, but she'd understood her mother's tears and in time she'd come to understand that he'd never be coming home.

She'd learned afterwards that her father had been a hero. A police officer, called to an armed robbery that had gone bad. He'd saved two of his fellow officers but he had been unable to save his own wife and child from the mistakes and hardships that had resulted from his death.

It was the best reason in the world not to get involved with Ben, a man who took risks for a living, like her father had. He might be mouth-wateringly handsome and Callie had always had a soft spot for men with a hard exterior and warm eyes. But he was very definitely on her not-to-do list this Christmas. It was okay for the camera to register his smouldering eyes but she wasn't going to think about them.

One of the firefighters let her into the station on a crisp, cold Christmas Eve morning. Callie made her way to the ready room, adding the two dozen mince pies she'd made last night to the pile of boxes of Christmas fare in the kitchenette. Then she sat down, her camera ready, waiting for something to happen.

No sprayed-on jeans this morning. If he'd known in advance, Ben might have thought that Callie in a pair of serviceable trousers, heavy boots and a thick red hoodie would be an easier prospect. But that would have been a mistake because she still looked quite terrifyingly gorgeous.

He'd made sure that the photo of himself, captioned 'Hunk of the Month', had been taken down from the ready room notice-board. Everyone had taken their chance to have a good laugh, and there was no need for Callie to see it.

She was sitting quietly in the ready room. Blending in, as he'd seen her do before. Watchful, observing everything. He'd bet the silver sixpence from the Christmas pudding that she'd already sized up the decorations and the small tree in the corner of the room, deciding how best they might be put to use in her photographs.

'You're here.' He suddenly couldn't think of anything else to say.

'Yes.' She turned her green eyes up towards him thoughtfully. 'So are you.'

That got the patently obvious out of the way. Ben sat down.

'Eve showed me her pictures.'

She reddened a little, seeming to know exactly which of the pictures he was referring to. 'You know that she called the shots?'

'Yes, Eve told me that you'd talked about it all at some length, and that she was happy with what you'd done.' Ben liked it that Callie was unsure what his reaction might be, and that she actually seemed to care what it was.

She nodded slowly, obviously pleased. 'She rang me and said she'd be happy for them to be included in the pictures for the calendar.'

'And what do you think?'

'I think they're exactly the kind of thing we want. But I'm going to leave it until after Christmas and give Eve some time to think about it. Sometimes people say yes to a proposal and then change their minds when it becomes a reality.'

'I'll leave you to sort that out with her.' Two weeks ago it had been unthinkable that he could leave Callie to negotiate directly with his team, but now... Maybe her photographs had worked a little magic on him as well.

'You're expecting to be busy today?' She asked the question with an air of innocence and Ben smiled.

'Yes, we're often busy over Christmas.'

'I'm hoping that you'll agree to my going with the crew on a call-out. The station commander gave me the go-ahead and I've signed the waiver. But the final decision's down to you.'

He'd been half expecting this. For someone who was so invested in how things looked, it was impossible that her own appearance didn't mean something. She'd even ditched the bulky camera, replacing it with a smaller one that might easily be stowed away inside a jacket.

'Can you earn it?' The words slipped out before he could stop them. He usually put things a little more tactfully than that, wrapping it all up in talk about basic fitness and health and safety procedures.

If it was the little tilt of her chin that he'd wanted to see, she didn't disappoint him. Neither did the defiance in her eyes.

'Just watch me.'

# CHAPTER THREE

CALLIE WOULD HAVE thought that four years working as a first response paramedic might have allowed some of the more basic procedures to go without saying. But it appeared that Ben took nothing for granted.

'Don't forget to stand where he tells you.' Eve's eyes flashed with humour as she whispered the words to Callie.

'Sorry about this…' The yard wasn't the place to be in this freezing weather, and everyone looked as if they'd rather be in the ready room, making inroads into the stack of Christmas food.

Eve grinned. 'It's not you. He does it with everyone. Everyone he likes, that is…'

Right. This was obviously the hurdle that she had to jump to gain entry to the team. She could respect that, there was no such thing as being too careful when your job involved the kinds of risks that the crew faced every day.

'Callie! Over there…' Ben shouted, and she started. She was already standing well out of the way of the fire crew, and the point he'd indicated precluded any good photographic shots of the imaginary conflagration.

She ran obediently to her allotted spot and he nodded, seeming to be fighting back a grin. 'All right. Thanks, everyone.'

The crew followed his lead, at ease now as they left their positions and started to meander back inside. Ben was suddenly one of them again, just another member of the crew, but Callie was under no illusions that as soon as the alert bell rang, he'd be their leader again.

'Did I pass?' She murmured the words to him as he strolled back across the yard towards her.

'Yeah. Full marks.' This time he allowed himself to smile. 'Make sure you do the same when this is for real.'

This wasn't for real? Full marks meant that she had a chance of going with the crew on their next call-out. That made it real enough.

They didn't have long to wait. When the alarm sounded, Callie was on her feet with the others, pulling on the high-vis protective jacket with 'Observer' written across the back of it.

She was familiar with the sound of a siren but it usually emanated from her own rapid response vehicle. The fire engine made more noise and she wasn't used to the sway of the vehicle or to being squashed between Eve and one of the other firefighters while someone else did the driving. Neither was she accustomed to feeling like a parcel, only there for the ride.

But she did as she'd been told, waiting for the firefighters to get out of the vehicle before she did. Smoke and flame plumed upwards from what looked like a storage yard behind a brick wall.

'Callie, stay right back. There are gas canisters in there.' There was a popping sound as one of the canisters exploded in the heat of the conflagration. Ben didn't look back to make sure that she complied with the instruction as he hurried towards the back of the fire truck, where the crew was already deploying two long hoses.

Water played over the top of the wall, another jet aimed at a gate to one side. Callie knew that the angles were carefully chosen to maximise the effect of the hoses, but it seemed that no one had actually made that decision. It was just a team, working together apparently seamlessly.

Photographs. That was what she was here for. She'd almost forgotten the camera in her hand in favour of watching Ben. In charge, ever watchful and yet allowing his crew to do their jobs without unnecessary orders from him. It was a kind of trust that she wished he might bestow on her.

He turned, waving her further back, pointing to a spot beside the police cordon. At least she was out of his line of sight now, and she could remove the heavy gloves that made it practically impossible to take photographs. Not that it mattered all that much. She was standing so far back that the people behind the cordon probably had as good a chance of taking a meaningful shot as she did.

*I hate this.* She was used to working on her own and making her own decisions. But if she proved she could comply with Ben's orders, he might ease up on her a bit.

In the meantime, she'd do what she could. Callie turned for a shot of the cordon, people lined up behind it watching anxiously. Some were passers-by who'd stopped, while others in bright-coloured sweaters and dresses rather than coats had obviously been evacuated from the houses closest to the blaze. Over the steady thrum of the fire engine and the roar of the flames she could hear a child crying and another babbling in excitement.

Panning back towards the firefighters, a movement caught her eye. A twitch of the curtains in one of the houses in the row next to the yard. When Callie pressed the zoom, she saw a head at the front window.

'Ben…!' She ran towards the fire engine, screaming above the noise, and he glanced back towards her. 'Over there, look.' She pointed to the window and he turned suddenly, making for the house. He'd seen what she had, that the police evacuation had left someone behind.

It appeared that since he'd given Callie no indication that she should move, he expected her to stay where she was. Forget that. Callie tucked the camera into her jacket and followed Ben.

'Go back. We've got it…' They met on the doorstep. The woman had disappeared from the window and without a second glance at Callie he bent down, flipping open the letterbox to look through it and then calling out.

'That's right, my love. Open the door. No… No, don't sit down. You need to open the door for me.'

Suddenly he puffed out a breath and straightened, turning to Eve, who had arrived at his side. 'We have an elderly woman sitting on the floor, leaning against the front door. We'll go in through the window.'

Eve nodded and Ben reached into his pocket, pulling out a window punch. It took one practised movement to break one of the small glass panes in the windows at the front of the house.

'Callie, I won't say it again. You're in the way…' He didn't look round as he reached in, slipping the catch and swinging the window open.

'Since when was a paramedic *in the way* when you have a possible trauma? You should be getting out of *my* way.' Callie resisted the temptation to kick him. Playing along with Ben at the fire station was one thing, but this wasn't the time or the place.

He turned quickly, a look of shock on his face. Then he took the helmet from Callie's hand, securing the strap under her chin and snapping down the visor. 'Put your gloves on. Stay behind me at all times. Eve, stay here and let me know if the fire looks as if it's coming our way.'

He pushed the net curtains to one side and climbed in, turning to help Callie through the window. She ignored his outstretched hand and followed him. When he led the way through to the hallway, Callie saw an elderly woman sitting on the floor behind the door. Her eyes were closed but her head was upright so she was probably conscious. Callie tapped Ben's arm to get his attention.

'Did she fall?'

'I don't think so. She just seemed to slide down the wall.'

'Okay.' Standing back wasn't an option now and neither was staying behind him. The house wasn't on fire and Ben's skills were of secondary use to her. Callie pushed past him and knelt down beside the woman, taking off her helmet and gloves. She wasn't used to working with these kinds of constrictions.

'Hi, I'm Callie, I'm a paramedic from the London Ambulance Service.'

The woman looked up at her with placid blue eyes. It seemed that the urgency of the situation had escaped her, and Callie saw a hearing aid, caught in the white hair that wisped around her face, with the ear mould hanging loose. She was clutching a pair of glasses that looked so grimy that they could only serve to obscure her sight.

Great. No wonder she hadn't responded when Ben had called through the letter box. Callie gently disentangled the hearing aid, putting it in her pocket. There was no time now to do anything other than make do with what the woman could hear and see.

'Are you hurt?' She tipped the woman's face around, speaking clearly.

'No, dear.'

'Have you fallen?'

The woman stared at her, her hand fluttering to her chest. Callie heard Ben close the sitting-room door so that more smoke didn't blow through the house from the broken window. The smell of burning was everywhere, filtering through every tiny opening from the outside, and Callie knew that the air quality in here wasn't good.

She felt a light touch on her shoulder. 'You're happy to move her?'

Suddenly Ben was deferring to her. Callie's quick examination had shown no sign of injury and the woman's debility and confusion might well be as a result of smoke inhalation. On balance, the first priority was to get her into the fresh air.

'Yes.'

Thankfully, he didn't waste any time questioning her decision. Ben used his shortwave radio to check with Eve that their exit was still clear and helped Callie get the woman to her feet. Her legs were jerking unsteadily and it was clear that she couldn't walk.

'Can you take her?' She'd be safe in Ben's strong arms. He nodded, lifting the woman carefully, and Callie scooted out of the way, opening the front door.

Outside, the fire in the yard was almost out, quantities of black smoke replacing the flames. Ben didn't slacken his pace until he'd reached the cordon, and as a police officer shepherded them through, a woman ran up to them.

'Mae… Mae, it's Elaine. Elaine Jacobs…' The older woman didn't respond, and the younger one turned to Ben. 'Bring her to my house. Over there…'

'Thanks.' Ben shot a glance at Callie and she nodded. There was nowhere else other than the police car to set Mae down and examine her.

Ben carefully carried his precious burden into the small, neat sitting room, and Mrs Jacobs motioned him towards a long sofa that stretched almost the length of one wall. He put Mae down carefully and turned to Callie.

'Ambulance?'

'Yes, thanks.'

'Okay, I'll see to it.' He turned to Mae, giving her a smile, and her gaze followed him out of the room.

'I'm all right.' Mae seemed to be addressing no one in particular, and Callie guessed that she was trying to reassure herself as much as anyone else. She touched her hand to catch her attention.

'I know you are. Just let me make sure, eh?'

# CHAPTER FOUR

HOWEVER HARD HE tried to put Callie into a box, she just seemed to spring straight out again. He'd thought her capable of steamrolling over him and his crew if he allowed her to, and then she'd shown herself to be sensitive enough to make a difference to the way Eve saw herself. Ben had tried to limit her to the role of observer, and she'd shown him that she wasn't just that either.

Perhaps he had trust issues. It made no difference what Callie did, he couldn't bring himself to trust the warmth that her mere presence sparked in his chest. Maybe he never would truly trust a woman that he was attracted to ever again.

When he knocked on Mrs Jacobs's front door, he meant to stay on the doorstep, but she wouldn't have any of it, ushering him inside and telling him that he couldn't possibly compete with the mess that her two teenagers were capable of making. Callie was kneeling beside Mae, chatting to her, and looked up when he entered the sitting room.

'Everything all right?'

'Yes. The fire's out and we're making everything safe.' He trusted his crew. He'd trusted Callie, back at the house, when she'd snapped suddenly into the role of paramedic. Maybe that was what he should remember, rather than the way her smile seemed to plunge his whole world into chaos.

'The ambulance is on its way?'

'Yes.'

Mae had turned her gaze up toward them, obviously following their conversation. By the simple expediency of cleaning her glasses and making sure that her hearing aids were seated correctly, Callie had wrought an amazing change in the elderly lady. Ben bent down, smiling at Mae.

'How are you feeling now?'

'Callie says I have to go to the hospital…' Her voice was cracked and hoarse, but it was difficult to tell whether that was the effect of emotion or smoke inhalation. 'On Christmas Eve…'

'It's best to be on the safe side. If it were me, I'd take her advice.'

He heard a sharp intake of breath behind him. Mae's presence in the room had probably saved him from the humiliation of one of Callie's put-downs.

Mae's questioning gaze focussed somewhere to his left, and he turned. Callie's smile was almost certainly for Mae's benefit, but still it made Ben's heart thump.

'I'll come to the hospital with you, Mae. We'll find ourselves a handsome doctor in a Santa hat, eh?'

'Thank you dear. You're very kind.' Mae managed a smile. 'I'll pick a nice doctor for you.'

Callie chuckled. 'Make sure you do. I don't want just any old one.'

He couldn't do anything to help with the journey to the hospital but he could make things a bit better for Mae's return. 'I know someone who'll board up the window for you. I'll write their number down…'

Mrs Jacobs rummaged in a drawer and produced a pen and paper. Ben scribbled the number on it and handed it to Callie. 'Tell them I gave you their details. They'll liaise with the insurance company and help get things moving.'

Mae shot him a worried look. 'How much will it cost?'

'It won't cost you anything. All part of the service,

Mae.' It wasn't officially part of the service. The number was for a local charity. It had been Ben's idea to contact them and set up a task force to help vulnerable people clean up after a fire, and he and a number of the station staff volunteered with them.

'And when you get back from the hospital, you'll stay here over Christmas.' Mrs Jacobs sat down on the sofa next to Mae. 'No arguments, now. Stan and the boys will go over to your place and help sort things out there.'

'But…it's Christmas.' Despite her neighbour's firm tone, Mae argued anyway.

'Exactly. It'll do them good to go and do something, instead of sitting around watching TV and eating. I'm sure Stan's put on a couple of pounds already so he can do with the exercise.'

'You're very kind.' A tear dribbled down Mae's cheek. 'All of you.'

'It's Christmas. We'll all pull together, eh?' Mrs Jacobs put her arm around Mae and the old lady smiled, nodding quietly.

Ben beckoned to Callie and she frowned. He glared back, beckoning again more forcefully, and she rolled her eyes and followed him into the hallway.

'What? I'm busy.'

The tight-lipped implication that she was just trying to do her job and that he was getting in the way wasn't lost on Ben.

'I just wanted to know… How *is* Mae? Really?'

Callie's angry glare softened slightly and she puffed out a breath. 'I've checked her over the best I can, and she doesn't seem to be having any difficulty with her breathing. But she has a headache and she seemed very confused earlier, and you can hear she's a bit hoarse. She needs to be seen by a doctor. I'm going to stay with her.'

The thought that Callie might not come back to the fire station once she had finished here filled Ben with unexpected dismay. He had no one but himself to blame if she made that decision.

'I shouldn't have said that you were in the way earlier. It won't happen again.'

'I can take care of myself in these situations. I do it all the time.'

'Got it. I apologise.' Ben saw her eyebrows shoot up in surprise. Was that what she thought of him? He was perfectly capable of saying sorry when the situation warranted it.

But prolonging the conversation now while she was still angry with him probably wasn't a good idea. He'd said his piece and he should go.

'I'll see you later?' Ben tried not to make a question out of it, but his own doubts leaked through into his words. Callie gave a nod and he turned, making for the front door. He guessed he'd just have to wait and see about that.

The wait at the hospital hadn't been too protracted, and after X-rays and lung capacity tests had been carried out, Mae was discharged. They arrived back at Mrs Jacobs's house to find that the charity task force that Ben had put her in touch with had already boarded up Mae's window.

She had no qualms about leaving Mae here. Two cups of tea and a plate of mince pies appeared, and a yelled exhortation brought Mrs Jacobs's son tumbling down the stairs, a board game in his hand. He and Mae began to sort through the pieces together, and Mae finally smiled.

Mae's Christmas would be just fine. Callie's was a little more uncertain. The success of her project at the fire station depended on clearing the air with Ben, and there was no time to sit quietly and wait for him to let her in. She had to do something.

She took a taxi back to the fire station. He wasn't with the others in the ready room and Callie found him alone in the small office with the door wide open. She tapped on the doorframe and he looked up.

Blue eyes. The most photogenic eyes she'd ever seen, flickering with warmth and the hint of steel. The kind of eyes that the camera loved and… That was all. The camera loved them but Callie was just an impartial observer.

'Everything okay?'

'Yes. Mae was discharged from the hospital and she'll be staying with Mrs Jacobs over Christmas. The charity task force has been great.'

'Good.' His gaze was fixed on her face. 'I've been thinking about what you might be wanting to say to me.'

Perhaps he was trying out a management technique. Put yourself in the other person's shoes. Callie sat down.

'Okay, I'll play. What might I be wanting to say to you?'

'That I'm not giving you credit for the experience that you have. You need access to be able to work and I'm being unreasonable in withholding it.'

Actually, that pretty much summed it up. Callie dismissed the rather queasy feeling that accompanied the idea that he'd been reading her thoughts.

'And… I guess that you'd say in return that you and the others rely on teamwork. That kind of trust isn't made over a matter of days and you're not sure of me yet.'

The look on Ben's face told her that she was right. More than that, he found it just as disconcerting as she did to hear someone else voice his thoughts.

'I'll…um… I'll be honest. I wasn't much in favour of you being here when the station commander first told me about it.'

'Really? You hid that well.' Callie risked a joke. Somehow she knew that he wouldn't take it the wrong way.

He narrowed his eyes. Maybe he *was* taking it the wrong way. Then suddenly Ben smiled. 'So we see eye to eye, then.'

Rather too much so. If he really could see what was

going on in her head... Callie gulped down the sudden feeling of panic. Of course he couldn't.

The awkward silence was broken by the alarm bell. Ben rose from his seat, making hurriedly for the door, and Callie followed him.

She took her turn climbing up into the fire engine and found Ben sitting opposite her. As the sirens went on and they started to move out of the fire station, he leaned forward, bracing his foot against the lurching of the vehicle and checking her helmet.

Callie frowned. He'd been the one to say it and he hadn't even listened to himself. He was still double-checking everything she did.

'If I get the chance, I'll take you in as close as I think we can safely go.' The light in his blue eyes kindled suddenly.

'Thanks for that, boss.'

Ben's eyebrows shot up as he realised that Callie was using the word 'boss' to make a point. Then he grinned. Maybe this *was* going to work after all.

The word 'boss' on Callie's lips could hardly be anything other than a challenge. But they'd both risen to it. Ben had motioned her to stand next to him as he directed the firefighters in extinguishing a small blaze at the back of a shop. Callie had become like a shadow, never giving him a moment's concern for her safety, and adroitly stepping out of the way of both equipment and firefighters.

'I got some good shots. They'll do you all justice.' She waited until he was about to tell her that they were leaving now, catching his attention for the first time since they'd been there.

'Good. Thank you.' He smiled, and she smiled back. Then she turned to join the rest of the crew climbing back into the fire engine, leaving Ben with the distinct impression that his legs were about to give way under him.

It took some time to persuade himself that this evening would be nothing to do with wanting to spend more time with Callie but simply a matter of showing her another side of the job. But for once she made things easy for him. As the night shift arrived she hung back in the ready room, flipping almost disinterestedly through the photos she'd taken that day, as if she were waiting for something.

Ben dismissed the thought that it might be him. But then he found himself caught in her clear gaze.

'I wanted to catch you before I left. To say thank you for this afternoon.'

'My pleasure. You have plans for tonight?' Ben tried to make the question sound innocent. He'd already heard Callie's answer when Eve had asked earlier.

'No, not really. It's an hour's drive home and I'll probably just curl up with some hot soup and decide what I want to try and shoot tomorrow. You?'

'I'm going carol singing. We have a decommissioned fire engine, which is kept at one of the other stations. It's used for charity and public awareness events and this evening it's parked up in town. You should join me.'

She gave a little shake of her head. 'Are you ever entirely off duty?'

These days…no. Ben had always been immersed in his job but he'd known where to draw the line between work and home. But in the last year his work had been a welcome relief from worrying about what Isabel might do next.

He reached inside his jacket, laying two hats on the table. 'Can't really be *on* duty when you're wearing one of these.'

Callie's hand drifted forward, her fingers brushing the white 'fur' around the edge of the Santa hat and then moving to the bells around the edge of the green elf hat. A sudden vision of texture and movement and the feel of

Callie's fingers on his skin drifted into his head. He could tell she was tempted to accept his offer.

'You get to pick. Elf or Santa.'

She smiled. 'I'll be Santa.'

Of course she would. He was beginning to understand that this was something they shared, and that she too never felt entirely comfortable unless she was holding the reins.

'Okay.' He handed her the Santa hat. 'Play your cards right and you might get to drive the sleigh.'

Green suited Ben. No doubt red would have done too, but Callie had to admit that he made a very handsome elf. No doubt he'd be the one who got presents wrapped twice as fast, without even breaking a sweat.

After the bustle of the fire station and the cheery good-byes of the crew she'd suddenly felt very alone. She'd had to remind herself that returning to her cold, dark flat was exactly the way she wanted it. No one to welcome her home meant that there was no one to pull the carpet out from under her feet.

She pulled on a down gilet for warmth and put on her coat and gloves, attaching her camera to a lanyard around her neck, ready for use. Tonight was about photos and not Christmas cheer, she told herself stubbornly.

The quickest and easiest way to get to the centre of London was by the Underground. They left their cars at the fire station and twenty minutes later they were in the heart of the city.

The fire engine was parked on the edge of a small square, flanked by bars and shops, and there were still plenty of people on the street. As they walked towards it through the crowds, Callie could see that one side of the vehicle had been decorated to turn it into Santa's sleigh. There were carol singers and people were crowding around a warmly clad man in a Santa costume, who was helping children up into the driving seat.

Ben greeted the men already there and introduced Callie. Their names were lost in the music and chatter, but there were smiles and suddenly it didn't much matter who she was or why she was here. She was just one of the team.

A bundle of leaflets was pressed into Ben's hands and he set to work, wishing everyone a happy Christmas, in between singing along with the carols in a deep baritone. He placed leaflets in everyone's hands with a smiling exhortation to read them on the way home.

Callie picked up a leaflet that had fluttered to the ground. On one side were wishes for a safe and happy Christmas from the London Fire Brigade. On the other side was some basic fire safety advice that was easy to read and follow.

'So all this has an ulterior motive?' She saw Ben looking at her and she smiled.

'You could call it that. Although I reckon that having a house fire is one of the unhappier things that can happen to anyone, so it's really just a practical extension of us telling everyone to have a happy Christmas...'

He turned for a moment as a woman tapped his arm, responding to her question. 'Yes, that's the British Standards safety sign. Always make sure your tree lights carry it.'

'Okay. I'll check mine when I get home.'

'Great.' Ben gifted her with the kind of smile that would persuade the angels themselves to switch off their heavenly lights if they weren't up to safety standards and wished her a happy Christmas.

'Can I take some of those?' Callie pointed to the leaflets in his hand.

'Yes, of course. Don't you want to take some photographs?'

That was what she was there for but her camera was zipped under her coat and taking it out seemed like taking a step back from the circle of warmth and light around the fire engine. Realistically it was impossible to reduce the children's delight as they were lifted up into the driving seat to just one frame, so instead she took the opportunity to just feel the joy.

'Later maybe. I've got an interest in this, too.' As a paramedic, Callie didn't fight fires but she'd seen some of the of the injuries they caused.

He handed half his stack of leaflets to Callie. Ben didn't say a word but his grin spoke volumes. No more fighting each other. The season of peace and joy seemed to be working its magic.

# CHAPTER FIVE

SUDDENLY IT FELT like Christmas. Callie was animated and smiling, approaching people on the edge of the crowd that had gathered around them and giving them leaflets. She seemed softer, warmer somehow. As if she'd dropped her defences and with them the hard edges that didn't quite suit her.

'Getting cold?' Even though she was never still, she couldn't disguise her red fingers. Gloves made it difficult to separate the leaflets and hand them out, and she'd taken hers off and stuffed them in her pocket.

'Yes, a little.' She smiled up at him, clearly not of a mind to let frozen fingers stop her.

'There are flasks with hot coffee...' He motioned up towards the cabin of the fire engine, which was now closed and dark. The families had all gone home now, and the crowd mainly consisted of revellers, wanting to squeeze the last moments from their pre-Christmas celebrations.

'So that's why everyone's been nipping up there every now and then? Why didn't you tell me sooner? I'd love some.'

'You have to give out at least a hundred leaflets before you get coffee.'

'Well, I've given out three handfuls. That must be a hundred so...' She gripped the front of his jacket in a mock threat. *'Give me my coffee, elf. Or else...'*

However much he wanted to warm up, standing his ground now seemed like a delicious moment that couldn't be missed. 'Or else what?'

'Or… I'll make you collect up all the old wrapping paper, peel the sticky tape off it and smooth it flat to use next year.' She grinned.

'In that case…' Submitting to the threat was another delicious moment that made the hairs on the back of Ben's neck stand to attention. 'This way, Santa.'

He led her over to the fire engine, opening the door for her, and Callie climbed up into the cockpit, sliding across to sit behind the wheel. Ben followed her, reaching for the three large flasks in the footwell. Two were already empty, but the third was heavy when he picked it up.

As he poured the coffee, he saw Callie's fingers touch the bottom of the steering wheel lightly, as if she was yearning to take hold of it and pretend to drive, the way kids did when you sat them in that seat. She was looking ahead of her, the bright Christmas lights reflecting in her face, softening her features. Or maybe it was just the look on her face.

'Thanks.' She wrapped her fingers around the cup, clearly wanting to warm them before she drank. Ben poured a second cup for himself and propped it on the dashboard. The only heat he wanted right now was the heat of her smile.

'You can try it out for size if you want.' He nodded towards the steering wheel. 'I won't tell anyone.'

The thought seemed tempting to her, but she shook her head. 'Bit late for that now.'

'It's never too late…' Ben let the thought roll in his head. It was an odd one, since he'd privately reckoned that it *was* too late for him.

And Callie seemed to think that too. She shook her head, turning to him with a smile. 'Did you sit in a fire engine when you were a kid?'

'All the time. My dad was a firefighter and he used to lift me up into the driving seat of the engines whenever my Mum took me to the fire station.'

'So you knew all along what you wanted to be when you grew up.'

'Yeah.' Ben wondered which side of her life had been a childhood dream. Photographer or paramedic. 'What did you want to be?'

'Safe…' The word had obviously escaped her lips before she had a chance to stop it, and Callie reddened a little.

'Safe is a good ambition.'

Her gaze met his, a trace of mockery in it. *Do you even know what safe is?* Ben realised that it was the last thing he'd have thought about wanting when he'd been a child. He always *had* been safe.

For a moment the questions he wanted to ask hung in the cold air. Then Callie shrugged, grinning. 'My dad died when I was six. He was a police officer and he was killed in the line of duty. That was when I found out that… anything can be taken away.'

'I'm sorry. I can't imagine how that must have felt.'

She shrugged. 'I'm not entirely sure how I feel about it either. How did *you* deal with the risks of your father's job?'

'I guess… I never had to think about them. He always came home.'

'And now? You must have thought about them when *you* joined the fire service.'

The question seemed important to her, and Ben thought carefully about his answer. 'There are some things that are important enough to take risks to achieve. Without that, a life can become meaningless. And we don't take risks for their own sake, you know that we're all about safety.'

Callie nodded silently. She didn't seem much convinced

by his answer and Ben had the feeling he hadn't heard the whole story.

'But you never felt safe? As a child?'

'I did for a while. Mum remarried and I thought that we'd go back to being a family.' She shrugged. 'Her new husband ran up a pile of debts and then disappeared. We lost our house and pretty much everything we owned. After that it was horrible. Mum worked all the time and I was scared to be in our bedsit on my own. We got back on our feet but it was a struggle for her.'

Callie spoke almost dispassionately, as if she didn't care that she'd lost her father and then her home. In Ben's experience that meant she cared a great deal.

Nothing he could say felt enough. He reached for her hand, feeling a deep thankfulness when she didn't snatch it away.

'Here…' He guided her hand to the steering wheel, wrapping his over it. 'How does that feel?'

She gave a nervous laugh. 'That feels pretty good.'

'Try the other one.' He reached across, taking her coffee from the other hand, and Callie took hold of the steering wheel and gazed out ahead of her. Suddenly she laughed.

'Okay. You've made your point. I'm sitting on top of… how many horsepower?'

'About two hundred and fifty.'

'That much? And I'm looking over everyone's heads. It feels good.'

'Is powerful the word you're looking for?' Ben remembered the feeling of sitting behind the wheel when he was a child. Of being able to do anything, meet any challenge. That seemed to be the ultimate safety.

'That'll do.'

Suddenly he wanted very badly to kiss her. If he really could meet any challenge then perhaps he could meet this one? But Callie took her hands from the steering wheel and the spell was broken. She reached for her cup, wrapping her fingers around it again, and sipped the hot coffee.

Large snowflakes began to fall from the night sky, drifting down and melting as soon as they touched the pavement. Ben ignored them in favour of watching her face. It tipped upwards as the snowfall became heavier, a sudden taste of the magic of Christmas. Callie wasn't as unreachable as she tried to make out.

'There's always one, isn't there?' She quirked her lips down suddenly, and Ben could almost see the real world taking over from the imaginary. He followed her gaze, looking towards a couple of men in business suits and heavy overcoats, clearly involved in a drunken argument.

'Yep.' He wanted to tell her to disregard them. To come back with him to the world where it always snowed at Christmas, and where it was still possible to make up for all the things Callie hadn't had during her childhood. But one of the men suddenly took a swing at the other.

A space opened up around them as people moved out of the way. The argument seemed to become hotter and the carol singers faltered as the men's shouts reached their ears.

'So much for comfort and joy...' Ben muttered the words angrily, pulling the door of the fire engine open and getting out. A couple of the other firefighters were already on their way over to break up the fight.

But the brawlers were determined. One broke away from the firefighter who was crowding him back and threw a punch. The other slipped and fell, rolling on the icy pavement and cursing loudly. He tried to get unsteadily to his feet, and Ben could see blood running down the side of his face.

The men were separated quickly, with a minimum of fuss, and Ben made for the one who'd been hurt. He was standing unsteadily now, half supported and half held back by two of the firefighters. Then Callie pushed past him, her head bare, the Santa hat protruding from her jacket pocket. She'd snapped back into paramedic mode.

'Let me see… Bring him over to the fire engine.'

Ben walked the man over to the truck, opening the door of the cabin and helping him inside. Callie climbed in on the other side and the man relaxed back into the seat, seeming to want to go to sleep.

'You're carrying a first-aid kit?'

'Yep.' It was about the only piece of working equipment that the fire engine still carried. He went to collect it, adding a flashlight, and handed both to Callie.

She carefully examined the man, trying to elicit a sensible answer to some simple questions, but he was too drunk to even tell her his name. Or he had a concussion. Ben knew that it was impossible for even Callie to tell.

The stench of sweat and alcohol filled the cabin but she seemed not to notice. She cleaned the blood from his face carefully, and it appeared that the cut on his forehead was deep but relatively minor.

Finally, she blew out a breath. 'He's probably just drunk, but he's hit his head and it looked as if he was unconscious for a few moments. He should go to the hospital. Is there anyone here with a car who can take him? I'd call an ambulance but on Christmas Eve…'

The ambulance service would be busy and there would be a wait. It was quicker to have someone take him.

'I think so. I'll ask…' Ben didn't want to leave her alone with the man. He was unpredictable, and at any moment he could lash out at her. He wound down the window and called to one of the men standing next to the fire engine.

'Hey…! Close it.' The cold air blowing into the cabin seemed to wake the man for a moment and he shivered.

'All right. We're going to take you to the hospital, so they can make sure you're okay.' Callie's voice betrayed a note of caring that the man almost certainly didn't deserve.

'No! Going home…' The man tried to climb over her

to get out of the cabin, and Ben caught his arm before he elbowed Callie in the face.

'Stay put. And be quiet. You do what the lady tells you.' The threatening note that he injected into his tone was enough to subdue the man.

'My hero…' Callie rewarded him with a flashed smile and the murmured words, and he felt his chest swell in response.

Outside, the discussion amongst the other firefighters seemed to have come to some conclusion, and Ben saw one of them signal that he'd take the man when they were ready. Callie made one last examination and then opened the man's coat, looking for an inside pocket. Finding the man's phone, she switched it on and scrolled through the contacts list.

'This is your home number?'

The man reached out to snatch the phone from her, and Ben caught his arm before he could touch her. If he laid one finger on Callie, Ben might forget his training and be tempted to hurt him.

'Don't even think about it,' he growled at the man, opening the door to get him out of the cabin. Callie shot him a smile and dialled the number, speaking quietly into the phone.

The car drew up and he propelled the man into the back seat. Two of the other firefighters got in and, seeing that he was outnumbered, the man sat quietly, seeming to fall back into a drowse.

'Wait a minute. Callie's got his phone.' Ben looked round and saw that Callie had ended the call and was walking towards him.

'Shall I go with them? To the hospital?'

'No. The guys all have basic medical training, they can handle it. Jim will give them a lift home once they've taken him to the hospital.'

Callie hesitated, turning the corners of her mouth

down. 'I spoke to his girlfriend and she said that he was meant to be home hours ago, and that we could leave him in a gutter for all she cared. She gave me his brother's number, though, and he says he'll pick him up from the hospital.'

'Fine. Just give the guys his number and they'll deal with it.'

Callie still looked unconvinced, but she handed over the phone to Jim, bending down to look into the back seat of the car to check on the man one last time. It seemed that she was repeating her offer to go with them and Jim was repeating what Ben had told her. The car started and Callie shrugged, turning her attention to the other man, who was sitting on a nearby bench, his elbows propped on his knees, staring at his feet.

'Are you okay?'

'No, not really. They're taking Carl to hospital?'

'It's just a precaution. We don't think he's hurt, but he's drunk and he's hit his head. He needs to be checked over.'

'My sister's going to kill me. Carl's girlfriend...'

Ben saw Callie's lips press together momentarily. 'I dare say that everything will work out.' She'd clearly decided not to share what Carl's girlfriend had said to her on the phone.

'Yeah, right. She'll start talking to my wife...' The man shook his head. 'She wanted me to be home before the kids went to bed. I said we were just going out for a quick drink...'

'We'll get a taxi for you.' Ben decided it was time to step in. 'You're sure you feel okay?'

'Dead man walking, mate. You know how it is.' The man grinned at Ben, as if he was in league with him.

He could almost feel Callie's anger. She took a step forward and he reached out automatically, touching her arm. She heeded the silent warning and turned suddenly, walking away.

She looked so alone suddenly, standing with the fire-fighters, who were still giving out leaflets to the last of the passers-by. It was getting late, and there were few enough of them now, and Callie seemed silent and preoccupied. Common sense told him that he should leave her alone for a moment and she'd cool down, but Ben couldn't do it.

'Forget it.'

She was staring at her feet now, shivering with cold. 'I just… It's Christmas, for crying out loud. Couldn't they have just taken one night off and gone home? Been where they ought to be?'

'I know. But you can't let it get to you. No one can change what happened to you when you were a kid, but you can take *this* Christmas back. Wrestle it to the ground if you have to, beat it into submission and show it who's boss.' He reached for the Santa hat, pulling it out of her pocket and putting it firmly back onto her head, pulling it down over her ears.

She looked up at him suddenly. For a moment he thought he saw the magic again, reflected in her troubled eyes, but it was probably only the lights strung along the side of the fire engine. Suddenly she smiled, adjusting the hat to a jauntier angle on her head.

'All right. Are there any leaflets left?'

'A few…' Ben picked up the last of them and split the pile into two, giving her half. 'You want to see who can get rid of theirs first?'

She rose to the challenge. Of course she did, she didn't know what else to do with a challenge other than meet it headlong. But when Ben turned to watch her, she seemed suddenly so very alone in a crowd where everyone seemed to have someone.

# CHAPTER SIX

CHRISTMAS DAY DAWNED bright and clear. Callie was up early and on the road almost before she was properly awake. The fire station was thrumming with noise and light when she arrived, but the noise was that of sirens, and the lights flashed blue in the morning mist.

It wasn't just another working day, though. Everyone smiled and wished each other a happy Christmas, and between calls there were mince pies and a roast dinner, eaten in haste before the next call came in. But peace and joy brought oven fires, wrapping-paper fires and even a patio fire, where one brave soul had thought it a good idea to finish the turkey off on the barbeque.

Ben had been relaxed and jocular—there was nothing that Blue Watch couldn't deal with easily and the arrival of a fire engine brought extra interest, people coming from their houses with Christmas fare and good wishes for the firefighters. A young boy was cut from where he'd got lodged in the park railings, with the minimum of fuss, and seemed none the worse for the experience.

Callie photographed it all, working side by side with the crew. It seemed that Christmas Day was going to end with no serious damage to life and limb, but just as darkness was beginning to fall, the call came.

There was no room for her in the disciplined scramble. Ben took a moment to call an address to her and then Callie was left to her own devices. She waited until the fire engine was out of the garage, the sirens retreating into the distance, and then got into her car.

When she arrived, Blue Watch was already in action, along with three other teams that were in attendance. Fire was spurting from the windows on one side of a large, two-storey block of flats. Callie didn't need to be told to stay back out of the way. She knew that her presence would only hamper the men and women who were struggling to get the fire under control. She could see the firefighters of Blue Watch donning breathing equipment, ready to go inside.

She raised her camera and then lowered it. This wasn't a scene for calendar shots. Maybe afterwards, once it was clear that there had been no casualties.

All the same, she watched. Counting the firefighters of Blue Watch in and hearing her heart beat out the seconds and minutes before she could count them back out again. Ben had been the first in and she hadn't seen him come out yet.

Then he appeared in the doorway, a small bundle wrapped in his arms, protected from the smoke that curled around him. Behind him came a woman, supported by two firefighters.

The ambulance crew ran forward and Ben delivered the bundle to them. The woman was being helped to the waiting ambulance, reaching towards the child that Ben had brought out of the building. Tears blurred Callie's vision and she felt a lump rise at the back of her throat.

He tore the mask from his face and bent over in a movement of sudden weariness. Callie knew that the heavy equipment and the difficult conditions inside the building could exhaust even the fittest man quickly. But Ben took only a moment to catch his breath, walking over to the tender and gulping down water from a bottle. Then he turned, motioning to another two of the firefighters, including Eve. He was going back in again.

Callie turned away. She couldn't watch this. But she couldn't not watch either. The thought that little Isaac might not see his mother tonight... Or that she might not see Ben again.

She had to get a grip. Ben was doing what he had to and he was part of a team. No one would be hurt and no one would be left behind. Callie had attended plenty of scenes like this and she'd done her job, tending to those who'd been hurt. It was not having any job to do that was killing her.

Looking around, she saw a small family group sitting huddled together on a bench. Holding each other tight as they watched silently. No one seemed to be taking much notice of them and Callie walked over.

'Hello. Have you been seen by anyone? I'm a paramedic.'

The man looked up at her and Callie saw tears in his eyes. 'Yes. Thanks. We got out as soon as we heard the alarms go off.'

'You must be cold.' The woman had a baby in her arms, which she was holding inside her coat. There was a little girl of about six, who was swathed in a coat that was obviously her father's and the man wore just a sweater.

He looked up at her as if the idea of warmth or cold didn't really register. Just shock, and concern for his family.

'Do you have somewhere to go?' Callie sat down on the end of the bench. If she could be of no help to the fire and ambulance crews, maybe she could do something here.

'Yeah. My wife's brother...'

'He's coming to collect us.' The woman spoke quietly. 'He's driving down from Bedford.'

'It'll be a little while before he arrives, then. My car's over there. Why don't you come with me and get warm?'

\* \* \*

The whole family had piled into the back seat, seeming unable to let go of each other. Callie had got behind the wheel and started the engine so she could put the heaters on full for a while, and as the windows started to mist up, the woman told her that her name was Claire and her husband was Mike. Then the little girl spoke up.

'What's your name?'

'I'm Callie. What's yours?'

'Anna.' Now that she'd emerged from the wrappings of her father's coat, Callie could see blonde hair tied up in a ponytail with a red and green ribbon, and a red pinafore dress over a green sweater. Anna was looking around her, adapting to her new situation with the kind of resilience that only a child could muster.

'Are you taking pictures?' Anna's eye lit on the camera in Callie's lap.

'Not at the moment. But I've been at the fire station today, taking photographs.'

Anna frowned, and her mother reached out to her, smoothing a stray lock of hair from her face. 'There's always someone at the fire station, even on Christmas Day, sweetie. When they hear that there's a fire, they come quickly and put it out.'

'But…' Anna rubbed the condensation from the window with her hand, staring outside. 'It's not out yet.'

'Sometimes it takes a little while. But they won't leave until the fire's out.' Callie tried to sound reassuring.

'I left my presents behind…in my room.' Tears began to form in Anna's eyes. Her parents had clearly tried to shield her from the gravity of the situation, and she didn't know how much she'd lost yet, but she was beginning to work it out for herself.

Mike held his daughter tight. 'Everything's going to be all right, button. We're going to Uncle Joe's and we'll stay there for a little while. All that matters is that we're safe and we're together, and when we come back again I'll make sure everything's as good as new.'

'You…promise?'

'Yes, darling. I promise.'

Callie swallowed down the lump that formed in her throat. Opening the glove compartment, she found the bar of chocolate that was usually stowed away in there. It was all she had to comfort the child.

'Hey, Anna. Would you like to share this with your mum and dad?' She tore the wrapper open and broke the chocolate into squares.

Anna took the chocolate, holding a square up to her mother's lips. Claire smiled and opened her mouth. The little girl solemnly fed her father a square and then picked the biggest one for herself.

As the flames subsided, it became possible for the fire-fighters to rest a little longer than just the time it took them to get back on their feet. Ben had waited until each of his crew had taken their turn to have a ten-minute break, and then his chance came. He stood alone, scanning the people who stood beyond the police line.

She wasn't there. Somehow Callie had opened up a hole in his life that hadn't existed before. Something missing, which he'd never thought about until now.

He should turn away and find something else to do. Taking his break, sitting down and getting his breath would be a good idea because he suddenly felt very weary. But when he looked again, he saw Callie's car parked some way up the street, shadows on the rear window indicating that it wasn't empty. Before he knew what he was doing, Ben had started to walk towards it, drawn by the inescapable urge to just see her.

As he passed through the police cordon he removed his helmet and gloves, finding that he was wiping his face with one hand. He hadn't bothered before, and there was no way he could wipe away the grime and soot, but still he ran his fingers through his hair to flatten it a bit, feeling it rough and caked with sweat and dirt.

As he approached, the car door opened and she got out, smiling breathlessly in a good imitation of the way that Ben himself felt.

'You're…okay?'

Warmth swelled in his heart. He was okay now.

'Yes.'

She took a step forward as if to hug him and Ben stepped back. The filth on his jacket would spoil everything. He wanted her just as she was now, untouched by the ravages of fire, a bright, gleaming reminder that life would go on. Now he understood why the parents in his crew went home and just stared at their sleeping kids.

He pointed to the car, searching for something to say that didn't betray his joy at seeing her. 'They escaped from the fire? Are they all okay?'

'Yes, they got out as soon as they heard the alarm. Their flat's on the ground floor…' She pointed to the left-hand side of the building in an obvious question. How bad was it? Ben could see a small head bobbing between the two adults who sat in the back seat and felt his heart bang in his chest.

'The fire damage isn't as bad on that side. But everywhere… It's all going to be waterlogged, Callie. Do they have somewhere to go?'

'Yes, they have family coming to collect them from Bedford. They'll be here soon.' Callie's look of disappointment couldn't have been more acute if it had been her own home.

There was nothing he could say. All Ben could do was wonder whether Callie was reliving the time when she'd lost her home as a child. The back door of the car opened and a man got out, holding a little girl in his arms. Instantly, the loss and the heartbreak on Callie's face was replaced by a smile.

'I want to thank you.' The man held out his hand to Ben and he shook it, muttering his regrets that they hadn't been able to save their home.

'That doesn't matter. My wife and my kids are safe. Everyone else got out?'

Ben nodded an assent. Then the little girl called his name.

How did she know? Perhaps Callie had seen him walking over and had told the family. Then Callie grinned. 'I've been showing Anna some of the pictures I took back at the fire station. I'm not sure *I* would have recognised you with all that grime on your face.'

Suddenly he felt self-conscious, as if he'd turned up for a date with a piece of broccoli caught in his teeth. Ben shook off the feeling. He'd just been fighting a fire, for goodness' sake, and Callie was no stranger to people not looking their best in an emergency situation.

'Daddy, I want to take a picture…'

The man laughed. It was an incongruous sound amongst the noise of destruction, but when he looked at his daughter the stress lines on his face disappeared for a moment. 'I'm sure that Ben has better things to do, sweetie…'

'That's okay. Everything's under control and I've got a short break.' Ben glanced behind him to check again that he wasn't needed for a few minutes.

'Why don't I take the picture? You can be in it.' Callie addressed the child and she nodded.

Her camera was on a lanyard around her neck, but she turned back briefly to the car, fetching something from the front seat. It was a small compact camera, and Ben wondered why she would choose that one. Anna was lowered from her father's arms and Callie took the warm coat, which was far too big for her, from her shoulders to reveal a red and green Christmas outfit.

'Go and stand next to Ben, Anna. Try not to touch him, you'll get yourself all dirty.'

Ben sank to his knees next to the child. She was fresh and clean and, above all, safe. *This.* This was why he'd chosen his job and why he continued to do it.

'This is what we do at the fire station.' He folded his arms, smiling into the camera. 'Comrades...'

Anna glanced at Callie and she grinned. 'Comrades means friends. Everyone stands in a straight line, folding their arms.' She clearly understood Ben's reticence to leave a smudge on the child's hand by holding it.

Anna got the idea. Standing to attention, as straight as she could, she folded her arms. Through a daze of fatigue Ben heard Callie laugh, and new strength began to surge through him.

She seemed to be taking her time, which was unusual for Callie, who saw a shot and took it almost as naturally as breathing. When she was done, and Anna ran back into her father's arms, he realised why. She'd used both cameras.

Anna's father called out a thank-you, wrapping the coat around his daughter again. Callie motioned them back into the car, giving them the compact camera in response to Anna's demands to see her pictures. He and Callie were alone again for a precious few moments.

'Where did she get the camera from?' Ben reckoned he knew. It seemed unlikely that the family, who hadn't stopped to pick up their child's own coat, would have chosen a camera as the one thing to save from their home.

Callie shrugged it off. 'I keep a back-up camera in the boot.'

'Looks brand new to me.' The camera still had some of the manufacturer's stickers on it. Ben shot her a glance, which said she couldn't get away with this act of kindness without someone noticing, and she reddened a little.

'So it's new. My old one was on its last legs, so I bought

a new one and happened to have it in the boot of my car. Knock it off, Ben. It's Christmas Day…' Callie's steel resurfaced, all the more captivating because he knew that it concealed a heart of gold, which knew what it was like to be a child with no presents on Christmas Day.

He lost the chance to tell her that she'd made a generous gesture. A shout behind him turned her attention to a man running up the road towards them and Anna's father got out of the car, waving in response.

'That must be their lift…'

And she would want to say goodbye to Anna. Maybe hug her. The thought didn't seem so outrageous as it would have a few days ago, now he'd seen the evidence of Callie's softer side. 'I've got to get on. You're going straight home from here?'

The thought that he wouldn't get to touch her tore at his heart. Maybe he wouldn't need to so badly after he'd had a shower and changed his clothes, but now it was all that Ben could think about.

'No, I thought I'd see them off and then go back to the fire station…' She shot him an agonised look, which effortlessly penetrated the layers of protective clothing that shielded his heart. Maybe Callie wanted to be close to him as much as he wanted to be close to her. The idea fanned the flames that flickered in his chest.

'I'll see you there, then.' With an effort, he turned his attention to Anna, who was sitting in the back seat of the car, cuddled up close to her mother. The little girl seemed tearful now, and perhaps the reality of leaving her home behind, which Callie had somehow managed to hold back, was dawning on her.

Anna managed a smile and a wave, and her father shook his hand again. Then Ben turned, not daring to take another look at Callie before he walked back to his crew.

# CHAPTER SEVEN

IT WAS LONG past the time when his shift had ended, but Ben seemed in no hurry. He'd made time to exchange a few words with every member of his crew, trading jokes and casual goodbyes, which had somewhat covered the fact that he was clearly checking on everyone.

Callie had reckoned that seeing him showered and dressed in clean clothes might dispel the image of him walking towards her car, clearly exhausted and caked in grime. She hadn't been in any danger but he'd seemed like a hero, coming to carry her away and save her.

But it didn't. He seemed just as handsome, just as much the kind of man who might buck the trend and show her that it was possible to rely on someone and not get hurt. Callie dismissed the thought, reminding herself that she'd needed saving a long time ago. Her life was on track now and she was just fine on her own. If seeing Ben smile at Anna had awakened the thought that Christmas could bring unexpected presents, then this one had arrived far too late to change anything.

'Did you take any photographs?' She was sitting in the ready room, fiddling with her camera, trying to pretend that she wasn't waiting her turn for Ben to speak to her. She wasn't a part of his crew so maybe he didn't reckon that was necessary.

'A big fire like that isn't really the kind of thing to put on a calendar. People get hurt…' She felt herself redden.

'Yeah. You came anyway.'

'Well, it turned out that I could make myself useful.'

He grinned, as if this was exactly the thing he'd wanted her to say. 'That little girl's going to remember the person who gave her a camera when she had nothing else on Christmas Day. Maybe it'll make another little girl feel a bit better, too.'

The other little girl being Callie. The fearful child who knew that life was quite capable of taking everything she had, if she wasn't careful.

'Enough, Ben. I'm not in the mood for deep and meaningful at the moment.' Callie picked up her camera. 'Can I have one last shot? You by the Christmas tree?'

'Now I'm a little cleaner?' He got the point immediately. It was all about the contrasts, the rigour of his work and the winding-down process afterwards. He went and stood by the tree in the corner of the room, folding his arms.

Callie raised the camera, took a couple of shots in the hope that might make him relax a bit, and then lowered it. 'That's not quite right. Perhaps you could try looking a bit more awkward?'

Ben laughed uneasily. Some people smiled when they looked into a lens and some people froze. He was a freezer. The only really good posed shot she'd been able to get of him had been the one she'd taken with Anna, when Ben had been too exhausted to think about feeling self-conscious.

He uncrossed his arms, shifted from one foot to the other and then crossed his arms again. 'What do you want me to do with my hands?'

There was an answer to that but Callie wasn't going to give it. 'Try… No, not like that. You look like my sixth form biology teacher.'

He shook his head. 'I have *no* idea what that means…' For a moment Callie thought that she was going to get the relaxed shot that she was looking for, and then he stiffened up again. If all his smiles were that cardboard, she'd have no problem resisting them.

She took another couple of pictures and then gave up. She'd have to sneak up on him later. 'Okay, that's good. Thanks.'

Ben relaxed and walked back towards her. *That* was the shot she wanted but she'd already put her camera down and it was too late.

'Are you ready to go? I'll walk you to your car.' He picked up his jacket from the back of the chair. Callie nodded, picking her coat up and following him out of the building.

The car park was deserted. Just him and her, and a biting wind. Ben stopped next to Callie's car, as if that was the most natural thing in the world.

'I'm glad you're safe.' She was closer to him now, the sleeve of her coat almost touching his.

'Me too. It's…' He shrugged. 'We balance the risks and eliminate them…'

'Yes, I know. I'm still glad you're safe.' Leaving now without touching him might just trigger another emergency situation. One where she'd have to be hauled clear and revived. Because Callie felt that she wouldn't be able to breathe without Ben.

He didn't want her to make a fuss. He did this kind of thing all the time and so did the other firefighters.

*Who are you trying to kid, Ben?* He wanted Callie to make as much fuss as possible. He wanted to comfort her and then have her make a fuss all over again.

She was so close and yet not close enough. His hand drifted to hers, his fingers brushing the back of her hand. And then suddenly she flung her arms around his shoulders.

'This doesn't mean...' She buried her face in his shoulder, holding him tight.

'Anything...' Ben used the same excuse as she did to wind his arms around her waist. The cool-down after an emergency, when everything seemed so much simpler. The adrenaline still coursing in his veins and the feeling that everyday concerns didn't matter so much.

But it *did* mean something. He brushed his lips across her forehead, knowing that was never going to be enough, and felt her body move against his as she stretched up.

When he kissed her lips, it felt like all the Christmases he'd ever had rolled up in one big, beautiful parcel. It felt like a summer breeze, an autumn chill and the raging heat of an open fire, crackling and spitting as the flames blew hot and hard. Callie responded to him with just the right measure of softness and passion.

And then the fire subsided. They'd reminded themselves what it was like to be alive and safe this Christmas, and now it was time to let her go. But Ben couldn't.

'When you get home...' he linked his hands loosely behind her back '...and you switch on the lights on your Christmas tree...'

She shook her head. 'No Christmas tree this year.'

'What?' The image of Callie sitting next to her Christmas tree, drinking a toast to him at the same moment that he drank one to her, dissolved. It had been his last chance of walking away from her.

'What kind of person are you?'

She smiled up at him. 'One who's working over Christmas?'

No. Callie was the kind of person who knew exactly what a bleak Christmas was like. The kind of person who could prove to herself that she was strong enough for it not to matter by not caring about Christmas now. He wouldn't allow it.

'I have a tree. With lights. And I have sherry, and turkey sandwiches, and Christmas cake...'

'No! What are you, the Christmas mafia?'

He bent, whispering in her ear, 'I have red and green paper napkins. And board games. They're quite old, though, they're the ones I used to play when I was a kid.'

She laughed, nudging at his shoulder with her hand. 'Enough! I could drop in for an hour, I suppose. Since we're not back on shift again until Boxing Day evening.'

'My thoughts exactly.' The watch rota was two days and then two nights, separated by a twenty-four-hour break. Ben usually stayed up as late as he could after the second day, sleeping in, so he'd be fresh for his first night's work.

He took her car keys from her hand, unlocking it, and opened the driver's door. 'You'll follow me?'

'Yes, I'll follow you.'

Ben had given her the address and watched her punch it into the satnav, but even so Callie had stayed behind him, following him into the east end of London. Two cars, almost alone on the dark streets, winding through the hodgepodge of old buildings, most of which had been refurbished and given a new lease of life, making the area a vibrant and exciting place to live. He drew up outside a pair of iron gates, and they swung open, allowing them into a small parking area.

'What is this place?' Callie looked around at the massive building, which seemed to once have housed something industrial.

'It's an old warehouse.' Ben punched a combination into a keypad and swung the heavy entrance doors open, leading the way through a small lobby. A staircase ran around a large, commercial-sized lift and he pulled back the old-fashioned gates.

'It's got a lot of character.' Callie looked around her as she stepped into the lift. The lobby was bright and clean, paint having been applied directly onto the exposed brick-work to preserve the industrial feel.

'That's the nice way of putting it. When we bought this place we didn't have the funds to do more than just clean up and get everything working properly.'

'You did this?'

'A group of us. A friend of mine is an architect, and the company that owned this place was one of his clients. They were going to convert it into luxury apartments, but they only got as far as stripping it out and adding the internal walls to form separate living spaces before they ran out of money. They were selling the building at a bargain price, so my friend got a group together and we bought it.'

They stood on opposite sides of the lift as it ascended slowly. The drive, and this talk about home improvements hadn't diminished Callie's desire to touch him again, but she was handling it. Callie cleared her throat.

'How many apartments here?' She tried to make the question sound as if the information was vital to her.

Ben's smile made her shiver. He knew that this was all just a delicious game, that they'd play for an hour and then she'd go. And he seemed okay with that.

'Twelve. They were just shells when we bought the place, and each of us had a lot of work to do. It helped a lot having an architect on the team, because he knew how to undertake a big building project, what we could do ourselves and what we needed a contractor and a project manager for.'

The lift drifted to a halt on the third floor, and Ben drew back the gates, turning right to one of the two doors at either side of the hallway.

Callie was expecting something unusual, but when he opened the door to his apartment, ushering her inside, she was still surprised. A large, open space, the vaulted ceiling supported by round pillars and heavy metal beams. At the far end, a mezzanine had what seemed to be a sleeping area above it and a kitchen and dining area below. And in here it was most definitely Christmas.

Ben flipped a switch and the tree standing by the tall windows lit up. Fairy lights from top to bottom glimmered against gold baubles and frosted-glass icicles. Swags of greenery, mixed with tinsel and fairy lights ran along the length of the metal railings that edged the mezzanine. He walked over to a large brick fireplace surrounded by easy chairs and a sofa and turned the gas fire on, the leaping flames making the ornaments on the tree sparkle.

'This is… It's like something out of a magazine. I couldn't do it.'

Ben laughed, stowing her coat away in one of the built-in cupboards by the door and making for the kitchen. 'You're the photographer. I think you could do a lot better.'

Maybe with the small things. But the grand plan was beyond anything that Callie could conceive of doing. 'I wouldn't have the courage to put everything into a project like this. I'd think about it and then decide to play it safe and stick with what I had.'

Ben lost interest in the contents of the fridge, looking round suddenly. 'That's a bit of a recurring theme for you, isn't it? Playing things safe. I'd guess it's something you've learned and it doesn't come naturally to you.'

He was breaking the rules. This game of dropping round on Christmas night for sandwiches and board games shouldn't include anything more personal than whether she wanted cranberry sauce with her turkey. She walked over to the breakfast bar and sat down on one of the high stools that faced into the kitchen.

'Okay, I'll play. Why don't you think it comes naturally to me?'

'Because… Most people with a talent for something would stay in the nine-to-five and think, *If only*. You've gone out and made a success of your photography, and that takes a bit of self-belief and a lot of guts.'

Callie hadn't thought of it that way. 'It's nice of you to say that. But I never really thought of my photography as a decision.'

'Don't you think that everything's a decision? Even if we don't really think about it?' Ben took a cold turkey breast from the fridge and started to cut slices from it.

'It didn't look as if you were stopping to make any decisions today when you went into that building.' She'd resolved not to ask Ben about that but she couldn't help herself.

He laid the knife down. 'I made that decision a long time ago, when I joined the fire service. I don't want to be the person who stands by and watches, not able to do anything to change things.'

'Despite the risk?'

'I take a calculated risk, which is always minimised by training and preparedness. You're a paramedic. How many of your patients walked out of their homes, assuming they were safe without even thinking about it, and then something happened to them?'

He had a point. 'Most of them.' Callie snagged a piece of turkey from the pile. She didn't usually talk about any of this. Correction. She *never* talked about any of this. But, then, she didn't do Christmas either, and here she was, eating cold turkey and admiring a tree.

'So what made you make the decision to put up a tree, cook a turkey breast for sandwiches, and then spend Christmas alone?'

'I was working. In case you hadn't noticed.'

'That's no excuse. And you're not working now.'

'I'm not on my own either. You're here.' Callie raised her eyebrows and he shrugged. 'I had a bad break-up just after Christmas last year. I decided to go this one alone.'

So there it was. Two people who wanted to be alone had ended up together. This Christmas just wasn't going to give up.

Ben finished making the sandwiches and took the mince pies from the oven, sliding them onto a plate. Everything went onto a tray, along with forks and side plates, and he carried it over to the easy chairs, which were grouped around a coffee table in front of the hearth.

'I have juice and ginger beer...' He walked back to the kitchen, taking two glasses from the cupboard and flipping the door closed. Callie remembered that she was intending to drive tonight.

'Ginger beer's fine. Don't let me stop you if you want a drink, though.'

He thought for a moment, obviously tempted, and then shook his head. 'No. I think I'll join you.'

# CHAPTER EIGHT

CALLIE HAD WOLFED down her sandwiches, slowing a little for the mince pies, and now she was relaxed, slipping off her boots and tucking her feet up under her. Ben reached for the bottle of ginger beer and refilled her glass.

'Thanks. Cheers.' She stretched across the table, clinking her glass against his, and took a sip. 'So, were you serious about the board games?'

'Deadly serious.' Ben gestured towards the cabinet that held games he'd played practically every Christmas since he'd been a child. 'You get to choose which one, and I get to beat you at it.'

'You wish.' She got to her feet, making a thorough inspection of the contents of the cabinet. 'Snakes and Ladders. I haven't played that in years…'

'Good choice. I always win at Snakes and Ladders.' Ben grinned at her, and she carried the box over, opening it and laying out the board and pieces on the table.

'I always win too. So watch out.' She dropped the dice into the plastic cup and pushed it towards him. Delicious, competitive tension suddenly zinged in the air between them, like the promise of something forbidden.

His first throw took him to an empty square and Callie's took her to a short ladder. Ben picked up the dice, blowing on his fingers, and threw a six, which took him to the foot of a long ladder stretching halfway up the board.

'It's like that, is it?' Her gaze was on his face as she threw the dice again, and when she looked down at the board she wailed in frustration. 'No! A snake!'

'Admit it now. You're going to lose…'

She made a face at him, sliding her piece down the snake's body before taking a sip of her drink and taking her sweater off.

Ben looked back into her face and saw a smile that was beyond mischief.

If she was trying to make him so befuddled that he couldn't even count the squares, she was making a good job of it. Ben shook the dice and moved his piece. Two more moves each, which proved beyond any doubt that when snakes became suddenly interesting, ladders and empty squares were all you got.

'Ha!' Callie exclaimed in triumph as his next move took him right into the mouth of a long red and green snake, which wound its way almost to the bottom of the board.

'It *is* getting warm in here.' He pulled his sweater over his head. One look at Callie told him that he hadn't needed to voice the disclaimer. They both knew exactly where this was headed.

She landed on a snake. Her hand drifted to the buttons of her shirt, and Ben felt a bead of sweat trickle down his spine before he realised that no gentleman would allow her to do this. 'You could… A sock would be just fine, you know.'

'Where's the fun in that?'

Right now a mere inch of bare flesh, even if it was just an ankle, was likely to drive him crazy. Buttons would be a point of no return.

'I didn't… This isn't why I asked you here…'

'It's not why I came.' She turned the corners of her mouth down. 'Should I go?'

'No…' If she went now, she'd tear away the greater part of him. 'I really want you to stay.'

'A little Christmas madness?' She regarded him with a clear-eyed gaze. Such beautiful eyes, which seemed to see right through him.

'Just because it's not for keeps, it doesn't make it madness.' When she'd kissed him, it had been sheer magic.

Maybe she felt the same as he did, that *not for keeps* gave them both the freedom to do whatever they wanted tonight. Callie unbuttoned her shirt slowly, seeming to know that he wanted to watch every movement she made.

Even though she was wearing a sleeveless vest underneath, her bare arms and the curve of her breasts beneath the thin cotton were almost more than he could bear. It was an effort to tear his gaze from her, but somehow he managed to throw the dice and count the squares, knowing that this game was far too good not to be pushed to the point where neither of them could stand it any more.

They played in silence, smiling at each other across the board. A ladder each, and then Callie landed on another snake.

'Just my luck!' She puffed out a breath, sliding her piece back down the board.

'Why don't you let me take this one for you…?' Ben unbuttoned his shirt, feeling suddenly self-conscious. He wanted more than anything for her to like what she saw.

She did. He could see it in her face. The muscles across his shoulders tightened as the temperature climbed steadily higher.

He worked out. Of course he did, he had to be fit for his job. But right now it seemed as if someone were unwrapping the best Christmas present she could think of right in front of her eyes. Callie wanted to jump across the table and tear at his clothes.

But she didn't. Their initial hesitancy had set the pace. Slow and so deliciously tantalising.

She watched as he cupped the dice in his hands, blowing on them for luck, while he grinned wickedly. Ben was unafraid of his own body, not bothering to suck his stomach in or square his shoulders. He didn't need to, he was perfect, and his lack of self-consciousness just made him even more so.

He landed on a ladder. Callie grinned.

'Winning move...' His smile was deliciously wicked. 'What have you got to divert my attention from that?'

'A sock?' She teased him.

'I'll take a sock. As long as I can be the one to take it off...'

'Yes...'

Suddenly he was all movement, pushing the board to one side and stepping across the table. Then he fell to his knees in front of her and Callie shivered. It was all she could do not to reach out and touch him.

Ben propped her foot on his leg, slowly pulling her sock off. And then the other one...

'Hey! Are you cheating?'

'Yep. Are you arguing?'

'No.'

Callie slid to the edge of the chair, winding her legs around his back and pulling him close. His skin was smooth and warm, brute strength rippling beneath its surface. In one bold, swift movement he pulled her vest over her head, kissing her as if she was the one thing in the world that he truly possessed.

Right now she was. When his movements slowed, tender now, she began to tremble. His hand lingered for a moment over the catch at the back of her bra in an implied question, and Callie reached behind her, undoing it for him. She felt his lips curve into a smile against hers as he gently pulled the straps from her shoulders.

'Your skin... *So* soft...' His fingers were exploring her back, her breasts crushed against his chest. Callie moved against him, desperate for a little friction, groaning in frustrated impatience when it wasn't enough.

'Look sharp...' She whispered the words that Ben called when he wanted to hurry the crew along, and he chuckled.

'Is this an emergency?'

'Yeah. I'm calling a Code Red...' she gasped into his ear, clinging to his shoulders.

He didn't let her down. Getting to his feet, he lifted her up in his arms, striding to the curved staircase. The mezzanine was dark, but in the fairy lights strung along the railings Callie could see a bed. That was all they needed.

He laid her down, pushing her hands away when she reached for the button on the waistband of his jeans. He was going to let her watch.

As he stripped off the rest of his clothes, the power in his body seemed to seep through her veins. She *had* to have him inside her. Callie wriggled on the bed, pulling at the zip of her trousers, but she was too slow. Ben had it, and was slowly drawing them down over her hips, kissing her burning skin as he went.

'One minute...' When she was finally naked, he backed away suddenly, grinning.

'What? Where are you going?'

He disappeared through a door leading to a walled-in space at the side of the open balcony. Bathroom? Callie heard the sound of glass crashing and breaking on a tiled surface, but Ben was clearly in too much of a hurry to stop and clear it up, because he appeared in the doorway moments later.

'You didn't forget these, did you?' He was holding a packet of condoms in his hand.

'You remembered for me...' Callie felt suddenly foolish. She never relied on a partner to take care of things like this.

'Only just.' He slung the condoms onto the bed, crawling towards her and covering her body with his. 'All I can think about is what I want to do with you.'

'And what I'll do with you?' She liked it that he was just as lost in this as she was.

'Yeah. Particularly that…' He guided her hand between her legs. Waiting for the clues she gave about exactly where and how she wanted to be touched, and when he had them his fingers took over from hers. *So* much better.

'Where else…?' He whispered the words against her ear, chuckling when Callie moved her hand to her breast. 'Of course…'

No more words now, because his tongue and lips were busy with an altogether more pleasurable exercise. Ben took her gasps as a challenge, pinning her down and turning them into moans. When he slipped one finger inside her, everything suddenly focussed on that one spot.

She fought the overwhelming urge to be taken, now, because there was something she wanted to do much more. Somewhere she found the strength to push him off her, over onto his back.

Her gaze held his as she planted kisses on his chest, moving downwards. His hands moved to her shoulders, his fingers trembling lightly on her skin. Callie watched the anticipation build in his face, and then his head snapped back suddenly, his body arching.

'Do that again…' It was practically a command.

'Do *what* again?' This time she used her tongue to caress him instead of her fingers. His groan told Callie that he was heading right to the place she wanted him. Joining her, on the edge of madness.

They pushed each other further. With each caress she wanted him more, until finally there was no resisting it. Ben held her down on the bed, fumbling with the condom with one hand. And then he was inside her, moving with all the urgency of a man with only one thought in his head.

She could feel herself beginning to come, and there

was nothing she could do to stop it. Nothing she wanted to do. Pinned down by his weight, she could only respond to his driving rhythm. Callie choked out his name, digging her fingernails into his back, and then let go. She let go of everything she'd ever cared about, everything she'd ever wanted, turning herself over completely to Ben.

# CHAPTER NINE

SHE WAS SO SWEET. So incredibly sexy. And physically they were a perfect match. She liked hot and hard, crazy desire that had blown Ben's mind to smithereens.

She liked lazy, tender lovemaking as much as he did, too. Feeling himself harden again inside her, and feeling her soften as he whispered in her ear. He told her she was beautiful and felt her cheek flush with pleasure against his. Callie's smile filled him with the kind of warmth that Ben knew he could only take for a little while. But that little while was now.

They made love until they were exhausted and then slept. Got out of bed to eat something and then made love again, and slept until the Boxing Day sun was low on the horizon.

'Do you know the way back to the fire station?' He swallowed down the hope that they might take just his car, leaving hers here so she'd have to return with him to pick it up.

She nodded. 'I'll find it. Maximum deniability, right?'

She had a point. Ben took the toast from the toaster and put two pieces on a plate, pushing it across the kitchen counter towards her. She nodded a thank-you and set about layering it with butter and apricot conserve.

'I like your hair…like that.' After they'd showered, her hair had dried in curls. It made her look soft and sexy, and

Ben ventured the compliment even though he guessed that straight hair went a little better with the image that she wanted to project to the world.

'Do you?' She rubbed her hand across her head. 'I always think it makes me look a bit ditzy.'

Ben snorted in laughing disbelief. 'No. A little softer but definitely not ditzy.'

She grinned. 'Maybe I'll leave it for today, then. Where are my clothes?' She was wearing his towelling robe, which Ben privately thought looked a great deal better on Callie than it did on him.

'I put them in the washer-dryer while you were asleep. They'll be dry now.'

'You are a dream. You buy apricot conserve, you have a full fridge and you do my washing. Any chance I might kidnap you?'

Something tugged hard in Ben's chest. The voice of reason had been strangely silent up till now, but it was back in full force, reminding him that he couldn't take even the slightest suggestion that he was ready for a full-time relationship.

'Not really...' He shook his head, and heard her laugh as he turned away from her, pretending that the coffee machine needed his immediate attention.

'I know. Only joking. I'm not looking to keep you for much longer.'

If he were in any other place in his life, the sudden re-appearance of the other side to Callie's nature, the hard shell that kept everyone at arm's length, would have been disappointing. The fact that it was strangely comforting reminded Ben that he was in no position to deal with anything other than temporary. He turned, leaning across the kitchen counter to kiss her forehead.

'That doesn't mean... Last night was everything, Callie. You are so much more than beautiful.'

She smiled, as if that was just what she'd wanted to hear. 'I couldn't get enough of you.'

That was what *he* wanted to hear. Despite the feeling that the world had spun a little slower over the last twenty-four hours, he couldn't help wanting more.

'We have an hour before we need to leave. Ten minutes to finish our coffee, and then twenty minutes to shower and dress....'

'Which means we'd have to be quick...' She grinned at him, taking a condom out of the pocket of his robe and holding it up. It was disconcerting the way she thought so much like him.

'That's thirty seconds you've saved already.' He rounded the kitchen counter swiftly, taking her toast out of her hand and putting it down on the plate. Picking her up off the stool, he carried her over to the sofa.

She was shrieking with laughter, wriggling in his arms, and when he tipped her down onto the cushions she made a lunge for him, pulling him down. This was how it had been all night, a heady give and take that they'd both revelled in.

'Not this time.' He pinned her down, grasping at her wrists with one hand and undoing the tie of the dressing gown with the other. 'This time's all for you...'

She stared into his gaze, suddenly still. The smile she gave, when she knew he was about to make love to her, had the power to break him. But having more of Callie, feeling her break him, was the one and only thing he wanted right now.

It wasn't just that every minute with Ben seemed like ten. Last night he actually *had* spent hours making love to her. And his idea of a quickie before they went to work was thirty minutes, dedicated to giving her an orgasm so devastating that she would have fallen off the sofa if she hadn't been safe in his arms.

It felt as if his scent were on her. Swirling around her in her car as she drove the longest route she could think of to the fire station, so that there would be no possibility of them arriving together. No one seemed to notice it when she joined the rest of the crew at the ready room table, making sure she sat with her back to Ben, but when she pulled her sweater over her head, draping it over the back of her chair, she shivered, sure that her shirt smelled of him.

It was just his washing powder. His soap on her skin. But still there was that indefinable extra element to it, which reminded her of Ben alone.

Perhaps she should go and do something useful, instead of awkwardly trying to pretend that he wasn't in the room. She grabbed her camera, standing up suddenly and almost cannoning into a wall of hard muscle.

'Oh… Sorry…' She jumped back in alarm, and Ben grabbed her arm to steady her.

'My fault. Are you okay?'

She glanced around the table, suddenly terrified that it would be obvious that they'd been making love less than two hours ago. If it was, no one seemed to care.

'Yes, I'm fine.'

He nodded, grinning. Then the pressure of his fingers tightened on her arm for a moment, before letting go. His lips formed a silent word, just for her, and then he turned away.

*Later…*

Later. Ben had kept himself busy tonight, and Callie had done the same, but that one word made all the difference. An acknowledgement that the last twenty-four hours couldn't just be forgotten now they were back at work. She wanted there to be a *later* too, even if it only meant half an hour alone to talk to him.

'Not another one…' Eve threw a half-eaten piece of

stollen in the bin as the bell rang and Ben called out that this was their second abandoned car fire of the night. 'What is it with Boxing Day and joyriders? Haven't they ever heard of "Silent Night"?'

'That was supposed to be last night, wasn't it?' The night after Christmas Day.

'Is it? I suppose we're making up for it now, then.' Eve was already collecting her gear, ready to go. 'Good shot at four o'clock.'

The crew had taken to pointing out what they reckoned were good camera shots. Mostly Callie smiled and took the picture anyway, knowing she could delete it later, but Eve had a good eye. When she looked in the direction that Eve had indicated, she saw Ben, working with one of the other men to heave some heavy equipment onto the tender.

It was a great shot, full of movement and urgency. Callie raised her camera and then lowered it. She hadn't taken a picture of Ben all day, feeling that somehow it crossed the line between professional and personal.

He glanced over, catching her watching him, and grinned. And then he was back at work, making sure that the crew had everything they would need and calling out to Callie to get on the truck *now* if she was coming with them.

The night shift was finally over. Callie had looked for Ben in the small office and bumped into Eve her way back to the ready room.

'Have you seen Ben?'

'You wanted him? He's gone.'

'Gone…?' The news hit Callie with an uncomfortable force.

'Yes, he got a text and then dashed off. Said he had to see to something.' It seemed that some of the shock of realisation had shown on Callie's face, because Eve was looking at her questioningly. 'He'll be back here tonight. Or call him if it can't wait.'

'It can wait.' Callie forced herself to smile. 'Sleep well. I'll see you tonight.'

Callie collected up her gear, walking alone to her car. She'd been so sure that *later* had meant the end of their shift. Maybe she'd been mistaken. But Ben could have given her just one smile before rushing away. Just one sign that he hadn't come to regret what had happened between them. Callie grimly shook her head as she got into her car. It wasn't as if they'd promised each other anything.

All the same, Ben's scent seemed to follow her all the way home. She showered, throwing her clothes into the washing basket, and still it stayed with her like a ghost of Christmas, curling around her senses when she closed the curtains against the morning light and got into bed.

Callie had tried to sleep and found it impossible. Cocoa hadn't helped, and neither had sitting in front of the television, watching daytime TV. In the end, she had eventually fallen asleep for a short stretch on the sofa, and woken with a stiff neck. She considered staying at home tonight, but thought better of it. If Ben didn't want to say goodbye that was fine. She still had to say her goodbyes to the rest of the crew.

She was late, missing roll-call and Ben's briefing. She popped her head around the ready room door, letting the firefighters know that she was there, and then made for the locker room.

'You made it...' Ben's voice behind her made her jump.

'Yes. Sorry, I was a bit delayed.' She turned to him, trying not to look into his face.

*Keep it professional. Get through tonight and then walk away.*

'Since you're not officially on the roster, you're at liberty to come and go as you please.' He took a step closer, his voice quieter. 'I want to apologise. For last night.'

Callie's mouth felt suddenly dry. 'That's all right. You're at liberty to come and go as you please as well.'

'You've every right to be angry...'

'I'm *not* angry, Ben.

'Let me explain—'

Oh, no. Explanations weren't something that either of them had signed up for. Explanations made everything complicated.

'There's no need to explain anything. We're not...' She felt herself redden as the words she wanted wouldn't come.

'Not what?' He raised his arm, planting it against one of the locker doors. It was an unequivocal sign that if she wanted to end this conversation, she was going to have to push past him, and that would involve touching him.

'I'm nothing to you. You're nothing to me.'

The look he gave her made her into a liar. She wanted him so badly that he could be everything to her if he would just reach out and touch her.

'That's not true—' He broke off as the bell rang, cursing quietly under his breath.

'Go. You have to go.' She'd been saved. By an actual bell, of all things.

He turned, and relief flooded through her as Ben began to hurry away. But it took more than a bell to dissuade Ben.

'We're not done, Callie. Not yet...' He shot the words over his shoulder.

# CHAPTER TEN

THEY *WERE* DONE. They had to be. They'd made love, and Callie had been hoping they might be friends. Maybe even lovers again, for a little while. But he'd walked away without a word, and that was something she couldn't deal with. Not when she'd been beginning to feel that she might just be able to depend on him.

It was a busy night again. There wasn't much time for photographs at the fire station, and when they were called out, Callie made sure that she took up the vantage point that Ben indicated, without looking at him. The crew's mood became silent and dogged, as if they were all wishing for the end of the shift as much as Callie was. This morning they could all go home and celebrate what was left of Christmas with their families.

When she said her goodbyes, trading hugs and promising not to be a stranger, Ben was nowhere to be seen. Callie emptied her locker and made for the car park.

He was leaning against her car, hands in the pockets of his jacket in the morning chill. Callie took a breath, trying not to alter her pace as she walked towards him.

'I'm off now. I'll see you around.' Callie had regretted her bitter words in the locker room earlier. There was no reason to be uncivilised about this.

'No, you won't. Not if you can help it, anyway.'

Right. So this was how he wanted it. 'Step aside, Ben. I'm going home.'

He moved silently away from the back door of the car, letting her open it and put her bag inside. Then suddenly he was there again, blocking her path to the driver's door.

'Ben!' Callie tried to inject as much warning as she could into her voice.

'Trust me, Callie. Just enough to come with me and let me explain.'

He knew that was impossible. He knew she couldn't trust.

But the look on his face told her that he wasn't going to give up. Callie puffed out a breath.

'All right. We'll go to the café on the corner and you can buy me a cup of tea.'

Ben had messed up. Big time. He'd been longing to see Callie alone, knowing from their quiet, exchanged smiles that she wanted to see him. And then his phone had pinged, and the text had sent him running for the hills. Scared and confused.

He owed her an apology, and an explanation. After that, she was at liberty to throw her tea in his face and tell him that he needed to get his act together, and that he couldn't treat people the way he'd just treated her. It was no less than he'd been telling himself all night.

She followed him wordlessly to the café. One of the few small cafés left in London, where just one kind of coffee was served, and you could get a traditional breakfast. The morning rush was over, and they could sit in one of the booths that were arranged along the side wall and get a little privacy.

He ordered tea, and coffee and a bacon sandwich for himself. Callie's beautiful eyes were studying him solemnly and they gave him the courage to broach a subject that he suddenly realised he'd kept secret from even his closest friends.

'I rushed off yesterday morning, because I had a text...' When he said it out loud the reason sounded even more flimsy.

'I know. Eve said.' She brushed it off as if it meant nothing, but the hurt in her eyes gave the lie to that. If he was going to make her understand, he had to tell her everything.

*Show* her everything. Ben took his phone from his pocket, tapping the icon for messages and then displaying the four texts that had come in moments apart yesterday from an unrecognised number. When he laid the phone on the table in front of her, Callie ignored it.

'They all say the same thing. They're from my ex-partner.'

She puffed out a breath and looked at the phone, frowning when she saw the texts.

Happy Christmas. Love Isabel x

'Ben, if you wanted to be with someone else then you could have just said. The only promise we made to each other was that...there were no promises.'

'I didn't want to be with her—' He broke off as the waitress chose that moment to put their cups down in front of them, adding a plate of bacon sandwiches for Ben. He managed to get a 'Thank you' in before she turned her back on them, and then they were alone again.

Ben pushed the bacon sandwiches to one side. There was something he needed to do more than eat. More than breathe, if he was honest. 'It's a long story...'

'Not too long, I hope.' She glanced at her tea in a clear indication that when she'd drunk it she would be gone.

'I'll keep it as short as I can. Isabel and I met eighteen

months ago, I know her brother slightly. We went out a few times, it was a pretty casual thing…'

'Because you don't do anything other than casual.' She shot him a cool glance.

'Things were different then. She was a lot of fun to be with, but it was never going to work between us. I said I'd like to see her again but just as a friend. Then I got this long rambling letter, saying that she knew I didn't mean it, and that she'd decided to take me back.'

'*Did* you mean it?'

'Yeah, I meant it. But the more I tried to step back, the more she seemed to cling to me. She said that it was only my shift patterns that were keeping us apart, and that she'd give up her job so we could be together.'

Callie took a gulp of her tea, concern registering in her face. Maybe she could already see the danger that Ben had failed to recognise at the time. 'I know shift work is hard on relationships but…most people find a way to work that out.'

She didn't know the half of it yet. 'I told her that neither of us were giving up our jobs, but she wouldn't take no for an answer. She started to write to me, cards and letters, two or three times a day. She called and texted me at work all the time, and in the end I had to block her number. I reckoned she'd get tired of me soon enough if I didn't respond…'

Just talking about it was making Ben feel sick with self-loathing, but when he looked into Callie's face he saw a warmth he didn't deserve.

'In my experience, when a woman acts like that, they generally don't get tired of it. It's more likely to be a result of what's going on with her, not anything you did.'

It was good of her to make excuses for him, but Ben knew exactly what he'd done. When she heard everything, Callie would too, and she'd see that what had happened between them had been *his* fault, and maybe stop telling herself that the world had it in for her.

'When Isabel started calling on the landline at work, I realised that I had to do something. So I went to see her and told her that it couldn't go on. No more calls and no more letters. The next evening I came home from work to find a bunch of flowers and a note, saying that she wouldn't call again.'

'That's...' Callie shrugged. 'I'm guessing it wasn't a sign that she was beginning to find some boundaries?'

'The flowers were in a vase, sitting on the kitchen counter. She'd let herself in with a key I didn't know she had.'

The sick feeling, that had overwhelmed Ben when he'd looked at the flowers returned. In that moment he'd begun to understand violation. He'd thrown the flowers away, looking around the apartment for signs of Isabel, and he'd found them. Dismay had turned to despair as he'd slowly begun to realise that someone had been through everything he owned.

'You changed the locks. Please tell me you changed the locks.'

'It was late and I was working the following morning. I didn't have a chance. I texted Isabel to tell her that she wasn't to let herself in again and...the following evening I got home and found her in my bed. Naked. I told her that she had to get dressed and go, and she told me she was pregnant.'

Callie put her head in her hands, rubbing her face in a gesture of helplessness. Ben thought that he'd probably done exactly the same thing himself.

'I always wanted kids but I knew this wasn't an ideal situation to bring a child into. I told her that I'd take care of them both but that we couldn't go back to being a couple. Then, a couple of weeks later, Isabel told me she'd made a mistake and she never had been pregnant. I didn't know how to feel...'

It had been a mixture of relief and sorrow. Concern for Isabel, although in truth she hadn't seemed to mind all that much, and guilt. Ben had never felt so deeply flawed, and so incapable of doing anything about it.

'Ben…don't take this the wrong way, but did it occur to you that she was just trying to make you stay with her?'

Callie had asked the question that Ben hadn't dared to even think. 'When a woman tells you she's pregnant and the baby's yours, disbelieving her isn't the best way to respond.'

'Yes, I know, but…' She puffed out a breath. 'You had to know that this wasn't normal.'

'I tried to get her some help, but she wouldn't take it. The next thing I knew I had a call from her brother, saying she'd locked herself in her flat and was threatening to take a full packet of paracetamol.'

Callie was shaking her head slowly. 'She needed professional help. Lots of it… He didn't call the emergency services?'

'Isabel was asking for me. I went round and broke the door down. As far as I could see, she hadn't taken anything, but we took her to A and E to be sure. She fought me and said she wanted to die…' Ben closed his eyes. Isabel had kicked and screamed, blackening his eye. In the end, that had turned out to be the only physical injury in a night that had taken a heavy emotional toll on everyone.

'She got the help she needed, though?'

'Yes. Her brother and I both stayed the night to keep an eye on her, and the counsellor I'd contacted agreed to see her the next day. He told me that it was best if I didn't have any further involvement, and that I should let him and her family give her the support she needed.'

'So that was it?'

'I speak to her brother regularly. He says she's doing well.'

'And these texts…' Callie nudged his phone with one finger. 'I imagine it was really hard to see them.'

Somehow Ben managed to smile. 'Yes. I called her brother and he says they're dealing with it.'

'But you can't help.' Callie turned the corners of her mouth down. 'That's pretty tough for someone like you, who's used to making a difference.'

She made him realise what really hurt. The helplessness, and his complete inability to make things right.

'It's the best way. Maybe she really did just want to wish me a happy Christmas…' Ben shrugged. 'But that doesn't matter. I want to tell you that the way I acted yesterday morning had nothing to do with you. And that I'm sorry.'

'I imagine it was a knee-jerk reaction.' She was looking straight into his eyes now. 'A bit like the one I had.'

'You had every right to be upset.'

'Don't make excuses for me.' She reached forward, picking up one of the bacon sandwiches from his plate. 'Have you talked about this with anyone?'

Ben shook his head. If he had then maybe he'd have found the perspective and understanding that Callie was so ready to give. Or maybe that wouldn't have made such a difference if it hadn't come from her.

'Maybe you should.' She reached out, taking his hand. 'Stop trying to pack it away in a box and forget about it.'

How did she know him so well, after so little time? Callie seemed to get the parts of him that even he didn't get.

He picked up the other half of the sandwich and they ate in silence. There was something about the silence between him and Callie. Warm and companionable, it was allowing them both to heal.

'Are we done, Callie?' Finally he found it in himself to speak.

'I...' She looked up at him, and he saw all the warmth in her eyes that he'd found when he'd made love to her. 'No. We're not done yet.'

# CHAPTER ELEVEN

CALLIE HAD FOLLOWED Ben's car back to his apartment,
and they stood quietly together in the old, creaking lift.
Her heart had gone out to him when she'd seen the pain
and guilt in his face when he'd talked about Isabel. He'd
been damaged...

But, then, she was damaged too. And somehow that
meant that they fitted together well. There was no danger that either of them would take this relationship beyond
what the other could handle.

Ben opened the door to his apartment, ushering her inside. Light was streaming through the high windows, making the ornaments on the tree glisten and gleam. Christmas
wasn't over yet.

Neither were they. Callie reached for him, and he moved
suddenly, taking her into his arms, his warmth flooding
through her and making her gasp. His keys clattered un-
heeded on the floor and he backed her against the wall, his
hand behind her head to cushion it from the exposed bricks.

'I have the next four days off. Will you spend them
with me?' He kissed the soft skin behind her ear, and
Callie shivered.

'That would be...wonderful.'

Tired from the night's work, they'd spent the rest of the
day and the following night sleeping and making love. And

when dawn had broken, Ben had got out of bed, promising her breakfast. Sausages, bacon, eggs…the works.

'That smells great.' Callie had put on her clothes, fresh from the washer-dryer, and had gone downstairs to find him standing at the cooker, wearing a towelling robe. 'You know the good thing about you is that you always have a full fridge.'

He leaned over, kissing her. 'The only good thing?'

'You know the others. I'm not going to repeat myself.'

'Okay. Will you watch the pan while I go and take a shower? I might be a while, I'll be needing to revive my broken ego.' He flashed her an irresistible grin and Callie laughed.

'Your ego's just fine.…' She called after him.

He reappeared in a pair of worn jeans and a crisp white T-shirt. Crisp and white suited him. It accentuated his dark hair and the softly smouldering look in his eyes.

'Why don't we go to the zoo this afternoon? I haven't been to Regent's Park in ages.' He crowded her away from the pan and Callie took two mugs from the cupboard to make the coffee.

'Sounds like a plan. I like the zoo. I'd like to pop home this morning and get a change of clothes.' Something a bit nicer than work boots and trousers perhaps.

'Okay. Leave your camera behind so that I know you'll come back.'

Callie laughed, winding her arms around his waist. 'I'll be back. I'll leave my tablet as well, so you can have a look through the photos if you like.'

He turned away from the pan to face her. 'Really? You told me that I was the last person on the list to get a look at them.'

'I was making a point. Everyone has to approve the photographs that feature them, but it doesn't matter if you

take a look. I'd really like to hear your thoughts, actually.'
They'd come so far since that first day.

'Ah. So you were putting me in my place, were you?'

'Only because you didn't want me around.'

He bent down, kissing her. 'I can't imagine what I was
thinking. I must have been crazy.'

'I thought you were nice looking with a bit of an attitude.'

'I thought you were gorgeous. But very scary.' Ben
wound one of her curls around his finger. She knew he
liked it better when she left it to curl naturally, and letting her defences down with Ben was becoming surprisingly easy.

They tramped all the way round Regent's Park, working up
an appetite for lunch, before going to the zoo. They then
spent the evening curled up on the sofa together, watching an old film, and then another night together. Ben was
sure that there must be something in his life that had made
him as happy as Callie did, but he couldn't call it to mind.

They got up early and went out for breakfast, then took
a stroll through the buzzing network of streets of the East
End to do a little window shopping. Now Callie was sitting
cross-legged on the sofa, wearing an oversized sweater and
a flowered skirt, which draped around her legs. She was
busy with a pad and pencil, listing and ticking off photographs. And Ben was busy watching her.

'So…you have a thing about fire engines, then? Or is
it firefighters?'

She looked up at him, grinning. 'You're the one with
the thing for shiny red and chrome. And I only have a
thing for *one* firefighter.'

Ben chuckled. Callie had a way of making him feel
good without really trying. 'What made you propose this
project at the fire station, then? I imagine you could get

much better rates elsewhere, and you're putting a lot of work into it.'

'Actually, I'm doing it free.' Her cheeks reddened, as if she'd been caught in a good deed and was slightly embarrassed about it.

'Really? So what made you do it?'

In the last two days they'd talked about everything, felt everything together. It seemed so natural to ask questions but this one made Callie hesitate for a moment.

'I want to make a difference with my photography, not just take good pictures. I think it's important to show the realities of the work the emergency services do.'

Ben suspected there was a little more to it than that. 'I would have thought the ambulance service would be closer to your heart.'

'I particularly wanted to come to a fire station because...of my dad. You take risks every day in the course of your work, and I wanted to understand that a little better.'

Something prickled at the back of Ben's neck. As if a door had just swung open, and he wasn't sure whether he wanted to go through it.

'And do you?'

She shrugged. 'Maybe. I heard everything you said about the choices you made, and I understand it. It's a bit soon to be feeling it, though.'

It was almost a relief to imagine the door swinging shut again. The possibilities behind it, what might happen if Callie found a place where she could contemplate a long-term relationship with a certain firefighter, weren't something that Ben had thought about.

Callie had gone back to her list now, clearly not inclined to say any more. Ben should concentrate on the here and now and make the most of that, not worry about an impossible future.

'You fancy some lunch? I'd really like to see the photographs you've chosen, and perhaps we could do that afterwards over a glass of wine.'

She nodded. Risk averted. 'Yes, thanks. That would be nice.'

Callie was happy with her choice. Two or three photographs for each month, featuring different aspects of the work. Some formal and others informal, with a flavour of the Christmas festivities at the fire station on the December page.

'I like these especially.' Ben pointed to the choice for November. 'Putting the one of Eve with Isaac right next to the one of her on duty makes them both stronger.'

He'd picked the ones she was most pleased with. 'I like them too.'

'You know, if you want to make a difference, you could think about doing more of this. You have a way of showing strength and beauty that could change lives.'

Callie hadn't thought of it that way before. 'Portraiture as therapy, you mean? That would be…amazing.'

'I think so too.' He grinned, putting his hand to his chest in a gesture of mock distress. 'Although I'm mortified to find that you no longer see me as either strong *or* beautiful.'

He'd noticed. Out of the hundreds of photographs she'd taken during the last two shifts at the fire station, there wasn't a single one of Ben. Callie tried to laugh it off.

'Sleeping with you and then taking photos… It didn't seem right somehow.' Callie had never *wanted* to take photographs of anyone she'd slept with. Giving that much of herself and then having the photograph to prove it after it was over didn't much appeal to her.

Ben nodded, not seeming to want to push the subject. But she could see that he was a little disappointed with her answer. And so was Callie. They'd been talking about giving her heart to her photography, and she'd shied away from the first opportunity.

She looked around the apartment. Ben was so perfect, so handsome that she wanted something imperfect to photograph him against.

'Do you have any more exposed brickwork? Like that?' Callie pointed up at the roof space, spanned by heavy metal beams and flanked on either side by bare bricks.

'I have plenty of exposed brickwork, if that's what you want.' He laid the tablet down on the sofa between them, reaching for the soft sheepskin boots that she'd slipped off and left by the sofa. 'You'll have to put those on, though.'

'Where are we going?' Callie pulled the boots on, reaching for her camera and a folding tripod from her bag. He didn't answer, getting to his feet and leading the way to the doorway under the stairs. It led to a small corridor where the spare bedroom was situated, and then another door that Callie had assumed must be a cupboard. When he unlocked it and swung it open, the chill of a large, unheated space brushed her cheek.

Ben flipped a switch and lights came on, pooling under metal shades. The floor area was almost as much again as that of the apartment, and the space was clearly a continuation of it, double height with a cavernous roof supported by the same metal beams. But it was entirely untouched, bare brick walls and metal window frames, caked with many layers of paint.

'What's this, Ben?'

'When I chose the space I wanted I thought that it would be good to have room to grow, if I ever needed it.' He shrugged diffidently, as if he didn't know now why *room to grow* had ever been a factor in his thinking.

Callie swallowed hard. This was the family home that Ben had once wanted but now couldn't contemplate having. If she'd crossed a line, by taking her camera out and trying to capture what he meant to her, then he'd crossed one too, by bringing her here.

Ben hadn't brought anyone else in here for over a year. He no longer had any need of the space that he'd once thought might accommodate the needs of a family.

He loved his apartment. Even if he didn't grow old here, he'd reckoned on growing a good bit older. But however old he got, he reckoned that this space would remain the same, ready for the next owner to make something of it.

Watching Callie taking photographs of the walls and windows calmed him a little. She saw it in terms of light and shade, texture and colour. It was just bricks and mortar to her.

'Over there…' She'd set the camera onto the tripod she'd brought with her and suddenly turned her attention to him, pointing to a stretch of wall by one of the high windows.

'Here?' Ben walked over to the wall, feeling suddenly awkward and under scrutiny.

'No, a couple of yards to your left. Closer to the window… That's good. Maybe just rest your hand on the windowsill.'

Every time Callie pointed the camera at him, his hands became suddenly clumsy and felt twice their usual size. At least he knew what to do with one of them now and he complied, feeling the chill of the tiled sill under his fingers.

She bent to adjust the lens, and he smiled in response. Being photographed was far easier when Callie just crept up on you and you weren't aware of it.

'Okay… You're a little wooden…' She wrinkled her nose, inspecting her camera as if adjusting the settings might make him feel more at ease. Ben waited and saw her face light up as she looked towards him again. 'Oh. Look.'

She pointed at the window and he turned. It was snowing, large flakes blowing against the window and already gathering at the bottom of the small panes of glass. He heard her boots, padding softly on the concrete floor, and felt her body next to his.

'It's lovely, isn't it?' She stared up into the dark sky. This was clearly one of those things that Callie just wanted to experience, rather than photograph.

'Yes, it is.' He took her in his arms. It would be… interesting…to make love with her here. Feel the cold of her hands on his skin, while heat exploded between them. It wouldn't be comfortable, but feeling the rough brickwork against his back, protecting her against it with his own body, seemed only to heighten the pleasure of the fantasy.

It *was* just a fantasy. Callie wasn't his to protect, and even doing it for a while would make him want what he was too afraid to take. Her presence made him realise that a few of his old dreams still lingered here, not yet banished with the ruthlessness that he'd swept them out of the other parts of his life.

She walked away from him, clearly set on the idea of photographing him and not the snow. Ben resumed his awkward-feeling pose, looking at the camera.

'Don't smile.' Her voice floated out from behind the lens and he pulled his face straight. She took a couple of photographs, but seemed unhappy with them.

'Look at me, Ben. Think about…the wall behind your back. How does it feel?'

'It feels…like a wall.'

'Okay. That's a start. How does the window feel?'

'It feels a little draughty.' Ben grinned at her. 'I don't have your ability to give walls and windows any more meaning than just…'

He broke off. Callie had stepped forward again, standing on her toes to kiss him. When he moved his hand to wind it around her waist she stopped him.

'Don't move…. Don't move.'

'You do this with all your portraits?'

'It's a new technique. Just for you.'

Ben liked that a lot. And he liked the way it was difficult to keep still while Callie planted her palms on his chest, kissing him. The way she pressed herself against his body, seeming to know that he was suddenly aching for her.

Hot and cold. The rough surface of the wall against his back and the softness of her skin. It was almost unbearable.

'Stay still.' She backed away from him, her gaze still locked with his. Her fingers moved to her lips, grazing them as if she was trying to recreate the feel of his mouth. 'Still…'

He felt it. The way that Callie brought emotion and meaning into everyday actions and things. The way she wove a fantasy into the hard facts of reality. As he gazed into her eyes, he was aware of nothing other than her.

She must have stretched out her hand and touched the camera, because suddenly she walked back towards him. 'I think I've got the shots I want.'

He wound his arms around her. Ben was still trembling slightly from an emotion that he couldn't quite describe. Whatever shot she'd taken, he imagined that it must show both their hearts, and he wasn't sure whether he could bear to see it. He'd told her that he liked the rawness of her photographs, but maybe this was a little too raw.

'It's cold in here.' It was the only excuse he could think of to move. Callie nodded, breaking away from him, collecting the camera and tripod as he ushered her back into the apartment, closing the door behind them and locking it. The lines that they'd promised not to cross had somehow been crossed, and the feeling that maybe they'd gone too far nagged at him.

'You want to see?' Callie had fitted the lead from her

tablet to the camera, and the photographs had already downloaded.

'I'm…not sure.'

'I can delete them.' She turned her mouth down, seeming to sense his discomfiture.

'No…' Ben held out his hand. How bad could it be? A regular guy, standing against a wall.

She walked over to the hearth, warming herself, while Ben looked through the photos. It was all there. His face, his eyes were just the same as the ones he saw in the mirror every morning, but there was a raw undertone of passion.

The shadows, the texture of the brickwork and the smooth white of his T-shirt. Snow falling at the window and warmth in his face. It was a mass of inconsistencies, which felt rather too uncomfortably like the truth.

He laid the tablet down on the sofa and walked across to the fire. 'They're great. You have a talent, Callie. Don't let it go to waste.'

She snuggled into his arms. The screen on the tablet dimmed and then shut down, but Ben couldn't shake the image in his head.

That night, Ben made love to her tenderly, almost regretfully. Callie woke in the early hours to find him lying on his back, staring at the ceiling, and when he realised that she was awake he turned over, curling his body around hers and whispering to her to go back to sleep.

In the morning, she woke to the sounds of him moving around downstairs. She stumbled into the shower, rubbing her face hard in the stream of water, trying to gather her splintered thoughts.

They'd stepped out of the bounds that they'd both set themselves and tried to touch the impossible. And the bond that had formed so naturally between them couldn't withstand that.

Callie closed her eyes, turning her face up into the stream of water. If they called it a day now, they could keep everything that was special. Carrying on would only destroy that, because at some point they'd find that their deeply held fears were stronger than their desire to be together.

She blow-dried her hair, tugging it straight. Then she dressed and packed her things away in her overnight bag.

He had coffee ready for her, along with toast and apricot preserve. The silence grew heavier by the minute.

'I think...' He broke off, realising that Callie had opened her mouth to speak at the same time as he had. Even in this, they seemed in perfect synchronicity. 'You first.'

'I should go home. I have some more work to do on the photos, and I need my computer and printer.'

He nodded. 'Yeah. There are a few things I need to do today too. Call into the fire station maybe...'

This was the final acknowledgement that it was over between them. Irretrievably broken. Callie didn't have to go home any more than he needed to go to the station. After all the honesty they'd shared, they'd started to make excuses to each other.

'Right, then. It's been...'

'It's been too good to last.' The sudden flash of warmth in his eyes was too much to bear, and Callie looked away. She gulped the rest of her coffee down and put her mug in the sink, then collected up her camera and tablet, stowing them away in her camera bag.

'I'll walk you to your car.' Ben picked up his keys, shoving them into the pocket of his jeans.

'No, thank you. I'd rather you didn't.' Callie pulled on her coat and turned to face him. 'Time to get back to our real lives. Live yours well, Ben.'

'You too, Callie.'

She was aware that he stayed in the doorway after the

lift had creaked its way up to collect her and she'd got in. As it crept slowly downwards, she heard his front door close. Callie took a deep breath, trying to stop herself from trembling.

It was done. They'd both lived up to their side of the bargain and the whole of the rest of her life was waiting for her. Somehow the rest of her life seemed an awfully long time to contemplate at the moment.

Ben was sure that this was the right thing to do. There was no way forward, he'd understood that last night when he'd showed Callie the other side of the apartment.

Christmas had been a fantasy bubble, where neither of them had needed to think about the difficulties and complications of real life. They'd been able to live for the moment, and that was why it had all tasted so intoxicatingly good. But if every day of the year was Christmas Day, the novelty of it would soon wear thin.

He watched her go for as long as he dared. Until the lift began to move downwards and he could no longer see her behind the metal trellis of the gates. Then he kept the promise he'd made and turned away. He would miss her, but this was what they both needed.

# CHAPTER TWELVE

THE DULL THROB of missing Ben hadn't eased off in over six weeks. Callie knew that she couldn't contemplate anything other than a parting, and neither could he, but that didn't seem to make things any better. But if she thought *that* was bad, there was worse to follow.

'How was your day?' Sophie, her best friend at the hospital, was sitting in the canteen, a cup of tea in front of her. They'd followed this routine for years, meeting up for half an hour after work every Thursday, whenever their shifts allowed. This Thursday the normality of it was comforting.

'Busy. Have you seen a red-haired boy? Acid burns to his stomach?'

Sophie nodded. 'Yes, he came up onto the ward at lunchtime. You brought him in?'

'Yes. How is he?'

'The burns are second degree. The doctor had a look at him and said that he doesn't need a skin graft. It'll be a while but he'll heal. How did a five-year-old manage to get burns like that?'

'Bottle of bleach under the sink. His mother said that she never screwed the lid back on properly because she couldn't get it open again when she wanted to use it.'

Sophie rolled her eyes. 'Great. Because the whole point

of child-proof containers is for so-called adults to leave them open.'

'Something like that. I don't think she'll be doing it again.'

'Bit bloody late now…' Sophie's blue eyes flashed with anger and Callie nodded.

'Yeah. Keep an eye on him for me, won't you? He's a brave kid.'

Sophie nodded. This was what they did. Talked a little and got the frustrations of a day's work out of their systems. Then Sophie went home to her husband, and Callie went home to…

Another worried, sleepless night. It was about time she grasped the nettle and found out, one way or the other.

'You want one of these?' Sophie pulled a packet of blueberry muffins out of her bag, and offered one to Callie.

'No, thanks. Feeling a bit sick.'

'Oh. Stomach bug?'

'No, I don't think so. I've been feeling like this for more than a week.'

'Probably not something you've eaten, then.' Sophie frowned. 'You're a bit young to be getting an ulcer, but it might be stress…'

'It's not stress.'

Sophie rolled her eyes. 'You don't always know it, these things creep up on you. So what do *you* think it is, then?'

'It's…worse in the mornings.' That should be enough of a clue. By now Callie's mother would have been on her way to the shops to buy wool to knit a pair of bootees.

'Worse in the mornings? If it's acid reflux, you really should go and see someone about that.' Sophie took a sip of tea.

Maybe it was a bit much to expect of Sophie. Callie had been like a rabbit caught in the headlights, immobilised and too afraid to do anything to either confirm or deny her increasing suspicions. Wanting her friend to step in and sweep her off on a tide of common sense when she didn't have all the facts wasn't entirely fair.

'I have amenorrhoea, nausea in the mornings and my breasts are a little swollen and tender.'

Sophie stared at her, her teacup suspended at a precarious angle in mid-air. 'You're pregnant?'

Finally! 'Well, I don't know for sure... Don't spill your tea.'

Callie grabbed the cup and set it down on the table. Sophie was still wide-eyed, obviously trying to decide which question to ask first.

'You haven't taken a test?' Her friend came through for her, asking just the question that Callie wanted her to ask.

'No, I... I was too afraid.'

Sophie's nursing training kicked in. Grabbing her coat and bag from the back of her chair and taking hold of Callie's hand, she marched her to the door of the canteen. 'You're coming with me. Now.'

They drove to Sophie's house, stopping on the way for a visit to the chemist. Jeff, Sophie's husband, greeted Callie warmly, asking if she was staying for dinner, and Sophie bundled him into the kitchen while Callie sat miserably on the sofa. Then she heard the front door bang shut.

'Jeff's gone to the pub.' Sophie appeared in the doorway of the sitting room, the paper bag from the chemist in her hand.

'Soph, I'm sorry. I didn't mean...'

'That's all right. It's quiz night, and his mates will be down there. Do you want a glass of water?'

'No, thanks. I think I'm good.'

'Right.' Sophie jerked her thumb towards the stairs. 'Come on.'

Callie handed the wand from the pregnancy test kit around the bathroom door without even looking at it. She heard Sophie walking downstairs and filled the basin, splashing water on her face, before following her back to the sitting room. Sophie waited for her to sit down and then glanced at the wand again, as if to confirm what she'd seen.

'You're pregnant. It says more than three weeks.' Sophie's voice was calm. That was good, Callie needed some calm.

'Right. Thanks.'

'Do you know when it happened? Was there a contraceptive failure?'

'I don't remember there being one. We used condoms… I left it to him.' She'd let herself rely on Ben. 'I'm so stupid.'

'Let's get one thing straight here, Callie. These things happen. Not often, but abstinence is the only thing that's one hundred percent and beating yourself up about it isn't going to help.'

Callie shrugged. 'Oh, so tempting, though.'

'I know. But only you would give yourself a hard time over finding a reliable guy and leaving it to him to take care of things. You're still with him?'

'No, it's over. We were together between Christmas and the New Year.'

'When you were doing the shoot for the calendar?' Sophie's eyebrows shot up. 'He's a fireman?'

'Firefighter's the correct term…' Callie felt numb. She was pregnant by a man who didn't want to see her again.

'Not in this case. It's clearly a fire*man*.' Sophie stood, plumping herself down next to Callie on the sofa, putting her arms around her shoulders. 'I'm reckoning you haven't told anyone yet. Not your mum?'

'No. You know what Mum's like, she'll think it's all a case of cherubs and wedding bells.'

'You've got a point.' Sophie pressed her lips together. 'You need to tell him.'

Callie shook her head. 'I can do this by myself.'

'Yes, you can. Doesn't mean you should.' Sophie pulled Callie into a tight hug. 'You have choices here, Callie.'

'Thanks, Soph.' Callie could feel tears pricking at the corners of her eyes.

'No problem. You've always got me, you know that, don't you?'

Callie cried a little, clinging to Sophie. Then Sophie made a cup of tea, putting an unnecessary amount of sugar into Callie's cup. Callie appreciated the gesture, even though despair was a more accurate description of her reaction than shock.

'So...have you thought about what you'll do?' Sophie finally asked the question, her tone gentle.

'I'm keeping it.' There had never been any question in Callie's mind about that.

'Good. What about work?'

'I don't want to give up medicine. But I've been thinking about developing my photography, maybe specialising in hospital settings or using it therapeutically.'

Sophie nodded. 'It would be good to have the option to work from home. And it's a great idea. What made you think of it?'

'Someone suggested it to me.' It had been Ben. It seemed that during their few days together he'd touched almost every part of her life. 'I don't know if it's viable.'

'If that's what you want to do then we'll find out. We'll read up on it, and I bet that Dr Lawrence, in the burns unit, would be able to advise you.'

'Thanks Soph. I don't know what I would have done without you.'

Sophie chuckled. 'You're usually the one who knows what to do in any given situation. You've seen me through a few scary times in my life, and I'm glad to return the favour.'

Callie sighed. 'I have to do this right. I'm the one responsible for this baby, and it's going to have a stable, secure childhood.'

'Not like yours, you mean.' Sophie pressed her lips together. 'Callie I know you don't want to hear this, but it is possible to find a man who'll step up and take care of you.'

'That's…complicated.'

'I've got time. I'd say I had a bottle of red in the kitchen but that's not much use at the moment.'

'Don't let me stop you. Have you got anything to eat?'

'You're hungry?' Sophie grinned. 'That's good. I've got some pasta and I'll make a Bolognese sauce. I'll drink for both of us while I'm cooking.'

'So…he's as much of a commitment-phobe as you are.' Sophie paused to stir the sauce and take a swig from her glass. 'Who knew that there were two of you?'

Callie smiled. Sophie had a way of making everything seem better, and she was beginning to feel that she might be equal to whatever was coming next.

'Well, it seemed a perfect fit at the time.'

'I'm sure it did. Which month is he in the calendar?' Sophie had already seen the photographs that Callie had taken, and her choices for the various months.

'He's one of the September ones.'

'September… September…' Sophie clicked her fingers, obviously trying to remember which photos Callie had selected for September. 'September! Mr Blue Eyes?'

'Yes.'

'You never said you slept with Mr Blue Eyes! Is he as gorgeous as the photo, or did you do something to it?'

'I don't airbrush my photos. He's…' More gorgeous. Callie swallowed down the thought, because that was only going to lead to heartbreak.

Sophie shook her head. 'All right, that's probably a bit too much information. Is he someone you'd want to be a father to your baby?'

'I can't tell him…' Callie felt a new, different panic start to overwhelm her.

'Don't you think he *should* know? At least give him the chance…'

'It's not that simple, Soph. His ex-girlfriend told him she was pregnant after they split up.'

'The one you said stalked him? He has a child with her?'

'After Ben told her that he'd look after her and the baby, but they couldn't be a couple, she said she'd made a mistake and that she wasn't pregnant after all.' Sophie's eyebrows shot up and Callie shrugged in answer to her unspoken question.

'I don't know, Soph. It didn't sound all that believable to me, but he's too honourable to say so. He said he knew the situation wasn't ideal, but he'd always wanted children and he was really upset when she told him she wasn't pregnant.'

Sophie thought for a moment. 'To be honest with you, Callie, if you were going to choose a father for your child, he doesn't sound like a bad bet. I know you grew up without your dad, but at least you know who he was. And this guy's honourable, and he wants kids…'

'That's just the problem, though. Suppose he does all the right things, and we get back together for the baby's sake. It didn't last at Christmas, and there's no reason why it should be any different next time around.' The only thing worse than not having Ben would be having him again and then losing him.

'Well…maybe make it clear that a relationship between you two isn't on the table. Tell him that it's just a matter of him knowing his child.'

'I suppose so.' It would be hard, but Callie could do it. For the sake of her child, she could do almost anything. 'I think… I'm going to leave it a little while, though. Until I'm more sure.'

'You mean until you're showing? So there's no question in his mind that you actually *are* pregnant?'

Callie nodded. It would remove one of the difficulties, and it would give her plenty of time to think about what she was going to say to Ben.

# CHAPTER THIRTEEN

*Six months later*

BEN HAD THOUGHT he'd caught a glimpse Callie. The woman had been sitting in the passenger seat of a car that had parked across the road to the entrance to his apartment building. He'd cursed himself roundly as he'd thought he'd stopped seeing her face in crowds and catching her scent when no one was there.

Maybe he shouldn't have ignored the text Callie had sent last month. Maybe he should have agreed to see her again, just once more, to lay the ghosts to rest. But Ben knew that it wasn't going to work that way. Seeing Callie again would just re-set the clock on the process of trying to forget her. Nothing had changed, and their ending would be exactly the same.

He entered his apartment, slinging his jacket onto the back of the nearest chair and opening a few windows so that a breeze would begin to circulate. It had been a long night, and this morning all he wanted to do was take a shower, then eat something and go to bed.

Ben heard the tap on his door as he walked back downstairs to the kitchen. Wondering who it was, he ran his hand through his wet hair to tidy it a bit and opened the door.

For a moment he wondered whether he *was* seeing

ghosts. Her corn-blonde hair was curling softly around her face now, instead of being blow-dried straight. The image of the woman he'd slept with kicked him hard in the gut, only to be followed a split second later with a blow that almost brought him to his knees. She wasn't just pregnant. She was *very* pregnant.

'Callie...!'

'Hi. I rang the bell downstairs and someone let me in.' Her hand fluttered nervously to her stomach.

'I was in the shower.' As if it mattered. But the conversation seemed to be continuing under its own steam, while Ben's mind screamed in disbelief.

'I'm sorry if this isn't a convenient time.' Her gaze was clear-eyed and determined. A stab of guilt accompanied the thought that he really should have answered her text.

'It's...it's fine. I'm off shift now for three days.'

She nodded. 'I know. I looked up the rota on the fire station's website.'

Ben hadn't been aware that the watch rotas were even published on the website. But, then, he never had much occasion to visit it. Callie had obviously carefully picked her time to come here, perhaps reckoning that he might need a couple of days off work to get over the shock.

Shock. That was it. That was why he was standing there gawping at her and thinking about websites when there were far more important things to consider. It was why his limbs felt that they'd lost the power of movement. He needed to pull himself together.

'Please. Come in.' He stepped back from the doorway, watching her as she walked inside. She wore leggings and a pair of trainers, with a light summer top that fell loose over her stomach, reaching down to her hips. Pretty and practical. Less guarded somehow than the image she'd clung to when...

When he'd had sex with her. *He'd had sex with her and now she was pregnant.* The idea that the latter might well be a direct consequence of the former screamed in his head.

'How are you?' She looked up at him. Her gaze was less guarded too.

'Fine. Good.' The thoughts crowding his head seemed to have left him unable to frame a longer sentence. Ben took a breath, making an effort to at least say something.

'Come and sit down. Would you like a cup of tea or some juice?'

'Some juice would be great, if you have it.' Callie walked over to the breakfast bar and clambered up onto a high stool, exerting a little more effort in doing so that he remembered. Before he turned away from her to open the fridge door, he caught a glimpse of her drawing something out of her handbag. Ben poured two glasses of juice and when he turned back to face her she pushed a folded sheet of paper across the counter towards him.

'Since there's an elephant in the room, and I appear to be it...' She gave him a smile, as if she understood that he was struggling. 'As you can probably see, I'm going to have a baby. It was conceived in late December, here's my due date from the prenatal clinic.'

'Just tell me, Callie. Is the baby mine? Ours...' Finally. He'd managed to say something that sounded vaguely like the right thing.

'Yes. There's no doubt. But I want you to be sure too. There's no question you can't ask me.'

Where to start? 'Why...did you wait this long? Before you told me?'

She pressed her lips together. Clearly some questions were harder to answer than others. 'At first I wanted to be sure. Then I wanted to think things through a little. Time got away from me...'

She'd been afraid. Afraid to tell him, in case he didn't believe her. Or he told her he wanted nothing to do with the baby. Ben didn't quite know what he wanted at the moment, but he was sure of two things. If Callie said that this was his baby, he believed her. And if it was his baby, he wanted to be a father to it.

'We should—'

'Don't!' Her tone was almost sharp, and she gave a nervous smile. 'There's no *we*, Ben. I came to tell you this because you have a right to know. I don't expect anything from you, and I know it's a shock so I don't want you to say anything before you've thought about it.'

Yes, it was a shock. And the greatest shock of all was the way that his heart was pounding with joy at the thought that Callie was pregnant with *his* child. The way he wanted to take her in his arms and protect her. Now. From whatever threat he could think of.

He took a gulp of juice from his glass. It didn't surprise him all that much that Callie had a plan, and right now he wanted to know what that was. Needed to know whether he had some part in it.

'It's the last thing I thought would happen, but…that doesn't mean that I'm not here for you, Callie.'

She nodded. 'It's your choice, Ben. I won't stop you from being involved with your child if that's what you want.'

Callie had clearly already ruled out the possibility of a relationship between them, and he could live with that. He had done for the last eight months. But this… This changed everything.

She drained her glass and started to wriggle uncertainly towards the edge of the stool. Ben rounded the counter, taking her arm and helping her down.

'Thanks.' She accepted his help but as soon as her feet were on the floor she moved away from him, delving into her bag and withdrawing another sheet of paper. 'This is my address and my phone number. When you've thought about things a bit, you can give me a call.'

'You're going?'

'It's probably best to leave you to think about this.'

She was right. He should marshal his thoughts before he said anything else, but the one thing he wanted her to know was that he'd be there for her.

'Tomorrow afternoon. May I come and see you then?'

'Tomorrow afternoon's fine. Does about two o'clock suit you?'

'Two it is. I'll be there.'

She nodded, making her way to the door. The sudden feeling that she couldn't—mustn't—go just yet seized Ben. 'How are you getting home now?'

'I came with a friend. She's waiting outside in the car.'

'Right. Well…be safe, Callie.'

She grinned at him. 'I always am. I'll see you tomorrow.'

'Wait…' She'd got almost to the door before Ben realised that there was one more piece of information that he had to know. 'Do you know whether it's a boy or a girl?'

'Yes. You'd like to know?'

'It doesn't make any difference to the way I feel but… Yes, I'd like to know.'

'It's a girl.'

She refused to allow him to see her downstairs and almost glared at him when he stood at the doorway, watching her into the lift. Ben waited until she'd disappeared from view before closing the door. Walking over to the sofa, he threw himself down on the cushions before his legs decided to give way.

He had a little more than twenty-four hours to get his act together. Ben stared up at the ceiling, too shell-shocked for anything other than one thought.

Callie was having *his* child. His daughter.

Callie was shaking. She'd made the step. *I'll do it tomorrow* had finally turned into *I'll do it today* and it hadn't been as bad as she'd expected it to be. She'd made her intentions clear, and Ben hadn't questioned whether he was the father of her baby. Maybe that would come later, after he'd thought about it a bit.

His car drew up outside her house at exactly two o'clock. It was something of a relief that he wasn't late. Callie had been sitting watching the road for the last half-hour, and she didn't think she could take much more of this. She watched him get out, and to her horror he reached back into the car, bringing out a bunch of flowers.

He didn't get it. This wasn't about flowers or promises. It was all about working out something that they could both live with long term, and having the gumption to stick with it. You didn't bring flowers to a business meeting, and Callie was determined to take the emotion out and be businesslike about this. She could think more clearly when she wasn't fantasising about his touch.

She took a deep breath as she walked to the door. Ben looked like a nervous suitor on a first date. He was wearing a tie and holding the flowers as if they were some kind of defensive measure.

At least they weren't roses. He proffered the bright yellow and orange blooms and she took them. She supposed that putting them in water would give her something to do with her hands, rather than clasping them together, her nails digging into her palms.

'How are you?' he enquired solicitously.

'Good, thank you.' If you didn't count the light-headedness and the constant feeling that she was about to be sick. That had been bugging her for a day or so now, and was probably more to do with Ben than her pregnancy.

'Have you just moved in here?' He was looking around the freshly painted hallway, and his gaze lit on the stack of mover's crates under the stairs.

'Yes, I…was thinking of selling my flat and getting a small house, and this place came up. It didn't seem quite the right time to be moving but it was too good to miss.'

'And you've been decorating?' There was a trace of reproach in his tone.

'I haven't been doing it myself. The last owner had a penchant for primary colours, which is probably why he had a problem selling it. I got the painters in and they did the whole place in cream. That'll be fine for the time being.'

'If you need any help…'

'Thanks, but no. The sitting room and bedroom are both sorted, and the kitchen and bathroom aren't my choice of colour but they're both pretty much new. I have all that I need.'

He nodded and followed her through into the kitchen, still looking around as if he was assessing the house to see if it was fit for purpose. Callie ignored him, fetching a vase from under the sink and dumping the flowers into it.

'Coffee?'

He shook his head. 'I've had too much coffee already this morning. Do you have tea?'

'About twenty different kinds. My mother's been bombarding me with tea for months.' She opened the cupboard to reveal the stack of boxes.

'Regular tea will be fine, thanks. Your mother… She knows about this clearly.'

'Yes, she and Paul have been great…' Callie bit her tongue. She deserved the look of reproach in Ben's eyes. Other people had known about this for months when he hadn't.

'Paul's her partner. They've been seeing each other since last year and… I think she's found someone at last…' Callie saw her hand shake as she reached for the teabags.

'I'm glad you have their support.' His face softened suddenly. 'You have mine too.'

He carried the tea into the sitting room, and Callie let him do it. If he wanted to help, he could do the things that didn't matter so much, the things that she wouldn't miss if he left. Then he produced a piece of paper from his pocket.

'I've written this down. What I'd like…' He handed the paper to her and Callie took it, unfolding the single sheet. There were just two sentences and numbering them seemed a little over the top.

'Number one… No. I don't need you to help support me and my baby.'

'*Our* baby,' he corrected her quietly.

He could say that when his ankles started to swell and he couldn't get comfortable in bed at night. When tying his shoelaces started to become an exercise in balance and reach, and he'd been prodded and pummelled by what seemed like a whole army of doctors and nurses. Callie let that point go in favour of the greater principle.

'My photography's going well and… I'm sure I can manage.' *Sure* was a little bit of an overstatement, *hope* was a bit more like it. But she'd explored her options and the photographs she'd taken at the fire station had added a different slant to her portfolio, which had helped a lot.

'My offer isn't negotiable.'

'Neither is my refusal.'

They'd fallen at the first fence. Quiet words, which showed how diametrically they were opposed in their approach to this. Callie stared at him and he stared back.

Ben was the first to break the impasse. 'Okay. I'll set up an account and pay the money into it monthly. If you need it, it's there. If not, it's there to cover her university tuition fees.'

'She's going to university?' Callie hadn't thought that far ahead. That was the difference between them, she was focussed on getting through the next few months and he didn't have to worry about that. He could afford a few big dreams.

'When she's eighteen she can do whatever she wants. The money will be there for her.'

'Okay. I…guess that's between you and her.' If it happened then it happened. If Ben lost interest, she could provide for her daughter.

'We're in agreement, then?'

'Yes.'

'And number two?' He was doing it gently, but he was pushing her.

'Yes. You can have regular access to her, that's not a problem. We can sort something out…'

'Can we do that now?'

'No. We have to see what works and…' She felt dizzy, and Ben was going too fast. Sudden pain shot across her belly.

'Callie…? Are you all right?'

'Yes!' She took a breath to steady herself. 'Yes, I'm fine. I dare say something's hit a nerve somewhere…' If this was a new pain, to add to the other nagging aches and pains, it was one that Callie could do without. Particularly when she was engaged in negotiating with Ben over her daughter's future.

She shifted on the sofa, feeling a sudden warmth between her legs. Before she could check to see what it was, Ben's face told her that something really *was* the matter.

# CHAPTER FOURTEEN

HE'D EXPECTED HER to agree to number one straight away, and then fight him on number two. It was just like Callie to do the opposite. She might look a little softer but she was still determined to do things her way.

And determined not to take his help. Her face had contorted in pain, but she'd just kept on insisting that she was all right and it was just one of those things.

Then she'd moved, and he'd seen the blood soaking into the pale fabric of the sofa cushions. That definitely wasn't one of those things, and she wasn't all right.

She knew it too. She looked at him with frightened eyes, perhaps realising that even her carefully primed defences couldn't stop this.

But she was still trying to deal with it alone. Callie tried to get to her feet, her hand reaching for her phone, and he gently sat her back down again. 'Stay still, Callie. I'm calling for an ambulance.'

'Yes.' There was no compliance in her eyes but there *was* fear. He'd take fear. Whatever allowed him to help her. Ben took his own phone from his pocket, dialling quickly.

'Tell them… I don't think I'm in labour yet. I feel light-headed and sick, and…' She looked miserably at the spreading stain on the sofa. 'Severe vaginal bleeding… Possibility of *placenta abruptio*.'

Ben relayed the information, adding that Callie was

a paramedic to justify the attempt at self-diagnosis. The woman on the other end of the line told him that someone would be there in ten minutes, and Ben begged her to ask them to hurry. He wasn't exactly sure what *placenta abruptio* was, but he knew enough to understand that it wasn't good.

'I'm just going to breathe and stay calm.' Callie took the words right out of his mouth. 'They'll be here soon.'

'That's exactly right. Do you want to lie down?'

'Yes… I think so.'

He gently helped her to lie down on the sofa. Then knelt down beside her and held out his hand.

'Go on. Take it. We can forget it ever happened.'

She quirked her lips downwards, and then she took his hand. 'Our secret, eh?'

'Yes. Our secret.'

For a moment the old understanding flashed between them. If Callie would accept this temporary truce, that was a beginning. Temporary could be stretched until it resembled permanent.

'I need to call my mum.' She gestured towards her phone again. Ben picked it up and switched it on, scrolling through the contacts and dialling the number before giving it to her.

It seemed almost wrong to listen to her conversation, but Ben wasn't going to leave her side. Callie was making an effort to downplay the situation, but when she handed the phone over to him so he could take her mother's number, the woman on the other end of the line sounded worried.

'Text me when you know which hospital they're taking her to. And don't you leave her alone for one second until I arrive.'

'I won't.' He wasn't even sure whether Callie's mother knew who he was, and she rang off before he could tell her. He should have let her know that he would do anything, if only Callie and the baby were all right.

He held her tightly when her face contorted with pain and didn't let go when it passed. Ben was used to waiting for medical help, he'd done it many times before, but this time… It had never felt that he was so inextricably linked with someone that his own survival was entirely dependent on theirs.

'They're here…' Blue flashing lights reflected through the windows and across the room. Ben hurried to the front door, wishing that the two men would walk a little faster up the front path.

He ushered them through to the sitting room and the older of the two knelt beside Callie. Their exchanged smiles made it clear that this was one of Callie's colleagues.

'All right, lass. Symptoms…'

Callie rattled her symptoms off, seeming to rally a little now that the ambulance was here. Someone she knew. And trusted. Ben stood back, out of the way, fighting the urge to be the one that she clung to.

'I think there's a possibility of *placenta*—'

'Give it a rest, Callie. I can't abide patients who tell me what's wrong with them, you know that.'

'So what do *you* think?'

'Possibility of *placenta abruptio*.' The paramedic gave her a reassuring smile. 'We'll get you to the hospital now, and they'll confirm it.'

Callie puffed out a sigh. 'That's a hospital stay at best. Or they may have to do a Caesarean…'

'We'll see. One thing at a time, eh? You know the doctors don't much like it when we tell them what to do, even if we do know better than them.'

'Tell me about it.'

Ben was at a loss. He couldn't walk away and leave the

medics to do their job, the way he usually did. He had to *know*. 'Please…what's wrong with her?'

The man flipped a querying look at Callie and she nodded. He turned to Ben. 'It's possible that Callie is suffering from *placenta abruptio*, which is where the placenta separates from the wall of the uterus. It's something we take very seriously.'

'What does that mean?'

'It means that I might have to have the baby by Caesarean section. Now, before it becomes distressed or I bleed to death.' Callie was obviously in no mood to beat about the bush.

'Right. Thanks. We'll go now?'

'Yes, my partner's gone to get a wheelchair. We'll get her there as quickly as we can.'

'I'd like to go with her.' The desperate feeling that he had no right to insist on anything, but every reason to, gripped Ben.

The paramedic's gaze flipped once more to Callie in an unspoken question and Ben held his breath.

'Let him come. He's the father.'

Callie was surrounded by nurses and a doctor as soon as she reached the hospital. The ambulance crew stayed for ten minutes before they had to leave for another call, leaving Ben standing alone in the corner of the cubicle.

'She'll be all right. She's in good hands.' A nurse patted his arm. She was obviously the one who'd been assigned to calm the nervous father.

'Thank you.' Ben craned his neck, trying to hear and see as much as he could of what was going on. If there were decisions to be made, he at least wanted to know what they were, even if it was unlikely that Callie would give him any say in them.

Finally, the doctor turned and explained to him that

Callie was bleeding heavily and that a Caesarean section was needed. He added that it was a straightforward procedure and that Ben could look forward to welcoming his baby a little earlier than he'd thought.

Ben nodded his thanks, omitting to say that he hadn't had a chance to think anything yet. The doctor hurried out of the cubicle, and finally Ben could take his place at Callie's side.

'Hey, there.'

'You're still here?' She looked up at him a little blearily.

'No, I'm just a figment of your imagination.'

'Okay. That's fair enough.' She smiled at him, squeezing his hand, and Ben felt his overworked heart in danger of bursting.

A nurse arrived to take Callie down to the operating theatre, and hard on her heels came a woman who bore a marked physical resemblance to Callie.

'Mum…' Callie called for her, holding out her hand, and Ben stepped back again, wondering what he was supposed to do now.

There was no chance to do anything. The nurse released the brakes on the trolley that Callie was lying on, and before Ben could tell her any of the things he wanted to say, the trolley was manoeuvred out of the cubicle. Callie's mother ran a few steps to catch up, taking Callie's hand as she was wheeled away.

He should be glad that her mother had arrived in time. Callie had clearly arranged that her mother should be there at the birth, and she needed her right now. But all Ben could see was that Callie was being taken from him.

A neatly dressed man of about sixty approached him. 'You're Ben?'

Ben nodded, keeping his eyes on the trolley and the retreating figures of the nurse and Callie's mother.

'I'm Paul. Callie's mother's partner. Shall we wait together?'

\* \* \*

Ben followed Paul to the waiting room in a daze, glad that at least someone seemed to know what to do next. Stopping to drop a few coins in the vending machine, Paul brought two cups of tea over and sat down next to Ben.

'The waiting's the worst part. It'll all be worth it, though.'

'You have children?' Ben took a sip of his tea, thankful that this kindly man was here. Without someone to talk to he'd probably be banging his head against the wall.

'Two girls. My wife died when they were teenagers.'

'So you brought them up on your own?'

Paul nodded. 'I didn't think I'd find anyone else. But then I met Kate, Callie's mother. Just goes to show…'

'Goes to show what?'

'That you never know what's around the corner, waiting for you.'

Ben allowed himself a smile. Callie had said that her mother had finally found the right man, and he was willing to grab at any slender proof that life might allow second chances. He had to believe that was the case, that Callie and their daughter would be all right, and that somehow they could find a way through this.

After what seemed an age, a nurse popped her head around the door of the waiting room, calling out Ben's name. He stared at her for a moment, almost afraid to hear what she'd come to tell him.

'Go on. What are you waiting for?' Paul spoke quietly.

Ben got to his feet and hurried over. The nurse smiled at him.

'Mother and baby are both doing well. Callie's had a Caesarean section, and she'll be very drowsy for a little while. Her mother's with her and they'll be taking her back to the maternity ward soon. You can go and see her there.'

'Thank you. And the baby?'

'It's a beautiful, healthy girl. She's a little premature, so she'll be looked after in the high dependency care unit for a few days, but that's just a precaution.'

'Can we see her?' Ben heard Paul's voice behind him. 'I'm sure Ben would like to see his daughter.'

'Yes. Very much.' He was feeling a little unsteady on his feet, but he shot a grateful look in Paul's direction.

'I'll take you there now.' The nurse began to walk briskly along the corridor, leaving Ben and Paul to follow.

The high dependency unit was a large, quiet ward, all gleaming surfaces and technology. The nurse guided Ben to an incubator, and he looked at the tiny baby inside, willing her to open her eyes.

'She doesn't need any help breathing, and she's a good weight for being a month premature. Six pounds exactly.'

Ben couldn't stop staring at his daughter. *His* daughter.

'Kate said that you were going to call her Emily.' The nurse spoke again.

'Emily?' Ben could feel tears forming in his eyes.

The nurse laughed quietly. The fact that Ben didn't even know his daughter's name didn't seem to bother her. Maybe all new fathers were this dumbfounded, or maybe she'd just seen everything. 'I'll leave you here to get acquainted.'

'May I take a picture?' Something to take away with him, to remind him that this was real.

'Yes, of course. Callie got to hold Emily for a little while in the recovery room, but I'm sure she'd like a photograph.'

Ben took his phone from his pocket. At last, there was something he *could* do.

Paul accompanied him back to the maternity ward and they waited outside Callie's room for a moment before Kate appeared, her face shining.

'I won't stay, she's still groggy. But she'd like to see you for a couple of minutes, Ben.'

'Thank you.' Ben wondered whether the suggestion had come from Kate or from Callie, but right now that didn't matter. He had his entry pass and he wasn't going to argue.

'I think we should be going. We can come back in the morning.' Paul put his arm around Kate. 'We'll see you then?'

Wild horses wouldn't keep him away. He shook Paul's hand, thanking him, and opened the door to Callie's room quietly. She was lying still on the bed but her eyes were open, following him as he moved towards her. He smiled and suddenly a broad grin lit up her tired face.

'You did it, then.'

'Yes. I did it.'

Their connection, which had seemed so remote over the last two days, seemed forged anew. Ben sat down beside the bed.

'And you made a great job of it. She's beautiful.'

Callie chuckled quietly. 'Yes, she is. She's got blue eyes...'

'Most newborn Caucasian babies have blue eyes.' It was one of the few things that Ben knew about babies. He was committed to knowing more as soon as he possibly could.

'She has a little bit of dark hair as well.'

Like her daddy. The thought made the world swim around Ben slightly. He wondered whether Callie would ever say them.

'I didn't see her hair, she had one of those little hats on.'

'She has a tiny birthmark on one of her fingers and she weighs six pounds. That's good for a late pre-term baby.' Tears formed in her eyes. 'I know I'll be able to see her in the morning but I just want to hold her now.'

'Of course you do...' There was no point in saying that this was for the best, and that their baby was being well looked after. Callie already knew that.

He reached into his pocket and brought out his phone. 'Here…' He'd taken a video of the tiny baby, keeping it running until the memory on his phone gave out. Holding it in front of Callie, he saw her immediately transfixed by the small screen, her face mirroring each movement and each of the tiny grimaces on her daughter's face.

'She knows how to pull a face already.' He reached for Callie's hand, squeezing it, and she squeezed back. The regulator on the transfusion lead attached to her arm dripped a little faster.

Tears formed in Callie's eyes. 'Yes, she does. Thank you, Ben. Thank you so much.'

'Keep watching. And keep squeezing my hand.'

She glanced at the regulator and nodded, then her gaze was fixed back on the small screen. When the tiny baby sneezed, her own face scrunched up, as if she was trying not to.

'How are you feeling?'

'Very numb still.' She tried for a laugh and then thought better of it. 'The bits of me that aren't numb are starting to hurt.'

'You'll feel better soon.' Ben had no idea whether or not that was correct, but it sounded like the right thing to say. 'You're strong. Like her.' *That* he knew.

'Play it again.' She nodded towards his phone.

'Okay.' Ben wanted to watch it again, too. 'Keep squeezing my hand.'

The nurse brought in a milky drink for her, and Callie took one taste and scrunched her face up. Ben laughingly encouraged her to drink, helping her hold the cup. She was weak and shaky still, and if she was going to be able to hold her baby, she needed to build up her strength.

She was fighting sleep, wanting to see the video a third time, but Ben switched it off and made her close her eyes. As they talked quietly, Callie's voice became slower, more slurred, and finally she drifted off to sleep.

Ben settled in the easy chair, watching her. He imagined Callie wouldn't like the idea of his standing guard over her while she slept, but since she *was* asleep, she didn't have much say in the matter.

He was beginning to relax, soothed by the sounds of Callie's regular breathing, when the door opened quietly and a dark-haired nurse entered. She smiled at Ben and walked over to Callie's bedside, reaching out to brush her forehead with her fingertips.

'I'm Sophie, Callie's friend. You must be Ben.' She spoke in a whisper.

Ben nodded. When Callie's family and friends were around, his claim to her seemed to grow more tenuous. If Sophie wanted to throw him out, she probably had the authority to do so.

'How is she?'

'The doctor said she's doing well. She's very tired…'

'Yeah, I'll bet she is. I came as soon as my shift ended.' Sophie sat down in an upright chair next to the bedside. 'How are you?'

'Me?' Ben wondered how much Sophie knew.

She grinned at him. 'I was in the car outside your apartment yesterday, waiting for Callie. She left it a bit too long before she told you so this must all be a shock.'

The impulse to defend Callie tightened in his chest. 'It's okay. She had her reasons.'

'All the same…' Sophie subjected him to a steady, enquiring look, and when Ben didn't reply, she let the matter drop. 'You've seen your daughter?'

'Yes. She's beautiful… Perfect.'

Sophie looked at him thoughtfully. 'You want to stay?'

Ben had nowhere else to go. The only home he had was with Callie and his little girl. And whatever Callie had told her friend about him, it couldn't be all that bad, because she seemed willing to let him remain here.

'Yes. I...' He shrugged. 'If the staff tell me to leave, I'll sit outside.'

'Okay, I'll have a word. They won't kick you out.' Sophie rose, stopping for one last look at her friend. 'I'll see you again?'

'Yes, you will. Quite a lot, I imagine.'

'Good.'

When the door closed quietly behind Sophie and Ben had settled back in his chair, it occurred to him that he'd passed some kind of test. There would be more to come, a lot more, but at least this was a start.

# CHAPTER FIFTEEN

BEN HAD BEEN there for her. He'd done more than possibly could have been expected of him over the last few days, coming to the hospital every morning and spending the day there. The joy and indignity of being a new mother had made Callie forget for a while that she'd promised herself that she could do this on her own.

When he'd told her that he was taking two weeks' emergency leave from work, she'd protested. But he hadn't listened, insisting that he wanted to be there. He clearly wasn't sleeping much and even though he smiled every time he looked at their little girl, there were dark rings under his eyes.

Callie watched him as he sat rocking their baby. She'd be released from the high dependency unit in a few days, and then Callie could take her home.

'I've been thinking. About her name.' Callie hadn't once called her daughter Emily, it didn't seem to suit her.

'Yeah?' Ben had steered clear of the decision-making. He was there, always listening, but he always deferred to Callie's opinion.

'Do you think that she really looks like an Emily?'

Ben considered the thought carefully. 'Most of the babies here don't really *look* like their given names. I dare say they'll grow into them.'

That was about as close as Ben was going to get to

speaking his mind. Callie pursed her lips. 'Only... I just can't get used to Emily. I love the name, but...it just doesn't seem to fit.'

Ben chuckled. He obviously thought the same. 'So what did you have in mind?'

'I don't know really.' Callie had thought of a few names she liked better, but she wanted to hear what Ben thought as well. 'Any ideas?'

He smiled and shook his head, answering too quickly to have thought about it at all. 'No, not really.'

'Go on. Don't you have any favourite names?'

Ben sat for a moment, holding the tiny baby. Then he drew in a breath. 'What about Riley? You probably don't like it...'

Callie said the name a couple of times, trying it out for size. She liked it a lot. 'What made you come up with that?' Perhaps one of the guys at the fire station had a kid named Riley.

'When my sister was pregnant, she wanted my brother-in-law to come up with a few names...he was a bit stuck and we went to the pub to brainstorm it. I liked Riley but he didn't, so it never made it onto the shortlist. It means *valiant*.'

That was exactly what Callie was going to teach her daughter to be. Valiant. 'I really like it.'

Ben looked shocked. 'Do you?'

'Yes, I do.' She cooed the name a couple of times, and the little girl opened her eyes. 'She likes it too...'

'She's probably just hungry.'

Callie ignored him. She knew what her daughter liked and didn't like. 'I think Riley's a great name. Let's call her that.'

He gave her a smile so bright and enchanting that there was no question about Ben's approval. And no question that he appreciated having been asked in the first place. 'If that's what you want, I think it really suits her.'

\* \* \*

Callie had brought Riley home when she was five days old. Her mother had moved in for a while to help with the baby and Ben had visited every day, busying himself with helping to unpack crates and finding jobs to do around the house when he hadn't been spending time with his daughter.

It had been time well spent. He and Callie had talked about access to Riley on an ongoing basis, and it seemed she was committed to making it easy for him and working around his shift patterns. And he'd fallen in love with his daughter.

All the same, the idea of going back to work was a relief. Helping make Callie's house into a home had been a little too much like having someone to build a home and family with. They were lost dreams, and he needed to get back to the realities.

But even the reality of going back to work had changed. When he walked into the ready room he found that Blue Watch had embraced the unexpected news that he was a father. A loud bang produced a shower of sparks and streamers and everyone crowded around to shake his hand.

Ben endured the jokes and friendly advice and managed to ignore the words 'dark horse' when he heard them. Eve had waited until he was alone again and proffered a brightly wrapped package that she'd been holding behind her back.

'Eve…thank you.' Ben didn't know what to say. This was an aspect of parenthood that he hadn't quite counted on.

'It's just a little something…for the baby.' Eve seemed as embarrassed as he was.

'I…' Ben stared at the package. 'Should I open it now?'

'No, boss! You're supposed to give it to Callie and let her open it.' Eve grinned suddenly. 'You haven't got the hang of this yet, have you?'

'No, I haven't. It was all a bit of a shock.' Ben wondered whether Eve would ask. He almost wished that she would. 'I didn't expect anyone to make a fuss…'

Eve shrugged. 'A baby's something special. It doesn't matter how it happens.'

All the same, Ben felt like a fraud. His only real contribution to Callie's pregnancy had been the obvious one at the very start. And now people were slapping him on the back and giving him presents.

'I don't know… How do you do this, Eve?' He'd take whatever advice was on offer.

'Babies don't come with an operations manual—you have to deal with everything as it comes. You'll be fine.' Eve shot him a smile and turned away.

He retreated to his office, making a mental list of all the things he needed to do now that he was back at work. Then his phone vibrated. Callie had sent a video of Riley. Ben stared at the notification, his finger hovering over the play icon. Then he threw his phone down onto the desk, hearing the bell ring as he did so.

The crew had been summoned to a small fire on one of the few pieces of waste ground left in the densely populated city. It was a simple enough job to extinguish the flames but it seemed somehow surreal.

'Steady on, boss…' Ben almost tripped over a coiled length of hose and he turned just in time to see Jamie flash a knowing smile towards Eve. Yeah, okay. He still had his baby head on.

And Callie hadn't exactly helped. He'd managed to get his head around not seeing her and Riley for five days, but now all he could think about was that video.

'Sorry…' Ben decided that if he couldn't watch where he was putting his feet the best place for him was out of the way, standing next to the tender. He was used to the fact that Blue Watch could operate perfectly well without him, he'd encouraged that during their training exercises. Being a liability was new, though.

This couldn't go on. Compartmentalisation was the way forward. When he was on duty he had to be a leader. Off duty was the time to be a father. Ben decided not to look at his phone again until the shift was finished.

That evening, when he retrieved his phone from his locker, there was another text from Callie. Before he had a chance to look at it, the phone buzzed again.

How was your day?

Callie was probably feeling the same as him, that all this was unbearably strange. They both had to find their feet, but it was just as well to start as they meant to go on.

Good. Can't text while working.

He sent the text before he had time to think that it sounded a little curt. His phone buzzed again, almost immediately.

Sorry.

Ben cursed under his breath. He'd upset her now.

It's okay. Busy day.

It hadn't been a particularly busy day. If he was starting as he meant to go on, a little honesty would be better than excuses. But the text had been sent now. He typed another.

Thanks for the video. Looking forward to seeing you on Wednesday. Eve sent a present. I'll bring it with me.

His phone buzzed again. It would actually be easier to call Callie but something stopped him.

That's so kind. What is it?

So Callie didn't know that they were supposed to open it together either. Ben smiled. They were both on a learning curve.

I don't know. She says you have to open it. Wait until Wednesday.

He added a smiley face and put his phone in his pocket, slamming his locker door shut. Wednesday seemed a long time away, and he'd just ruled out any possibility of more texts in the meantime. That was how it should be, though. They were both adults, and surviving for a few days on their own shouldn't be that hard.

# CHAPTER SIXTEEN

IT HAD BEEN five days since she'd seen Ben, and Callie had spent much of that time thinking about him. Perhaps it was her hormones.

The texts had been a mistake. Ben had made it very clear that he didn't want to indulge in the to and fro of sending videos and *How are you?* messages on the days he was working. And Callie had decided that she needed to clear the air, leave nothing unspoken, because it was the things that were left unsaid that generally did the most damage to a relationship.

He was on her doorstep at exactly two o'clock on Wednesday afternoon. Ben was nothing if not prompt.

'How are you?' That was always his first question, and always accompanied by a tight smile.

'Fine, thanks.' Callie stood back from the door to allow him in. As he passed her in the hallway she caught a delicious curl of his scent. She needed to ignore that. He was Riley's father, and that was bound to flip a switch somewhere.

'Where's Kate?' He walked into the sitting room, looking around.

'She's popped out for some shopping. Riley's sleeping.' Maybe he wouldn't notice that this opportunity to talk had been carefully contrived.

If he did, he gave no hint of it. Ben's smile was inscrutable, calculated not to give anything away. Inscrutable was probably a lot easier for him than it was for her at the moment as he didn't have raging hormones to contend with.

'I wanted to say...' Callie lowered herself carefully onto the sofa. 'I'm sorry about the texts.'

He shook his head. 'It doesn't matter. That was a great video of Riley.'

It *had* mattered. Callie had known it almost as soon as she'd sent it, and when he hadn't replied straight away it had confirmed her fears.

'Ben, I wish that...'

'What?' He gave her an innocent look.

'I wish that we could have an adult conversation. There are things that we need to work out and... Can't you just tell me how you feel about this?'

'I don't matter. You and Riley are the ones who matter.'

'Stop it. You *do* matter.' Callie could feel tears in her eyes and she blinked them away impatiently. 'Look, there's no walking-away option here. Not for me anyway. Riley will always be my daughter and you'll always be her father.'

He looked at her thoughtfully. 'I don't have a walking-away option either.'

'Right, then. In that case we both need to say how we feel. Because that's the only way forward.'

'You're right.'

Callie puffed out an exasperated breath. Ben had been letting her off the hook about things, telling her that everything was okay for the last three weeks. He couldn't keep this up and at some point he was going to explode.

If he couldn't do it now, maybe he'd think about it and do it later. Callie wondered whether she should get up and make a cup of tea, and decided that the effort of standing could wait a little longer.

'I'm angry.' His quiet words didn't sound all that angry but at least he'd said them. It was a start.

'About?' Callie felt herself starting to tremble.

Ben sucked in a deep breath. 'Were you really so afraid of me that it took eight months to work up the courage to tell me you were pregnant?'

'I'm not afraid of you. After what you went through with Isabel, I decided to wait until…you could be sure.'

'I imagine it had been obvious for a while.' He shook his head, clearly trying to understand but unable to. 'Isn't it just that you wanted to be the one to provide for Riley? You didn't want me to have any part in her life?'

The quiet vehemence in his tone shocked Callie. But this was what she'd wanted, to clear the air between them and for Ben to tell her how he felt.

'Yes, I want to be able to provide for Riley on my own. There's nothing wrong with that, is there? But you had a right to know, and you have a right to be able to see her as well. You're her father.' The sudden thought that Ben might have been questioning that struck Callie. 'You can take a test if you're in any doubt…'

His face softened suddenly. 'I'm in no doubt. I trust you, Callie, but I just wish you'd trusted *me* a bit more.'

'I tried. I sent you a text but you didn't reply.' Now she thought about it, not replying to uncomfortable texts was Ben's modus operandi. She should have taken that into consideration.

'It was one text.' He spread his hands in disbelief. 'You said you wanted to meet for lunch, not that you were pregnant.'

'Because it would have been such a good idea to tell you that I was pregnant by text, is that what you're saying?'

They fell silent, staring at each other. Callie was the first to give in. 'Look I know I did this badly but I did the best I could at the time. I'd hoped that we'd have a bit more time to get used to this but… I failed there as well, I couldn't even make the full term of my pregnancy…'

The nurses had told her that it was common for women

who'd undergone emergency deliveries to feel a sense of failure. She'd said the very same thing to women herself when she'd attended emergency calls. Callie hadn't realised just how all-consuming and corrosive the feeling was until now.

Ben shook his head, running his hand through his hair in a gesture of frustration. 'That's not a failure, Callie. But not telling me...it made *me* fail. I wasn't there for you during your pregnancy and now...it's a lot to get my head around in such a short time. I'm struggling and I need some...distance.'

Callie's mouth felt suddenly dry. Failure. Distance. It hadn't taken Ben long to change his mind and now he was backing away.

'What kind of distance?'

'I just need to compartmentalise a little. When I'm at work I need to concentrate on that. When I'm here I can concentrate on you and Riley.'

That didn't sound so bad. One box for Ben's job and another for her and Riley. Callie could live inside that box for Riley's sake. She'd even decorate.

'That's okay. I can live with that.'

'Really?' He looked almost surprised.

'Yes. I need some time to myself too and...that sounds like a good arrangement.'

Her head approved of it at least. Her heart and her hormones wanted to know where he was at any given point in the day and wanted Ben here when he wasn't at work. But her head was her best and strongest ally.

The sound of a key in the front door made them both jump. Ben smiled a hello as Callie's mother walked past, towards the kitchen, and then he got to his feet. 'I should go...'

'No, Ben. You're not going anywhere.'

'Your mum's here and I don't want to argue.' His face was impassive again. Closed off.

'Fair enough. But you're here to see Riley and I don't want her to be one of those kids who gets caught up in her parents' problems. Whatever happens between the two of us shouldn't ever affect your time with her.'

He nodded. 'You're a great mother, Callie.'

The compliment made her want to burst into tears. Not now. Not when they seemed to be making progress.

'Then be a good father and go and fetch her. I dare say that Mum's making a cup of tea.'

Ben had smiled a lot since Riley had been born, but none of his smiles had had the carefree warmth about them that Callie had seen in his face last Christmas. But this one... He was getting there. A weight had obviously been lifted from his shoulders.

They were making progress. Maybe not quite in the direction that Callie had imagined, but that was what compromise was all about.

# CHAPTER SEVENTEEN

AGAINST ALL ODDS, they were making it work. Ben wondered if that would be the one thing that he looked back on as the crowning achievement of his life.

They were doing it for Riley. She meant more than his anger and Callie's independent streak. More than their confusion and the feeling that neither of them were a match for the situation. And he told himself that Riley meant more than the tenderness that he saw in Callie's eyes from time to time, and which echoed in his own empty heart.

As late summer gave way to autumn and then winter, they were turning their uneasy truce into a way of life. Callie started to organise afternoon photography shoots, starting with portraits and visits to the hospital to talk about the possibility of using her portraiture as therapy. She always worked on Ben's days off, and after some weeks of having Kate there to help him look after Riley while Callie was gone, he took the plunge and cared for his baby daughter alone.

The times that Ben had come to treasure were when Callie wasn't working. When all three of them could spend time together. The everyday things that had meant so little to him took on a touch of magic. Going shopping for food or for a walk in the park. Watching as Riley began to notice that there was a world around her, and seeing her discover it.

'I have to pop in to the hospital before we drop Riley off with my mum. There are some notes I need to pick up from Dr Lawrence in preparation for this evening.'

'You're sure your mum's happy to look after Riley this evening?' Callie was working, taking photographs with a man who was recovering from severe burns.

'She's always happy to look after Riley. I don't know what time I'll finish, and you're working tomorrow.'

'You're going to be great.' He could see that Callie was nervous. He'd felt much the same when he'd gone back to work after Riley was born, and he'd had far less reason. This new project, in partnership with the burns unit at the hospital, had taken a lot of work and planning.

'Thanks. I just hope… I just want to do this right.'

Callie gave him an apprehensive smile. This was one of the times when he wanted to fold her in his arms and tell her that he believed in her. But Ben couldn't, because hugs were for Riley. If he and Callie happened to touch during that process, it was an electric pleasure that he never allowed himself to think about.

'Trust me. You'll do it better than right.' Ben shook off the temptation that was pounding in his veins and lifted Riley out of her baby bouncer.

Watching him trying to bundle Riley into her snow-suit seemed to take Callie's mind off her own self-doubt for a moment. Ben heard a stifled giggle behind him as the little girl managed to pull her left arm back out of the sleeve for the third time.

'I think she must get this from you,' Ben joked, finally managing to get both Riley's arms into the snowsuit at the same time and pulling the zipper up.

'And I thought that she'd inherited her uncooperative streak from her father.' Callie laughed and Riley started to wave her arms, joining in. That was one thing that the little girl definitely got from her mother. Her smile, and the way that it made Ben's heart turn to mush.

Ben concentrated on his daughter, leaving his feelings for Callie out of the equation. 'Do you want to walk to the hospital or take the car?'

'Shall we walk?'

'Yes. I could do with stretching my legs.' His arms and legs still ached a little from his efforts at a factory fire two days ago. But that wasn't for Callie to know.

As they drew near the hospital gates she seemed more buoyant, talking about her work and the new opportunities and challenges it would bring. That was Callie all over— the closer at hand the challenge, the better she rose to it. It was good to hear her so excited now. Maybe in time he'd share some of the challenges that his work brought…

No. Keeping that separate worked for both of them. Ben didn't function well at work when he was thinking about Callie. They'd been through that already.

In front of them a car wove across the road. Ben instinctively put his arm out, pushing Callie and the pram behind him, although the car wasn't going at any great speed. It drifted to a halt halfway across the pavement, pointing towards the entrance to the hospital.

He felt Callie start forward and he pulled her back, gripping her arm tightly. 'Stay here with Riley. I'll go and see…'

She looked as if she was about to protest and then she nodded. Ben ran towards the car, seeing a man slumped across the steering wheel as he neared it.

He tried the door and it was locked. But the front window was slightly open, as if the car's occupant had been in need of some air. He forced it down, reaching in to switch off the engine and open the driver's door.

'He hasn't crashed, the airbag hasn't even been activated,' Ben called back to Callie, knowing somehow that she'd wouldn't have stayed right where he'd left her. She couldn't help coming a little closer.

'Maybe taken ill at the wheel.' Callie's voice was even closer than he'd expected and when he looked around she was craning to look inside the car, one hand on the pram.

'Callie, will you—?'

'Stay back? No.'

Ben gave in to the inevitable. Callie was better qualified to do this anyway. He took hold of the pram while she knelt down beside the car, examining the man quickly.

'Looks as if he's had a heart attack. Maybe he felt unwell and tried to drive himself to the hospital.' She looked up at Ben. 'Get my phone, will you? It's tucked in the side of the pram.'

Ben felt for the phone and found it. Callie grabbed it from him and made a call, speaking quickly. Then she put the phone back into her pocket.

'They're sending someone down straight away.' She unzipped the man's jacket, pressing her head to his chest, her fingers searching for a pulse. 'We can't wait. He's in cardiac arrest.'

'We need to get him out of the car?' If they were going to attempt resuscitation, they couldn't do it while the man was still in the driver's seat.

'Yes.' Callie pre-empted Ben's next thought and stood back. 'You can lift him better than I can.'

Ben knew that the scar from the Caesarean still pulled a little sometimes, and reaching into the car meant she'd have to lift and pull at the same time. He let her take charge of the pram, thankful that she hadn't ignored her better judgement. Carefully he manoeuvred the man out of the car, laying him down on the pavement, and Callie slipped a baby blanket under his head.

'Should I start resuscitation?' He wasn't going to allow Callie to do that either. Ben had enough training to do the job.

'Yes. You want me to count?'

'Yep.' Ben felt her eyes on him as he positioned his hands on the man's chest in the way he'd been taught. Callie started to count and he followed the rhythm that she set for him.

'Keep going, you're doing great. They're coming…' He heard Callie give an impatient huff. 'Stay back, will you? There's nothing to see here. Let the paramedics through.'

Ben smiled grimly, briefly aware that the small crowd that had formed behind them on the pavement had suddenly begun to disperse. There was the sound of voices and then a man knelt down beside him.

'Swap on three.' Callie counted the beats and Ben sat back on his heels, letting the paramedic take over. An ambulance was approaching the gates and its crew were unloading a trolley, ready to take the man into the hospital.

He stood up, retreating to where Callie stood with the pram. She smiled up at him and Ben felt her hand slip into his.

'Good job, Ben.'

'Great counting.' He smiled down at her. 'I'm impressed by the standing back, too.'

'Don't push it.' He felt her elbow in his ribs and a sudden tingle ran down his spine.

Riley's first medical emergency. She'd come through it with flying colours, dozing in her pram the whole time. He and Callie had come through it too, relying on each other and working as a team. It had stirred an ache in Ben's chest. Memories of when they'd been more to each other than just Riley's mum and Riley's dad.

Callie reappeared from her meeting with Dr Lawrence, a manila envelope in her hand. It was only a short walk to Kate's house, and once they'd handed Riley over to her grandmother there was no reason for him to stay. He'd pick up his car keys from Callie's and go home.

As they walked up her front path, Callie's phone rang. She answered it, cradling the phone between her ear and her shoulder as she opened the front door and motioned him inside, listening intently to someone at the other end of the line.

'No… No, Eric, that's absolutely fine. We'll do this when you're ready, not before… It's no inconvenience. It's really important that you take whatever time you need.' She was smiling into the phone. 'Give me a call tomorrow when you're feeling better. If you want to talk about things a bit more, I can always drop in and see you…'

A few more reassurances and then Callie finished the call. As she met Ben's enquiring gaze, the smile faded from her face.

'What's up?'

'The guy I was going to take photographs with this evening just cancelled. He's had a bad day and doing things when he isn't ready is just going to be counterproductive.' Callie shrugged. 'That's okay. He still wants to do it, just not this evening.'

She was clearly disappointed. Callie had prepared for this so carefully and now that it wasn't going to happen she seemed at a loss as to what to do next. Ben made for the kitchen. 'I'll make you a cup of tea before I go.'

There was no excuse to keep Ben there now but Callie suddenly didn't want him to go. That was a sure sign that she should send him on his way as soon as politely possible.

'It's good that he felt able to phone and cancel.' She sat on the sofa, her coat and gloves next to her on the cushions. 'I suppose I'd better go and get Riley.'

Ben put two mugs of tea down on the coffee table. 'Drink your tea first. There's no rush. Kate's got a full programme of baby activities planned, and she won't much like it if you turn up on the doorstep before she's had a chance to try Riley out with the baby learning centre.'

Callie chuckled. 'True. Mum's determined that she's going to be a genius.'

'I'll settle for her being able to do whatever she wants.'

'Yes, me too.' That was one thing that she and Ben could agree on without any danger of their shared ambitions starting to look like a relationship.

'I know you've done a lot of preparation for this evening. You must be disappointed.' He leaned back on the sofa cushions, sipping his tea.

This crossed the boundaries that she and Ben had set for themselves. But maybe she needed him to put a toe across those lines at the moment.

'I just feel…' She shook her head, trying to work out exactly how she did feel. 'I'm rather hoping I haven't lost my edge. That man this afternoon…'

'Lost your edge? Seriously? From where I was standing, it looked as if you were in charge the whole time.'

It was nice of him to say so. She'd stood by, counting helplessly, clinging to the pram, while he'd done all the real work. 'I'd have had him out of the car and started resuscitation without even thinking about it once upon a time.'

'And you'll do it again, but not before you're fully fit.' He held up his hand as she protested. 'I know you feel as if you are, but these things always take a bit longer than you think. You were exactly where you needed to be, and where Riley needed you to be.'

What would she have done if Ben hadn't been there, though? Callie dismissed the thought. He wasn't the only person who could have helped, even if, at the time, it had felt that he was the only person she needed in the world.

'Do you want to stay and watch a film with me?' She could allow herself that at least. 'Then I'll go and pick Riley up.'

It was a departure from their usual way of doing things,

and he took a moment to think about it. Then he nodded. 'I'd like that. Why don't you choose something and I'll go and get us some snacks from the kitchen?'

# CHAPTER EIGHTEEN

CALLIE'S IDEA OF snacks while watching a film usually extended to opening a packet of crisps. She flipped through the list of films, trying not to smile. It wasn't exactly unexpected that the man with the best-stocked fridge she'd ever seen had found the packet of popcorn at the back of the cupboard, and from the sound of it was putting it to use.

She still hadn't settled on a film when he appeared in the doorway of the sitting room, holding a bowl of popcorn in one hand and a large platter in the other.

'What's this?' She moved her coat so that he could sit down beside her.

'Just popcorn. And I raided your chocolate stash and found some bits and pieces in the fridge...'

To good effect. A thick, melted chocolate goo was in a small bowl in the centre of the platter, surrounded by an assortment of fruit, chopped and arranged carefully. Callie grinned at him.

'When it's time to teach Riley to cook, will you promise to do it?'

Ben chuckled. 'Taste it before you say that.'

He reached forward, taking half a strawberry from the pile and dipping it into the chocolate. When he held it to her lips the warm and cold sweetness, coupled with the scent of having him close, made her forget about everything else.

'Mmm… That's…very good.' Too good. Callie could feel heat rising to her cheeks, and she covered her confusion by reaching for the TV remote. They could draw back now and nothing would be lost. It would just be a moment that meant nothing.

'Have you chosen a film?' If Ben had felt anything then he too seemed unwilling to acknowledge it.

'How about this?' The first one on the list looked as good as any other, and when Ben nodded she pressed the start button. They'd watch the film and then she'd collect Riley and Ben would be on his way.

This was strong magic. The wish to take Callie's mind off her disappointment had turned into the sudden feeling that kissing her was the absolute next thing to do. If that was just an illusion, it was a hard spell to break.

He held out as long as he could. But Callie seemed about as interested in the vivid special effects on the TV screen as he was. All he could see was her.

'Carrots? Really?' They'd worked their way through the fruit on the platter now.

'I used whatever I could find…'

'So this is an experiment?' She dipped the baton into the chocolate and tried it. 'It's….different.'

Ben couldn't move. He didn't have the strength to resist when she dipped the rest of carrot into the fondue and held it to his lips. And by some sorcery he thought he tasted only Callie.

He should stop before he was completely beguiled. But the look in her eyes kept him motionless. And then the touch of her finger on the side of his mouth, wiping away a smear of chocolate, turned his blood to fire.

He could kiss her now, and then they could forget all about it and go back to what they'd been for the last three months. What had worked. *Yeah. Tell yourself that…* Ben ignored the voice of warning echoing softly in the back of his head.

She dipped one finger into the chocolate and put it into her mouth. And he was lost. When he reached for her, Callie was there, melting into his arms as if there had never been any other place she'd wanted to be.

Her body was different now, but it hadn't forgotten what it was like to feel Ben close. However had she thought it could?

She felt Ben's hands spreading across her back. Just the way they had before...

Not *just*. It was more. All they'd been through since last Christmas, all the hurdles they'd managed to overcome lent a depth and an exquisite tenderness to his kiss. A slow burn, which couldn't be quenched.

He was holding her away from him a little, but seemed helpless to stop her when she moved closer, feeling his body hard and trembling against hers. Callie kissed him again or maybe Ben kissed her. They were so connected, so much at one with each other, that it was impossible to tell.

'I've missed you so much, Callie. But...'

Did there always have to be a *but*? Always some reason why they couldn't do what they both wanted to do? Callie couldn't bear to pull away from him. If he was going to reject her, he'd have to do it while she was still in his arms.

'But what?'

In the heat of his sudden smile nothing could hurt her. 'You couldn't be any more beautiful to me than you are now, Callie. But you've just had a baby and...to be honest, I don't even know the right questions to ask.'

It was all right. Everything was all right again. Callie put her finger over his lips and shifted onto his lap. Face to face, staring into his eyes.

'You want to ask whether I'm ready. And how far we can go together.'

Ben chuckled softly. 'I knew I could count on you to come to my rescue. I don't suppose you have the answer, as well as the question?'

'My answer is that I feel ready, and I trust you to be with me and take each moment as it comes.' She kissed him, a new warmth flooding her body. She was safe with Ben, he'd never hurt her. And he'd never hurt Riley.

'I'm following your lead. One word from you and we stop. I'm trusting you to say that word.'

'Do I get to say "Come upstairs" as well? "Let me take your clothes off"?' she teased him.

'Yeah. You can say that as soon as you like.'

Their lovemaking hadn't been so physically active this time around. But Ben's tenderness had been deeper and wilder than before. He'd told her all the things she wanted to hear, that she was beautiful and that he desired her. And the connection was stronger than ever as he watched for her every reaction.

She wanted to stay curled up in his arms but the evening had slipped away in a slow burn of delight and it was getting late.

'I should go and fetch Riley.' She nudged at his shoulder.

'I can go if you want to stay here.' He opened his eyes sleepily.

'No, I'll do it. Mum's expecting me.'

Ben nodded. Maybe he too wanted to keep this between the two of them. Callie wasn't ready to make it a part of her everyday life, not just yet.

His gaze followed her as she got out of bed. Picking up her clothes from the floor, she instinctively held them across her stomach, hiding the scar and the stretch marks.

'Don't cover them up.' His murmured words made her

stop. 'Or am I going to have to take a photograph to convince you?'

Callie dropped her clothes back onto the floor.

He grinned, blinking his eyes as he imitated the sound of a camera shutter. 'That's the picture I want…'

Ben refused to think about the complications. This felt right. Getting out of bed, he threw his clothes on and went downstairs. The sitting-room light was still on and he cleared away the scattered remains of the popcorn and fondue. Still wrapped in the satiated warmth of their lovemaking, he sat down on the sofa and began to doze.

He didn't hear Callie coming back. When he felt tiny fingers on his face, his eyes snapped open in alarm and he heard Callie's laughing admonition.

'Don't punch Daddy in the face, sweetie.'

Two different pieces of his life crashed together headlong. He rubbed his eyes, trying to make sense of the gorgeous chaos.

'Sorry.' Callie was sitting on the edge of the sofa, one hand on Riley's back to steady her. 'Did we startle you?'

'I must have dozed off.'

And woken to find that the simple, comforting rules that he'd built his life around didn't hold true. He could follow the pattern he'd used to keep his work and his private life separate, and put his relationship with Callie and his relationship with his daughter into two separate boxes all he liked. Keeping them there was an entirely different prospect.

But somehow it didn't matter. He reached for Riley, picking her up for a hug. It seemed suddenly possible to hold everything that he most loved in the world in his arms. When Callie moved closer, nestling against him, that possibility became a reality that took his breath away.

'This…is nice.' Callie looked up at him as he put his arm around her shoulders. 'Different…'

He kissed Callie's cheek and then bent to kiss the top of Riley's head. 'You want to take a moment to get familiar with it? I'd like to.'

She laughed suddenly, and Riley imitated the sound in her own sing-song way. 'Yes. I could definitely get used to this.'

Riley was crying. And then the bed heaved as Ben got out of it and she heard the sound of him pulling on his jeans.

'I'll go…'

Callie muttered an acknowledgement. This moment ranked with all the others that she wanted to keep. She could hear Ben singing quietly, and when she opened her eyes she saw his silhouette, rocking their baby in his arms.

'I'll take her downstairs. You get some sleep.'

She heard Ben chuckle. 'You'll do no such thing.'

The bed moved again as he sat down on it, and Callie wriggled over towards him, still wrapped in the duvet. All the love in the world seemed to reside within the circle of his arms.

Love? Was this what this was? Or was it just two people thrown together who wanted to make a family from the materials to hand? At the moment the future seemed like a distant ogre that could be fought later.

'I'll have to go soon.' Ben's voice rang with regret and Callie glanced at the clock beside the bed. It was an hour's drive home and then he had to get to the fire station to start his shift.

'How long?'

'Not yet. Half an hour.'

He seemed to want that half-hour to last as much as she did. Riley quietened suddenly in his arms, as if she too knew that this was something special.

'When will I see you again?' The question she'd been determined not to ask came naturally suddenly.

'Maybe we can…spend the day together when I'm next off shift?'

Five days. Probably six, to give him the chance to sleep after his night's work. It seemed like an age but Ben was probably right. This was too fragile a thing, too precious, and they should go slowly.

'Yes, I'd like that. Give me a call then?'

She felt him move and his lips brushed her forehead. 'Yeah. I'll give you a call.'

# CHAPTER NINETEEN

No THOUGHT WENT into it. Ben's training kicked in as soon as he realised he was falling, and he bent his knees, landing on his feet and then rolling.

The pain came soon enough. He couldn't stand so he crawled, dragging his useless leg behind him. There was only one aim in his head. Get out. If he wanted to hold Callie and Riley in his arms again, he had to get out...

Blind, dogged effort gave way to relief when he felt himself being lifted and carried the final few yards out of the building. Eve's voice penetrated the haze of pain. 'Stand down, boss. We've got you.'

He realised that he'd been fighting, still trying to get to his feet even though he was well clear of the building now and he could see the sky. Hands found the place where his ribs hurt most and he groaned...

Sirens. The ambulance was running on a siren and it was making his head hurt. Why couldn't they just turn it off? He managed to pull the oxygen mask from his face, getting out just one word before the ambulance paramedic gently put it back in place.

'Callie...'

Callie ran from the hospital car park, making straight for the ambulance crews' entrance into A and E. She hadn't heard from Ben since he'd left her early yesterday morning, and she hadn't expected to. When Eve had called, it had felt like a physical blow.

As luck would have it, her mother had been there, and she'd been able to leave Riley with her. The roads had been clear and she'd made the drive to the hospital in just over half an hour.

An ambulance had drawn up and the crew was wheeling a gurney through the automatic doors into A and E. She recognised Ben's shock of dark hair and put on a final sprint for the doors before they swished closed again, feeling the scar across the base of her stomach pull a little as she ran.

'Callie Walsh. I'm a paramedic...' She fumbled in her bag, showing her ID to the ambulance driver, who was standing next to the gurney. 'I'm...with him.'

Luckily *with him* was a good enough explanation. Callie wasn't sure how else to describe herself.

'Okay. We're finding a doctor now....' The driver nodded towards his partner, who was navigating through the melee of people, all of whom seemed to have something to do.

'How is he?' Callie could see dressings on Ben's arm and an immobiliser on one of his legs. An oxygen mask obscured his face and his eyes were closed.

'He's breathing on his own, no critical injuries that we can see. His arm's burned and his leg's broken.' The man allowed himself a tight smile. 'I'm glad you're here.'

Before Callie could ask why, Ben stirred. He seemed to be trying to reach for something, and she caught his flailing hand, telling him to stay still. At the sound of her voice he opened his eyes suddenly.

'Callie...?'

'Everything's all right, Ben. You're at the hospital and you're safe.'

He seemed to only half comprehend what she was saying but half was enough. Ben's fingers tightened around her and the urgency of his movements subsided.

'What happened?' Callie murmured the question to the ambulance driver.

'A floor gave way and he fell from the first to the ground floor. He crawled a fair way before the crew could get to him and bring him out.'

And Ben was still on autopilot. That steely determination of his hadn't quite worked out that he was safe yet.

'He's been like this all the way here?'

'Yeah, he's been drifting in and out. When he was awake he was thrashing around, calling for you. And Riley...?'

'That's our daughter.'

'Right.' The ambulance driver looked round, seeing his partner approach with a young doctor. 'Here we go...'

Callie followed as the doctor shepherded them into a cubicle with the gurney. She could hardly breathe. Ben hadn't called out for his work family, the team he'd come to rely on. He'd wanted her and Riley.

It was nothing, an automatic reaction. She'd heard patients call out for all kinds of people. The doctor introduced himself as Michael, and Callie flashed her paramedic's ID again, when it looked as if the next thing he would do was to tell her to stand back.

The doctor thought for a moment. 'We're very busy and it's not as if I couldn't do with your help.'

Could she keep her tears under control and think like a medic? Right now she'd do whatever it took. 'I won't get emotional.'

Michael nodded. 'Okay. I want you to step back if that changes, Callie. We all have our limits, and I can deal with whatever needs to be done.'

Barely. It would be quicker and better with two. But Callie nodded her head. 'I understand.'

'In that case, I want you to try and keep him conscious and focussed.'

Michael was giving her a task that involved as little medical intervention as possible. That didn't matter, as long as she could be close to Ben. And it would be a lot easier for the doctors and nurses if he could react to their questions, rather than alternating between a semi-conscious state and trying to fight them.

As Michael turned his attention to the nurse who had just arrived with a burns trolley, Callie surreptitiously reached for the penlight on the counter. Keeping him conscious wasn't so very different from checking for a concussion.

She tapped his cheek with her finger. 'Ben… I've got you now, and you're safe. Look at me…'

He opened his eyes. Clear blue, in stark contrast with the grime streaking his face. They held all the need that she'd seen when he'd cried out for her in the night, but this time he needed her in a different way, one that was a lot harder to respond to. He was hurt, and it was up to Callie to pull him back from a precipice that she hadn't dared think about.

Callie swallowed hard. She knew her job, even if she knew nothing else at the moment. She just had to do her job.

'Do you know where you are, Ben?'

His lips formed one word. 'Hospital…'

'Great. That's right.' Callie caught his free hand in hers. 'I want you to squeeze my hand if you feel any sudden pain.'

He nodded, his gaze fixed on hers. When she shone the penlight, his pupils reacted correctly to the light and Ben appeared to know what was going on around him. More than that. His gaze seemed to know everything, the way it always had…

Tears threatened, and Callie made an effort to stop

thinking that way. If she showed any signs of distress, Michael would have to make her stand back.

'What's the date today?' She covered her confusion with a question, moving the face mask a little and leaning in to hear the answer.

'First of December. The monarch is Queen Elizabeth. My name's Benjamin David Matthews and my daughter's name is Riley.' Ben caught his breath in pain. 'She has the cutest smile.'

Okay. She got it. Ben had been through this procedure before and he knew all the answers to the questions.

'Your middle name's David, is it?' She forced a smile. In all the hundreds of little details about their lives that they'd exchanged, middle names had never come up.

'Yes.'

'Just stay still for a moment…' Callie let his hand drop and felt him clutch at her blouse. Fair enough. How many other patients had reached for her, holding on as if that was all that was keeping them safe. She carefully examined him for any cuts or bumps on his head, finding nothing.

'Your leg and your arm hurt…' She could see from his eyes that they did. 'Anything else?'

She was caught again in his gaze. 'Nothing…hurts.'

Nothing had been able to hurt her either when she'd been in his arms. 'Ben, cut the macho act. What else?'

His eyelids fluttered down in a sign of acquiescence. 'My side…'

Callie turned, and saw that Michael had uncovered a large, rapidly forming bruise on his ribs. It could be a sign of a cracked rib or even internal bleeding. He was probing it with his fingers and Ben groaned, his hand clutching tighter onto her shirt.

'I want you to breathe in…' Michael caught his attention and Ben's gaze turned to him. But however hard she tried, Callie couldn't get him to loosen his grip on her.

\* \* \*

As Callie had anticipated, the break was a bad one, and his leg was going to need surgery. The doctor thought that they could get Ben down to the operating theatre straight away, and left Callie with him to wait for news.

He was slowly coming around. Warm, and about as comfortable as pain killing drugs and pillows could make him, Ben began to loosen his grip on her shirt. Then he let go.

'It won't be long now.' Callie had gone to speak to one of the nurses to find out what was happening.

'I'm sorry, Callie.'

'Be quiet. You have nothing to apologise for.' Callie heard a tense edge to her voice. Ben must know as well as she did that her greatest fear was that the father of her child wouldn't come back one day, and that it was agony to see how close he'd been to that possibility today.

'You should go… Riley…'

'Riley's fine, she's with Mum. You're the one I'm worried about.' She bit her lip as tears sprang to her eyes. Callie had resolved not to mention the word 'worry'.

He reached for her hand, squeezing it tightly. 'I'll be okay…'

She wanted to raise his fingers to her lips, but she couldn't. Instead, she laid her hand lightly on his forehead. It was a gesture of comfort that didn't seem too dangerous at the moment.

'I'll be here when you come out of surgery. I called Eve to let her know how you were doing and she said that some of the crew would be coming down here later as well.'

'No fuss, Callie…'

'You're not the boss here, Ben. You'll do as you're told and we'll make as much fuss as we want to. You're in no position to stop us.'

He frowned, clearly searching for an argument. Then Ben's lips quirked into a smile. 'Yes, ma'am.'

'That's better.'

When she was alone she could cry. She could think about the ramifications of seeing the father of her child injured in the line of duty. How it felt more awful than she could ever have thought it would. But for now she had to be strong.

Yesterday afternoon and evening was a blur. The only thing that had been in really sharp focus was Callie. Ben had woken up in his hospital bed this morning, and as Eve had promised him before she left last night, he was hurting in places he hadn't even known he had.

Ben submitted to all the doctors' and nurses' requests of him, but his mind was elsewhere. His injuries had changed everything between him and Callie. She'd done everything to reassure him, but he had seen through the façade. He'd made a reality out of her worst fears.

When visiting time came, he couldn't help but watch for her, almost hoping that she'd decided not to come. But she did, and when she walked through the doors of the ward, carrying Riley in a sling, his heart took over from his head and beat wildly.

He couldn't take his eyes off her. As she sat down next to his bed, she smiled at him. 'How are you today?'

'Much better, thanks. What about you?' Callie looked tired. As if she hadn't had a wink of sleep last night.

'I'm fine.' The hint of protest in her voice told Ben that she very definitely wasn't fine. He reached for her hand, feeling it cold in his.

'No, you're not.' He flashed her a *Don't argue* look, and she quirked the corners of her mouth down. 'I know that this isn't where you ever wanted to be.'

He'd put her here, though. He'd made love to her, and now she was sitting by his hospital bed. The different strands of his life had become tangled and knotted and it was time to unravel them.

'I don't know what you mean.' She bent down, reaching into the bag she'd brought with her, but she couldn't disguise the flush in her cheeks.

The worries that had been swirling in his head consolidated into certainty. Callie would make an effort to ignore her fears, but she couldn't overcome them. She might stay with him because of love, or from a misplaced sense that it would be better for Riley. She might stay to nurse him back to fitness. Whatever the reason, she'd get to the point where concerns over his safety made her feel threatened and unsafe, the way she had when she'd been a child, and that would break them apart. There could only be one thing worse than never having the family he wanted, and that was having them and then losing them.

'We have to talk about this, Callie.'

She puffed out a breath, one hand moving protectively to the back of Riley's head. The little girl was curled against her chest, fast asleep.

'Okay. It's difficult, Ben, is that what you want to hear? I'm dealing with it.'

No. She wasn't. The only way forward was to rely on what he knew worked. Compartmentalisation.

'Callie, neither of us can deal with this, we both need to back away. What happened between us the other night can't happen again. We can't take that risk.'

She caught her breath. He could see the question in her eyes. *Don't you care?* If she didn't know that he cared for her, she didn't know anything about him, but Ben couldn't say it. Callie could ask him anything, but that was the one question he wouldn't answer.

'We can't take the risk with Riley, you mean?' Eventually she settled on an easier question.

'No, we can't. We promised that our relationship wouldn't ever hurt her, and a week ago that promise was easy to keep. I think we should make sure it stays that way.'

'But…we already…' She looked around at the other

beds, as if to check that no one was taking an interest in their conversation. 'We've already spent the night together and things were fine... They weren't just fine, they were great.'

'And now they're not. After one night we can go back and pick up our lives. After six months or a year... I couldn't make it back from that.'

'But what if we *can* make it work?' She was frowning, her face haggard with lack of sleep. Callie was so intent on just getting through this, but he could see in her eyes that she was fighting a losing battle with herself.

'Can you honestly tell me that this is what you want for Riley? Having her mother worry like this every single day? Because it's not what I want for her and it isn't what I want for you and me either.'

'I...' Callie's protest died on her lips. 'No. It's not what I want.'

'So let's make things easy, shall we? Go home. I'll give you a call in a couple of days when I'm out of here. We'll work from there.'

Her back stiffened suddenly. 'I can't do that. You need someone to look after you, Ben.'

That was the least of his worries right now. He reached for his phone, switching it on and showing her the texts. 'What I *need* is an appointments system.'

She flipped through the texts, a tear rolling suddenly down her cheek. 'I guess the fire service looks after its own.'

'Yes, we do.' Ben had always thought of his crew as family. Now they seemed a shadowy second-best to the one he was sending away. The one that couldn't ever be.

'Okay.' She began to unclip Riley's sling, running her finger across the little girl's cheek to wake her. Then she held her closer to the bed so that Ben could reach her. 'I want you to kiss your daughter, Ben. Tell her you'll see her very soon.'

* * *

'So how's Ben?'

It was a natural enough question. When Callie had accepted an invitation to lunch at Eve's, she'd expected she would ask and had her answer ready.

'I haven't seen him for two weeks. My mum and her partner have been taking Riley over to see him. We decided that it's best for all of us if we just stick to our access arrangements.'

'That's what he said when I saw him last. I just wondered what your side of the story was.' Eve flashed Callie an apologetic smile.

Even in the quiet agony of their parting it seemed that she and Ben were maintaining a united front. Callie hugged Riley tight. She was the one thing that made any sense in any of this.

'It is what it is. He's a great father to Riley, and that's what matters.'

'Yep. I can't imagine Ben would be anything else.' The oven timer sounded from the kitchen and Eve got to her feet. 'That's our lunch…'

Thankfully, there were no more questions about Ben. But Callie was learning that not talking about him didn't stop her from thinking about him. All roads seemed to lead back to him at the moment.

'Doesn't your husband worry? About your job?' Eve had been talking about how they managed Isaac's care when she was on shift, and Callie couldn't help asking the question that was pounding in her head.

'Yes, he worries. I worry about him as well.' Eve grinned in response to Callie's questioning look. 'He's a civil servant. Desk jobs can be tough, too.'

'Not as tough as your job surely?'

'I don't know about that. He's not as fit as I am, and he doesn't get to work off the stress. I'm a bit concerned about his cholesterol.'

'What level is he?' Callie asked automatically, and then thought better of it. 'Sorry. Professional interest.'

'That's okay. He's at five point five.'

'That's not so bad. It could be lower, particularly at his age, but a bit less saturated fat in his diet and some exercise should bring it down.'

'I'm sending him to the gym.' Eve grinned. 'I reckon that I might as well get the benefit of this health kick of his, and I'm looking forward to a little finely toned musculature.'

Callie almost choked on her food. Ben did finely toned musculature well. Very well. Thinking about it wasn't going to help.

'So it's not really an issue for you, then?'

'Yes, of course it's an issue. But I was a firefighter when I met Danny, and we both knew what we were signing up for when we got married.' Eve shot Callie a knowing glance. 'And I'm not Ben.'

'Is there a difference?'

'Ben's a leader. He's responsible for everyone, and he's the one who makes the hard decisions. Do you know why it was him who fell through that floor the other day and not his partner?'

'No. Why?' Callie almost didn't *want* to know.

'Because Ben goes first. He always does. He never asks any of us to do anything that he won't do, and he never gives up. That's not an easy thing to live with.'

Callie could feel the flush spreading across her cheeks. Ben was a true hero. That *was* hard to live with, but she couldn't be more proud of him.

'If you see him…'

'I'm dropping in tomorrow. The guys are great at going round there and ordering in a pizza, but Ben's probably worked his way through most of the fresh food I left him last time. You want a status report?'

'Yes… Yes, please. But please don't tell him.' The least

that Callie could do was to watch over Ben from afar. It couldn't hurt if he never knew about it.

'I won't. I'll call you tomorrow evening.'

# CHAPTER TWENTY

*Christmas Eve*

BEN WAS SPRAWLED on the sofa, looking miserably at the Christmas tree. It was still bare, looking like something that had wandered in and settled itself by the hearth but had no real place there.

He'd had such hopes for this Christmas. This year, Blue Watch had Christmas Eve off, and he'd been planning to see both Callie and Riley. The day would be full of sparkle, all the pretty things that Riley loved. After their night together, he'd briefly hoped that he and Callie would be able to share some magic of their own, too. It would be the best day of the year.

Instead, it was shaping up to be the worst. Ben shifted uncomfortably on the sofa, the cast on his leg cumbersome. His leg throbbed and the burns on his arm were still painful.

The buzzer sounded and Ben laboriously made his way over to the intercom. That was one of the disadvantages of a large, open-plan living area. Everything was so far away.

Whoever it was didn't buzz again. They must know that he was slow at the moment. Perhaps it was one of his crew, coming to try and cheer him up. He'd done his best when Eve had popped round the other day with her little boy, but when she'd left he'd felt even more upset and alone.

'Ben. Are you there?' Despite the crackle of the inter-com, he recognised Callie's voice.

'I'm here.' His hand hovered over the door release and then dropped to his side. He'd made his decision about see-ing Callie, and he wasn't going to change it just because he was at a low ebb.

'Are you going to let me in?'

'No. Go home, Callie.'

'I've just come from home. It's taken me an hour to get through the traffic…' Her voice rang with dismay. 'I have Riley with me, and she's freezing cold. And she's crying.'

Ben couldn't hear any crying. But Callie obviously wasn't going away and he couldn't leave her on the door-step. Despite himself, Ben felt a little thrill of excitement as he pressed the button to release the main door.

'Thank you!' He heard Callie's final words before the intercom cut out. They were laced with frustration and he could just imagine her rolling her eyes.

It would be a few minutes before she got herself and Riley into the lift and back out again. Ben used the time to stack that morning's breakfast things into the sink and dump the newspapers that littered the sofa onto the cof-fee table in something that resembled a tidy pile. It was the best he could do to make it look as if he was manag-ing for himself.

He'd barely got settled, back onto the sofa, when the door drifted open and Callie appeared. She was carrying Riley in a body sling over her red coat, a richly patterned skirt grazing the tops of her fleece-lined boots and a large bag over her shoulder. Riley was dressed in green, with a little elf hat on her head. When Callie pointed towards Ben, Riley stretched one arm out and began to chuckle.

Ben hardly dared move. He watched as Callie kicked the door closed behind her and walked towards him. A short struggle with the body sling and then she put Riley down on the sofa next to him. 'Look, Riley, there's Daddy.'

Riley reached for him, and Ben lifted her onto his lap. He hugged his little girl tight, kissing her.

'She doesn't look as if she's been crying.' He decided to call Callie's bluff.

'She cheered up when she saw you.'

From the little jut of her chin it seemed that Callie found Riley's sudden change in mood just as unlikely as he did. She shrugged, looking around the apartment.

'Nice tree. You've decided to go for the minimalist look this year?'

'The guys brought it round but they had to get to work and I haven't got around to decorating it yet. Sorry about the mess, I wasn't expecting company.'

'That's all right. I can tidy up a bit…' Callie seemed intent on finding something to do.

Enough. He couldn't bear this. 'Callie, why are you here?'

'I knew you'd be disappointed about not seeing Riley, and Mum's busy. I brought some shopping as well. Eve said you were running out of a few things…'

'*Eve* said?'

'You know I speak to Eve.' She flushed, putting her bag onto the kitchen counter and starting to empty it.

He knew it. Callie and Eve had struck up a friendship, and had seen each other regularly since Riley had been born. It had been hard, in the last three weeks, not to ask Eve how Callie was and clearly Callie had been similarly tempted.

'Callie, you didn't need to come all this way to restock my cupboards. And it's great to see Riley, but that could have waited until Kate was free to bring her.'

She froze, staring down at the groceries that she'd taken out of her bag. 'Yes. You're right.'

'So what *are* you doing here?'

* * *

Callie felt her cheeks burn. This was the biggest risk she'd ever taken in a life dedicated to avoiding risk.

She swallowed hard. If he was going to send her away, she might as well say what she'd come to say first.

'I've made a decision, Ben. I couldn't do anything about it when I lost my father or my home, but I can do something about losing you. You said to me once that there are some things that are important enough to take risks to achieve, and without that a life can become meaningless...'

Callie stopped for breath. Ben was staring at her, and Riley was suddenly still in his lap. The little girl was looking intently at her too, knowing maybe that this was a moment that could change their lives.

'Go on, Callie.' At least he was going to hear her out. That was something.

'Eve told me that you were injured because you always go in first. You never ask anyone to do anything you won't do.'

Annoyance flashed across his face. 'That's not quite how it is.'

'Don't try to protect me, Ben, that's exactly how it is. And you're exactly the kind of man that I want in Riley's life. Someone who isn't afraid to lead and who'll be there for her whatever happens.'

He nodded. 'I *will* be there for her.'

Callie took a deep breath. Now or never... 'You're exactly the kind of man I want in *my* life, too.'

'Callie, we've been through this already—'

'Yes, we have. But I was wrong to let you go. All I could think about was that I might lose you, but... I never thought that the only person who could make me happy enough to deal with my fears was you.'

He shook his head. She'd messed up all over again. Callie began to panic, as the consequences of the risk she'd taken began to swell in her heart.

'Say something, Ben. If you want me to go…'

Suddenly he smiled. 'Stay here, Callie. With me.'

She could feel heat spreading from her cheeks to her ears and then around the back of her neck. She'd taken the first step, and Ben had responded with another one. She wanted to fling herself into his arms, but it was all too soon for that. If he just let her stay for a little while, she could show him that she wasn't going to pressure him any more.

'Right, then. So you'll tell me where the decorations are?'

Ben nodded towards the door that led to the other side of the apartment. 'There's a big cupboard. Through there…'

She hadn't been through there since last Christmas. Then it had seemed a concrete reminder for Ben of all the things he hadn't believed in any more. Now maybe it was a reason for hope.

'I'll…go and get them, shall I?' She was still standing yards away from him, in the kitchen area, but Callie couldn't shake the feeling that they were closer now than they'd ever been.

'That sounds great. We can decorate the tree together.'

That sounded wonderful. Callie almost ran towards the door, twisting the key feverishly in the lock, before Ben changed his mind.

It seemed that Callie couldn't sit still. Ben knew exactly how she felt, but it was a little more difficult for him to give in to the temptation to quiet the pounding of his heart with physical activity.

Callie had changed everything. The tearful grin she'd given him had made him realise why his life had been so dark recently. Without her, Christmas was just another drab winter day. But she'd turned it into a time of hope.

In a whirl of energy she fetched the decorations and examined the contents of his fridge, while the coffee machine dribbled the last of his fresh coffee into two cups. Then she declared the food situation to be worse than she'd imagined and decided they should go out, because he couldn't possibly go without turkey sandwiches at Christmas time.

'It's too late. We'll never get a turkey on Christmas Eve.'

'It's early still and when I drove down the High Street the shops were heaving. Look at Ebenezer Scrooge—he managed to find a turkey on Christmas morning.'

Ben chuckled. 'As I remember, he sent a boy to find the turkey. And that was a long time ago. Things have probably changed.'

'Yes, they've changed. We have supermarkets now. Do you have a sock that I can put over your cast to keep your foot warm?'

Ben gave up. It was hard enough to resist Callie when she wasn't around, and now it was downright impossible.

'Upstairs. I'm afraid it's a bit of a mess...'

Callie chuckled. 'I'll survive. Running up and down the stairs to tidy up isn't exactly a priority when you're on crutches.'

'I'll have you know that my physiotherapist was very impressed with my grasp of stair climbing techniques. She may even have mentioned the word *perfect*...' He called after her.

Ben could hear the sounds of pillows being plumped and the duvet being rearranged. 'Don't bother with that. Socks are in the top drawer of the dresser.'

'Okay...' It sounded as if Callie was ignoring him because she was still walking around, probably picking up the clothes he'd left on the floor. 'We'll go shopping and then we'll decorate the tree.'

Callie knew that she was pushing things further than she'd meant to go. But Ben was smiling, that luminous blue-eyed smile that she remembered from last Christmas. The moment he stopped, she'd take a step back, but she couldn't while it was still on his face.

Ben's car was bigger than hers and he could get into the passenger seat more easily. Callie manoeuvred the SUV into a parking space as close to the supermarket entrance as she could. It went without saying that leaving him in the car with Riley while she got the shopping was too much time apart. And even if everything did take a little longer, Ben made good use of the opportunity, dropping things they didn't need into the trolley and making faces at Riley.

'I can hear carol singers.' He was looking around as Callie loaded the boot of the car, trying to work out from which direction the voices were coming.

'Perhaps we can drive past...'

'Can't we take a walk over?' They must be at the Market Square on the High Street.

'How far is it? Can you make it?'

He nodded. 'This is Riley's first Christmas. I'll make it.'

Riley had seen carol singers already, but Callie decided not to take away the magic. This was the first time she'd see them with her father. She flipped the remote to lock the car doors and put Riley into the body sling, feeling her daughter's hands to make sure that she wasn't too cold. The little girl was as warm as toast and as cute as a button in her green elf hat.

The carol singers were obviously an established choir and they had a band with them. The music swelled as they got closer, and the crowd around them let Ben through when they saw his crutches. Callie stood close. Even if he couldn't hold Riley, he could at least touch her.

She began to hum along with the carols, and Riley followed her example, tuneless and wavering, not pausing when the singers finished and the band turned the pages of their music sheets. Ben's smile made Callie's heart quiver.

Maybe it was just Riley who made him smile. But Ben slipped the crutch out from under his left arm, putting it with the other one under his right. Callie felt his arm curl lightly around her waist, a little tighter when she nestled against him. She'd missed this so much, his scent and the taut strength of his body. It had seemed like an impossible dream that he would hold her again, and that Riley should be with them in a circle of warmth between her mother and father.

But they couldn't stay long. Ben began to shiver, from the cold and the effort of standing like this, and when Callie led him away, he didn't protest. It had been a few precious minutes, but whatever the future held for them, that could never be taken away.

# CHAPTER TWENTY-ONE

IT WAS ALL his Christmases rolled into one. Callie had decorated the Christmas tree, and Ben had helped as best he could. Riley had wanted to touch all the decorations, and he'd carefully held them in front of her, allowing her to play with the felt ones he'd bought for her.

'*Ew...* This one's all slimy.' Riley had handed Callie a fabric star, pointing at the tree. She was getting the hang of this quickly. 'She's been sucking it, hasn't she?'

'Yes, I think she's hungry.'

'I'll make up a bottle.' Callie grinned at him and headed for the kitchen.

'Don't bother with that, I'll make myself scarce. She's already had one bottle today.' However much he wanted to recreate the feeling he'd had watching Callie feed Riley at the hospital, he shouldn't rush things. If Callie wanted this space, he had to respect it.

'Don't you want to feed her?'

'Yes, but…' He realised suddenly that it wasn't space that Callie wanted. She'd suggested a bottle so that he could feed Riley. Warmth rushed through his veins and he nodded.

'Well, then.'

Callie prepared a bottle and put Riley into his arms. The little girl tugged at his shirt, pressing herself against him. This was the best time in the week. Along with all the other best times that he had with Riley.

He glanced up at Callie, and suddenly the world tipped and he slid helplessly into her smile. *She* was watching *him*.

Riley had fallen asleep, and Callie reckoned she'd have at least an hour before she woke up again. She knew that Ben wouldn't do this in front of his daughter.

'Let me see your arm.'

'No need. It's okay.' Apparently he wasn't intending to do it in front of Callie either. But if Riley clearly had her father wrapped around her little finger, Callie had a few more weapons in her arsenal. Being able to form words was a start.

'When did you last have it dressed?'

'A few days ago. It'll be all right until after Christmas.'

'I'm sure it will be, but *I* want to take a look. The health visitor left some sterile dressings?'

Ben grinned. 'In the cupboard, over there. You treat all your patients like this?'

'Not all of them. The firefighters are generally the worst, they're a pretty stroppy crowd. I keep my special tactics for them.'

'Special tactics?' He chuckled, and Callie fought to keep a straight face.

'You don't want special tactics. You're not up to it at the moment.'

'No, I don't think I am.' He undid the zip of the warm sweater he was wearing and slipped it from his shoulder, rolling up his sleeve.

Callie carefully peeled off the tape that secured the dressing pad, making sure that nothing was stuck to the wound. The burn looked better than she remembered it, but it was still red and painful.

'And the health visitor's happy with your progress?'

'I don't much care what the health visitor thinks. Since you've decided to take a look, I'd like to know what *you* think.'

Callie stared at his arm. She wasn't accustomed to being fazed by any degree of injury, a paramedic who was wouldn't be of much use. But this healing burn had turned her stomach to jelly.

'I think…you're doing well. If it keeps healing like this there won't be any scar. How's your leg feeling?'

'It feels…like a broken leg. It'll heal.'

'And I don't need to make a fuss?' She grinned up at him, and saw laughter reflected in his eyes.

'Consider it your sole prerogative to make as much fuss as you like.'

Callie re-dressed the burn as gently as possible. Ben didn't make a sound, although she knew it must still hurt.

'How does that feel? Not too tight?'

'No, it feels fine.'

She pulled his sleeve back down again carefully. As she reached to help him back into his sweater, she felt his fingers on the side of her face, tipping it up to meet his gaze. All the tenderness that she'd missed so much.

'Thank you, Callie.'

She felt her fingers turn clumsy. Liquid fire was running through her veins, not burning but warming her after what seemed like a very long winter.

'How's your side? Since it's my prerogative to make a fuss.'

'Still a bit painful. They said that this kind of bruising would take a little while to heal.'

Callie nodded. 'It is healing, though?'

He nodded, pulling the side of his shirt up a little, and Callie carefully pulled it a little farther. The bruise that had covered most of his left side was blotchy and beginning to disperse. Callie felt a tear run down her cheek and turned her face downwards so he wouldn't see it.

'Hey. What's this?' His fingers brushed her face again, and this time they were trembling. 'Please, Callie. Don't cry, I'm not going anywhere. Riley's going to have to put up with me for a good while longer. So are you, for that matter.'

'Of course we are.' Callie wiped her face with her sleeve. 'I think I just needed to look and… I needed to face what happened to you. I never really did, not at the hospital, I was too afraid of breaking down.'

'And now you have faced it?' Ben's voice was tender.

'I can leave it behind.' She sat down next to him on the sofa, feeling his arm curl around her shoulders. She already had more than she could have hoped for, but she was greedy. Callie wanted one more thing.

'I was going to take Riley over to Mum's tomorrow morning for lunch with her and Paul. She asked me if you'd like to come.'

'She…did?' He raised his eyebrows in disbelief.

'Well… Actually, she said it was a shame that you were alone this Christmas, and she wished you could be with us. If she knew I was here, she would have told me to ask you to come.'

'You're sure about that?'

'Yes, positive. You'll be more than welcome, Ben. And it's Riley's first Christmas. If you'd like to come, I can pick you up in the morning.'

He was silent for a moment. Callie felt her heart thump in her chest.

'I'd love to come. But you can't make a two-hour round trip on Christmas morning.'

'It's okay. The roads will be clear.' Perhaps she shouldn't push it.

'You could, but if you'd like to stay here tonight, you and Riley can take the spare room.'

'I suppose…that might be more convenient.' The pounding of her heart seemed to be blocking her throat.

'Let's do that, then. Thank you.'

Ben's head felt as if it was about to explode. Was it really possible that so much could change in the course of just a few hours?

When she'd looked at his injuries, she'd cried. She'd let herself feel something, and that had helped her to move on. If Callie could be that brave, he could too. Whatever difficulties stood ahead of them, they could be no match for love. He could face the risk of losing her if it meant he had a chance of keeping her.

Suddenly, from being sure about nothing, Ben was very sure about everything. Last Christmas had seemed like a bubble and the New Year a return to reality. But it was the other way around, and Christmas was the reality.

'I need you to do something…' He wondered if she'd guess what it was.

She moved in his arms, looking up at him. 'What's that? You'd like something to drink?'

'No.'

'Switch the gas fire on? It's getting a little chilly in here…' Callie grinned suddenly. She knew now, and she was just teasing him. Making the delicious anticipation last.

No.' Ben tightened his arm around her shoulders in case she took it into her head to move anyway.

'This?'

She moved closer, pausing before their lips finally met. The thought that this was so much more than he could ever deserve flitted briefly through his mind. And then there was no thought, just the feel of her arms around his neck and her body pressed close to his.

The kiss lasted until they were both breathless. And when she drew back, the look in Callie's eyes was almost as intoxicating.

'You're going to do that again?' Ben needed to be reminded that this wasn't all a dream.

'How soon?'

'Now...'

There was no doubt any more. When Callie kissed him again, he knew that this was a promise that wouldn't be broken.

'Please don't ever doubt me, Callie. I love you, and that's never going to change.'

'I love you too, Ben. That's never going to change either.'

Ben wound his arms around her. The here and now had just turned into for ever.

Ben's kiss was all she needed. Callie almost danced through the evening, cooking for them while he played with Riley, and Christmas carols echoed softly from the sound system. She'd taken the wreaths from the boxes of decorations and wound them around the balustrades at the edge of the mezzanine floor, the way they'd been last year.

He helped her bathe Riley and put her down to sleep, and then the evening was their own. Callie returned to the sofa, and Ben's arms, and he kissed her.

'There's something missing.'

'What's that? I'll fetch it immediately.'

He laughed. 'You'll need superpowers, if you're going to make it snow.'

Tonight it felt as if Callie really could conjure up snow. She could do anything she wanted to.

'I'll attend to the snow a bit later. I have something a little more pressing on my schedule.'

'Yeah? What's that?'

As if he didn't know. Callie kissed him, and Ben trailed

kisses across her jaw. She felt his mouth on her neck and she shuddered with pleasure.

'You remember last year, lying in bed, with just the Christmas lights from the balcony...?'

She remembered. He'd traced the patterns that they made across her skin with his finger. And she'd watched the smooth ripple of light and shadow that had accompanied every move he'd made.

'Why do you suppose I put them up there?'

He chuckled. 'I'm not sure I can manage what came next...'

Callie put her finger over his lips. 'I doubt you can, but this'll be better. I'll arrange a few pillows to make you comfortable... You don't have to worry about anything, you'll be in the hands of a trained paramedic.'

He gave her a questioning look. 'That...could work.'

'Then...' she leaned in, whispering in his ear '... I'll rip your clothes off, and have my way with you. You might hurt a bit in the morning...'

He pulled her against his chest, holding her tight in his arms. 'That's very definitely going to work. Tomorrow can take care of itself.'

Just the two of them. Together. Callie had a feeling that everything was going to be just fine.

## EPILOGUE

*Two years later. Christmas Eve*

THE PARTY FOR Ben and Callie's first wedding anniversary had wound down. Plates and glasses were stacked in the dishwasher, and after Riley had fallen asleep in her father's arms, Ben had put her to bed. He walked up to the mezzanine and found Callie, wearing a bright red cosy dressing gown and sitting cross-legged on the bed, stuffing Riley's Christmas stocking.

'That's very cute.' The dark blue felt stocking had an appliquéd Santa and his sleigh on it, along with sparkly snowflakes and shining golden stars.

'Isn't it just? Mum made a great job of it. Are you going to put it in her bedroom now?'

'I thought I'd give it an hour. Just to make sure she's fast asleep.'

Callie nodded, putting the stocking to one side. 'One year, Ben.'

'It couldn't have been a better one.' He took the small package out of his pocket, sitting down on the bed next to her. 'Happy anniversary, darling.'

She turned his gift in her hands, shaking it to see if it rattled. Her shining excitement made Ben smile. Then she undid the wrappings and opened the box, her hand flying to her mouth when she saw what it was.

'Ben! This isn't paper!'

'I couldn't wait another fifty-nine years to give you diamonds. I reckoned it would be good enough if I just wrapped them in paper.'

'They're beautiful, thank you.' She wrapped her arms around his neck, kissing him. 'So do you want me to try the earrings on or the paper?'

'Earrings first. If you don't like them we always have the wrapping paper to fall back on.' Ben watched as Callie took off her stud earrings and replaced them with his present. 'You look gorgeous.'

'Thank you. I love them. Would you like to come and see yours?'

'I have to come and see it?' Ben wondered what on earth Callie could have given him that he had to go to it, rather than it coming to him.

She took his hand and led him downstairs, tiptoeing past the open door of Riley's room and unlocking the door to the other side of the apartment. She'd been overseeing the last of the building works here while Ben had been busy with work. Every time he'd thought of coming in here to see the progress that was being made, Callie had headed him off, telling him she wanted him to wait until it was finished.

The faintest smell of new paint still hung in the air, and Callie led him past the new bedrooms and the playroom to the door that led to the new master bedroom. She made him close his eyes and then guided him into the room.

'You can look now.'

Ben opened his eyes and his breath caught suddenly. 'A wall? You've given me a wall! It looks fabulous…' The simplicity of the cream colour scheme set off the far wall perfectly. It had been sandblasted and sealed, something that Ben and Callie had talked about doing but had decided that they didn't have the funds.

'It's not just the wall.' She almost danced over to the

far end of the room to a line of four photographs hung in plain, dark frames. The first was the one that Callie had taken of Ben that first Christmas at the fire station. Then Riley's first Christmas, followed by a photograph of Ben and Callie's wedding day. The fourth was one that Callie had taken of Ben and Riley together just a few days ago.

'We'll add to it. One photograph every year.' She was hugging herself, grinning broadly at Ben's delight.

'There's plenty of space…'

'Then we'll have to make a lot of memories to fill it, won't we?'

A whole wall of Christmas memories. This was their future together, the one that they'd both taken a leap of faith to make possible.

'I love you, Callie.' However often he said it, those four words still seemed to take on a deeper, richer meaning every time. And Ben never tired of her reply.

'And I love you.'

He took her in his arms, holding her tight. 'It's been the best year, Callie. Your book deal, and the recognition of your work with burns patients.'

'And your new job. I hope you'll have a bit more time to spend at home now that the initiative's off the ground.'

'I will. Depend on it.' Ben had accepted a new job, heading up a task force to promote fire safety for the elderly. Callie been concerned that he might be taking it for her sake, and had insisted that he follow his own heart. But this was what he'd wanted to do, and the position had turned out to be even more challenging, and rewarding, than he'd hoped.

'I'll be wanting you here.' She stretched up, kissing his cheek. 'We've just built three new bedrooms, and I can't fill them all on my own…'

A little brother or sister for Riley. If Ben could have predicted the one night of the year when that shared dream would come true, it would be this one. He smiled, gazing into her eyes.

'Are you ready for it, darling? Our future?'

She smiled up at him, and his heart almost burst with happiness. 'I can't wait…'

\* \* \* \* \*

# MIDWIFE'S MISTLETOE BABY

**FIONA McARTHUR**

Dedicated to my darling husband, Ian.
Because I love you
xx Fiona

# PROLOGUE

*March*

RAYNE WALTERS BREATHED a sigh of relief as he passed through immigration and then customs at Sydney airport, deftly texted—I'm through—and walked swiftly towards the exit. Simon would be quick to pick him up. Very efficient was Simon.

He'd had that feeling of disaster closing in since the hiccough at LA when he'd thought he'd left it too late. But the customs officers had just hesitated and then frowned at him and waved him through.

He needed to get to Simon, the one person he wanted to know the truth, before it all exploded in his face. Hopefully not until he made it back to the States. Though they were the same age, and the same height, Simon was like a brother and mentor when he'd needed to make life choices for good rather than fast decisions.

But this choice was already made. He just wanted it not to come as a shock to the one other person whose good opinion mattered. He wasn't looking forward to

Simon's reaction, and there would be anger, but the steps were already in motion.

A silver car swung towards him. There he was. He lifted his hand and he could see Simon's smile as he pulled over.

'Good to see you, mate.'

'You too.' They'd never been demonstrative, Rayne had found it too hard——but their friendship in Simon's formative years had been such a light in his grey days, and a few hilarious hell-bent nights, so that just seeing Simon made him feel better.

They pulled out into the traffic and his friend spoke without looking at him. 'So what's so urgent you need to fly halfway around the world you couldn't tell me on the phone? I can't believe you're going back tomorrow morning.'

Rayne glanced at the heavy traffic and decided this mightn't be a good time to distract Simon with his own impending disaster. Or was that just an excuse to put off the moment? 'Can we wait till we get to your place?'

He watched Simon frown and then nod. 'Sure. Though Maeve's there. She's just had a break-up so I hope a sister in my house won't cramp your style.'

Maeve. Little Maeve, Geez. It was good to think of someone other than himself for a minute. She'd been hot as a teenager and he could imagine she'd be drop-dead gorgeous by now. All of Simon's sisters were but he'd always had a soft spot for Maeve, the youngest. He'd bet, didn't know why, that Maeve had a big front of confidence when, in fact, he'd suspected she was a lot softer than the rest of the strong females in the house.

Though there'd been a few tricky moments when she'd made sure he knew she fancied him—not politic when you were years older than her. He'd got pretty good at not leaving Simon's side while Maeve had been around. 'I haven't seen Maeve for maybe ten years. She was probably about fifteen and a self-assured little miss then.'

'Most of the time she is. Still a marshmallow underneath, though. But she makes me laugh.'

She'd made Rayne laugh too, but he'd never mentioned his avoidance techniques to Simon. He doubted Simon would have laughed at that. Rayne knew Simon thrived on protecting his sisters. It had never been said but the *Keep away from my sisters* sign was clearly planted between them. And Rayne respected that.

'How are your parents?' It was always odd, asking, because he'd only had his mum, and Simon had two sets of parents. Simon's father, who Rayne had known as a kid, had turned out to be Simon's stepdad and he remembered very well how bitter Simon had been about all the lies. Bitter enough to change his last name.

But Simon's mum had chosen to go with someone she'd thought could give her accidental child the life she wanted him to have, and had been very happy with Simon's wealthy stepdad. Simon's birth father hadn't known of his son's existence until Simon had accidentally found out and gone looking for him.

No such fairy-tale for himself. 'Your father is dead and not worth crying over,' was all his mother had ever said.

'You know Dad and Mum moved to Boston?' Simon's voice broke into his thoughts. 'Dad's bypass went well and Mum's keeping us posted.'

'Good stuff.' Rayne glanced at his friend and enjoyed the smile that lit Simon's face. Funnily, he'd never been jealous of Simon's solid family background. Just glad that he could count this man as his friend and know he wouldn't be judged. Except maybe in the next half-hour when he broke the news.

Simon went on. 'And Angus and the Lyrebird Lake contingent are great. I saw them all at Christmas.' More smiles. He was glad it had all worked out for Simon.

Then the question Rayne didn't want. 'And your mum? She been better since you moved her out to live with you?' Another glance his way and he felt his face freeze as Simon looked at him.

'Fine.' If he started there then the whole thing would come out in the car and he just needed a few more minutes of soaking up the good vibes.

Instead, they talked about work.

About Simon's antenatal breech clinic he was running at Sydney Central. He'd uncovered a passion for helping women avoid unnecessary Caesareans for breech babies when possible and was becoming one of the leaders in re-establishing the practice of experienced care for normal breech births.

'So how's your job going?' Simon looked across. 'Still the dream job, making fistloads of money doing what you love?'

'Santa Monica's great. The house is finished and looking great.' Funny how unimportant that was in the big picture. 'My boss wants me to think about becoming one of the directors on the board.' That wouldn't happen now. He shook that thought off for later.

'The operating rooms there are state-of-the-art and we're developing a new procedure for cleft pallet repair that's healing twice as fast.'

'You still doing the community work on Friday down at South Central?'

'Yep. The kids are great, and we're slipping in one case a week as a teaching case into the OR in Santa Monica.' He didn't even want to think about letting the kids down there but he did have a very promising registrar he was hoping he could talk to, and who could possibly take over, before it all went down.

They turned off the airport link road and in less than five minutes were driving into Simon's garage. Simon lived across the road from the huge expanse of Botany Bay Rayne had just flown in over. He felt his gut kick with impending doom. Another huge jet flew overhead as the automatic garage door descended and that wasn't all that was about to go down.

He'd be on one of those jets heading back to America tomorrow morning. Nearly thirty hours' flying for one conversation. But, then, he'd have plenty of time to sit around when he got back.

Simon ushered him into the house and through into the den as he called out to his sister. 'We're back.'

Her voice floated down the stairs. 'Getting dressed.' Traces of the voice he remembered with a definite womanly depth to it and the melody of it made him smile.

'Drink?' Simon pointed to the tray with whisky glass and decanter and Rayne nodded. He'd had two on the plane. Mostly he'd avoided alcohol since med school but he felt the need for a shot to stiffen his spine for the conversation ahead.

'Thanks.' He crossed the room and poured a finger depth. Waved the bottle in Simon's direction. 'You?'

'Nope. I'm not technically on call but my next breech mum is due any day now. I'll have the soda water to keep you company.' Rayne poured him a glass of the sparkling water from the bar fridge.

They sat down. Rayne lifted his glass. 'Good seeing you.' And it was all about to change.

'You too. Now, what's this about?'

Rayne opened his mouth just as Simon's mobile phone vibrated with an incoming call. Damn. Instead, he took a big swallow of his drink.

Simon frowned at him. Looked at the caller, shrugged his inability to ignore it, and stood up to take the call.

Rayne knew if it hadn't been important he wouldn't have answered. Stared down into the dregs of the amber fluid in his glass. Things happened. Shame it had to happen now. That was his life.

'Sorry, Rayne. I have to go. That's my patient with the breech baby. I said I'd be there. Back as soon as I can.' He glanced at the glass. 'Go easy. I'll still be your mate, no matter what it is.'

Rayne put the glass down. 'Good luck.' With that! He had no doubt about Simon's professional skill. But he doubted he'd be happy with his friend when he knew.

Rayne watched Simon walk from the room and he was still staring pensively at the door two minutes later when the woman of his dreams sashayed in and the world changed for ever.

One moment. That was all it took. Nothing could have warned him what was about to happen or have prevented him, after one shell-shocked moment, standing up. Not all the disasters in the universe mattered as he walked towards the vision little Maeve had become.

A siren. Calling him without the need for actual words. Her hair loose, thick black waves dancing on her shoulders, and she wore some floating, shimmering, soft shift of apricot that allowed a tantalising glimpse of amazing porcelain cleavage—and no bra, he was pretty sure. A flash of delicious thigh, and then covered again in deceptive modesty. He could feel his heart pound in his throat. Tried to bring it all back to normality but he couldn't. Poleaxed by not-so-little Maeve.

Maeve paused before entering the room. Drew a breath. She'd spent the day getting ready for this moment. Hair. Nails. Last-minute beauty appointments that had filled the day nicely. When Simon had told her yesterday that Rayne was coming she'd felt her spirits lift miraculously. Gone was the lethargy of self-recriminations from the last month. She really needed to get over that ridiculous inferiority complex she couldn't seem to shake as the youngest of four high achieving girls.

Here was one man who had never disappointed her. Even though she'd been embarrassingly eager to pester him as a gawky teenager, he'd always made her feel like a princess, and she wanted to look her best. Feel good about herself. Get on with her life after the last fiasco and drop all those stupid regrets that were doing her head in.

She hoped he hadn't changed. She'd hero-worshiped the guy since the day he'd picked up the lunch box she'd dropped the first time she'd seen him. Her parents' reservations about Rayne's background and bad-boy status had only made him more irresistible. At fifteen, twenty had been way out of her reach in age.

Well, things should be different this time and she was going to make sure they were at least on an even footing!

Maybe that's where the trill of excitement was coming from and she could feel the smile on her face from anticipation as she stepped into view.

That was the last sane thought. A glance across a room, a searing moment of connection that had her pinned in the doorway so that she stopped and leant against the architrave, suddenly in need of support—a premonition that maybe she'd be biting off more than she could chew even flirting with Rayne. This black-shirted, open-collared hunk was no pretty boy she could order around. And yet it was still Rayne.

He rose and stepped towards her, a head taller than her, shoulders like a front-row forward, and those eyes. Black pools of definite appreciation as he crossed the room in that distinctive prowl of a walk he'd always had until he stood beside her.

A long slow smile. 'Are you here to ruin my life even more?'

God. That voice. Her skin prickled. Could feel her eyebrows lift. Taking in the glory of him. 'Maybe. Maybe I'm the kind of ruin you've been searching for?'

Goodness knew where those words had come from but they slid from her mouth the way her lunch box had dropped from her fingers around ten years ago. The guy was jaw-droppingly gorgeous. And sexy as all get-out!

'My, my. Look at little Maeve.'

*And look at big Rayne.* Her girl parts quivered.

'Wow!' His voice was low, amused and definitely admiring—and who didn't like someone admiring?—and the pleasure in the word tickled her skin like he'd brushed her all over. Felt impending kismet again. Felt his eyes glide, not missing a thing.

She looked up. Mesmerised. Skidded away from the eyes—too amazing, instead appreciated the black-as-night hair, that strong nose and determined jaw, and those shoulders that blocked her vision of the world. A shiver ran through her. She was like a lamb beckoning to the wolf.

Another long slow smile that could have melted her bra straps if she'd had one on, then he grew sexy-serious. 'Haven't you grown into a beautiful woman? I think we should meet all over again.' A tilt of those sculpted lips and he held out his hand. 'I'm Rayne. And you are?'

Moistened her lips. 'Maeve.' Pretended her throat wasn't as dry as a desert. Held out her own hand and he took her fingers and kissed above her knuckles smoothly so that she sucked her breath in.

Then he allowed her hand to fall. 'Maeve.' The way he said it raised the hair on her arms again. Like ballet dancers *en pointe*. 'Did you know your name means *she who intoxicates*? I read that somewhere, but not until this moment did I believe it.'

She should have laughed and told him he was corny but she was still shaking like a starstruck mute. Finally she retaliated. 'Rain. As in wet?'

He laughed. 'Rayne as in R.A.Y.N.E. My mother hated me.'

'How is your mother?'

His eyes flickered. 'Fine.' Then he seemed to shake off whatever had distracted him and his smile was slow and lethal. 'Would you like to have a drink with me?'

And of course she said, 'Yes!'

She watched him cross the room to Simon's bar and that made her think, only for a millisecond, about her brother. 'Where's Simon?' Thank goodness her brother hadn't seen that explosion of instant lust between them or he'd be playing bomb demolition expert as soon as he cottoned on.

'His breech lady has gone into labour and he's meeting her at the hospital.'

Maeve ticked that obstacle out of the way. A good hour at least but most probably four. She was still languid with residual oxytocin from the Rayne storm as she sank onto the lounge. Then realised she probably should have sat in Simon's favourite chair, opposite, because if Rayne sat next to her here she doubted she'd be able to keep her hands off him.

He sat down next to her and the force field between them glowed like the lights on the runway across the bay. He handed her a quarter-glass of whisky and toasted her with his own. Their fingers touched and sizzled and their eyes clashed as they sipped.

'Curiouser and curiouser,' he drawled, and smiled full into her face.

OMG. She licked her lips again and he leaned and took her glass from her hand again and put it down on the coffee table. 'You really shouldn't do that.' Then lifted his finger and gently brushed her bottom lip with aching slowness as he murmured, 'I've been remiss.'

He was coming closer. 'In what way?' *Who owned that breathy whisper?*

'I didn't kiss my old friend hello.' And his face filled her vision and she didn't make any protest before his lips touched, returned and then scorched hers.

In those first few seconds of connection she could feel a leashed desperation about him that she didn't understand, because they had plenty of time, an hour at least, but then all thoughts fled as sensation swamped her.

Rayne's mouth was like no other mouth she'd ever known. Hadn't even dreamt about. Like velvet steel, smoothly tempered with a suede finish, and the crescendo was deceptively gradual as it steered them both in a sensual duel of lips and tongue and inhalation of whisky breath into a world that beckoned like a light at the end of the tunnel. She hadn't even known there was a tunnel!

Everything she'd imagined could be out there beckoned and promised so much more. She wanted more, desperately needed more, and lifted her hands to clasp the back of his head, revel in his thick wavy hair sliding through her fingers as she pulled him even closer.

His hands slid down her ribs, across her belly and up under and then circling her breasts through the thin fabric of her silk overshirt. His fingers tightened in deliciously powerful appreciation then he pulled away reluctantly.

'Silk? I'd hate to spoil this so I'd better stop.'

'I'll buy another one,' she murmured against his lips.

Rayne forced his hands to draw back. It was supposed to be a hello kiss. Holy hell, what was he doing? He'd barely spoken to the woman in ten years and his next stop was definitely lower down. They'd be naked on the floor before he realised it if he didn't watch out. 'Maybe we should draw a breath?'

She sat back with a little moue of disappointment, followed by one of those delicious tip-of-the-tongue lip-checks that drove him wild. He was very tempted to throw caution to the winds, and her to the floor, and have his wicked way with the siren. Then he saw Simon's glass of sparkling water sitting forlornly on the table and remembered his unspoken promise. Forced himself to sit back. He'd be better having a cold glass of water himself.

'I'm starving!' He wasn't, but appealing to a woman's need to feed a man was always a good ploy to slow the world down.

She shrugged and he wanted to laugh out loud. Still a princess. Gloriously a princess. 'Kitchen's through there.' A languid hand in vague direction. 'I'm not much of a cook but you could make yourself something.'

Observed her eyes skid away from his. Decided she was lying. 'Don't you know the way to a man's heart is through his stomach?'

'And the way to a woman's heart is more of that hello kissing.' She sighed and stood up. 'But come on, I'll feed you. And then I'm going to kiss you again before my brother comes home. You'll owe me.'

He did laugh at that. 'I'll pay what I have to pay.' And he thought, I am not sleeping with this woman but thank God I brought condoms.

\* \* \*

Maeve had lied about not being able to cook. She'd done French, Italian and Spanish culinary courses, could make anything out of nothing, and Simon's fridge was definitely not made up of nothing. 'Spanish omelette, French salad and garlic pizza bread?'

'Hold the garlic pizza bread.'

She grinned at him, starting to come down from the deluge of sensations that had saturated her brain. She'd planned on being admired, building her self-esteem with a safe yet sexy target, not ending up in bed with the guy. 'Good choice.' Heard the words and decided they applied to herself as well. It would be a good choice not to end up in bed either.

Then set about achieving a beautifully presented light meal perfect for a world traveller just off a plane.

'Oh, my.' He glanced down at his plate in awe. 'She cooks well.'

'Only when I feel like it.' And spun away, but he caught her wrist. Lifted it to his mouth and kissed the delicate inside skin once, twice, three times, and Maeve thought she was going to swoon. She tugged her hand free because she needed to think and she hadn't stopped *feeling* since she'd seen this man. She mimicked him. 'He kisses well.'

He winked at her. 'Only when he feels like it.'

She leaned into him. 'We'll work on that. Eat your dinner like a good boy.' *While I get some distance, fan my face and figure out why I'm acting like he's my chance at salvation. Or is that damnation?*

Five minutes later Rayne sat back from his empty plate. He had been hungry. Or the food was too good to possibly leave. 'Thank you.'

He needed a strategy of space between him and this woman. What the heck was going on to cause this onslaught of attraction between them? His own dire circumstances? The thought that she might be the last beautiful thing he would see or touch for a long time?

And her? Well, she was vulnerable. Simon had suggested that. But vulnerable wasn't the word he would have used. Stunning, intoxicating, black-widow dangerous?

He stood up and put his plate in the sink. Rinsed it, like he always did because he'd been responsible for any cleaning he'd wanted done for a long time, and internally he smiled because she didn't say, *Leave that, I'll do it*, like most women would have. She leant on the doorframe and watched him do it.

'Simon said you've just finished a relationship?' Seemed like his subconscious wanted to get to the bottom of it because his conscious mind hadn't been going to ask that question.

'Hmm. It didn't end well, and I've been a dishrag poor Simon had to put up with for the last month. You've no idea the lift I got when Simon said you were coming.'

No subterfuge there. He had the feeling she didn't

know the meaning of the word. 'Thank you. But you know I'm here only for one night. I fly back tomorrow.'

She turned her head to look at him. 'Do you have to?'

That was ironic. 'No choice.' Literally. 'And I won't be back for a long time.' A very long time maybe.

She nodded. 'Then we'd best make the most of to-night.'

He choked back a laugh. 'What on earth can you mean?'

'Catch up on what we've both been doing, of course. Before Simon monopolises you.' She was saying one thing but her body was saying something else as she sa-shayed into the lounge again, and he may as well have had a leash around his neck because he followed her with indecent haste and growing fatalism.

'Simon will be back soon.' A brief attempt to re-turn to reality but she was standing in the centre of the room looking suddenly unsure, and that brief fragility pierced him like no other reaction could have. Before he knew it he had his arms around her, cradling her against his chest, soothing the black hair away from her face. Silk skin, glorious cheekbones, a determined little chin. And she felt so damn perfect in his arms as she snuggled into him.

'Take me to bed, Rayne. Make me feel like a woman again.'

'That would be too easy.' He kissed her forehead. 'I don't think that's a good idea, sweetheart.'

'I'm a big girl, Rayne. Covered for contraception. Unattached and in sound mind. Do I have to beg?'

He looked at her, squeezed her to him. Thought about the near future and how he would never get this chance again because things would never be the same. He would never be the same. Searched her face for any change of mind. No. Bloody hell. She didn't have to beg.

So he picked her up in his arms, and she lifted her hands to clasp him around his neck, and he kissed her gorgeous mouth and they lost a few more minutes in a hazy dream of connection. Finally he got the words out. 'So which bedroom is yours?'

She laughed. 'Up two flights of stairs. Want me to walk?'

'Much as I have enjoyed watching you walk, I'd prefer to carry you.'

And with impressive ease he did. Maeve rested her head back on that solid shoulder and gazed up at the chiselled features and strong nose. And those sinful lips. OMG, did she know what she was doing? Well, there was no way she wanted this to stop. This chemistry had been building since that first searing glance that had jerked and stunned them both like two people on the same elastic. She tightened her hands around his neck.

He felt so powerful—not pretty and perfect like Sean had been—but she didn't want to think about Sean. About the pale comparison of a man she'd wasted her heart on when she should have always known Rayne would stand head and shoulders above any other man.

Speaking of shoulders, he used one to push open the door she indicated, knocked it shut with his foot, and strode across the room to the big double bed she thought he would toss her onto, but he smiled, glanced around the room and lowered her gently until her feet were on the floor.

His breathing hadn't changed and he looked as if he could have done it all again without working a sweat.

Ooh la la. 'I'm impressed.'

He raised his brows quizzically and freed the French drapes until they floated down to cover the double window in a flounced bat of their lacy eyelids and the room dimmed to a rosy glow from the streetlights outside. Slid his wallet out of his pocket and put it on the windowsill after retrieving a small foil packet.

Then he pulled her towards him and spun her until her spine was against the wall and her breasts were pressed into his hardness. Shook his head and smiled full into her eyes. Felt her knees knock as he said, 'You are the sexiest woman I have ever seen.'

She thought, *And you are the sexiest man*, as she lifted her lips to his, and thank goodness he didn't wait to be asked twice. Like falling into a swirling maelstrom of luscious sensation, Maeve felt reality disappear like a leaf sucked into a drainpipe then she heard him say something. Realised he'd created physical distance between them. Her mind struggled to process sound to speech.

'Miss Maeve, are you sure you want to proceed?'

It was a jolting and slightly disappointing thing to say

in the bubble of sensuality he'd created and she looked up at him. Surprised a look of anguish she hadn't expected. 'Are you trying to spoil this for a particular reason?'

A distance she didn't like flashed in his eyes. 'Maybe.'

She pulled his head forward with her hands in his hair. 'Well, don't!'

Rayne shrugged, smiled that lethal smile of his, and instead he lifted her silk shift over her head in a slow sexy exposure, leaving the covering camisole and the dark shadow of her breasts plainly visible through it.

He trailed the backs of his fingers up the sides of her chest and she shivered, wanted him to rip it off so she could feel his hands on her skin. And he knew it.

This time the backs of his fingers trailed down and caught the hem of the camisole, catching the final layer, leaving her top half naked to the air on her sensitised skin.

She heard him suck in his breath, heard it catch in his throat as he glimpsed her body for the first time— and the tiny peach G-string that was all that was left.

Her turn. He had way too many clothes on and she needed to look and feel his skin with a sudden hunger she had no control over.

She reached up and danced her fingers swiftly down the fastening of his black shirt, as if unbuttoning for the Olympics way ahead of any other competitor, because she'd never felt such urgency to slip her hands inside a man's shirt. Never wanted to connect as badly as now with the taut skin-covered muscle and bone of a man. The man.

This was Rayne. The Rayne. And he felt as fabulous as she'd known he would and the faster she did this the faster he would kiss her again. Her fingers seemed to glow wherever she touched and she loved the heat between them like a shivering woman loved a fire.

While her fingers were gliding with relish he'd unzipped and was kicking away his trousers. They stood there, glued together, two layers of mist-like fabric between their groins, two flimsy, ineffectual barriers that only inflamed them more, and his mouth recommenced its onslaught and she was lost.

Until he shifted. Moved that wicked mouth and tongue lower, a salutation of her chin, her neck, her collarbone, a slow, languorous, teasing circle around her breast and exquisite tantalising pleasure she'd never imagined engulfed her as he took the rosy peak and flicked it with delicate precision.

She gasped.

His hands encircled her ribs, the strong thumbs pushing her breasts into perky attention for his favours. Peaks of sensitive supplication and he took advantage until she was writhing, aching for him, helpless against the wall at her back, unable to be silent.

She. Could. Not. Get. Enough.

Rayne lifted his head, heard the moan of a woman enthralled, saw the wildness in her eyes, felt his own need soar to meet hers, dropped his hands to the lace around her hips and slid those wicked panties slowly down her legs, savoured the silk of her skin, the tautness of her thighs under his fingers, and then the scrap of material fell in a ridiculously tiny heap at her feet. There was something so incredibly sinful about that fluttering puddle of fabric, and he'd bet he'd think about it later, many times, as he reached for the condom and dropped his own briefs swiftly.

Then his hands slid back to her buttocks. Those round globes of perfection that fitted his hands perfectly. Felt the weight of her, lifted, supported her body in his hands, and the power of that feeling expanded with the strain in his arms and exultantly, slowly, her back slid up the wall and she rose to meet him.

Rayne slowly and relentlessly pinned her with his body and she wrapped her legs around him the way he had known, instinctively, she would, and it felt as incredible as he'd also known it could be, except it was more. So much more. And they began to dance the ancient dance of well-matched mates.

The rising sun striped the curtains with a golden beam of new light and Maeve awoke in love. Some time in the night it had come to her and it was as indestructible as a glittering diamond in her chest. How had that happened?

Obviously she'd always loved him.

And it was nothing like the feelings she'd had for

other men. This was one hundred per cent 'you light my fire, I know you would cherish me if you loved me back, I want to have babies with you' love. So it looked like she'd have to pack her bags and follow the man to the States.

At least her mother lived there.

But Rayne was gone from their tumbled bed and someone was talking loudly downstairs.

Maeve sat up amidst the pillows he'd packed around her, realised she was naked and slightly stiff, began to smile and then realised the loud voice downstairs was Simon's.

A minute later she'd thrown a robe over her nakedness and hurried into Simon's study, where two burly federal policemen had Rayne in… handcuffs?

The breath jammed in her throat and she leant against the doorframe that had supported her last night. Needed it even more now.

Simon was saying, 'What the hell? Rayne? This has to be a mistake.'

'No mistake. Just didn't get time to explain.' Rayne glanced across as Maeve entered and shut his eyes for a moment as if seeing her just made everything worse. Not how she wanted to be remembered by him.

Then his thick lashes lifted as he stared. 'Bye, Maeve,' looked right through her and then away.

Simon glanced between the two, dawning suspicion followed swiftly by disbelief and then anger. 'So you knew they'd come and you…' He couldn't finish the sentence. Sent Maeve an, 'I'll talk to you later' look, but the federal policemen were already nudging Rayne towards the door.

Simon was still in the clothes he'd left in last night so he hadn't been home long. Rayne was fully dressed, again in sexy black, and shaved, had his small cabin bag, so it looked like he'd been downstairs, waiting. She would never know if it was for Simon or the police.

She wondered whether the police hadn't come he would have woken her to say goodbye. The obvious negative left her feeling incredibly cold in the belly after the conflagration they'd shared last night and her epiphany this morning.

He'd said he was going and wouldn't be back for a while but she'd never imagined this scenario.

Then he really was gone and Simon was shaking his head.

# CHAPTER ONE

*Nine months later.*
*Looking for Maeve.*

RAYNE'S MOTHER DIED of a heroin overdose on the fifteenth of December. He was released from prison the day after, when the posted envelope of papers arrived at the Santa Monica police station, and he put his head in his hands at his inability to save her. The authorities hadn't been apologetic—he should have proclaimed his innocence, but he'd just refused to speak.

Her last written words to him…

> *My Rayne*
> *I love you. You are my shining star. I would never have survived in prison but it seems I can't survive on the outside either with you in there. I'm so sorry it took me so long to fix it.*

With the other letter and proof of her guilt she'd kept, the charges on Rayne were dropped and he buried her a week later in Santa Monica. It had been the only place she'd known some happiness, and it was fine to leave her there in peace.

He had detoured to see his old boss, who had been devastated by the charges against him, explained briefly that he'd known she wouldn't survive in jail, and the man promised to start proceedings for the restoration of his licence to practise. Undo what damage he could, and as he'd been able to keep most of the sensation out of the papers, that was no mean offer.

Then Rayne gave all his mother's clothes and belongings to the Goodwill Society and ordered her the biggest monumental angel he could for the top of her grave. It would have made her smile.

Then he put the house up for sale and bought a ticket for Australia and Maeve. The woman he couldn't forget after just one night. Not because he was looking for happily ever after but because he owed it to her and Simon to explain. And if he was going to start a new life he had to know what was left of his old one. If anything.

All he knew was the man he was now was no fit partner for Maeve and he had no doubt Simon would say the same.

On arrival it had taken him two days of dogged investigation before he'd traced Maeve to Lyrebird Lake and he would have thought of it earlier if he'd allowed himself to think of Simon first.

Simon's birth father lived there and Simon often

spent Christmas with them—he should have remembered that. With Maeve's mother in the US it made sense she was with her brother.

Who knew if she'd say yes to seeing him after the way he'd left, if either of them would? He guessed he couldn't blame them when they didn't know the facts, but he had to know they were both all right. Maybe he should have opened the letters Maeve had sent and not refused the phone calls Simon had tried, but staying isolated from others and keeping the outside world out of his head had been the only way he'd got through it.

Looked down at the wad of letters in his hand and decided against opening the letters now in case she refused to see him in writing.

Two hundred miles away from Lyrebird Lake, and driving just over the legal speed limit, Rayne pressed a little harder on the accelerator pedal. The black Chev, a souped-up version of his first car from years ago, throttled back with a throaty grumble.

He didn't even know if Maeve had a partner, had maybe even married, but he had to find out. She would refuse to see him. It was ridiculous to be propelled on with great urgency when it had been so long, but he was. He should wait until after the holiday season but he couldn't.

The picture in his head of her leaning against the doorframe as he'd been led away had tortured him since that night. The fact that he'd finally discovered the woman he needed to make him whole had been there all the time in his past, and he'd let her down in the most cowardly way by not telling her what would happen.

He couldn't forgive himself so how did he think that Maeve and her brother would forgive him? All he just knew was he had to find her and explain. Try to explain.

So clearly he remembered her vulnerability before he'd carried her up those stairs. Blindingly he saw her need to see herself the way he saw her. Perhaps it was too late.

If she had moved on, then he would have to go, but he needed her to know the fault was all his before they said a final goodbye. It wasn't too late to at least tell her she couldn't have been more perfect on that night all those months ago.

A police highway patrol car passed in the opposite direction. The officer glanced across at him and Rayne slowed. Stupid. To arrive minutes later after nine months wouldn't make the difference but if he was pulled over for speeding then the whole catastrophe could start again. International drivers licence. Passports. He didn't want the hassle.

It was lucky the salesman had filled the fuel tank last night because he'd only just realised it was early Christmas morning. Every fuel stop was shut. He had no food or drinks except the water he'd brought with him. Big deal except he was gatecrashing Simon's family at a time visitors didn't usually drop in. Hopefully the rest of the family weren't assembled when he arrived.

It wasn't the first time he'd done this. He remembered Simon taking him home to his other parents' one year while they'd been in high school. Rayne's mother had ended up in rehab over the holiday break, it had always been the hardest time of the year for her to stay straight, and his friend, Simon, had come to check on him.

He'd been sixteen and sitting quietly watching television when Simon had knocked at the door, scolded him for not letting him know, and dragged him reluctantly back to his house for the best Christmas he'd ever had.

Simon's parents had ensured he'd had a small Christmas sack at the end of his bed on Christmas morning and Maeve had made him a card and given him a Cellophane bag of coconut ice she'd made for everyone that year. He'd loved the confectionary ever since.

Well, here he was again, gatecrashing. Unwanted.

It was anything but funny. The truly ridiculous part was that in his head he'd had an unwilling relationship with Maeve for the last nine months. She'd made an irreversible imprint on him in those hours he'd held her in his arms. Blown him away, and he was still in pieces from it. He'd kept telling himself they'd only connected in his last desperate attempt to hold onto someone good before the bad came but he had no doubt she would always hold a sacred piece of his heart.

In prison he'd separated his old life out of his head. Had kept it from being contaminated by his present. Refused any visitors and stored the mail. But when his defences had been down, when he'd drifted off to sleep, Maeve had slid in beside him, been with him in the morning when he'd woken up, and at night when he'd dreamt. He'd had no control over that.

But he'd changed. Hardened. Couldn't help being affected by the experience, and she didn't need a man like he'd become—so he doubted he'd stay. Just explain and then head back to Sydney to sort out his life. Start fresh when he could find some momentum for beginning. Wasn't even sure he would return to paediatrics. Felt the need for something physical. Something to use up the coil of explosive energy he'd been accumulating over the last nine months.

So maybe he'd go somewhere in between for a while where he could just soak up nature and the great outdoors now that he had the freedom to enjoy it.

Funny how things were never as important until you couldn't have them. He'd lusted after a timeless rainforest, or a deserted mountain stream, or a lighthouse with endless ocean to soothe his soul.

Or Maeve, a voice whispered. No.

# CHAPTER TWO

*Maeve*

MAEVE PATTED HER round and rolling belly to soothe the child within. Christmas in Lyrebird Lake. She should have been ecstatic and excited about the imminent birth of her baby.

Ecstatic about the fact that only yesterday Simon had declared his love to Tara and was engaged to a woman she couldn't wait to call her sister. She put her fingers over the small muscle at the corner of her eye, which was twitching. But instead she was a mess.

Her only brother, or half-brother, she supposed she should acknowledge that, seeing she was living in Lyrebird Lake where his birth father lived, was engaged to be married. That was very exciting news.

And it wasn't like Simon's family hadn't made her welcome. But it wasn't normal to land on people who didn't know you for one of the biggest moments of your life even if Simon had always raved about Lyrebird Lake.

The place was worth raving about. She'd never been so instantly received for who she was, even in her own family, she thought with a tinge of uneasy disloyalty, but that explained why Simon had always been the least judgemental of all her siblings.

Until she'd slept with Rayne, that was.

Simon's other family didn't know the meaning of the word judgmental. Certainly less than her mother, but that was the way mum was, and she accepted that.

And she and Simon had re-established some of their previous closeness, mostly thanks to Tara.

The fabulous Tara. Her new friend and personal midwife was a doll and she couldn't imagine anyone she would rather have in the family.

She, Maeve, was an absolute bitch to be depressed by the news but it was so hard to see them so happy when she was so miserable.

She gave herself a little mental shake. Stop it.

Glanced out the window to the manger on the lawn. It was Christmas morning, and after nearly four weeks of settling in there was no place more welcoming or peaceful to have her baby.

So what was wrong with her?

It was all very well being a midwife, knowing what was coming, but she had this mental vision of her hand being held and it wasn't going to be Simon's. Have her brother, in the room while she laboured? Not happening, even if he was an obstetrician.

No. It would be Tara's hand that steadied her, which

was good but not what she'd secretly and hopelessly dreamt of.

That scene she'd replayed over in her head a thousand times, him crossing the floor to her after that first glance, and later the feel of his arms around her as he'd carried her so easily up the stairs, the absolutely incredible dominance yet tenderness of his lovemaking. Gooseflesh shimmered on her arms.

She shook her head. The birth would be fine. It was okay.

She tried to shake the thought of needing Rayne to get through labour from her mind but it clung like a burr and refused to budge as if caught in the whorls of her cerebral convolutions.

Which was ridiculous because the fact was Rayne didn't want her.

He'd refused to answer her letters or take the call the one time she'd tried to call the prison, had had to go through the horror of finding out his prison number, been transferred to another section, the interminable wait and then the coldness of his refusal to speak to her.

Obviously he didn't want her!

Simon had told her he'd found out he would be in prison for at least two years, maybe even five, and that the charges had been drug related. She, for one, still didn't believe it.

But she hated the fact Rayne didn't want to see her.

Her belly tightened mildly in sympathy, like it had been tightening for the last couple of weeks every now and then, and she patted the taut, round bulge. *It's okay, baby. Mummy will be sensible. She'll get over your father one day.* But that wasn't going to happen if she stayed here mooning.

Maeve sat up and eased her legs out of the bed until her feet were on the floor. Grunted quietly with the effort and then smiled ruefully at herself for the noisy exertion of late pregnancy.

She needed to go for a walk. Free her mind outside the room. Stay fit for the most strenuous exertion of her life.

It was time to greet Christmas morning with a smile and a gentle, ambling welcome in the morning air before the Queensland heat glued her to the cool chair under the tree in the back yard. The tables were ready to be set for breakfast and later lunch with Simon's family and she would put on a smiling face.

She wondered if Tara was up yet. Her friend had come in late last night with Simon, she'd heard them laughing quietly and the thought made her smile. Two gorgeous people in love. The smile slipped from her face and she dressed as fast as she could in her unbalanced awkwardness and for once didn't worry about make-up.

Self-pity was weak and she needed to get over herself. She was the lucky one, having a baby when lots of women ached for the chance, and she couldn't wait.

It wasn't as if she didn't have a family who loved her, even if her mum was in the States.

But she had dear Louisa, Simon's tiny but sprightly grandmother, spoiling them all with her old-fashioned country hospitality and simple joy in kinfolk. She, Maeve, was twenty-five and needed to grow up and enjoy simple pleasures like Louisa did.

Once outside, she set off towards the town and the air was still refreshingly cool. Normally she would have walked around the lake but it was Sunday, and Simon liked the Sunday papers. Did they print newspapers on Christmas Day? Would the shop even be open? She hadn't thought of that before she'd left but if it didn't then that was okay.

It was easier not to think in the fresh air and distractions of walking with a watermelon-sized belly out front cleared the self-absorbtion.

Maeve saw the black, low-to-the-ground, old-fashioned utility as it turned into the main street and smiled. A hot rod like you saw at car shows with wide silver wheels and those long red bench seats in the front designed for drive-in movies. It growled down the road like something out of *Happy Days*, she thought to herself. The square lines and rumbling motor made it stand out from the more family-orientated vehicles she usually saw. Something about it piqued her curiosity.

She stared at the profile of the man driving and then her whole world tilted. Shock had her clutching her throat with her fingers and then their eyes met. Her heart suddenly thumped like the engine of the black beast and the utility swerved to the edge of the road and

pulled up. The engine stopped and so did her breath—
then her chest bumped and she swayed with the shock.

It was Maeve! The connection was instantaneous. Like
the first time. But she was different. He blinked. Pregnant! Very pregnant!

Rayne was out of the car and beside her in seconds,
saw the colour drain from her face, saw her eyes roll
back. He reached her just as she began to crumple.
Thank God. She slumped into his arms and he caught
her urgently and lifted her back against his chest, felt
and smelt the pure sweetness of her hair against his
face as he turned, noticed the extra weight of her belly
with a grimace as he struggled with the door catch
without dropping her. Finally he eased her backwards
onto the passenger seat and laid her head gently back
along the seat.

He stared at the porcelain beauty of the woman he'd
dreamed about throughout that long horrible time of
incarceration.

Maeve.

Pregnant by someone else. The hollow bitterness of
envy. The swell of fierce emotion and the wish it had
been him. He patted her hands, patted her cheek, and
slowly she stirred.

Unable to help the impossible dream, he began to
count dates in his head. He frowned. Pushed away a
sudden, piercing joy, worked out the dates again. But
they'd both used contraception. It couldn't be…

She groaned. Stirred more vigorously. Her glorious long eyelashes fluttered and she opened her eyes. They widened with recognition.

Then she gagged and he reached in and lifted her shoulders so she was sitting on the seat and could gag out the door. She didn't look at him again. Just sat with her shoulders bowed and her head in her hands.

He reached past her to the glove box and removed a small packet of tissues. Nudged her fingers and put them into her hand. She took them, but even after she'd finished wiping her mouth she still didn't look at him and he glanced around the street to see if anyone had noticed. Thank God for quiet Sunday mornings. Quiet Christmas morning, actually.

Well, that was unexpected. Something going right!

Seeing Maeve outside and alone. So unplanned. Looking down at her, he couldn't believe she was here in front of him. His eyes were drawn to the fragile V of the nape of her neck, the black hair falling forward away from the smoothness of her ivory skin, and he realised his heart was thumping like a piston in his chest. Like he'd run a marathon. Like he'd seen a vision of the future that was so bright he was blinded. Fool.

It felt like a dream. A stupid, infantile, Christmas fantasy... In reality, though, the woman of his dreams had, in fact, fainted and then thrown up at the very sight of him! He needed to get a grip.

# CHAPTER THREE

*After faint...*

'WHERE DID YOU come from?' Maeve opened her eyes.
Barely raised her voice because her throat was closed
with sudden tears. She kept her head down. Couldn't
believe she'd fainted and thrown up as a first impression. Well, he shouldn't have appeared out of nowhere.

'America. Earlier this week. You're pregnant!'

*Der.* 'Does Simon know?'

'That you're pregnant?'

She sighed. Her head felt it was going to explode.
Not so much with the headache that shimmered behind
her eyes but with the thoughts that were ricocheting
around like marbles in her head. Just what she needed.
A smart-alec answer when she had a million questions.

Awkwardly she sat straighter and shifted her bottom on the seat in an attempt to stand. Frustratingly
she couldn't get enough purchase until he put his hand
down and took hers.

She looked at his brown, manly fingers so much

larger than the thin white ones they enclosed. Rayne was here. She could feel the warmth from his skin on hers. Really here.

He squeezed her fingers and then pulled steadily so she floated from the car like a feather from a bottle. She'd forgotten how strong he was. How easily he could move her body around. 'I assume you caught me when everything went black?'

'Thank goodness.' She looked up at the shudder in his voice. 'Imagine if I hadn't.'

She instantly dropped her other hand to her stomach and the baby moved as if to reassure her. Her shoulders drooped again with relief.

'You're pregnant,' he said again.

Now she looked at him. Saw the rampant confusion in a face she'd never seen confusion in before. 'I told you that. In the letters.'

His face shuttered. A long pause. 'I didn't open your letters.'

Maeve was dumbstruck, temporarily unable to speak. He hadn't opened her letters? The hours she'd spent composing and crunching and rewriting and weeping over them before she'd posted them. Wow!

That explained the lack of reply, she thought with a spurt of temper, but it also created huge questions as to just how important she'd been to him. Obviously not very. Not even being locked away in prison had been enough to tempt him to open her letters. She felt the nausea rise again.

He'd refused to talk to Simon too and she knew her brother had been hurt about that. He had hoped for some reassurance from Rayne that somewhere there was an explanation.

The guy was lower than she thought. She needed to protect Simon from being upset a day after his happiest day. That was a real worry. Or a diversion for her mind.

She tried to compose herself, get her thoughts together…

'I don't think you should see Simon until I can warn him you're back.'

Rayne straightened. Lifted his chin. 'I'm not going to hide.'

'It's not about you.' She could feel the unfairness expand in her. This was not how she dreamed their first meeting would be. Why couldn't he have warned her he was coming? Given her a chance to have her defences sorted? Dressed nicely? Put her make-up on, for goodness' sake? She'd just walked out of the house in her expander jeans and a swing top. And trainers. She groaned.

'Are you okay?'

She looked up. Saw the broad shoulders, bulging muscles in his arms, that chest she'd dreamt of for three quarters of a year. He was here and she wanted to be scooped up and cradled against that chest but he wasn't saying the right things. 'You can't see Simon yet. He's just got engaged. He's happy. I won't let you do that. You've upset him enough.'

He'd upset her too, though upset was an understatement. Hurt badly. Devastated. But then you reappeared at the right moment, a tiny voice whispered. The exact right moment. Just in time.

She saw a flicker of pain cross his face and she closed her eyes. What was she doing? Why was she being like this? Was she trying to drive him away?

She needed to think. It overwhelmed her that Rayne was here. As if she'd conjured up him by her need this morning and now she didn't know what she should think. And he hadn't known she was pregnant!

Rayne was having all sorts of problems keeping his thoughts straight. He could see she was at a loss too. 'Maeve!'

'What?'

He needed to know. Couldn't believe it but didn't want to believe it was someone else. 'Are you pregnant with my baby?'

She hunched her shoulders as if to keep him out. 'It's my baby. You didn't want to know about it.'

He pulled her in close to him and put both arms around her. Lifted her chin to look at him. 'For God's sake, woman.' Resisted the urge to shake her. 'Are you pregnant with my baby?'

'Yes. Now let go of me, Rayne.' His loosened his fingers. Felt her pull away coolly. Create distance between them like a crack from a beautiful glacier breaking away from its mountain, and his heart, a heart that had been a solid rock inside him, cracked too.

Maeve turned her back on him and climbed awkwardly into his car. The realisation that she couldn't protect Simon from this shock forever hit her.

'Come on. Let's get it over with. You need to see Simon and then we need to talk.'

Simon came out of the house when the car pulled up and a petite blonde woman followed him. Rayne remembered now that Maeve had said Simon was engaged. This would be some first introduction.

Rayne climbed out and walked around to open the passenger door; he glanced at his old friend, who looked less than pleased, and then back at the woman's hand he wanted to hold more than anything else in the world.

For an icy moment there he thought she wasn't going to allow him that privilege—right when he needed her most—but then she uncurled her closed fist and allowed her fingers to slide in beside his. By the time Simon had arrived she was standing beside him. Solidarity he hadn't expected.

'They let you out?' There was no Christmas spirit in that statement, Rayne thought sardonically to himself, though couldn't say he could blame him, considering Maeve's condition.

He stared into Simon's face. Felt the coolness between them like an open wound. 'I wanted to explain.' He shrugged. 'It just didn't happen.'

'Instead, you slept with my sister.'

'There's that.' To hell with this.

He just wanted it over. Tell Simon the truth. Let Maeve know at least the father of her baby wasn't a criminal. At the very least. Then get the hell away from here because these people didn't deserve him to infect their live with the disaster that seemed to follow him around.

'When my mother died there wasn't a reason for me to be in there any more. She told them the truth before she overdosed and they dropped the charges.'

Maeve's breath drew in beside him. 'Your mother died?' Felt her hand, a precious hand he'd forgotten he still held, tighten in his. She squeezed his fingers and he looked down at her. Saw the genuine sympathy and felt more upset than he had for the last horrific year. How could she be so quick to feel sorry for him when he'd ruined her life with his own selfishness? That thought hurt even more.

'You took the rap for your mother!' Simon's curt statement wasn't a question. 'Of course you did.' He slapped himself on the forehead. Repeated, 'Of course you did.'

He didn't want to talk about his mother. Didn't want sympathy. He spoke to Simon. 'I understand you not wanting me here.'

He forced himself to let go of Maeve's hand. 'Take Maeve inside. She fainted earlier, though she didn't fall.' He heard Simon's swift intake of breath and saw the blonde woman, from hanging back, shift into gear to swift concern.

He felt Maeve's glance. Her hand brushed the woman's gesture away. 'No. We need to talk.'

'I'll come back later when you've had a chance to rest. I'll find somewhere to stay for tonight.'

And give myself a chance to think, at least, he thought. He reached into his wallet and pulled out a piece of paper on which he'd written his number. 'This is my mobile number. Phone me when you've rested.' And then he spun on his heel and walked away from the lot of them, wishing he had warned them he was coming, though he wasn't sure it would have gone over any better if he had.

Well, they knew the truth now. He'd done what he'd come to do. Learnt something he'd never envisaged and was still grappling with that momentous news. He allowed himself one long sweeping glance over the woman he had dreamed about every night, soaking in the splendour that was Maeve. Her breasts full and ripe for his child, her belly swollen and taut, and her face pale with the distress he'd caused her.

Maeve allowed Tara to steer her back inside, up the hallway to her bedroom, because suddenly she felt as weak as a kitten. Simon was still standing on the street, watching the black utility disappear down the road with a frown on his face, but she'd worry about Simon later.

An almost silent whistle from Tara beside her drew

her attention as she sat down on her bed. 'So that's Rayne. Not quite what I imagined. A tad larger than life.' Tara squeezed her arm in sympathy. 'You look pale from shock.'

Maeve grimaced in agreement. Glanced at Tara, calm and methodical as usual as she helped her take off her shoes. 'It was a shock. And highly embarrassing. Not only did I faint but then proceeded to throw up in front of him.'

She felt the assessing glance Tara cast over her. 'For a very pregnant lady you've had a busy morning and it hasn't really started yet.'

It was barely seven o'clock. 'Lucky I got up early. It was supposed to be a gentle Christmas morning walk for Simon's newspaper.'

'The shop won't be open. But your Rayne is a Christmas present with a difference.' Tara laughed. 'What was it you said when you described him to me? A head taller and shoulders like a front-row forward and those dark eyes. No wonder you fell for him, boots and all.'

A fallen woman. And still in love with him, boots and all. 'Is it mad that even after ten minutes with him after all this time, I wanted to go with him? That I feel like we've been together for so much more than one night? That I can even feel that when he's just been away? When even I know that's too simplistic and whitewashed.'

She saw Tara look towards the bedside table, cross to her glass of water and bring it back for her. 'Even from where I was standing, I could feel the energy between you two. I wouldn't be surprised if Simon felt it too.'

'Thanks for that, at least.' She took a sip of water and it did make her feel a little clearer. 'Problem is, I was okay to sleep with but not okay to tell that he was going to prison.'

'Well.' Tara looked thoughtful. 'It seems he has got an explanation if he took the blame for his mother. And things are different now. He can't just walk away and think you'll be better off without him without even discussing it.'

She touched Maeve's shoulder in sympathy. 'And you have been carrying his child. So I guess at least a part of him has been with you since then.' Tara gave her a quick hug. 'He looks tough and self-sufficient but doesn't look a bad man.'

She knew he wasn't. From the bottom of her heart. 'He's not. I believe he's a good man.' She stroked her belly gently. 'I have to believe that if he's going to be part of our lives. And until this...' she patted her belly again '...Simon wouldn't hear a wrong word said about him.' She glanced at Tara and smiled to lighten the dramatic morning. 'And we both know Simon has good taste.'

Tara blushed but brushed that aside. 'Did he say he wants to be a part of your lives?'

In what brief window of opportunity? 'We didn't get that far. What with me fainting like a goose at the sight of him.' Maeve shook her head. Thought about it. 'He said he hadn't opened my mail. That he didn't know I was pregnant.' She thought some more. 'But he didn't look horrified when I told him.'

'Helpful. Though why he wouldn't open your mail has me puzzled.'

*Me, too.* 'I'll be asking that when he comes back. And it's Christmas morning.' She suddenly thought of the impact of her commotion on everyone else's day. That's what Lyrebird Lake did to you. Made you begin to think more of other people. 'I hope it doesn't spoil your first Christmas with Simon. I feel like I'm gatecrashing your engagement celebrations with my dramas.'

'Nothing can spoil that.' A lovely smile from Tara. 'I'm just glad we're here for you. No better time for family. And Simon will be fine.'

Tara had said family. The idea shone like a star in a dark night sky. It was a good time for family. Tara had probably meant Simon's family but Maeve was thinking of her own. Rayne and her and their baby as a family.

To Maeve it had felt like she'd been marking time for Rayne to arrive and now he was here he was her family. As long as he could handle that idea. Well, he'd just have to get used to it.

She heard Simon's footsteps approaching and as he paused at her bedroom door Maeve felt his assessing glance.

She looked at him. 'Rayne went to gaol for his mother! That's what he'd come to tell you that night.'

Simon nodded. 'So it seems. Fool. He didn't get around to it and if he had I would have tried to talk him out of it. I'm not surprised he didn't rush into an explanation. He knew I would have told him that taking the blame for his mother wouldn't help her at all.'

What kind of man made that sort of sacrifice without flinching? Actually, her man. 'He went to prison for her. Lost his job and his reputation.' And me, she thought, but didn't say it. Well, he hadn't lost her yet.

Simon rubbed the back of his head. 'That news just makes me more angry with him. But I'll get over it.' He rubbed again. 'Obviously I'm still battling with the idea I didn't suspect Rayne would do that. Now it's glaringly obvious. So I let him down too.'

He put his finger up and pointed at her. 'Maybe you should do what he suggested. Lie down. You're as pale as a ghost and the family won't be here for another two hours for breakfast.'

Maybe she would. Because she had plans for tonight. 'I want Rayne to spend Christmas with us.'

Simon didn't look as surprised as she'd thought he would. He glanced at Tara and Maeve caught the almost imperceptible nod between them. 'Thought you might—just don't rush into anything,' was all he said.

Rayne threw his duffle bag on the floor of the sparse hotel room and himself onto the single bed on his back. He'd had to knock on the residence door to ask if they were opening today. The guy had said not officially and let him in. Given him a room and said he'd fix him up tomorrow.

Rayne pulled the packet of letters from his pocket and eased open the first one. Started to read about Maeve's pregnancy. After ten minutes, and an aching, burning feeling in his gut, he loosened his belt and lay down on the bed. His mind expanded with images, good and bad, of his time with Maeve and what she'd gone through because he hadn't been there for her. He couldn't stomach it. He searched for something else to think about until he got over the pain.

He reached his hands arms up behind his head and sighed. One thing about prison, you lost your finicky ways about where you could sleep.

It was a typical country pub. With typical country hospitality, seeing he could be sleeping on a park bench if they hadn't let him in.

Squeaky cast-iron bedframe with yellowed porcelain decoration in the middle, thin, lumpy mattress, used-to-be white sheets and a wrinkled bedspread. A hook for clothes and a bathroom down the hall to share, except that no one else was such a loser they were in there for Christmas.

He wouldn't be here long. Wasn't sure he should be in Lyrebird Lake at all. But thank God he'd come.

*Maeve was having his baby. Maeve, who was anything but 'little Princess Maeve'. How the hell had that happened when they'd been so careful?*

Funnily, he didn't even consider it could be anyone

else's because the dates matched and after what they had shared—Lord, what they had shared in one incredible night—if a persistent sperm was going to get through any night that would be the one. He half laughed out loud—a strangled, confused noise—thankful that nobody else would hear or care about it.

A ridiculous mix of horror that a child had been dumped with him for a parent, regret at how distressed Simon must have been at his supposed friend's perfidy, ghastly regret that Maeve had had to face Simon without him and spend a pregnancy without his support.

But on top, like a life-raft shining light in the dark ocean, was an insidious, floating joy that glorious Maeve had kept his child and he was going to be a father. And she'd held his hand in front of Simon.

Though the next steps held a whole bag of dilemmas. What was he going to do about it? What could he do about it? Of course he would support them, money wasn't a problem. Hell, he'd buy her a house and put it in her name, or the baby's name, whatever she wanted. But what else?

Suddenly his whole world had changed, from that of a lost soul who hadn't been able to help his own mother—the one person he'd tried so hard to save—to a social pariah without any commitments and little motivation to slip back into his previous life, and now to a man with the greatest responsibility of all. Protecting another woman, keeping in mind he hadn't been able to save the last one, and this time his child as well, was something which scared him to the core.

Of course, that was if they could possibly work something out, and if she'd let him, but at least she wanted to talk. He wasn't so sure Simon wanted to and he really couldn't blame him.

It was a lot to take in. And a lot to lose when you thought you'd already lost it all.

Maeve saw Rayne arrive because she was standing at the window of her bedroom, waiting. It was nine-thirty and everyone had arrived for breakfast and the huge pile of family presents were to be opened after that.

She shook her head as the black car stopped, so antique it was trendy again, big and bulky and mean looking, very *James Dean, I'm a bad boy*, Rayne really needed to get over that image. Especially now he was going to be a father. She smiled ironically through the window. Though if Rayne had a son her child would probably love that car as he grew up.

She turned away from the window and glanced at the mirror across the room. So it seemed after only one sight of Rayne she was thinking of her child growing up with him.

She saw her reflection wincing back at her. The worried frown on her brow. Saw the shine reflected on her face and she crossed the room to re-powder her nose.

Was she doing the right thing, going with her feelings? she thought as she dabbed. Should she believe so gullibly that there might be a future with Rayne? Take it slowly, her brother had said. Maybe Simon was right.

She reapplied her lip gloss. At least she'd been the first point of call as soon as he was free, and that had been before he'd known she was having his baby.

Or was she having herself on. Maybe it was Simon, his best friend from his childhood, not her he'd really come to see. He had travelled across the world last time for a conversation with Simon that hadn't happened. This morning he'd just seen her on the side of the road first.

When it all boiled down to it. how much did Rayne know about her or could care after just one night? One long night when they hadn't done much talking at all.

Nope. She wasn't a stand-out-in-the-crowd success story.

With a mother who expected perfection and three older, very confident sisters, she'd always wanted to shine in the crowd. Had hidden her shyness under a polished and bolshie exterior that had said, *Look at me*, had forced herself to be outgoing. Maybe that was why her relationships with men had seemed to end up in disaster.

Once they'd got to know her and realised she wasn't who they'd thought she was.

That was her problem. Being the youngest of five very successful siblings, she'd always seen herself falling a little short. But finally, when she'd settled on midwifery, incredibly she'd loved it. But her job had gone down the tube with this baby for a while yet—so she'd blown that too.

The hardest thing about Rayne walking away without a backward glance had been those voices in her head saying it had been easy for him to do that. Too easy.

She turned away from the mirror with a sigh. And then there was Rayne's consummate ease in keeping the whole impending disaster of his court appearance and sentencing from her.

But what if she had the chance to show him the real woman underneath? Maybe he'd show her the real man? Maybe it could work because there was no doubting physical chemistry was there in spades between them. Or had been before she'd turned into a balloon. They'd just have to see if that was enough to build on with their child.

She slid her hand gently over the mound of her stomach and held the weight briefly in her palm.

*You are the most important person, baby, but maybe your daddy just needs to have someone with faith in him to be the perfect father. And I do have that faith and he'll have to prove otherwise before we are going to be walked away from again.*

# CHAPTER FOUR

*Christmas Day*

RAYNE PULLED UP outside the place Maeve had called the manse. The phone call had come sooner than he'd expected. Apparently he was down for family breakfast *and* lunch. He wasn't sure if could mentally do that but he'd see how it turned out.

As he gently closed the door of the car he glanced at motorised nodding animals in the Christmas manger on the lawn and shook his head. There was a little straw-filled crib with a tiny swaddled baby in it, and for a minute he thought it was a real baby; rubbed his eyes and, of course, it was a doll. He was seeing babies everywhere. Not surprising really.

But there were definite adoring looks and nods from the mechanical Mary and Joseph, and the three wise men and those crazy manger animals nodded along.

He could imagine during the weeks leading up to Christmas it wouldn't be unusual for children to drop by on the way home from school to check out the display.

He'd sort of noticed the display but not really when he'd been here earlier. He stopped for a moment and took in the full glory of the scene. Geez. Now, that was schmaltz with a capital S.

It was so over the top, with the solar mini-train circling the yard carrying fake presents, the fairy-lights all over the house and around the manger, and the giant blue star on the main building roof, totally the opposite of Maeve and Simon's mother's idea of colour-coordinated, understated elegance. Or his own poor mother's belief it was all a waste of time.

Imagine a family who was willing to put that much effort into decorations that only hung around for a month and then had to be packed away again. He couldn't help but speculate how much they'd be willing to put into things that were really important.

It was so hard to imagine that sort of close-knit caring. The kind he'd seen between Maeve and Simon's family every time he'd visited their house.

He'd always told Simon he was lucky, having two families and six sisters, and Simon had said he could share them as long as he didn't chat them up.

Well, that one had been blown out of the water with Maeve, he thought with a grimace, though he and Maeve hadn't done much chatting.

He sighed. Pulled back his shoulders and lifted his chin. Started to walk again. Not something to be proud of. Well, that's what he was here for. To make right what he could. Maeve had said they needed to talk but he wasn't so sure Simon was going to come to the party.

The front screen door opened and Simon met him as he came up the steps. And held out his hand. There was a definite welcome there he hadn't expected. Holy hell. Rayne's throat burned and he swallowed.

Simon shrugged and smiled. 'Can't say I've been happy but it is good to see you.' Then he stepped in and hugged him.

Rayne's choked throat felt like someone had shoved a carpenter's wood rasp down his neck, not that he'd ever cried, even when he'd buried his mother, so it was an unfamiliar and uncomfortable feeling, but he hadn't expected this. He gripped Simon's hand so hard his friend winced and he loosened his fingers. Dropped the handshake.

'Um. Thanks. That was unexpected.'

'I've had time to cool down. And I'm sorry about your mother.' A hard stare. 'You taking the blame for her is something we'll talk about another time.'

His throat still felt tight. He so hadn't expected this. 'Maeve is incredible.'

Simon snorted. 'Or incredibly stupid. We'll see which one.' He shrugged, definitely warmer than earlier that morning, and gestured to the door. 'Now come in. It's Christmas and you're about to meet the rest of the family. By the way, my dad knows all about you.' Simon raised his brows.

Raised his own back. 'Nice.' Not. Rayne glanced

over his shoulder at the road but there was only his car on the street. He'd hoped as there were no other cars he could come and go before the family arrived.

Simon must have seen his look because he said, 'Everyone walks most places around here. They're all out the back.'

They walked through the house down a central hallway, past some mistletoe he needed to avoid unless Maeve was there, with at least three rooms each side, and into a large kitchen, heavily decorated for Christmas, complete with multi-coloured gifts under the tree. At the kitchen bench a tiny, round, older lady with a Santa hat on her white hair was carving ham slices onto a plate. The young blonde woman he'd seen earlier that morning was piling fried eggs onto another carving plate.

'This is Rayne, Louisa. My grandmother, Rayne.'

The older lady looked up and glowed at Simon and then with twinkling eyes skimmed Rayne from head to toe with apparent delight. 'Maeve's mystery man. You are very welcome, my dear. And just in time for breakfast. Merry Christmas.'

Just in time for breakfast? His stomach rumbled. He hadn't even thought about food. She was a jolly little thing and jolliness had been hard to come by lately. He couldn't help a small smile. 'Merry Christmas to you.'

Simon's voice warmed even more. 'And this divine being is my fiancée, Tara. Tara's a midwife at the birth centre and has been looking after Maeve's pregnancy since she arrived. If you're good, we might even invite you to our wedding.'

'Hello, Rayne. Welcome. Merry Christmas.' And Tara, a much younger small blonde woman with wise eyes, smiled a smile that said, *I know how hard it is for you at this moment*. And, incredibly, he actually believed her. Now, that was strange.

Tara handed him the heaped plate. 'Take this out with you when you go, could you, please, and try to find a spot on the table for it.'

He took the plate and she gestured Simon to a basket of rolls, which he obligingly picked up right after he'd kissed her swiftly on her mouth. She laughed and shooed him off and Rayne looked away. He couldn't ever imagine being so easy with Maeve.

There was a brief lull in the conversation when they opened the screen door out into the back yard, but Rayne had spotted Maeve and the voices were fading anyway as his eyes drank in the sight of her.

Damn, she looked amazing in a red summer dress, like a ripe plum, the material ballooned over her magnificent belly and shimmered when she shifted. A green Christmas scarf draped her gorgeous shoulders. She looked like his fantasy Mrs Santa Claus and he had to hold himself back as Simon introduced him to his other family.

A tall, powerfully built man crossed to them. He put his hand out to Rayne and he took it. Shook firmly and stepped back. Yep. That had to be Simon's natural father. Same mouth and nose. A chip off the old block, and he reminded him of an army major he'd know once. 'Pleased to meet you, sir.'

'Angus, not sir. And I understand you're a paediatrician?'

'Not for nearly a year.'

'Maybe we'll get a chance to talk about that while you're here. You could think of having a breather here while you settle back into some kind of routine.'

Not likely. He already wanted to run. 'Perhaps.'

A vivacious redhead swooped in and gave him a hug. He tried awkwardly to return it but he'd never been a hugger. Her head only came up to his chin. 'Merry Christmas, Rayne. I'm Simon's stepmother, Mia.'

She stepped back and waved to two young miniatures of herself at the table. 'And our daughters Amber and Layla. So there will be nine of us for breakfast.'

It felt like a lot more but, really, the only person he wanted to talk to there was Maeve, who was watching him with an enigmatic expression, and it looked like they'd have to eat before he'd get any chance of that.

Tara and Louisa brought the last two plates and they all began to sit at the long table under the tree, but as he crossed to Maeve she moved towards the table as if she felt more confident there. With definite intent he held her chair and then settled himself beside her.

He glanced around and hoped nobody could see he really didn't want to be here, then he pulled himself up. It was Christmas.

One of the little girls said grace, and he acknowledged the nice touch, especially as he would have been stumped if someone had asked him, and the table groaned with food. He hadn't seen this much food since that Christmas at Simon's all those years ago.

When grace was over he turned to Maeve. She was why he was here. Funny how Simon had slipped back into second place, though it was good to see him too. His only friend in the world, and he'd thought he'd lost him.

But Maeve. She looked even better up close. Much more colour in her cheeks than earlier. He lowered his voice because he imagined she wouldn't want to draw attention to the fact she'd fainted that morning. 'Are you okay?'

A brief glimpse of her confusion as she looked at him. 'I'm fine.'

'Fine as in Freaked Out, Insecure, Neurotic and Emotional?' He tried a poor attempt at a joke.

A longer look. 'They been showing you movies in there?'

He felt his face freeze. His body go cold with the memories. 'No.'

Then he saw the distress that filled her eyes and her hand came across and touched his. Stayed for a second, warmed him like an injection of heat up his arm, and then shifted back to her lap. 'I'm sorry. It was a stupid joke.'

'Ditto. From another movie.' He forced a smile. 'It's fine.'

Her face softened. 'You sure? You know what "fine" means?'

He so didn't want to play, even though he'd started it. 'How long do we have to stay? I need to talk to you.'

She glanced around to make sure nobody had heard. It wasn't a problem because everyone was talking and laughing full steam ahead and the little girls were bouncing in their seats. Maeve's eyes softened when she looked at them. 'Until after the presents, and then I don't have to be back here until this afternoon.'

'So you'll come with me for a couple of hours. Talk in private? Sort what we can?'

He felt her assessing look. 'We can do that. Not sure how much we can sort in a couple of hours. As long as you get me back here before Christmas lunch at three o'clock. I promised to make the brandy sauce.' She glanced under her brows at him. 'I can cook when I feel like it, you know.'

'Oh. I know.'

It was all still there. Maeve could feel the vibration of chemistry between them. Just an inch or two between her skin touching his skin and even then his heat was radiating into her shoulder in waves without the contact. And all this at the Christmas breakfast table in front of Simon's family.

How could this man make her so aware of every part

of her body, and why him? He curled her toes, made her nipples peak, her belly twist and jump, and that was without the baby doing its own gyrations in there. It was darned awkward and the only consolation was he didn't look any more comfortable than she was.

But this was way more important than incredible sex. This was about the future, and even she had to admit she hadn't given the future a thought last time they'd been together. He'd been pretty adamant there hadn't been a future if she remembered rightly, though she had expected a little more pillow talk the next day rather than him being marched away by federal police.

She caught Tara's concerned eyes on her and shrugged. She'd be okay. Early days yet. But to think that this morning she'd been crying into her pillow, wanting him to be here for the birth, and here he was within an inch of her. It was a lot to take in. And she couldn't help the tiny beam of light that suggested she'd been given a blessing to be thankful for.

Someone asked her to pass a plate of tomatoes. There was a lot of eating going on all around them and she and Rayne hadn't started yet. Maybe they'd better.

Rayne must have thought the same because he passed her the ham and she took a small piece, glanced at his plate, and saw at least he was preparing to be fed. Then he passed her the eggs and she took one of those as well. Though she didn't feel like putting anything into her mouth. Her belly was squirming too much.

People were putting their knives and forks together

and sitting back. Leaning forward again and pouring coffee and juice. Maeve reached over and brought the rolls over in front of her, gave one to Rayne and one to herself without thinking and then realised she was acting like an old housewife looking after her husband.

He lifted his brows and smiled sardonically at her and she shrugged. 'Enjoy.' Reminded herself that she'd been a confident woman the last time he'd seen her and she needed to keep that persona even more now she was fighting for her baby's future. But what if she wasn't enough? What if he still left after their talk today? Surely he wouldn't leave this afternoon after just getting here.

'How long can you stay around here?'

He paused with his fork halfway to his mouth. Good timing at least. 'When is the baby due?'

'Tomorrow.'

His face paled and she thought, *Tell me about it, buster, I'm the one who has to do it.* 'But I expect I'll go overdue. Does it matter what date?'

He shook his head, clearly rattled by the impending birth. Put his fork down. Couldn't he see her belly looked like it was about to explode?

Then he said quietly, aware that a few ears were straining their way, 'I have no commitments, if that's what you mean.'

She sniffed at that. 'You do now.'

He glanced around the table. Saw Simon and his

father watching them. 'I'll be here for as long as you want me to be here. It's the least I can do.'

If only he hadn't added that last sentence. The relief she'd felt hearing him say he'd stay as long as she needed him was lost with the tone of sacrifice. Before she could comment, and it would have been unwise whatever she'd been going to say, at the very least, he touched her hand.

'Sorry. That came out wrong. It's just that I'm still getting used to you expecting a baby. And this table is killing me.'

Just then Mia stood up. 'The girls want to know how long before everyone is finished.'

Maeve pushed her plate away thankfully. 'I'm done.'

Rayne stood up. 'Let me help clear.' And he began very efficiently scraping and collecting plates, and she remembered him rinsing his plate at Simon's house.

At least he was house-trained, she thought with an internal smile as she began to gather up side plates, probably a lot more than she was. It was a warming thought that maybe there was stuff that they could do for each other, maybe there were things they could share between them that they'd find out and enjoy as well.

Within a very short time the dishwasher was loaded, the leftovers were stowed in the fridge and the kitchen clean. The big sunroom area of the back room at the end of the kitchen had been cleared when the kitchen table had gone outside and the Christmas tree was surrounded by lots of presents, as well as chairs and cushions so everyone had a niche to perch to watch the fun.

Simon had Tara on his lap, Mia and Angus were sitting with Louisa on the lounge they'd pulled in, and the girls were hopping and crawling around the tree as they shared out the presents one at a time.

Everyone sat except Rayne. He leant against the wall to the left of Maeve so he could watch her face, and he knew she wished he'd take the chair Simon had offered and sit down next to her. But he didn't. He didn't deserve to be a part of the circle. Felt more of an outsider than he ever had, despite the efforts of others. It was his fault he felt like that and he knew it. Just couldn't do anything about it.

He watched Simon take a present from the eldest child and hand it solemnly to Tara. When she opened it he saw her eyes flash to Simon's, saw the tremulous smile and the stroke of her finger down the painted face of the Russian doll. Those dolls that had other dolls inside. This looked like a very expensive version of those.

Cute. But a strange present to give. Though he had no idea about giving presents himself. He frowned, realising he should have thought about that on the way here. He didn't have any to give.

Tara didn't seem to know about the tinier dolls inside and Simon laughed and showed her how they came apart and another pretty painted doll was removed from the centre. And another and another. Until there was a dozen little painted dolls in a line along the arm of the chair. Simon's little sisters had eyes wide with wonder and he suspected there was a little moisture in Tara's eyes, and even Maeve's. He was missing something here.

Maeve shifted her body so she was closer to him and gestured for him to lean down.

'Tara's parents died when she was six. So she was in an orphanage until she grew up. Since then she's never owned a doll.'

Damn! No wonder she understood a little of his awkwardness on arrival. He wasn't the only one who'd had it hard. He'd always been grateful his mum had stayed straight long enough to keep him out of care. Even though he'd been the one doing the caring at home. At least it had been his home and he had had a mother.

The present-giving moved on and Maeve was given a little hand-made wheatpack, a drink bottle with a straw, and a pair of warm socks as comfort aids for labour, and they all laughed.

He watched Maeve smile and thank Tara, but the little twitch in her eyelid made him wonder just how calm the woman having his baby really was about the approaching birth.

His own uneasiness grew with the thought. It wasn't like neither of them didn't know a lot about birth. He'd been at many, but mostly he had been the paediatrician there for Caesarean babies or other newborns at risk.

And Maeve had done her midwifery so she was well versed in what would happen. But it was a bit different when it was this close to home. There were those other times when the unexpected happened.

He really needed to talk to her about that. He glanced at the clock. Fifteen minutes since last time he'd looked at it. Not too bad. And then it was over. The paper was collected, hugs were exchanged and everyone sat back. Louisa asked about fresh coffee or tea and Maeve shifted to the edge of her chair. He put out his hand and helped her up.

Her hand felt good in his. He tightened his grip.

'We're going for a drive.' She said it to the room in general and there was a little pause in the conversation. Then she looked at Louisa and smiled. 'I'll be back by two-thirty to make that brandy sauce.'

Simon groaned. 'Make sure you are. That sauce is to die for.' Everyone laughed again and Rayne wondered, with dry amusement, if he really was the only one who got the warning directed their way.

Louisa said, 'Hold on for a minute.'

And Maeve shrugged and said, 'I'll just go to the loo before we go.' He thought they'd never get away.

Then Louisa was back with a small basket. Quickest pack he'd ever seen. 'Just a Thermos of tea and a cold drink. Some Christmas cake and rum balls in case you get hungry.'

He looked at her. 'I'm pretty sure nobody could be hungry leaving this house.' Looked at her plump cheeks, pink from exertion. Her kind eyes crinkled with the pleasure of giving her food. 'Thank you.' He lowered his voice so that nobody else heard. 'I was going to take Maeve to the seats by the boatshed. This is perfect.'

She held up a finger. 'One more thing, then.' And within seconds was back with a small brown paper bag. 'Bread scraps for the ducks.'

He shook his head. He had never ever met anyone like her. 'You are my new favourite person.'

Then Maeve came back and he tucked the paper bag into his pocket so he could take her hand and carried the basket in the other.

# CHAPTER FIVE

*The lake*

DRIVING AWAY FROM the house, he felt like a load fell from his shoulders. He never had done other people's family events well and the feeling of being an outcast had grown exponentially when he'd had to add the words 'ex-inmate' to his CV.

He realised Maeve was quiet too, not something he remembered about her, and he looked away from the road to see her face. Beautiful. She was watching him. He looked back at the road. Better not run over any kids on Christmas morning, riding their new bikes.

'So where are we going?'

'I saw a boathouse down on the lake. Thought we'd just sit on one of the park benches beside the water.' He looked at her again. 'That okay?' He could smell the scent of her hair from where he was sitting. He remembered that citrus smell from nine months ago.

'Sure.' She shrugged and glanced at the seat between them. 'What's in the basket?'

He had to smile at that. Smile at the memory of Louisa's need to give. 'Emergency food supplies Simon's grandmother worried we might need.'

Maeve peered under the lid and groaned. 'She put in rum balls. I love rum balls. And I can't have them.'

He frowned. She could have what she liked. He'd give her the world if he had the right. 'Why can't you have rum balls?'

She sighed with exasperation. 'Because I'm pregnant and foetuses don't drink alcohol.'

He looked at her face and for the first time in a long time he felt like laughing. But he wasn't sure he'd be game to.

Instead, he said, trying to keep his mouth serious, 'I hope our baby appreciates the sacrifices its mother has been through.'

Tartly. 'I hope its father does.'

That was a kick to the gut. He did. Very much. He turned into the parking area of the boatshed and parked. Turned off the engine. Turned to face her.

'Yes. I do. And I am sorry I haven't been here for you.'

She sighed. 'I'm sorry you didn't know. That I couldn't share the pregnancy with you.'

He thought of his state of mind in that prison if he'd known Maeve was pregnant and he couldn't get to her. God, no. 'I'm not.' He saw her flinch.

'Surely you don't mean that now. That's horrible.' She opened the car door and he could feel her agitation.

Regretted immensely he'd hurt her, but couldn't regret the words. Saw her struggle to get out of the low car with her centre of balance all haywire from the awkwardness of the belly poking out front.

Suddenly realised it sounded harsh from her perspective. He didn't know how to explain about the absolute hell of being locked up. About the prospect of staying locked up for years. About his guilt that his mother had died to get him out and he'd actually been glad. He still couldn't think about the load of guilt that carried. He opened his own door and walked swiftly round to help her out.

Finally Rayne said very quietly, 'I would have gone mad if I'd known you were pregnant and I couldn't get to you. There was a chance I wasn't coming out for years and years.'

She stopped struggling to get herself from the car. Wiped the tears on her cheek. Looked up at him. 'Oh. Is that why you didn't read the letters?'

'I lost access to everything, Maeve. I was a faceless perpetrator surrounded by men who hated the world. I'd never hated the world before but I hated it in there. The only way I could stay sane in that toxic environment was to seal myself off from it. Create a wall and not let anything in. The last thing I needed was sunshine that I couldn't touch and that's what your letters were to me. That way led to madness and I had to stay strong behind my wall.'

'I shouldn't have sent them, then?'

It certainly hadn't been her fault for sending them. She was an angel—especially now he'd read them. 'You couldn't have known. But they were something I looked forward to. I was going to open them when I got out. As soon as I got out. But then I got scared you would tell me not to come and I needed to see you and Simon one more time to explain. So I decided to open them after I saw you.' He rubbed the back of his neck. 'I'm so sorry I caused you pain.'

Maeve looked up at Rayne and saw what she'd seen nine months ago. Big shoulders under a black shirt, black hair cut shorter to the strong bones of his head, dark, dark eyes, even more difficult to read, but maybe they were only easy to read on the way to the bedroom. And that wicked mouth, lips that could work magic or drop words that made her go cold.

This was going to be tougher than she'd expected it to be. Something Tara had said to her a couple of days ago filtered back into her memory. Something about her knowing men who had been to prison and were harder, more distanced from others when they got out.

The problem was Rayne had already been distanced from people before he'd been wrongly convicted.

But when he'd said he was glad he hadn't opened her letters, and she'd responded emotionally with the hurt of it, she'd been thinking about herself. Not about why he would say something hurtful like that. Not about what he'd been through. She promised herself she would try to help heal the scars that experience had left him with—not make the whole transition more difficult.

Guess she'd have to learn to filter her reactions through his eyes. And that wasn't going to be easy because she liked looking at things her way.

But it should be easier with him here, not harder. The thought made her feel cross. 'For goodness' sake, help me out of this damn car.' Not what she'd intended to say but now she thought about it she'd be a whole lot more comfortable with him not standing over her.

The dirty rat laughed.

But at least he put his hand out and again she sailed upwards with ridiculous ease until she was standing beside him.

'You really are a princess, you know that?'

She glared at him as she adjusted her dress and straightened her shoulders. Re-establishing her personal space. 'You have a problem with that?'

He looked at her, and if she wasn't mistaken there could even be a little softening in that hard expression. 'Nope. I love it.'

Warmth expanded inside her. There was hope for the man yet.

Rayne shut the door behind her and picked up the basket. Tucked her hand under his other arm, and she liked that closeness as they sauntered across to the lakeside seats.

Like nothing was wrong. She let it go. She'd always been a 'temper fast and then forget it' person so that was lucky because she had the feeling they had a bit of getting used to each other to come.

Further down the shore, a young boy and his dad were launching an obviously new sailing boat into the lake and a small dog was barking at the ducks heading their way away from those other noisy intruders.

'I love ducks,' Maeve said. 'Always have. I used to have a baby one, it grew up to be an amazing pet. Used to waddle up and meet me when I came home from school.'

'What did you call it?'

She could feel a blush on her cheeks. He was going to laugh. Maybe she could make up a different name. A cool one.

He bumped her shoulder gently with his as if he'd read her mind. 'I want the real name.'

She glared at him. 'I was going to give you the real one.'

'Sure you were.'

Quietly. 'Cinderella.'

Yep, he laughed. But it was a good sound. And so did she. Especially for Christmas morning, from a man only a few weeks out of prison who'd recently lost his mother and found out he was going to be a father. Going to be a father very soon. It felt good she'd made him laugh.

'Imagine,' he said. Then he turned and studied her face. His eyes were unreadable but his voice was sombre. 'Thank you for even thinking of giving me a chance.' And when she saw the sincerity, and just a touch of trepidation, now she felt like crying.

Wasn't sure she should tell him about this morning—what if she scared him?—but couldn't resist the chance. 'You know, I woke up today and all I wanted for Christmas was to be able to talk to you.'

His eyes widened in shock. And something else— she wasn't sure but it could have been fear. Yep, she'd scared him. Fool.

She felt her anger rise. Anger because it shouldn't be this hard to connect with a guy she'd been powerless to resist and it wasn't like he'd been doing something he hadn't agreed to either that night they'd created this baby together. So there was a force greater than them that she believed in but she wasn't so sure it worked if only one of them was a convert. 'It's not that hard to understand. I'm having a baby and there is supposed to be two of us. And if you don't hate me, think about it.'

She turned away from him. Didn't want to see anything negative at this moment. She watched the little boy jumping up and down as his little sailing boat picked up the breeze and sailed out towards the middle of the lake.

Nope. She needed to say it all. Get it out there because if it wasn't going to happen she needed to know now. She turned back to him. 'So what I'm saying is thank you for coming, even though you didn't know I was pregnant, thank you for driving all this way on Christmas to see us.'

'That's nothing.'

'I haven't finished.'

He held up his hands. 'Go on, then.'

'If you want to do the right thing, do something for me.' She took a big breath. 'I'm asking you to stay. At least until after the birth. Be with me during the birth, because if you're there I will be able to look forward to this occasion as I should be—not dreading the empti-ness and fear of being alone.'

Rayne got that. He also got how freaking brave this woman was. To lay herself out there to be knocked back—not that he would, but, sheesh, how much guts had it taken for her to actually put that request into words? He felt the rock in his heart that had cracked that morning shift and crack a little more.

Heck. 'Of course I'll stay. Just ask for anything.' Well, not anything. He didn't think he was the type of guy to move in with, play happy families with, but he could certainly see himself being a little involved with the baby. He was good with babies. Good with children. For the first time in a long time he remembered he had an amazing job helping children and their parents and maybe it was a job he should go back to some time.

But he had no experience about making a family. No idea how to be a father. No idea what a father even did, except for those he'd seen at work. Simon's father had just seemed to be 'there'. He didn't know how to do 'being there'.

He glanced around the peaceful scene. Another little

family were riding shiny pushbikes along the path. They all wore matching red helmets. The dad was riding at the back and he guessed he was making sure everyone was okay. That seemed reasonable. Maybe he could do that. The birds were chirping and hopping in the branches above his head like the thoughts in his brain.

This place had an amazing vibe to it. Or it could be the collective consciousness of celebrating Christmas with family and friends creating the goodwill. But he'd never felt anything like it. He looked at Maeve. Or seen anyone like her.

She was staring over the water into the distance but there was tension in her shoulders. Rigidity in her neck. And he'd put that there. He'd need to be a lot better at looking after her if he was going to be her support person in one of the most defining moments of her life. Of both their lives.

He stepped up behind her and pulled her back to lean into his body. Lifted his hands to her shoulders and dug gently into the firm muscles, kneaded with slowly increasing depth until she moaned and pushed her bottom back into him until her whole weight was sagged against him.

She moaned again and he could feel the stir of his body as it came awake. Down, boy. Not now. Definitely not now. He could barely get his head around any of this, let alone lose the lot in a fog of Maeve sex.

'That feels *so-o-o* good,' she said.

He just knew her eyes were closed. He smiled. 'I'd

need to get lots of practice to build up my stamina for the event.'

'Mmm-hmm,' she agreed sleepily.

He shifted his fingers so that they were circling the hard little knot in her neck and she drooped even more.

'You might need to sit down.' He could hear the smile in his voice. Drew her to the bench they were standing beside and steered her into a sitting position. Went back around the bench so he was standing behind her—which helped the libido problem as he wasn't touching her whole body now.

He began again. Slow circular rotations of his fingers, kneading and swirling and soothing the rigidity away, for her, anyway. His body was as stiff as a pole.

He'd never had this desire to comfort and heal a woman before. Plenty of times he'd wanted to carry one to bed with him, but this? This was different. His hand stilled.

'Don't stop.'

He stepped back. Created distance from something he knew he wasn't ready for. Might never be ready for. 'I remembered the bread.' Pulled the brown paper bag from his pocket and gave it to her. A heaven-sent distraction to stop her interrogation into why he'd stepped back.

'For the ducks,' he said.

'Oh.' He heard the disappointment fade from her voice. Watched her straighten her shoulders with new enthusiasm. She was like a child. And he envied her so much. He couldn't remember when he'd felt like a child.

Then she was into planning mode again. 'You'll have to stay at the manse so I can find you when I need you.'

Just like that. Room, please. 'I can't just gatecrash Simon's grandmother's house.'

She threw a knobby crust of bread at a duck, which wrestled with it in a splash of lake water. 'Sure you can. Locum doctors and agency midwives come all the time when one of the hospital staff goes away. That's where they stay. The manse has lots of rooms and Louisa loves looking after people.'

Unfortunately too easy. He'd said he'd be there for the birth. He said he'd be her support person. He'd said he'd do anything and the second thing she asked for he was thinking, No!

H pushed back the panic. It would be better than the hotel. And not as bad as just moving into a house with Maeve and having her there twenty-four seven as his responsibility not to let anything happen to her.

Now, that was a frightening thought.

He wasn't on a good statistical run with saving people, which would be why he was an orphan now, and he went cold. Couldn't imagine surviving if anything happened to Maeve on his watch.

He did not want to do this. 'Sure. If Simon's grandmother says it's fine.' He thought about his friend. 'If Simon doesn't think I'm pushing my way into his family.'

'Simon spends every available minute with Tara.

Which reminds me. Tara is my midwife. I might ask her to run through some stuff with us for working together in labour. She's done a course and it works beautifully for couples.'

His neck tightened and he resisted the impulse to rub it. Hard. Or turn and run away. Couple? Now they were a couple? She must have sensed his withdrawal because she made a little sound of distress and he threw her a glance. Saw a pink flood of colour rise from her cleavage. Was distracted for a moment at the truly glorious sight that was Meave's cleavage, and then looked up at her face.

She mumbled, 'I meant a couple as in you are my support person in labour.'

Hell. He nodded, dropped his hands back onto her shoulders. Tried not to glance over the top of her so he could see down her dress. He was an emotionally stunted disgrace, and he had no idea what Maeve saw in him or why she would want to continue seeing him. He needed to be thankful she was willing to include him at all.

But he couldn't come up with any words to fix it. He watched her throw some more bread scraps to a flotilla of black ducks that had made an armada towards Maeve. They were floating back and forth, their little propeller legs going nineteen to the dozen under the water. A bit like he was feeling, with all these currents pulling him every which way.

Across the lake the Christmas sailboat was almost

at the other side. He could see the father and the little boat boy walking around the path to meet it. That father knew what to do. He wasn't stressing to the max about letting his kid down. What training did he have? Maybe, if bad things didn't happen, if he didn't stuff up, if Maeve didn't realise she deserved way better than him, he'd do that one day with his own son.

Or kick a ball. Ride bikes with him and buy him a little red helmet.

Or maybe Maeve's baby would be a little miniature Maeve. That was really scary. Imagine having to keep her safe? The air around him seemed to have less oxygen that it had before, leaving him with a breathless feeling.

'Want to see what's in the basket?' Maeve was pulling it onto the seat beside her. 'We'd better eat something out of it before we go back.'

She handed him the rum balls. 'Eat these so I don't.' Began to put mugs and spoons out.

He took them. Battened down the surge of responsibility that was crowding in on him as Maeve began to make a little picnic. Like any other family at the side of the lake. He didn't know where the conversation should go or what he was supposed to do. She handed him a cup of tea and he almost dropped it.

He felt her eyes on him. 'Relax, Rayne.' Her voice was soft, understanding, and he wasn't sure he deserved that understanding but he did allow his shoulders to drop a little. 'It's all been a shock for you. Let's get through the next week and worry about long term later. I'm just glad you're here and that you've said you'll stay for the labour.'

She was right. He felt the stress leach away like the tea seemed to have soaked into the brown dirt. He sat down beside her.

She handed him the bag of crumbs. 'Bread-throwing is therapeutic.'

Like a child. 'You are therapeutic.' But he took the bag. Before he could throw more crumbs, a tiny, yapping black-curled poodle came bounding up to them, the red bow around his neck waving in the slight breeze. He raced at the ducks and stopped at the edge of the water, and the black ducks took off in a noisy burst of complaint because they'd just found another benefactor in Rayne and now they had to leave.

A little girl's tremulous cry called the dog from further down the street and the black dog turned, cocked an ear, and then bounded off towards his mistress.

'So much for duck therapy.'

'Poor Rayne. Come, snuggle up to me and I'll make you feel better.'

He smiled and was about to say something when they heard the quack of another duck from the bushes beside them. He frowned and they both looked.

'Is it a nest?'

'Could be tangled in something.' He was about to stand up and check the bush when the sound came again and the branches rustled with movement. He stilled in case he frightened whatever was caught in there and they watched the bushes part until a little brown bird appeared, not a duck at all, a slim bird with a long drooping tail that shook itself free of the undergrowth.

'Ohh…' Maeve whispered on a long sigh of delight. 'It's not a duck making that noise—it's a lyrebird.'

Rayne watched in amazement. 'A lyrebird mimic? As in Lyrebird Lake? I guess that figures.' But there was something so amazing about the pure fearlessness of a wild creature glaring at them as it moved a step closer and cocked his head to stare their way.

Then the little bird, no larger than a thin hen, straightened, spread his fan-shaped tail in a shimmer of movement and proceeded to dance at the edge of the lake for Maeve and Rayne.

A gift for Christmas.

Backward and forward, shimmering his harp-shaped tail as it swayed above his feathered head, and Rayne had never seen anything like it in his life as he clutched Maeve's hand in his and felt the tight knot in his chest mysteriously loosen the longer it went on. He glanced at Maeve and saw silver tears glistening.

He hugged her closer, drank in the magic without questioning why they were being gifted with it. All too soon it was over and the tail was lowered. One more stern look from the bird and he stepped nonchalantly back into the bush and with a crackle of foliage he disappeared.

They didn't speak for a moment as the moment sank into both of them.

'Wow,' whispered Maeve.

'Wow is right,' Rayne said, as he turned and wiped away the silver droplets from Maeve's face. Leant over and kissed her damp cheek. 'I feel like we've just been blessed.'

'Me, too.' And they sat there in silence for a few minutes longer, in an aura of peace between them that had been missing before, and slowly the real ducks came floating back.

# CHAPTER SIX

*Back at the manse*

WHEN THEY GOT back Maeve disappeared into the kitchen to make her brandy sauce. Most of the family were out in the back yard—apparently the Christmas lunch table was set out there again—and the little girls were engrossed in their new possessions.

Simon waylaid Rayne and steered him back out the door away from the family. 'So what have you two decided?'

Rayne wasn't sure he'd decided anything. Maeve had done all the planning and now it was up to him to keep his end of the bargain. 'Maeve wants me to stay for the birth. I've said I will.' Simon looked mildly pleased. 'It's the least I can do.' There was that statement that had upset Maeve and it didn't do anything positive to Simon's frame of mind either if the frown across his friend's brow was an indication. He had no idea why it kept popping out.

'Is it that hard to commit to that? You slept with her.' His friend was shaking his head.

He held up his hand. 'Simon, I'm sorry. The last time I saw you it was an awful night. My world was about to implode. I didn't intend to end up in bed with Maeve.' He paused. Looked back in his mind and shook his head. 'But you should have seen her. She was like some peach vision and she poleaxed me.'

Simon glanced sardonically at him. 'And she dragged you off to bed?'

'Nope.' He had to smile at that memory. 'I carried her.' And she'd loved it.

Simon raised his brows. 'Up two flights of stairs?' Then he put his hand up. 'Forget I asked that. Tara says the sparks from you two light up the room. I get that. I get being irresistibly drawn to someone. And I get that you don't do commitment.'

Simon laughed dryly. 'But I thought I didn't do commitment until my Tara came along.'

Rayne looked at his friend's face. Had never seen it so joyous. As if Simon had finally found his feet and the whole world. Rayne couldn't imagine that. 'I meant to say congratulations. Tara seems a wonderful woman.'

Simon's smile grew. 'She is. And she so tough and...' He stopped, shook his head ruefully. 'Nice diversion. But this is about you.' Simon searched his face and he flinched a little under the scrutiny. 'Are you in for the long haul?'

Freaking long haul. Geez. He didn't know if he would last a week. 'I'm in for the labour. I'm in for what I can do to help Maeve for the birth. But as soon as I cause problems in her life I'm out of here.'

'And if you don't cause problems in her life?' The inference was he had already let her down, and he guessed he had.

'I didn't know she was pregnant.' Thank God.

Simon shrugged. 'Tara said you didn't open the mail. And I know you wouldn't answer my calls. Why?'

It was his turn to shrug but his bitterness swelled despite his effort to control it. 'I didn't want to bring her into that place. Either of you. I had to keep the good things pure. And when I got out, I didn't want to read that she might refuse to see me. So I came here first.'

'Have you read the letters now?'

'Yes.' Could feel the long stare from Simon. Those letters just reiterated how much he was capable of stuffing up other people's lives.

Simon sighed long and heavily. 'I love you, man. I'm even getting used to the idea that you will be in Maeve's life now. In all our lives. But don't stuff this up.'

So he'd read his mind? Rayne almost laughed, even though it was far from funny. 'That's the friend I remember.'

'Yeah. Merry Christmas.' Simon punched his shoulder. 'Let's go ask Louisa if you can stay. She'll be over the moon. She likes you.'

'I get the feeling your grandmother likes everyone.'

Simon laughed. 'Pretty much.'

Maeve had already asked Louisa.

'Of course he can stay,' Louisa enthused. 'So he'll be with you when you have the baby.' She sighed happily. 'Things have a way of working out.'

Maeve grimaced on the inside. *Things weren't 'working out' yet*.

There were a lot of things she and Rayne had to sort yet, not the least his attitude of *It's the least I can do*. *Grrr*. But, she reminded herself, this morning she'd been on her own. And he was here!

The magnitude of that overwhelmed her for a moment and she paused in the rhythmic stirring of thickening liquid in the bowl and just soaked that in. Rayne was here. And he was staying. At least until after the birth, and that was all she could ask for. Yet! She wondered if they would actually get much alone time.

Wondered if he was up for that. Wished she was skinny and gorgeous and could drag him off to bed. Or be carried there by her gorgeous sex object 'partner', round belly and all.

*Partner*. She'd always been uncomfortable with that sterile word. Not that Rayne was obviously sterile. And he wasn't her boyfriend. He certainly wasn't her lover.

'You want me to do that?' Louisa's worried voice. Maeve jumped and stirred again in the nick of time before she made lumps in the sauce.

'Wool-gathering.' Louisa's favourite saying and she'd picked it up. It described her state of mind perfectly. Little floating fibres of thought creating a mess of tangles in her brain. Mushing together to make a ball of confused emotions and wishes and fears and silly impossible dreams. Like the flotsam of leftover wool collected from the bushes where the sheep had walked past.

Well, Rayne was nobody's sheep. He'd never been a part of the flock, had never followed the rules of society except when he'd taken his incredibly intelligent brain to med school at Simon's insistence.

Men's voices drifted their way.

And here they came. Simon and Rayne. Two men she loved. The thought froze the smile on her face. She really loved Rayne. Did she? Fancied him, oh, yeah. The guy could light her fire from fifty paces away. But love?

Maybe brotherly love. She looked at her brother, smiling at something Louisa had said. Nope. She didn't feel the way she felt about Simon. And there was another bonus. She could stop fighting with Simon now that Rayne was back. Fait accompli.

Her mind eased back into the previous thought. The scary one. That she did really love Rayne. There was no 'might' about it. She really was in no better spot than she had been this morning because though Rayne was physically here she wasn't stupid enough to think he was in love with her. And he could leave and have any woman he wanted any time he wanted.

The sauce was ready and she poured it into the jug.

The beauty of this recipe, the reason she was the only one who made it in her family, was the secret ingredient that stopped the film forming on the top. So it didn't grow a skin.

That was a joke. She needed the opposite. She needed to grow ten skins so she could quietly peel away a new layer of herself to show Rayne so that she didn't dump it all on him at once. Because she knew it would require patience if she wanted to help him see he had a chance of a future he'd never dreamed about.

That he could be the kind of man any child would be proud to call his or her father. The kind of man any woman wanted to share her full life with—not just the bedroom.

What was with these pregnancy hormones? She needed to stop thinking about the bedroom. She ran her finger down the spoon handle on the way to the sink. Coated her finger in the rich golden sauce. Lifted it to her lips and closed her eyes. Mmm…

Rayne tried not to stare at Maeve as she parted her lips to admit a custard-covered fingertip. Watched her savour the thick swirl. Shut her eyes. Sigh blissfully as she put the spoon in the sink. Geez. Give a guy a break. If the day hadn't been enough without the almost overwhelming urge to pick her up from amidst all these people and ravish a heavily pregnant woman.

Louisa was talking to him. 'Sorry.' He blinked and turned to the little woman and he had the idea she wasn't blind to what had distracted him if the twinkle in her eyes was anything to go by.

'I said if you would like to follow me I'll show you your room. It's small but I think you'll like the position. And all the rooms open out onto a veranda and have their own chair and table setting outside the door.' She bustled out of the kitchen and he followed.

'That's the bathroom. It's shared with Maeve and Simon and Tara.'

He nodded and paid a bit more attention to the fact that this old country manse had to be at least a hundred years old. The ceilings were a good twelve feet high and the wood-panelled walls looked solid and well built.

Louisa gestured to a door. 'Maeve said she didn't mind there was a connecting door between the two. Do you?' She twinkled up at him.

'Um. No. That will be fine.'

'I thought it might be. Especially as she's getting near to her time and if she wanted to she could leave the door open between you.'

It was a good idea. That look of nervous anticipation he'd seen in Maeve's eyes this morning, he didn't like to call it fear, did need addressing. And it wasn't like he hadn't seen her without clothes. He brought his mind sternly back to the present.

If he could help by being close then that would give him purpose as he tried to come to grips with becoming an unexpected part of a large, noisy, hugging family—all that contact took a bit of getting used to.

He still couldn't believe they weren't all wishing him back to prison away from Maeve. But he knew for a fact Maeve was glad to see him. Maybe too glad, considering the prize she'd won.

Louisa opened the door next to Maeve's and, sure enough, it was a small room, but it did have a double bed against the wall and a chest of drawers. All he needed. 'Thanks, Louisa. It's great. Can I fix you up for it?'

'Lordy, no. I don't need money. I'm well looked after. But you may end up working every now and then for Angus at the hospital if he gets stuck. Everyone helps everyone in Lyrebird Lake.'

Well, not where he'd come from. He felt like he'd fallen into some religious sect and they were going to ask for his soul soon, except he knew that Simon was regular. And Maeve. And this sweet, generous older lady was obviously sincere. So it looked like he had a casual job as well as a place to lay his head. Though he couldn't see him being needed much at the hospital. 'Maybe I can help around the house. Or the garden? I wouldn't say no to be able to burn off some energy.'

She looked at him, a good once-over that had him wishing he'd tucked his shirt in and shaved, but she nodded. 'I have a pile of wood I need chopped before winter. The axe is in the wee shed under the tank stand. It's a bit early in the year but whenever you feel the need you just go right ahead and chop.'

He grinned. Couldn't help himself. Of all the things he'd thought might happen as he'd driven through the night to get here, getting a job as a woodcutter hadn't figured in the speculations.

He followed her out. 'Have I got time to nip back to the pub and let them know I won't be staying?'

'Have you left anything there?'

'No.' You didn't leave things in pub accommodation. Or maybe you did in Lyrebird Lake. Who knew?

'Well, that's fine. Denny Webb will be over visiting his wife at the hospital. Angus will pass the message on to the ward sister.'

Louisa waved to his car out in the street. 'You could bring your things in and then wash in the bathroom if you want.' She had noticed the bristles. 'And we'll see you back in a few minutes because it's nearly time for Christmas lunch.'

Obediently Rayne walked out to his car and brought in his overnight bag. The rest of his stuff—one small suitcase—was under the tarpaulin in the back of the truck. Not that he had much. He'd pretty well given everything else away. Had never been one for possessions. Wasn't quite sure what had influenced him to buy the old Chev. He'd passed it in a car yard on his way in from the airport and it had reminded him of his mother in happier times.

After his sleep in the motel for eight hours he'd walked back to the car yard an hour before closing time. Had told the guy if he could arrange a full mechanical check by a third party, transfers and insurance and tank of petrol in the time they had left, he'd pay the full price.

By the time he'd had a feed and returned, his car was waiting for him. So he did have one possession.

And an exit strategy. Both good things.

Walking back through the kitchen and outside, it seemed that Christmas lunch would be even noisier than breakfast.

Simon offered him a beer before they all sat down and, to hell with it, he took the glass and it was icy cold, and even though they were in the shade from the trees, it was pretty warm outside.

It was Christmas in Queensland and the beer tasted like Australia. Strong and dry and producing a sigh of momentary content. He noted some corny Christmas music on the CD player and Maeve was holding one hand over her left ear, pleading for it to stop. Tara was laughing and Louisa looked offended.

He leaned towards her. 'So you don't like carols?'

'Not twenty-four seven for the last month,' she whispered. 'Save me.'

He laughed. And gave her a quick squeeze as she went past with another jug of sauce to put on the end of the table. She glanced back and she looked at him like he'd given her a present. *Be careful there,* he thought to himself. Expectations and what he could actually deliver could differ.

Angus came up and stood beside him. Raised his glass. 'Lemonade. I'm on call.' He grimaced. 'But cheers. I hear you're staying.'

'Cheers.' He lifted his beer. 'Staying until after the baby at least.'

'Good.'

That was unexpected approval. 'Thank you.'

'It's for Maeve. And Simon. But I'm guessing it's not all easy on your side either. Not easy to get used to all this when you didn't expect it.'

Rayne glanced around. 'It's taking some.'

Angus nodded. 'Just chill. This place is good at helping the chill factor. Maeve has a lot of support so you won't be doing it on your own. And Tara is a good midwife.'

Change of subject. Great. 'Which reminds me. Congratulations on your new daughter-in-law-to-be. I haven't seen Simon look this happy, ever.'

Angus nodded. Glanced at his son, who had Tara's hand clasped firmly in his. Tara was laughing up at him. 'Best Christmas present I could wish for.' Then he glanced at his own wife and daughters. 'Finding the right woman is hard but incredibly worth it.'

'Okay, everyone,' the woman he was regarding said. 'Sit.' He inclined his head at her, gave Rayne a faint smile, and moved away to hold Louisa's chair, and then his wife's. He sat at the head of the table and Louisa sat on his left, with Mia on his right.

Simon sat at the other end with Tara next to him and Maeve on the other side. Rayne was in the middle opposite the two little girls, who were giggling at something Simon had said.

After this morning, he wasn't surprised when the elder of the two girls said grace, and for a fleeting moment he wondered with an inner smile whether, if he had a daughter, he would ever hear her piping little voice bless this table at Christmas. His throat thickened and he drew a quiet breath, and in a reflex he couldn't control he blocked it all out. Blocked out the tinny Christmas music, the laughing people, the beautiful woman expecting his baby beside him.

Maeve felt the distance grow between her and Rayne and wanted to cry. There had been moments there when he'd seemed to be settling into the day better than she'd expected. Especially when she'd noted his obvious rapport with Louisa, but, then, who didn't feel that? Louisa was a saint. Even when she'd first arrived and been at her most prickly and morose, Louisa's gentle, good-natured kindness had won her round before she'd known it.

She'd seen him talking to Angus. Well, since she'd arrived she'd decided Angus was a man's man, so that wasn't surprising. Rayne hadn't really spoken to the girls or Mia since they'd been introduced, but in fairness he hadn't had much chance. She couldn't help hoping he would exhibit some signs he was good with children. The guy was a paediatrician, for goodness' sake. And soon to be a father.

Tara leaned across the table and distracted her by offering the end of a Christmas cracker to pull. 'I'm not sure how many of these I'm supposed to pull,' she said in a quiet aside. 'I just did it with Simon and of course he won. And with Amber and she won. But I want a hat.'

Maeve smiled. 'You can pull any bon-bon offered. It's the bon-bon owner's choice who they want to pull them with. So take any you can.' Maeve had pulled a lot of bonbons in her time. The two young women had tested their strength against each other, and Tara had been a little more competitive than Maeve had expected, and that made her smile.

Maeve pulled harder and the bon-bon banged and split in half. Tara got the bigger half and the hat and prize. This time Tara crowed as she won. Simon clapped. He didn't miss much where Tara was concerned, Maeve thought with a pang. She glanced at Rayne. He was watching but his face was impassive and she got the feeling he wasn't really there.

Not so flattering when she was sitting beside him. 'Would you like to pull a bonbon with me?' Darn, did she have to sound so needy?

He blinked. 'Sorry?'

'A Christmas cracker.' She waved the one that was on her plate. 'See who wins.'

'Oh. Right. Sure.'

Such enthusiasm, she thought, and realised she was becoming a crotchety old woman by waiting for Rayne to behave like her fantasies.

'It's okay. Don't worry. I'll pull it with Tara. She loves them.' She meant it. No problem. Then he surprised her.

'Oi. I love them, too.'

That was the last thing Maeve had expected him to say. 'You love bon-bons?'

'Yeah. Why not?' His eyes crinkled and she sighed with relief that he was back with her. 'Not like I had that many family lunches over the years. That Christmas at your place was the first. You made me coconut ice.'

He remembered. The thought expanded in ridiculous warmth. 'I made everyone coconut ice at Christmas. For years. But it's very cool that you remembered.'

He held his hand out for the end of her Christmas cracker and she waved it around at him. 'I want to win.'

They pulled it and Rayne won. 'Oops,' he said. 'Try mine.' They realigned themselves to pull again and she could tell he tried hard to let her win but the cracker broke the larger end on his side. He got the prizes. Life sucked when you couldn't even win in a cracker-pull.

'Can I give it to you?'

'Not the same.' Shook her head. Pretended to be miffed.

He raised his brows. 'But I can't wear two hats.'

Then she said, 'Men just don't understand women.'

Rayne looked at the woman beside him, 'I'm hearing you.' He held out the folded hat. She took it reluctantly, opened it out and put it on. He'd given her the red one to match her dress and she looked amazing in a stupid little paper hat. How did she do that? He felt like an idiot in his.

He decided to eat. It seemed they were last to reach for the food again but, then, they'd made inroads into the basket Louisa had sent with them to the lake. He was starting to feel sleepy and he wasn't sure if it was the fact he'd driven all night, though he'd slept most of yesterday after the flight. Or maybe Louisa's rum balls were catching up with him. He stifled a yawn.

'I'm a bitch.'

The piece of roast turkey that was on the way to his mouth halted in mid-air. 'Sorry?'

'You're tired. I'd forgotten you haven't slept.'

He had to smile at her mood swings. The idea that life would not be boring around Maeve returned with full force.

They ate companionably for a while, he answered a question from Louisa on how the drive had been and gradually relaxed a little more with the company. 'I'll snooze later. Isn't that what everyone does after Christmas lunch? Wash up and then lie around groaning and doze off until teatime?'

'You're eating off a paper plate. The washing up's been done.' She smiled at him and his belly kicked because he was damned if there wasn't a hint of promise in that smile. More than a hint.

She bent her head and spoke softly into his ear. 'Not everyone sleeps.'

Geez. He wasn't making love with Maeve when Simon's room was two doors down. Imagine if she went into labour and everybody knew he'd been the one responsible for the induction. His neck felt hot and he couldn't look at anyone at the table.

'Rayne?' She laid her hand on his leg and it was all he could do not to flinch. Since when had he ever been at this much of a loss? The problem was his libido was jumping up and down like a charged icon on a computer.

She yawned ostentatiously and stood up. 'Happy Christmas, everyone. I think I'll go put my feet up.'

'Bye, Maeve.' From Simon and the girls.

'Don't go into labour, Maeve. I'm too full,' Tara said.

She turned back to Rayne. 'You coming? I think we need to talk some more.'

His ears felt hot. He needed to get himself back on an even footing here. It seemed she'd turned into a militant dominatrix and while the idea of submitting to sex wasn't too abhorrent, it didn't fit with the very late pregnancy visual effect. And he wasn't enamoured by the smothered smiles of his lunch companions.

'Sure. I'll just help Louisa clear the table first.'

She narrowed her eyes at him. 'Fine.'

Hell. She'd said, '*Fine.*' Which meant she was emotional and he might just have heard a tiny wobble in the word, which meant maybe he should go and comfort her.

Louisa shooed him away. 'You cleared at breakfast. Off you go and help that girl put her feet up.'

He caught Simon's perplexed glance at his grandmother and then at him. They both shrugged. How did you help someone put their feet up? Either way, he'd had his marching orders from two women. Maybe he should get his own place or they'd have him emasculated before New Year.

He stood up. Gave Simon a mocking smile and walked after Maeve.

# CHAPTER SEVEN

*Resting after lunch*

MAEVE HAD GOT as far as slipping her shoes off, she'd been stupid, telling him to follow her, and she'd better learn from her mistakes pretty damn quick if she didn't want to drive him away.

She stewed on that thought for a minute until she heard Rayne's quiet footsteps coming down the hall and she didn't know whether to sit on the bed, stand at the window, looking decorative, or just freeze where she was looking at the closed door like a rabbit in head-lights.

Time took care of that because Rayne knocked, paused and then opened the door and put his head around. She didn't get time to do anything except feel her heart thumping like a bass drum.

It was the Rayne from nine months ago. Black brows slightly raised, eyes dark and dangerous, a tiny amused tilt to those wicked lips. 'Louisa said you needed a hand to get your feet up?'

She licked dry lips. 'You can come in.' But when he did push open the door and shut it again the room shrank to the size of a shoebox and they were two very close-together shoes. 'Um. I am a bit tired.'

He glanced at the queen-sized bed then back at her. Looked her over thoroughly. 'Want a hand getting your dress off?'

'Thanks.' She turned her back and once he'd worked out there was no zip and she only wanted him to help her lift it over her head, the task was accomplished in no time.

No real seduction in that swift removal. She tried not to sigh. While he was draping the dress carefully over the chair she was thinking as she sat on the bed, *Thank goodness I changed my stretchy granny undies for the cute lace pair.*

He seemed to be staring at her chest. 'Nice cleavage.' Well, at least he appreciated something.

He was so big and broad standing over her and she patted the quilt she was sitting on. She wished he'd take off *his* shirt. 'Are you staying?'

'Staying? As in coming to bed with you?'

'You did say everyone lies down after Christmas lunch?'

He sat on the bed beside her. Then he turned his head and looked her full in the face. 'I'm not going to have sex with you but I'm happy to lie beside you while you rest.'

She pulled a face at him. Her own desire to snuggle

up to him was withering like a dehydrating leaf. 'I wouldn't want to force you to do anything you didn't want to.'

He grinned at her but there was a definite flare in his dark eyes that left her in no doubt she was wrong. A flare that made all the saggy disappointment feelings sit up and take notice again. 'It's not that I don't want to get closer.' He was telling the truth and at least that made her feel a little bit better. 'But I think we need to talk a whole lot more before we fall into...' he hesitated, didn't even offer a word for what they were both thinking about '...first.'

Talk? When she was sitting here in her lacy bra and panties—admittedly with a huge shiny belly out in front—behind a closed door with all those pregnancy hormones saying ooh-ah. 'Talk?' She fought back another sigh. 'That sounds more like a girl thing than a guy thing.'

He shrugged, stood up again and then leaned down, slipped an arm behind her knees and the other under her shoulders and placed her in the middle of the bed. Oh, my, she loved the way he did that.

Then he bent, unlaced his shoes and removed them, loosened his belt and then sat back down on the bed in his jeans. Reached for the folded light sheet at the bottom of the bed she'd been resting under in the afternoons, swung his legs up and draped the sheet over both of them.

Then he slipped his arm around her shoulders so her head was resting on his chest and settled back.

She was still smarting from the 'not having sex with you' comment. 'Is this the pillow talk I missed out on last time?'

He didn't seem perturbed. 'You do have a nasty little bite when you don't get your own way, don't you?'

She hunched her shoulders. 'It comes with not knowing where I stand.'

'Well,' he said slowly, 'I see that. But I can't tell you what I don't know. And if you want me to make something up then you're resting your head on the wrong chest.'

It was not what she wanted to hear and yet it was. And this particular chest felt so good to lean on. She relaxed and snuggled in a little closer. 'So you're saying you won't lie to me.'

The sound of his heart beating in a slow, steady rhythm reverberated under her ear. God, she'd missed this. 'I won't lie to you.'

She lifted her other hand slowly and ran her fingertip down the strong bulge of his bicep. An unfairly sexy bicep. Her girl parts squirmed in remembered ecstasy. Conversation. Remember conversation. 'Not lying to me is a good start.'

'You're supposed to say you won't lie to me either.' She could tell he was dead serious. Fair enough.

She wriggled awkwardly, trying to shift her weight

until she'd managed to roll and could see his whole face. Said just as seriously, 'I will not lie to you.'

She couldn't read the expression in his eyes but his mouth was firm. 'So if you want me to go, you tell me. Not telling me is a lie too.'

She frowned at him. 'I'm not sure I want to hear about it if you want to go.' Then she sighed and lay back down again. 'But I guess that's fair.'

He was shaking his head. 'You don't understand and you need to get where I'm coming from. I may not be good at this whole father thing, Maeve. I'll try but I don't have a lot of family experience, and no paternal role model, to draw on.' She could hear the slight thread of panic in his voice. Had to remind herself that a few hours ago this guy had had no idea he would be having a child some time in the next few days.

She thought about his 'no family experience' statement. Well, she guessed he'd never had a father to learn from or even subconsciously copy. Maybe he was finding that pretty daunting. 'Did you know your father at all?'

'Nope. I asked. All my mother said was he was dead and didn't offer any clues. Not even his name. And my mum wasn't into men staying over so no "special" uncles. If she spent the night with a man, she usually stayed out.'

Maeve thought about that. 'So when you were young you stayed home alone? At night?'

Maeve squeezed his arm in sympathy and Rayne

could feel himself begin to freeze her out. Had to force himself to let her offer comfort because if he was going to try to make this work he had to at least attempt to learn to do these things too. Apparently it was what families did and he needed to at least give it a shot.

He dispelled the myth that he had been alone. 'We lived in a dingy block of flats. You were never alone. You could always hear people in the other units.'

She nodded against him. 'So you never got scared on your own at night?'

He nearly said no. But he'd said he wouldn't lie. 'When I was younger I got scared. Especially if someone was shouting or I could hear someone yelling on the footpath. The worst was if a woman screamed down on the street. I always worried it was my mum and I wasn't doing anything to help her.'

He'd never told anyone that. Didn't know why he'd told Maeve. He moved on and hoped she would forget he'd said it. 'Guess I'd make sure my kid was never left alone until they wanted to be left.'

She squeezed him again. 'Perhaps your mum thought the people she was with were more disturbing than the idea of you being alone.'

His mum had actually said something like that. He hadn't believed her. Had there been a grain of truth in it after all? And Maeve had picked up on it all these years later. 'You don't judge her, do you? My mother?'

Maeve shrugged on his chest. 'Who am I to judge? I know nothing about her. I just know I've always admired you and she must have had a part in that. She was your mother.'

That heavy carpenter's rasp was back down his throat. Sawing up and down and ripping the skin off his tonsils. Or at least that's what it felt like as his throat closed. He searched for some moisture in his mouth. 'Even when I said I'd been in prison because of her, you were sad for me that she was dead.'

He'd been thinking about that a lot. Couldn't get his head around the fact that Maeve saw the part of him he hadn't shown to many people. Except Simon. But he doubted her brother would have discussed it with his little sister.

She snuggled harder and his arm protested and began to cramp. He told it to shut up.

Then she said, 'Even though you didn't meet your father, I think you'll be a good dad. And you certainly tried to look after your mum from a very young age. You're probably better father material than many men who had dads.'

He grimaced at the fact that maybe he had become a little parental with his mum, but that didn't change the fact he hadn't been able to save her.

Maeve was like a dog with a bone. 'You'll be fine. You're a paediatrician so at least you're good with kids.' She settled back. The law according to Maeve.

'At least I'm that,' he said dryly. 'I'm good with sick kids.' And especially the ones who were left alone and needed company.

She went on, 'I was too young to understand about how you grew up. You always looked tough and capable when I saw you.'

Rayne listened to her voice, the husky tigress lilt tamed a little now, and thought about what she'd said. So he'd appeared tough and capable. He guessed he had been. By the time she'd been in her early teens he'd almost grown out of his, and his mum had begun to need a bit more care taken of her. A couple of dangerous overdoses. A problem with her supplier that had left her badly bruised. The way she'd forgotten to eat. She'd had two close shaves with the law and had told him if she ever got convicted she would die if she went to prison.

The last years had been a downward spiral and he'd tried most things to halt it. The number of rehab centres, fresh towns, health kicks they'd tried. Things would go well for a few months and he'd get tied up at work. Miss a couple of days dropping in then she'd start to use again.

The best she'd been had been in Santa Monica. She'd looked young for the first time in years. Had got a job as a doctor's receptionist at one of the clinics he worked from in the poorer area, a place where kids who needed care they normally couldn't afford could access a range of different doctors. And she'd been good at it.

She had connected well with the people who didn't need anyone to look down on them. He'd valued the once a week he'd donated his time there, away from the upmarket private hospital he'd worked in the rest of the time. And he'd cheered to see her making a life for herself. Fool.

Until the day she'd worked and gone home early. It had been his day as well and he'd finished late. Locked up. The investigation had been well in progress by the time he'd found out all the drugs had been stolen. Had known immediately who it had been. He hadn't been able to track her down anywhere until finally she'd rung him. Pleading. Promising she would never, ever, touch anything ever again, if he would say it was him. That this was her chance to go clean for life.

He'd hoped maybe it was true and that she would stop using. Then had begun to realise the fingers had been pointing to him anyway. So he'd made a conscious decision to try a last attempt at saving her.

He'd tried ringing Simon so he wouldn't find out from someone else that he would probably be going to prison. Hadn't been able to give the explanation on the phone and had had that ridiculous idea to fly out, explain and then fly back in twenty-four hours. He'd thought he should have just about that much time before it all came crashing down. Before the police came for him!

'Hey,' Maeve whispered, but she wasn't talking to him. The belly beside him rolled and shifted and his eyes fixed on the movement, mesmerised. He glanced quickly at Maeve, who was watching him with a gentle smile on her face, lifted his hand and put his palm on the satin skin. And the creature below poked him with something bony.

Geez. He looked back at Maeve.

'Cool, isn't it?' she said softly. And put her hand over his. And he realised with a big shift of emotion that the three of them were together for the first time. 'He likes you.'

His eyes jerked to her face. 'It's a he?'

She laughed. 'I really don't know. Just find myself calling him he. Maybe because you weren't here.' He winced at that.

'Might be a girl.' She shrugged. 'I really don't care which.'

'I hope she looks like you.'

She looked at him as if she were peering over a pair of glasses at him. 'Why on earth would you want your son to look like me?'

'Okay. A boy could be like me but it would be very sweet to have a little girl who looks like you.' Then he spoilt it all by unexpectedly yawning.

She laughed. 'You need a nap more than I do. Why don't you take your jeans off? We can talk more later. Then you can roll over and I'll cuddle you.'

'Bossy little thing.' But suddenly he felt morbidly tired and he did what he was told, not least because his arm had gone totally to sleep now and his jeans were digging into him.

When he climbed back onto the bed and rolled to face the door, she snuggled up to him as close as her big tummy would allow. It actually felt amazing when his child wriggled against him. Geez.

Maeve listened to Rayne's breathing change and she lay there, staring at his dark T-shirt plastered against his strong shoulders as he went to sleep.

She tried to imagine Rayne as a little boy, from a time when his first memories had begun to stick. Dark, silky hair, strong little legs and arms, big, dark eyes wondering when Mummy would be home.

It hurt her heart. She wanted to hug that little boy and tell him she'd never leave him scared again. How old had he been when his mother had begun to leave him? She had a vague recollection of hearing Simon say to her parents that Rayne's mum hadn't started using drugs until after something bad had happened when Rayne had gone to school.

She wondered what had happened to Rayne's poor mum. Something that bad? It couldn't have been easy, bringing up a child alone with very little money.

Her childhood had been so blessed. Always her hero brother Simon and three older sisters to look after her, as well as both well-adjusted parents, although her mum was pretty definite on social niceties.

Her dad was a fair bit older than her mum, but he'd always been quietly there, and her mother had come from a wealthy family and always been a determined woman. She'd been spoilt by her dad, but had sometimes felt as if she wasn't quite enough of a star for her mother. Hence the try-hard attitude she really needed to lose.

She would be thankful for all her blessings of family and now having this gorgeous, damaged man appear just when she needed him. He hadn't run. He'd promised to stay at least until after the birth. Had tried to fit into a strange family's Christmas Day, which must be pretty damn hard when he was still reeling from being in prison and adjusting to society again, and he'd just found out he'd fathered a child.

She stared again at the powerful neck and short hair in front of her eyes and the way the thick strands clung to his skull like heavy silk. Resisted the urge to move her hand from around his chest to touch it as she didn't want to wake him, but her fingers curled.

She could imagine her baby having hair just that colour, though, of course, hers was black like her dad's as well, so the kid didn't have much choice. But she would think of it as his father's hair. Would he have Rayne's eyes and mouth too?

Imagine.

A long slow pulling sensation surged in her belly from under her breasts down to her pubic bone, growing tighter and then after a while easing off. Just one.

Braxton-Hicks. Practice contractions. Not painful. Just weird, as if the baby was stretching out straight. But she knew it wasn't. Soon they would come more frequently. Maybe for a couple of hours at a time and then stop. For a few days probably. She'd told other women this so many times, but it was strange when it was yourself you were reassuring.

This time she'd welcomed it without the accompanying flare of nervousness she'd been fighting for weeks. Giving birth was a job that needed to be done and now that Rayne was here the time was right. Whatever happened, whatever her birth journey was meant to be, Rayne would be there to share it all. The best Christmas present of all.

Rayne woke an hour later, straight from dreaming about Maeve. Like he'd woken nearly every day for the last nine months. Except this time he really had her in his arms, his hands really were cupping her glorious breasts, her taut backside really was snuggled into his erection, which was growing exponentially with confirmation of the contact.

They must have rolled in their sleep.

She murmured drowsily, not yet awake, and languidly backed into him a little more. Unconsciously, his hands slid over her belly, pulling her closer.

The little person inside that belly nudged him and he recoiled in startled appreciation of where his actions were leading. 'Sorry,' he murmured, and slid his hands down to the sides of Maeve's abdomen, but Maeve was having none of it. Took his hands and placed them back on her breasts. Wriggled into him.

'Have mercy, Maeve,' he whispered in her ear, but he couldn't help the smile that grew on his face. She wriggled against him again and he groaned. Slid his rear end across the bed to make room for her to shift and turned her to face him. 'You are a menace.'

'And you feel so good against me,' she whispered back drowsily. Then tilted her face for a kiss, and there was no way he could resist those lips, that mouth, or keep it to one kiss. And the gentle salute turned into a banquet of sliding salutations and memories that resurfaced from all those months ago. How they matched each other for movements, timing, a connection between them that had him pulling her closer, but the big belly in the middle made everything awkward, yet erotic, and he must be the most debauched man on earth to want to make love to this woman who was so close to giving birth.

As if she'd read his mind, she said, 'If we don't make love now, you'll have to wait for ages.'

He really hadn't thought of that. 'Maybe we should wait.' But he seriously didn't want to. And she obviously didn't. Nine months of fantasy and the woman of his dreams was demanding he make love to her.

No-brainer really.

In the Maeve fog that was clouding his mind he wasn't really sure what he'd been thinking to knock her back before.

Still in the fog, he slid from the bed, ripped his T-shirt off his head in one movement and kicked off his briefs. Knelt back down and dropped a big kiss right between Maeve's awesome assets. Geez, he loved her breasts.

He slid his hands around her back and unclasped her bra. Sighed as the two gorgeous spheres eased out of the restraining material like big, soft plump peaches. The circular areolas surrounding her nipples were dark peach, highlighted for a tiny baby to find easily, and he skimmed his fingers across in awe while she watched him with a womanly smile as old as the ages.

He swallowed to ease the dryness in his throat. 'They say pregnant women in the third trimester of pregnancy have erotic dreams and surges of erotic desires.'

'That's very true,' she whispered, pulling him closer and tilting her mouth for him to kiss again. When they paused for breath there was no concept of stopping. But he was doing this right, and gently, and he wanted to show her just how beautiful she was in his mind and in his heart. 'Then we'd better take our time.'

# CHAPTER EIGHT

*Labour and birth*

WHEN MAEVE WOKE up Rayne was gone. But the contraction tightenings weren't gone. That darned love hormone.

She did not want to have this baby on Christmas Day. It was okay for baby Jesus. He'd never been materialistic, but Maeve knew how she'd feel about the one day of the year that belonged to everyone, in her corner of her world anyway. But it was her own fault.

Still, she could not regret this afternoon in Rayne's arms. She smiled a long, slow, satisfied smile. Regret definitely wasn't the word that sprang to mind.

Revel, ravish, rolling around with… Scraping the bottom of the barrel there, but *reaaaalllyyy* amazing just about covered it. Her skin flushed at the thought of how wonderful he'd been, so unhurried, showing her a world of gentleness that had brought tears to her eyes. He had paid homage to her body, coveted her belly, and just plain loved her, something she'd missed so badly as her body had changed, and he had banished for ever the idea he wasn't the man for her.

Which was an excellent thing if she was about to have his baby.

Another contraction followed on the thought. That love hormone again.

She glanced at the clock. It was seven-thirty in the evening. Almost sunset. Less than five hours until midnight. 'Hang in there, baby.'

She climbed awkwardly out of bed. Pulled on a robe and gathered something light to wear for the evening. Something comfortable like a sarong. They'd probably sit out the back or go for a leisurely walk along the lake. Another contraction tightened her belly, this time with a little bit of discomfort.

They were still not lasting long but she guessed she wasn't going to go too far from home. At least there was no car journey involved, like there would have been if she lived in the city. Here, they'd just pick up Tara from the room down the hall—she grinned at that, same house—then walk across the road to the birth centre. It was all pretty streamlined, actually. Almost a home birth without the organising of equipment involved.

Rayne would be stressed. Simon would worry. But she would be calm. Could be calm now because she deputised other people to do the worrying and from this moment on she would have faith in her body, in a natural process she was designed to achieve. It was exciting really. And Tara would be there. She giggled. She hoped Tara had digested her lunch by now.

She thought about giggles. That's right. In early labour you apparently felt like giggling. The fact labour had finally arrived after all the waiting. Happy hormones. She grinned in the mirror. Actually, she did feel like giggling. Even the fact that she knew this would pass onto harder and stronger contractions was funny. At the moment, anyway. No doubt she'd change her mind later.

She slipped out of the bedroom door and into the bathroom with a smile on her face. She could hear the rumble of Simon and Rayne's voices coming from the kitchen. The thought made her feel warm. She would not have believed the change in her world in the last day. It was like she'd been released from her own prison. That thought put her feet back on the ground. She shouldn't joke about it. Rayne really had been released from prison.

She hung the robe on the hook at the back of the door, climbed into the shower and relaxed again as she revelled—there was that word again—in the hot water that soothed any tension away from her shoulders. Another contraction started its slow rise in intensity and consciously she sent all the negative thoughts down the drain with the soapy water, and breathed out.

Still ten minutes apart, plenty of time to tell people. She just wanted to hug the excitement and her baby to herself. This was the last day that she and her baby would be together so intimately. A miracle in itself.

She stayed in the shower for a long time.

Until Rayne knocked on the door. 'You okay in there?' A hint of concern in his voice.

She had to wait for the contraction to stop before she could answer. They were getting stronger but that was a good thing. More powerful, not more painful, she reminded herself. A tiny voice inside muttered about that not being true but she ignored it. The pain eased.

'I'm fine.' Wow. Her voice sounded kind of spacy. Endorphins.

'Can I come in?'

'Sure,' she breathed. Then had to repeat it a bit louder. 'Come in.'


Rayne pushed open the door and a cloud of steam billowed out past his head. He waved it away and stepped into the bathroom. 'You've been in here for ages.' He crossed the tiles to the corner shower. Stood outside the curtain. 'Is there something I should know?'

He waited. She didn't answer and he could hear her breathing. Eventually he pulled back the curtain so he could see her. She smiled at him and he thought she looked almost half-asleep. Looked again. Now, that was something you didn't see every day. A glistening wet, very rounded, amazingly breasted, porcelain pregnant lady naked in the shower, with her black hair curling on her shoulders.

She said, 'If we ever live together, you'll need a very large hot-water system.'

He had to smile at that. He assumed Louisa did own one of those if this house could sleep twelve. 'I'm getting that.'

'And also,' she went on in the same distant voice, 'my contractions are about seven minutes apart.'

His heart rate doubled and then he slumped against the wall. Sex fiend. He'd done that. Come on. Pull yourself together. You're a doctor, for crikey's sake.

'Is that a good thing?' he asked cautiously. Who knew what Maeve was thinking? He was trying to be supportive because that was his job, and he'd agreed without coercion when, in fact, he wanted to run screaming to Simon.

'As long as baby waits till after midnight, that's fine.'

Rayne glanced at his watch. Eight o'clock. Four hours until midnight. Of course she'd have her own way and the baby would wait. Four hours of stress.

'Shall I go and tell Simon? Or Tara?'

'No hurry.'

It was all very well to say that, along with some heavy breathing, and he observed, as if from a long way away, that his fingers were white where he was clutching the handrail. 'You sure?'

'Mmm-hmm…' Loud exhalation.

Geez. Rayne prised his fingers off the towel rail and

straightened off the wall. 'Um. Might just mention it to them in case they want to go out.' Though where they would go on Christmas night was a mystery.

Quietly, on an out breath, an answer came from the shower. 'Okay.'

Rayne left and he wasn't quite jogging. He skidded into the kitchen but it was empty. Typical. This house had crawled with people all day and now he couldn't find anyone when he needed them. Even Louisa was missing but he guessed she, out of all of them, deserved a rest.

Poked his head out the back door but the darkening yard, a space that had seen so many Campbells, was deserted.

He went back inside, walked down the hallway, but both Simon and Tara's doors were ajar and he guessed if they were in there they'd have closed the doors. He went out to the front veranda in case they were sitting on that bench, looking at the nodding animals, and he was distracted for a minute by the fairy-lights that had come on with the sunset. Nobody there. He glared at the manger. Mary and Joseph had had their baby in a manger, with animals and wise men, so what was his problem?

He ran his hand distractedly through his hair. Took a deep breath. It was okay. Maeve was calm. Happy even. The hospital was across the road for pity's sake. He could see the porch lights. All he had to do was be a support person.

It would have been nice to have that 'couples' discussion with Tara that he'd had a knee-jerk reaction about today before Maeve had gone into labour. But, *no-o-o*, Maeve had had to have nookie.

What was it he'd learnt in med school? A first-time mum, after a slow start while the contractions got sorted out, dilated about a centimetre an hour. To get to ten centimetres was ten hours. Right? Or maybe she was already six centimetres then it would be four hours. Or less if she'd got there this quickly. His mind was spinning faster than the wheels of the new Christmas pushbike some happy, oblivious-to-the-drama-inside kid was pedalling past too late to be out.

He forced himself to take another breath. Yesterday he would not have believed all this was going to happen. Yesterday he had been wondering if she would see him. Today she was his responsibility.

Well, he'd been in at the beginning so he had to stay for the hard part.

'Rayne?' He spun round and Maeve was leaning on the door to the front veranda. She looked like she'd just stepped off a plane from Fiji, with a hibiscus sarong wrapped around her and not much else. He could see her cleavage from here.

'Why are you staring at the manger?'

He wasn't looking at the manger now. Cleavage. 'Umm. Looking for Tara and Simon.'

She leant her head on the doorframe. 'They're on

the side veranda outside their rooms, watching the stars come out.'

He strode back across the lawn and up the steps to her side. 'Okay. You okay?'

'I'm fine. But I'd sort of like you to stay with me.'

'Yep. Of course.' He was obviously really bad at this support-person caper. Where was the midwife? 'So did you tell Tara?'

'I wanted to find you first.'

Not the choice he would have made. 'Fine. Let's do it now.'

'You said *fine*...'

She leant against his arm and smiled up at him and as if she'd pressed a button he leant down and kissed her lips in an automatic response. Just one day and they had an automatic response?

He stepped back. Must have picked up on some of her endorphins because he could feel his panic settle a little. *Fine.* Yep, he had been feeling freaked out, insecure, neurotic and emotional.

His voice softened, lowered, and he gently turned her back towards the house. 'How can you be so calm?'

'I've had nine months to think about this happening. You've had twelve hours.'

Had it only been twelve hours? It felt like twelve days. But, then, that's how things seemed to happen around Maeve and him. Acceleration with the pedal pressed and they were driving off into the future at a hundred miles an hour.

'Do you do anything slowly?' he said as they walked down the hall. He grinned at her. 'Apart from the way you're walking up the hallway now.'

'I put my make-up on slowly.'

'Does that mean if I took you out I'd be one of those guys hanging around waiting for his woman to get ready?'

'I might speed up for you.' Then her face changed and she stopped, closed her eyes as she leant against him. He lifted his hand and rested it on her arm and her shoulder dropped its tension beneath his fingers as if he'd told her to relax, and it startled him.

She sighed out, 'Boy, I can tell these contractions are doing the job.'

That was good. Wasn't it? 'We still waiting for midnight?'

'No choice now. It's all up to baby. You just have to hold my hand for the ride.'

He could do that. Glanced down at her hand, thin and suddenly fragile looking, as they set off again. 'It would be an honour,' he said very quietly. And it would be. She was blowing him away with her strength and serenity.

Simon and Tara, also holding hands again—spare me, he thought—appeared in the hallway and Maeve had a contraction before he could say anything.

Tara let go of Simon's fingers with a smile and went towards them. No need to say anything. So he didn't. Wasn't really his place anyway.

And they didn't ask. Their restraint was amazing and he could only follow their lead.

When the contraction was over, Tara murmured, 'Good job. When did they start?'

'About an hour ago.'

'So what do you feel like doing?' Tara was walking beside Maeve as they drifted down the hallway to the kitchen. Simon smiled at Rayne.

'You should see your face.'

'Shut up.' But there was relief and he felt the smile cross his own face. 'Geez, mate. Yesterday none of this was happening.'

'I know. In that context you're actually doing well. But open your letters next time.'

Rayne gave him a hard look. 'Try being where I was and you might not feel so sure about that.'

The smile fell from Simon's face. 'You're right. But I would never do something as stupidly noble as that. But I should have known you would. I'm sorry I was so quick to believe in your guilt.'

Rayne heard Maeve laugh at something Tara had said and looked at Simon and dropped the whole subject. This wasn't about him. Or Simon. 'How can she laugh?'

They both walked towards the kitchen. 'See, that's why I chose obstetrics over paediatrics.'

Rayne thought about the stress he'd been under already. 'You think giving birth is funny? It's a wonder you haven't been killed.'

Simon laughed again and it felt good to loosen the tension between them. The dynamics were certainly tricky. Especially if he didn't make the grade to stay around for the long haul. But he would worry about that later.

'Rayne?' Maeve's voice.

He quickened his pace and left Simon behind. 'I'm here.'

'I want to go in the bath and Tara thinks it might be easier if I don't have to move from this bath here to the one in the birth centre. So maybe we should go over there fairly soon.'

'Sounds sensible to me.' Sounded amazingly sensible. A hospital, or a birth centre at least with a hospital next door.

Louisa appeared. Caught on very quickly what was happening. 'I'll pack a hamper.'

He looked at her. Felt more tension ease from his shoulders. 'You have a feeding fetish.'

'Must have.' She winked at him. 'I'm too old for any other kind of fetish.'

Simon and the two girls looked at her in comical surprise but Louisa was off to do her stuff.

'I'll see you over there,' Tara said. 'I'll go ahead and run the bath and then come back. We can check baby out when you get there. Take your time, unless you feel you have to hurry.'

What sort of advice was that? Rayne thought with a little flutter of his nervousness coming back. He for one felt like they had to hurry. But Maeve was nodding and doing a go-slow. She didn't even look like making a move.

Simon said he'd leave them to it. Maybe go and see his dad and let him know what was going on.

Rayne watched him go and thought, So the obstetrician leaves? He looked towards Maeve's bedroom. 'Do you have a bag packed?'

'Yep.' She was just standing there with a strange little smile on her face, looking out the window at the Christmas fairy-lights in the back yard. The clock on the wall ticked over a minute. And then another. He felt like ants were crawling all over him.

'Um. You want me to go and get the bag?'

She turned her head and smiled vaguely at him. 'You could.'

So how was he supposed to find it? This must be the kind of stuff normal people talked about when they were planning to have a baby. People who had more than twelve hours' notice they were going to be a support person in a labour. The woman would say, "My bag is in my wardrobe if we need it. My slippers are under the bed." Bathroom kits and baby clothes would have all been discussed. Baby names!

He tamped down his panic again. 'Where is the bag?'

'Behind the door.'

At last. He could do something. He looked at Maeve as if she might explode if he left, and then turned and strode up the hallway for the bag. Was back within seconds.

'Do you need anything else?'

She blinked. Smiled. 'Are you trying to organise me?'

Sprung. 'Uh. Just making sure everything is ready when you want to go.'

'It's really important—' she was speaking slowly as if to a child who wasn't listening '—that the birthing woman is the one who decides when to go to the birth centre. She has to feel like she *needs* to be somewhere else before she leaves the place she feels safe in *now*.'

'So this is what you tell women in antenatal classes? About when they go to the hospital?'

'And the men,' she said with a patronising smile.

They went across to the birthing centre at nine o'clock. Walked across the road, slowly, because Maeve had to stop every few minutes. The stars were out. Christmas night. The air was still warm and Maeve was wearing the sarong.

He had her overnight bag over his shoulder, the hamper from Louisa in one hand and Maeve's elbow in the other.

'It's a beautiful night,' Maeve said after a very long drawn-out breath.

*Yes. Yes, beautiful,* he thought. *Come on.* 'Yep. You okay?'

She had another contraction and they stopped again.

Tara met them at the door. Nobody else was in labour so they had the place to themselves.

The midwife on duty was over at the hospital but would come across for the birth.

Angus was the doctor on call for obstetrics and would wait outside the door in case they needed him. All these things he found out in the first three minutes because he had requests, too! He really didn't know if he could handle a lifetime of responsibility for Maeve. What if something went wrong?

Tara sent him to make tea because Maeve needed to go to the ladies and he was pacing outside the door.

He was back too quickly.

He could feel Tara's eyes on him and he looked at her.

'Maeve is low risk, Rayne,' Tara said. 'It's her first baby. She's here on the day before the baby is due. Her waters haven't broken. She has no infections. Her blood pressure is normal. She's only been in labour for two hours at the most.' A sympathetic look. 'Why are you worried?'

'It's my first baby too?'

'Sure. I get that.'

He didn't think she did. 'I'm a paediatrician. They only called me for the babies that might need help and I've seen a lot of very sick babies. I guess my idea of normal birth is a bit skewed.' Or more than a bit, and in any case he'd only found out about this baby today.

'I get that too. But Maeve's baby will be fine.'

He wanted to believe that. 'What if it isn't?'

'Then we will manage. It's what we do.' She glanced around the homey birthing room for inspiration, or at least something that would reassure him. 'Why don't you check the equipment? And the resuscitation trolley? All the drugs on the trolley? Check the suckers and oxygen.'

He couldn't help his horror showing in his face. 'You haven't checked those?'

She actually laughed. 'Yes, Dr Walters, I have checked those. But I'm trying to distract you!'

'Oh.' Now he felt dumb. 'Sorry.' He put his finger under the collar of his T-shirt because suddenly it felt tight.

Tara's voice was gentle. 'Maybe doing those things would be helpful if Angus called you in an emergency in the next few weeks.'

He sighed. Get a grip. Thank goodness Tara did have a sense of humour. 'Sorry. It's just been pretty sudden. I'm not normally such a panic merchant.'

She looked at him. 'I have no doubt that's true. I think you've done exceptionally well, considering the scenario you've fallen into. But here's the thing.' Her voice dropped and her face was kind but serious and she glanced at the closed bathroom door. He started to wonder if Maeve and Tara had cooked up this pep talk for him between them.

He guessed he'd never know.

'I need you to be calm. I need you to be Maeve's rock. You don't need to say much—just be here. Agree with her. She really wanted you to be here. And hold her hand when she wants you to. Rub her back when she wants you to. Okay?'

He took a big calming breath. 'Okay.'

'No more panic vibes, please. And in the meantime you can familiarise yourself with the equipment only if you need distraction.'

Okay. He got that. The bathroom door opened and Maeve came out. He sat quietly in the corner of the room while Tara felt Maeve's abdomen, discussed the lie of the baby, which was apparently pointing in exactly the direction and attitude they wanted, and listened to his baby's heartbeat.

Geez. That was his baby's heartbeat. Cloppety, cloppety, clop. It was fast. He knew foetal hearts were fast. But was that too fast?

Calm. He needed to be calm. Dissociate. That was the answer. Pretend it wasn't his baby. Okay. He felt calmer. In fact, he felt in total control. It was cool. Normal heart rate.

'Rayne?'

'Yes, Maeve.'

'Can you hear our baby's heartbeat?'

'Yes, I can. It seems very fast!'

Tara looked at him with eyebrows raised.

He racked his brains. 'Baby must be as excited as we are.'

Maeve laughed. 'That is so cute.'

Cute. Geez. He stood up. Might go check the equipment.

* * *

The next hour was traumatic.

Then Maeve decided to get out of the bath and the hour after that was even worse.

But baby was fine. Heart rate perfect, with no slowing after contractions. Rayne's heart rate slowed after the contractions because during the contraction it doubled. And not just because he was rubbing Maeve's back non-stop.

Between contractions Maeve was calm. Rational. Gathering her strength for the next wave. During contractions it was hell.

Noisy. Intense. Painful when she had his hand in hers and dug her nails in.

Tara was the rock. Quiet. Steady. Unflappable. Like the calm in the storm. He'd look across at her when a contraction was at its height and she would be smiling. Gentle and calm. This was Maeve's profession as well. How did these women do this day in, day out?

'I am so going to be at your birth, Tara,' Maeve ground out as the contraction finally eased.

'Good. We'll swap places.'

Rayne shook his head. How could they carry on a normal conversation when two minutes ago she was ready to rip all their heads off?

And then it was time to push. Eleven forty-five p.m. He looked at Maeve. It had been incredibly hard work. Perspiration beaded her brow, and he leant across and wiped it.

'Hey, Rayne,' she said softly. 'You okay?'

How could she possibly care about him when she was going through hell? 'As long as you're okay, I'm okay.'

'I'm fine.'

He smiled. 'I'm *fine* too.'

She smiled back wearily. 'Home straight now.'

There had been a bit of a lull in the contractions after a series of torrid strong ones. 'So why has it stopped?'

'Nature's way of giving us a break before the last stretch.' Then her face changed. 'Oh.'

The next twenty minutes would be forever etched in his mind. Angus was outside the door in case he was needed. He'd checked, but they didn't see him. Simon had arrived as well but was waiting to be invited in afterwards. He'd bet there was some pacing happening out there. As much as he was suffering in here, it would have been a hundred times worse imagining outside the door. Especially with the Maeve soundtrack they had playing.

With each pushing contraction a little more of the baby shifted down. The excitement was building and Maeve was much more focused now she could use the contractions to make things happen. If there was one thing his Maeve could do, it was make things happen.

Maeve was impatient. No surprise there. She moved position several times, kneeling, leaning on a ball, leaning on Rayne. Even sitting on the toilet, but that stressed him out until Tara smiled and put a towel over the toilet seat so he could stop envisaging his baby falling into the toilet bowl. But eventually they were standing beside the bed, and he could actually see the hair on his baby's head.

'You're doing well,' Tara said.

*Well? Doing well? She was freaking amazing, incredible.* 'Come on, Maeve. You're nearly there, babe.' He saw her glance at the clock and register it was a few minutes after midnight. She'd got what she wanted, and she looked at him.

Triumph, thankfulness and new determination, and he realised it would never be the same between them again. But that was okay. He could admit she was stronger than him. In some ways, anyway. Maeve turned to face him. 'I want to sit back on the bed against the pillows.'

So he lifted her and put her back on the pillows. 'Love that,' she panted, and even in that moment their eyes met and she tempted him. Then she relaxed back against the pillows, hugging her knees, and gave one long outward sigh. And suddenly the crown appeared then a head of black hair, stretched into a face, one shoulder and then the other.

'Want to take it from here, Rayne?' Tara murmured, and he got it instantly. He stepped in and put his hands under his baby's armpits and, gently eased with the pressure Maeve was exerting, his baby entered the world with his own hands around him in a rush of belly, thighs, long legs and feet and a tangle of cord and water—and suddenly in a huge internal shift and crack through the wall of years of keeping emotion at bay, tears were streaming down his face.

Maeve was staring down with surprise and he lifted the squirming buddle of…? He glanced between the legs, grinned. 'It's a boy!' His eyes met hers and for that moment, when she looked at the baby, and then him and then the baby again, he didn't see how anything could ever stand between them.

His son cried. Loudly and lustily, and Maeve gathered him and snuggled him up against her breasts, and the baby's cries quieted instantly.

*Boob man. Chip off the old block.* He experienced such a swell of emotion his heart felt like it was going to burst.

In shock he saw the second midwife—where had she come from?—lean in to dry the little legs and arms and belly and rub the damp hair before she stepped back and replaced the damp towel with a warm bunny rug over them both until the baby was in a Maeve skin and bunny-rug sandwich.

Tara delivered the placenta and then a big warm hospital blanket covered Maeve's legs and belly and arms until finally her baby was tucked snugly with just his downy cheek against his mother, turned sideways toward Rayne, with big dark eyes and little squashed nose, and deep pink rosebud lips and a gorgeous mouth like Maeve's. And it was done.

His chest felt tight. 'Hello, there, buddy,' Rayne said softly.

He glanced at the clock. Ten past twelve. Boxing Day baby. Eighteen hours after arriving in Lyrebird Lake here he was—a father. New responsibility swamped him.

# CHAPTER NINE

*Emergency*

MAEVE LAY THERE with the weight of her son on her chest, feeling the little wriggles on the outside of her body instead of the inside as he shifted. Could smell the unmistakable scent of new babies, and blood, and almost taste the relief in the room.

Why were they all worried? She had this. She looked at Rayne, who was sinking into the chair beside the bed that Tara had pulled up for him, unnaturally pale. His hand was halfway to the baby and hung suspended in the air as if he didn't know whether to touch or not.

'He's your son,' she whispered. Wishing he would kiss her. As if he'd heard her, he half stood and leaned across and kissed her lips. His hand drifted down and he touched the downy cheek of their child.

'Thank you. He's amazing. You were incredible.' He blinked a couple of times. 'Are you okay?'

'Buzzing,' she said, and grinned at him, and he shook his head and sank back in the chair. Looked like Rayne had aged ten years, she thought to herself. Still, the years sat well on him.

She glanced at Tara, who was taking her blood pressure. Waited until she was finished and then caught her hand. 'Thanks, Tara.'

Tara smiled mistily. 'I'm going to hold you to that promise.'

'Why? Because you know you'll be much quieter than me?'

Tara laughed. 'You always will be more outspoken than I am. You tell it like it is. Fabulous birth. I loved it.'

She glanced back at Rayne, who was looking at them both as if they were mad.

Tara said, 'Can Simon and Angus come in now? Then everyone will go away so you three can get to know each other.'

Maeve looked at Rayne, who left it up to her, so Simon and Angus came in.

After congratulations Tara took Angus aside, and Maeve could distantly hear that they were discussing the labour and birth, the blood loss, which had been a little more than usual but had settled now, and she saw Simon pump Rayne's hand.

'You look ten years younger, Simon.' Maeve teased him, as he leaned in to kiss her.

'I gave them to Rayne. You, sister, dear, are a worry that thankfully is not mine any more.' He slapped Rayne on the back. 'Welcome to parenthood, Rayne. It's never going to be the same again.'

Rayne still looked in shock. For a tough guy that was pretty funny. 'I get that premonition.'

'You look pale,' Simon said.

'I feel pale.' Rayne glanced across at the new baby, a baby with his own huge dark eyes and maybe it was his mouth.

Maeve remembered a new mother telling her once that when her baby had been first born she could see all the familial likenesses but after a couple of hours she'd only been able to see her baby as whole. Maeve tried to imprint the separate features before that happened. She could see his father's stamp as plainly as if there was a big arrow pointing to it. The brows and nose were from her side.

Rayne shook his head and smiled at her and she soaked up like a hungry sponge the amazed awe he was exuding in bucketloads. She must look a mess but for once she didn't care.

Maeve relaxed back in the bed, letting the euphoria wash over her. She'd always loved watching the way new mums seemed to have this sudden surge of energy, and now she was feeling it herself. She did feel that if she needed to, she could pick up her baby and run and save them both. Probably needed a few more clothes on for that, though, or she'd be scaring people.

She'd discarded the sarong hours ago. Clothes had seemed too much of an annoying distraction in the maelstrom of labour. Her baby wriggled and began to suck his fingers on her chest. His head lay between her breasts with his cheek over her heart, and she smiled mistily down at him. Next he would dribble on his fingers then he would start to poke and rub her with his wet hands as his instincts began to take over.

Yep, he was doing that now, she was careful not to distract him as his little head lifted and he glanced around.

Simon and Angus left and she barely noticed as she saw her baby look and sniff for the dark areolas and the nipple he would find a way to arrive at.

'Watch him,' she whispered to Rayne, who leaned closer. 'He'll bob his head and wriggle and find his own way to where he needs to go.'

The baby's hands were kneading the softness of her breast under his tiny fingers, and his pink knees had drawn up under his belly as if he was going to crawl. 'Can't you just move him there?' Rayne said quietly.

'I could, but he needs to do a sequence. He needs to learn to poke out his tongue before he attaches, and he'll get there under his own steam at just the right moment.'

'He's only half an hour old.'

'That's why a baby stays skin to skin on his mother's chest for that first hour. Shouldn't get nursed by anyone else or have needles or get weighed or anything. It gives them the chance to do all this and the breast-feeding rates go through the roof if the baby attaches by himself. You watch.'

Baby was bobbing his head up and down like a little

jack-in-the-box, and Maeve saw him narrow his gaze on the left nipple and lean towards it. Tiny jerking movements, and shoulder leans, and hand scrunching, and slowly his body changed angle, his neck stretched, and incredibly he was almost there. Another wriggle and head bob and stretch, a series of little tongue peeps as he began to edge closer.

'Come on, little guy,' his father whispered, and she had a sudden vision of Rayne on the sideline of a tiny tots soccer game, being the dad yelling, 'Go, son!'

'Do you like Connor as his name?'

Rayne looked at her. Grinned. 'Spelt with two ns.'

'Lord, yes. As much as I like the Irish version of Conor, this child will not go through life having to spell his name, like I did.'

'Or have people say "Rain, as in wet?"'

'I was teasing.'

'Beautifully.' He leaned across and kissed her and in that moment her world was complete. 'I think he looks very much like a Connor.'

'You can choose the second name.' She saw his face shutter. Felt the withdrawal.

'I didn't do enough to warrant that privilege.'

She felt the slap of reality right when she didn't want to. Acknowledged he was feeling inadequate, and maybe even vulnerable at the moment but, hey, she was the one with no clothes and had exposed herself to the world. She narrowed her eyes at him. 'Then try harder.'

She searched in her mind for a way to make him see

that unless he wanted to, they would never lose him. 'Besides, he's going to cost you a fortune.'

He grinned and she saw the tension fall from his shoulders. Saw his look at her and the comprehension of how adroitly she'd manoeuvred him. Given him something he really could do, regardless of his parenting skills. His smile had a touch of the old bad-boy Rayne who'd been missing for the last few hours. 'In that case, how about the middle name of Sunshine?'

She knew he was kidding. She hoped he was kidding. 'Is that Sunshine from Rayne?'

Just then Connor found the nipple, poked out his tongue, opened his mouth wide and swooped. On! And didn't let go. Maeve gasped and smiled. 'That feels really weird.'

Rayne sat back in wonder. Tara leaned in from passing by and nodded. 'Good work, young man.'

'Connor.'

'Nice name. Welcome, Connor.' And she smiled at them both.

'Connor Sunshine.'

'Really?' She grinned at Maeve, who glared briefly at Rayne before looking back at her son. 'Awesome.' Then Tara had a brief feel of Maeve's belly, to check her uterus was contracting, gave it a little rub, then went back to sorting the room and writing the notes.

'You should've seen your face.'

But Maeve had moved on. Was gazing down at her son, whose jaw was working peacefully, his hands each side of his mouth, fingers digging into her breast every now and then. And all the while his big dark eyes stared up into her face. A swell of love came out of nowhere. Like a rush of heat. Her baby. She would protect this tiny scrap of humanity with her last breath.

'He's incredible,' she whispered, and all joking disappeared as they both watched him.

The next fifteen minutes were very peaceful. They didn't talk much, mostly just stared, bemused at the new person who had entered their lives and would change them as people for ever.

Until Maeve felt the first wave of dizziness and realised the wetness beneath her was spreading and she was beginning to feel faint.


Rayne watched the downy jaw go up and down on Maeve's breast and marvelled at the dark eyes watching his mother. He could feel his heart thawing and it wasn't comfortable. Maeve had had his baby.

He thought about the last twenty-four hours. Driving to Lyrebird Lake, not knowing if she would see him. Or knowing if that powerful current between them from the night so long ago had been real or instigated by the events that he'd known would follow.

Then seeing her this morning, pregnant, catching her as she'd fallen, daring to calculate on the slightest chance it could possibly be his child when Maeve should never have conceived. His fierce exultation that had drowned out his shock.

The swell of emotion was almost a physical pain in his chest as he went over the last tumultuous few hours of labour and finally the birth. Now here he was. A father with his son. A helpless newborn with him as a father. At least Connor had a father.

'Take him, Rayne.'

'He's still drinking.' Rayne was glued to the spectacle but something in her voice arrested him.

'Started bleeding,' she said faintly. 'Get Tara.' Her eyes rolled back, and she fainted like she had when he'd first seen her, only this time he caught his son.

Rayne's heart rate doubled. 'Tara!' Hell. He scooped Connor off his mother's chest as Maeve's arms fell slack, wrapped him in the bunny rug that had covered them both under the big blanket and hugged him to his chest as he leaned over Maeve.

Connor bellowed his displeasure at being lifted off his mother and automatically he patted his bottom through the rug.

Tara scooted back to the bed from her little writing table in the corner, lifted the sheet and sucked in a breath at the spreading stain on the sheets that just then flowed down the sides of the bed. 'Hit that red button over there for help and grab the IV trolley. We'll need to insert cannulas.' He saw her slide her hand over Maeve's soft belly, cup the top of her uterus through the abdominal wall and begin to rub strongly in a circular motion as he forced himself to turn away and do what needed to be done.

Once he'd pushed the emergency bell, he strode into

the treatment room he'd cased earlier and grabbed the IV trolley and pushed it back towards the bed, not as fast as he'd have liked because it was awkward with his son tucked like a little football against his chest. Connor had stopped crying and when Rayne glanced down at him his dark eyes were wide and staring.

Put the cannulas in. That he could do. He glanced around for somewhere to put Connor. Saw the little crib and tucked him in quickly. Connor started to cry.

'Sorry, mate.' He could find and secure veins on tiny infants so he should be able to do it on someone bigger. Someone he couldn't afford to lose.

'What size cannulas do you want?'

'Sixteen gauge. Two.'

Right. Found the size, the tourniquet, the antiseptic. Saw the tubes for blood tests. 'Which bloods?'

Another midwife hurried in after him and Tara glanced up and spoke to her. 'Get Angus back here first, then lower the bedhead so she's tipped down, give her oxygen, then draw me up a repeat ten units of syntocinon. Obs we'll get when we get a chance.'

Tara hadn't taken her hand off the uterus and the flow had slowed to a trickle but the loss from just those few minutes of a relaxed uterus had astounded Rayne with its ferocity. At least two litres had pooled in the bed.

She turned to him. 'Purple times two, one orange and one blue. Coags, full blood count, four units crossmatch.'

'Angus is on his way,' the other midwife said, as she lowered the bed and slipped the oxygen mask onto

Maeve's white face. 'Just some oxygen, Maeve.' The girl spoke loudly and as he withdrew the blood for the tests he realised Maeve might be able to hear.

'Hang in there, Maeve. Don't be scared. We'll get it sorted.' Incredibly his voice sounded confident and calm. Not how he was feeling on the inside. He wondered if Tara was as calm as she seemed.

Angus hurried in. Took over from Tara down the business end, checking swiftly to see if there was any damage they'd missed, but the sheer volume and speed of the loss indicated a uterus that wasn't clamping down on those powerful arteries that had sustained the pregnancy. Tara began assembling IV lines and drugs. She gave one bag of plain fluids to him and he connected and secured it. Rayne turned the flow rate to full-bore volume replacement until they could get blood.

An orderly arrived and the nursing supervisor who carried the emergency record started writing down times and drugs as she listened to Tara who spoke as she sorted the emergency kit.

The second midwife was writing Maeve's name on the blood-test tubes. When she was finished she wrote out a request form and sent the samples on their way. Then she hooked Maeve up to the monitor and they all glanced across at the rapid heartbeats shooting across the screen in frantic blips. Her blood pressure wasn't too bad yet but he knew birthing women could sustain that until it fell in a sudden plunge. His neck prickled in the first premonition of disaster.

Angus looked up at the second orderly. 'Bring back two units of O-neg blood. We'll give those until we can cross-match.'

'I'm O-neg if you need more.' Blood. She needed blood, Rayne thought, and wondered how often this happened for them all to be so smooth at the procedures. He glanced at Maeve's face as she moaned and began to stir with the increase in blood flowing to her brain from the head-down position change.

He wanted to go to her but Tara handed him the second flask loaded with the drugs to contract the uterus. 'Run it at two hundred and fifty mils an hour,' she murmured, and he nodded, connected it and set the rate. Then stood back out of the way. The whole scene was surreal. One moment he had been soaking in magic and the next terror had been gripping his throat as Maeve's life force had been seeping away.

'Given ergot yet?' Angus was calm.

'No. But it's coming.' Tara was drawing up more drugs. Rayne's legs felt weak and he glanced across at Connor roaring in his cot. He picked him up and the little boy immediately settled. He hugged his son to him.

'You okay?' Angus looked at him.

No, he wasn't, but it wasn't about him. He crossed to sit back in the chair beside Maeve's head so he could talk to her as she stirred. They didn't need him staring like a fool and fainting, with his son in his arms. Couldn't imagine how frightening this would be for her. 'It's okay, sweetheart. Just rest. Angus is here.'

Her eyelids flickered and for a brief moment she looked at him before her eyelids fell again. 'Okay,' she breathed.

He looked at Angus. 'Why is she still bleeding?'

'Might be an extra lobe of placenta she grew that we missed.' Angus was massaging the uterus through Maeve's belly like Tara had been doing. 'Or could just be a lazy uterus. Or could be a tear somewhere. We'll try the drugs but if it doesn't settle, because of the amount of loss, we'll have to take her to Theatre.'

Angus glanced at the nursing supervisor. 'Call Ben and Andy, clue them in, and have operating staff standing by. We can always send them home.'

Nobody mentioned it was early Boxing Day morning. The supervisor nodded and picked up the phone. 'And phone Simon,' Angus said, with a quick glance at Rayne. 'We'll need his consent.'

Consent for what? Operating theatres? He could give that consent. No, he couldn't. He had no legal claim on Maeve or his son. He had nothing except Maeve's permission to be here. He was no one. Shook himself with contempt. It wasn't about him.

And what would they do? But he knew. They would do what they needed to do to save her life. And if Maeve could never have children again? He thought of the powerful woman who had majestically navigated the birth process with gusto. Imagined her distress if the chance would never be hers again.

He imagined Maeve dying and reared back from

the thought. They would get through it. She had to get through it.

'She's started to bleed again,' Angus said to Tara. 'Get me the F2 alpha and I'll inject it into her uterus.' To the other midwife, he said, 'Check the catheter isn't blocked and I'll compress the uterus with my hands until we can get to the OR.'

The next two hours were the worst in Rayne's life. Worse than when they'd come for him in Simon's house and he'd seen Maeve's distress, worse than when he'd been sentenced to prison, worse than when he'd found out his mother had died.

Maeve went in and for a long time nobody came out. Simon sat beside him in the homey little waiting room that was like no other waiting room he'd ever seen.

It had a big stone water cooler and real glasses to drink from. A kettle and little fridge to put real milk in your tea and a big jar of home-made oatmeal biscuits. And a comfortable lounge that he couldn't sit on.

He paced. Connor didn't seem to mind because he slept through it in his bunny rug. Rayne couldn't put him down. Not because Connor cried but because Rayne couldn't bear to have empty arms while he waited for Maeve to come through those doors.

'Do you want me to take Connor?'

'No!' He didn't even think about it. Looked down at his son asleep against his chest. Doing at least something that he knew Maeve would like while he waited. 'What's taking them so long?'

'She'll go to Recovery when they've sorted everything. Then Dad will come through and talk to us. Or maybe Ben or Andy.'

'Are they good?'

'Superb.'

'I feel so useless. I worried about being a good enough father. That's nothing in the big picture.'

'It's not a nothing. But this is bigger. But you'll be fine. She'll be fine.'

Rayne heard the thread of doubt in Simon's voice and stopped. Looked at the man who would become his brother-in-law. Because he would marry Maeve. If she'd have him. He didn't deserve her. Would never have presumed to think she'd have him. But after this fear of losing her he'd take her faith in him and hold it and be the best dad a man could be. And the best husband.

Surely that would be the start of good enough?

He had a sudden vision of waking up in bed beside Maeve for every morning to come for the rest of his life. How the hell would he get out of bed?

But Simon. He'd forgotten that Maeve was the sister Simon was most protective about. How could he forget that in the circumstances? Because he needed to think of other people in his life now. He wasn't alone. He had Maeve, and Connor, and apparently a whole family or two. He glanced down at his son again and then at Simon.

He stopped where Simon was sitting. 'Can you hold him for a sec? My arm's gone to sleep.' It hadn't but he could see Simon needed something to hold as well. Tara was in the operating theatre with Maeve and she couldn't help him.

He watched his friend's face soften as he took the sleeping infant. Saw the tension loosen in the rigid shoulders. He missed the weight of Connor but was glad that Simon had him for the moment. Funny how a tiny helpless baby could help both of them to be stronger.

And then the doors opened and Angus came out. He looked at Simon first and then at Rayne.

'She had a spontaneous tear in her uterus. Probably a weakness in the muscle she was born with. It took a while to find it and she lost a lot of blood. But she's stable now.'

Rayne felt his body sag. Was actually glad that Simon held Connor.

'No more normal births for her. And a Caesarean in a bigger centre next time in case it does it again.'

So they had saved her uterus. Not bad for a tiny country hospital. 'So more blood transfusions?'

'And fresh frozen plasma and cryo. They'll need some of your blood over at the blood bank because we've used nearly all of theirs.'

It was the least he could do.

'Do we need to ship her out to a bigger hospital?' Simon had stood and his father was smiling at him with his nephew in his arms.

'I don't think so. And I would if I thought she needed to go. Would have spirited her there half an hour ago if I could have, but the crisis is past.' He grinned at Simon, who was swaying with the baby. 'Can't you men put that baby down?'

Rayne glanced at his friend. The relief was soaking in slowly. 'We're sharing the comfort. So she'll be fine?'

'She'll have to spend a few more days in hospital than she expected but she'll be spoiled rotten in Maternity.'

Rayne thought of going back to the manse without Maeve and Connor. 'Can I stay there, too? In the room with her and Connor? Help her with the baby?'

Angus raised his brows. 'Can't see any reason why not. Might mean that Tara will hand her over because she's not budging and I think she's nearly out on her feet.' He glanced at his son with a tired smile. 'Tara did a great job, Simon.'

So many amazing people here. So many he had to thank. Rayne stepped up to Angus and shook his hand. How could he ever repay them? 'Thank you. Thank the other guys.'

'We'll call in a favour if we need it.' Angus smiled.

Rayne looked at him. Saw a man who would be ruthless if he needed something for his little country hospital, and understood that. Smiled at it. Got the idea that resources could be hard to come by here when life threw a curve ball but those who had chosen to live here had saved his Maeve. They could have him any time they wanted.

He saw that he'd been accepted and was therefore fair game. He could deal with that. Thought for the first time about where Maeve might want to live and that, for the moment, if it was here he could cope with that.

Ten minutes later Simon took Tara home and Rayne carried Connor back to the room that would be Maeve's. The night midwife, Misty, took him through to the nursery and they finally got around to weighing Connor and giving him his needles, then she ran her hands all over him, checking that everything was fine.

She listened to his heart and handed the stethoscope to Rayne with a smile. 'Tara said you were a paed.'

Rayne listened. His son's heart sounded perfect. No valve murmurs. No clicks. He ran his own hands over him as if he were a baby he had been asked to check. But this wasn't a baby of some other lucky couple. This was his son. His hands stilled. This child depended on him for all the things his own father hadn't given him and he would deliver.

Misty handed him clothes and he looked at the tiny singlet. Thought of Maeve.

'Maeve's missing this. Wish she was here to share it.'

'Have you got your phone?'

He looked at her blankly. It wasn't like he could ring her. It must have shown on is face.

Misty laughed. 'You are tired. I can take photos of you dressing Connor and you can show her later.'

He shook his head. He should have thought of that. Handed her the phone in his pocket and Misty started snapping.

Rayne glanced at the sink as he lifted the singlet to stretch it widely over Connor's head. 'So when do we bath him?'

Misty shook her head. 'Not for twenty-four hours. He still smells like Mum and it helps him bond and feel secure and remember what to do when he goes for his next feed.'

Rayne vaguely remembered that from something Maeve had said, along with the skin to skin with Mum in the first hour.

Connor stared sleepily up at him as he dressed him. 'And what if he gets hungry before Maeve comes back?'

'He'll be fine. Tara said he fed well at birth. That's great. He could sleep up to twelve hours before he wakes up enough to feed again this first day. It's made such a difference letting them have that one long sleep after birth. Breastfed babies feed at least six to ten times a day and he'll catch up later.'

'I should know this stuff.' He shook his head. 'I've been out of it for nearly a year and in the States the doctors don't really discuss breastfeeding issues.'

She laughed. 'Everyone does everything here.'

He captured and pulled Connor's long fingers gently through the sleeve of the sleeping gown. All the experience came back as he turned the little boy over onto his front and tied the cords of his nightgown. Made him feel not so useless. He could do this for Maeve. He folded the gown back carefully so it wouldn't get damp if he wet his nappy. 'Don't you use disposable nappies here?'

'Not until after they do their first wee. Those new disposables are too efficient and it's hard to tell sometimes.'

'Fair enough.' He clicked the pin with satisfaction and tugged the secure nappy. Good job.

Misty nodded approvingly. 'You can even do a cloth and pin nappy without help. Not many dads could do that the first day.' The phone rang and she handed him a clean bunny rug. 'Excuse me.'

She poked her head back into the nursery. 'They're bringing Maeve back now.'

Rayne felt relief sweep over him as he wrapped Connor and put him snugly back into his little wheeled cot. Tucked him under the sheets so he didn't feel abandoned. His eyes were shut. Misty had put nappies and wipes and assorted linen under there in case he needed it in the room overnight and Rayne trundled the cot out the door and down the hallway, where two men were pushing a wheeled bed into the room.

His first sight of Maeve made him draw in his breath. She looked like Snow White, icily beautiful, but deeply asleep and as white as the sheets she lay on with her eyes shut. Her black hair made her look even paler and his heart clutched in shock. Unconsciously his hand went down until he was resting it on Connor's soft hair, as if he needed the touch of his son to stay calm.

She stirred as the bed stopped against the wall of the room. Blinked slowly and then she opened her eyes, focused and saw him. Licked her dry lips. Then softly, barely perceptibly, she murmured, 'Hi, there, Rayne.'

'Hi, there, Princess Maeve.' He pulled the cot up to the side of the bed. 'Your son is beautiful.'

'Our son,' she whispered.

'I love him already.' He didn't know where the words had come from but he realised it was somewhere so deep and definite in him that it resonated with truth and the smile on Maeve's face as she closed her eyes assured him it was the thing she most wanted to hear.

'Then I can leave him to you while I sleep.'

'I'm here. I'm not going anywhere.'

'Thank you.' And she breathed more deeply as she drifted back to sleep.

He watched her chest slowly rise and fall. Glanced at the blood running into a vein in her left arm and mentally thanked the donor who had provided it. Checked the drugs running into a right-arm vein. Watched Misty as she straightened the IV lines, the monitor leads and the automatic blood-pressure machine, set to record every half an hour, until they were all in a position she could glance at every time she came into the room.

Rayne shifted his intended chair slightly so he could see too. Frowned over the fact that Maeve's heart rate was still elevated, her blood pressure still low. But

respirations were normal. And even as she slept just a
tinge of colour was returning to her face.

He pushed Connor's cot quietly towards the big chair
beside the bed and sank back into it. Then pulled the cot
halfway between the bed and the chair so that either of
them could stretch out their arm and could touch their
son. Then he settled down to watch Maeve.

# CHAPTER TEN

MAEVE WOKE AND the room was quiet. It was still dark through the windows outside and her belly felt like it was on fire. At first she thought Rayne was asleep but he shifted and sat straighter when he saw she was awake and she wondered vaguely if he'd been awake all this time. Watching over her. It was an incredible thought.

'Hi.' She couldn't keep a frown off her face.

'Pain not good?'

She decided shaking her head would be too much movement. 'Eight out of ten.'

He stood up. 'I'll get Misty.' Left the room in a few long strides and she tried to lessen the tension in her body. What the heck happened to her beautiful natural birth? And how had she ended up being sore both ends? Now, that sucked. Closed her eyes and decided to worry about it tomorrow.

Misty came back in with Rayne and brought some tablets and a bottle of water with a straw.

Rayne slid his arm under her shoulders and eased

her up so slowly and gently that it barely hurt to move. She swallowed the pills and savoured the water as it ran down her throat as he laid her down again.

Misty checked all her observations then Connor's, without rousing him, and then lifted the sheets and checked her wound and her bleeding and nodded with satisfaction at both. 'Looking beautiful.'

She heard Rayne, say, 'You midwives are weird.'

It would hurt to laugh. Misty laughed and left the room and Maeve smiled. She turned her head carefully and looked at Connor. Sleeping like a baby. Hugged that thought to herself then looked at Rayne, who was watching her. There was something different about him.

'You okay?'

He smiled and there was so much caring in the look he gave her that she felt herself become warm. 'I'm okay, as long as you are,' he said.

Meaning? 'Been a pretty torrid day?'

He stood up. Smiled down at her. Took her hand in his and turned it over. Careful of the IV lines, she thought. It was just a hand. Then he kissed her palm and it became a magic hand.

Then he said, 'A first for me as well. You scared the daylights out of me.'

Funnily, she hadn't been scared. 'I wasn't scared. You said not to be. Thank you for being there.'

He shook his head. 'Connor is amazing.' He looked towards the door. 'These people are amazing.' He glanced at her. 'You are beyond amazing.' Then he leaned down. Kissed her dry lips and tucked her in. 'Go back to sleep.'

When she woke in the morning Rayne was still there. His eyes were closed but for some reason she didn't think he was asleep. The drips had stopped feeding blood and had changed to clear fluid, so she guessed that was a good thing.

Connor was still sleeping. She reminded herself that babies could sleep up to ten or twelve hours after the first feed to get over the birth and she didn't need to feel guilty she hadn't fed him again. Remembered he'd probably make her pay for it later by feeding every time she wanted to put him back in his cot. Though she couldn't imagine wanting to put him back in his cot. It felt so long since she'd held him in her arms.

'Good morning.' Rayne's eyes were open. 'How do you feel?'

'I must look like a dishrag.'

'You look beautiful. A little pale and interesting as well.'

'At least I'm interesting.' She winced as she smiled too hard.

'I'll get Misty.' He left and came back with Misty, who was almost ready to hand her over to the morning staff.

So they repeated the whole Rayne lifting her, tablet taking, observation thing, and this time she didn't want to go back to sleep afterwards. She wanted to change out of her horrible gown and get into her nightie. Get up and shower, but she didn't think she'd be able to do it.

Could feel herself getting cross. 'Why don't you go back to the manse and have a sleep?'

Rayne lifted his brows and looked at her. Smiled. 'Later. When you have a wash, and get into your nightie, and have Connor's next feed. I don't know you well but I know you enough to see you want to be fresh, and hold your son, soon.'

He looked at her and shrugged. 'I want to help you, and help the midwife helping you, and I can be the muscle so you don't have to hurt yourself trying to do all those things.'

She looked at him. Flabbergasted. Was this guy for real? 'Aren't you tired?'

'No more than you. I'll sleep later.'

'I can't let you do that.'

Another enigmatic smile. 'You're not running this show, Princess Maeve. I am.'

Ooh. Bossy. She was too weak, and it was hard not to sort of like it. 'Then maybe later, if you're good, you can put me in the shower,' she said with a tired smile.

'I don't think you'll be up to a shower but we'll see.'

But she dug her heels in. 'I'm not being washed in bed like a baby.' They all looked at Rayne for help.

'Fine,' he said.

So they agreed on a compromise before Misty went off. Once Maeve's pain tablets had kicked in and she wasn't too sore, they disconnected her IVs for the few minutes it would take, and Rayne lifted her to the edge of the bed then carried her to the shower chair and the hand-held shower nozzle, and gently hosed her all over, washed her back and her legs, until she began to feel human again. Amazing what some hot water and a change of position could do.

Misty made her bed up with fresh sheets and plumped up her pillows so that when Rayne had helped her dry and dress again she could sink back and relax.

'I'm walking back to the bed under my own steam.' She glared at him. He held up his hands.

'Your call. I'm happy to watch.'

So she eased herself into a standing position, and it wasn't too bad now that she'd loosened up. She tentatively took a few steps, knowing there was no way he would let her fall because his arms were right behind her. Not a bad feeling to have.

She straightened up more and she felt tender, but okay. She could do this. She looked up at Rayne to poke out her tongue, but then a wave of faintness caught up with her.

He must have seen the colour drain from her face because he said, 'No, you don't.' Before it could get too disastrous she found herself back in her bed, with Misty pulling up the sheets and saying, 'Someone needs to tell you about the blood you lost last night.'

When the world stopped turning she looked up to see Rayne frowning darkly at her. She thought vaguely that he was still too damn good looking even when he frowned. 'You're a stubborn woman.'

But Misty smiled at her as she tucked the sheets in. 'Stubborn women are the best kind because they never give in.'

Rayne rolled his eyes. 'Another mad midwife saying.'

Five minutes later Connor made a little snorting noise, and they both turned their heads to see, watched him shift in his cot, blink and then open his eyes.

'He's awake.'

Rayne saw the longing on Maeve's face and was so glad he'd stayed for this.

'Good morning, young man. Your mother has been through a lot while she waited for you to wake up.' He reached down and untucked the sheets and opened the bunny rug. A black tar train wreck lay inside. Was even glad he'd stayed for this. He'd cleaned up enough dirty nappies in his time to make short work of even the biggest mess and it seemed his son had quite a capacity. Go you, son.

Connor grumbled but didn't cry, as if confident of the handling he was receiving.

Rayne looked across at the bed and Maeve was holding her stomach to stop herself laughing, and they grinned at each other in mutual parental pride. Then he pinned up the new nappy efficiently and lifted Connor away from his bunny rug in his hospital clothes so

Maeve could see his long legs and feet as he tucked him carefully in her arms.

Rayne watched her face soften and her mouth curve into such a smile, and the ball in his chest tightened and squeezed. This stuff had turned him into a wimp but he wouldn't have missed it for the world. He tucked a pillow under Maeve's arm so she didn't have to hold Connor's weight and watched as she loosened her neckline to lift out a breast.

Now, there was a sight he'd never tire of as Connor turned his head and poked out his tongue. Rayne put his hand under Connor's shoulders to help Maeve manoeuvre him closer until Connor opened his mouth, had a few practise attempts and then a big wide mouth and onto the breast. Just like that.

Maeve sighed and rested more comfortably back on the pillows, and Rayne sat back with wonder filling him until he thought he would burst.

My God.

How had this happened? Yesterday he had been lost, without purpose or future, a social misfit and almost-pariah, following his instinct towards a woman who so easily could have turned him away.

Now he had a family, Maeve and Connor and him—his family. And this morning he knew there would be battles of will, adjustments to make, discoveries and habits and ideas that might clash, but he could never doubt he had love for this incredible woman he had almost lost as soon as he'd found her, and that love would only grow bigger—probably daily. The future that was theirs stretched before them like a miracle. A Christmas miracle.

Rayne looked with wonder at the big country-style clock on the wall and watched the hand click over to six-thirty a.m. Exactly twenty-four hours since his car had rolled down the street and swerved towards the woman he'd been searching for as she'd walked towards him.

'Rayne?' Maeve's voice was softly concerned. 'You okay?'

He shook his head. The room was blurry. Stood up and stepped in close to the bed, leant down and slid his arm around the two of them and gently rested his cheek on Maeve's hair. He'd just discovered that she made him feel brand new. That he could do anything. And he most certainly was the only man for this job of looking after his family. 'I need to hug the most important two people in my life.'

She rested back into his arms with a contented sigh. 'Feel free any time.'

Over the next day there were a lot of firsts.

Connor's first bath, a joyous occasion where Maeve sat like a princess packed up in pillows and watched while Rayne deftly floated and massaged and swirled his son around like he'd been doing it for years.

'You're so good at that,' Maeve said approvingly. 'Still, I always tell the mums it's nice to shower with your baby. One of the parents undresses and hands baby in to go skin to skin with the person in the shower and the other—that will be you Rayne.' She grinned up at him. 'You lost. You just get to take him back and dry and dress him while I have the fun part.'

Rayne grinned. 'Poor me. I have to watch the naked lady with the awesome breasts in the shower with my baby.' Maeve held her tummy and tried not to laugh.

Then came the visitors with hugs and kisses of relief.

Also along came things for Connor. His first knitted set of bonnet, booties, cardigan and shawl all lovingly created by his step-great-grandmother, Louisa, who also brought food just in case the hospital ran out.

His first pair of tiny jeans and black T-shirt to match his dad's, from Uncle Simon and Tara.

Goodness knew where he'd got it from, because he'd barely left her side, but Rayne produced a bright yellow rubber duck for Connor's bath because his mother loved ducks.

Tiny booties shaped like soccer boots with knitted bumps for spikes from Mia and the girls at morning teatime and a welcome-baby card that had a three-dimensional baby actually swinging in a seat from a tree that the girls had fallen in love with.

But the excitement all took its toll.

'You look exhausted. Enough. I'll go back to the manse and you sleep.' Rayne stood up.

It was lunchtime, and Maeve was ready for a sleep.

Rayne kissed her. 'I'll come back any time you need me. If you want to get out of bed or Connor is unsettled and you want someone to nurse him, I'm the man. Ring me.' He looked at her. 'Promise.'

'Bossy.'

'Please.'

'Okay.' Not a bad back-up plan. She watched him go with a prickle of weak tears in her eyes and sighed into the bed.

'He did well,' Tara said, as she closed the blinds of the room.

'He did amazingly.'

'You did amazingly. But I agree with you and with him. It's time for sleep.' She checked Connor was fast asleep after his feed and quietly backed out.

As the door shut Maeve relaxed back into the bed and glanced at her downy-cheeked son. It had happened. She couldn't tell if he looked like either of them because now he looked like her darling baby Connor.

The whole labour and birth were over. And the next stage was just beginning.

The beginning of shared parenthood with a man she knew she loved. She didn't know if Rayne felt the same, but she was too tired and tender to worry about that now. That he was here was enough.

Rayne's solid support had been a thousand times stronger than she'd dared to hope for, his pre-birth nerves were a precious memory to keep and maybe occasionally tease him about, and she could see that Rayne would take his responsibilities to Connor and to her very seriously.

Lying in Rayne's arms yesterday seemed so far away in time with what had happened since then but as she drifted off to sleep she knew there was so much they could build on. She just needed to be patient, she thought with sleepy smile on her face, and trust in Rayne.

# CHAPTER ELEVEN

FOUR DAYS LATER Maeve went home with Connor and Rayne—her family. Home being to the manse and the fabulous cooking of Louisa, who had decided the new mother needed feeding up.

Rayne, being fed three meals a day at least, was chopping wood at an alarming rate to try and keep his weight down from Louisa's cooking.

Simon went back to Sydney for work and planned to return each alternate weekend, and Tara was going to fly down to Sydney on the other weekends until their wedding in four weeks' time.

Selfishly, Maeve was glad that Tara had stayed with them, instead of following Simon to Sydney, and with Rayne booked to do the occasional shift over in the hospital on call, she had ample back-up help with Tara and, of course, Louisa, who was in seventh heaven with a baby in the house.

They'd shifted Connor into Rayne's room with the connecting door open and Rayne bounced out of their bed to change and bring Connor to her through the night.

Life took on a rosy glow of contentment as she and Rayne and Connor grew to be a family. The joy of waking in the morning in Rayne's tender arms, the wonder on his face when he looked at her with Connor, the gradual healing of her body, the steady increase of confidence in breastfeeding, managing Connor's moods and signs of tiredness, and the ability to hand him to his father's outstretched hands all gelled. Life was wonderful.

Her brother's wedding approached and their mother was coming. It was four weeks after the birth of Connor and Maeve was suddenly nervous.

Rayne decided Maeve had been twitchy all morning. Her mother was due to arrive along with Maeve's three older sisters. He'd seen her change her clothes four times and Connor's jumpsuit twice before the expected event.

On arrival her mother kissed Maeve's cheek and an awkward few moments had passed right at the beginning when she looked Rayne over with a sigh and then stepped forward and shook his hand.

'Hello, Rayne. Maeve said you were very good when Connor was born.'

So this was what Maeve would look like when she was older. Stunning, sophisticated and polished, though Desiree was blonde, perhaps not naturally because she had dark eyebrows, but a very successful-looking blonde.

He glanced at Maeve and the woman holding his

son had it all over her mum for warmth. 'It was Maeve who was amazing.'

A cool smile. 'I'm glad she's happy.'

'So am I.' Which left what either of them really meant open to interpretation.

Maeve broke into the conversation. 'You remember my sisters, Ellen, Claire and Stephanie.'

'Ladies.' He smiled at the three women, who were cooing at Connor.

Maeve hung onto his hand and Connor was unusually unsettled, probably receptive to the vibes his mother was giving off.

Luckily Desiree was swept up into the final wedding preparations and they all managed to ease back on the tension for the rest of the afternoon.

The next day Simon and Tara's wedding was held in the little local church and most of the town had come to celebrate with them.

It was a simple and incredibly romantic celebration. The church ladies had excelled themselves with floral decorations. Tara looked like the fairy on top of the cake, thanks to the absolute delight Mia, Simon's stepmother, had taken in spoiling her, and beside him, Simon nearly cried in the church when she entered.

A big lump had come to Rayne's throat when he thought about his friend finding such happiness and he couldn't help his glance past the bride and groom to the chief bridesmaid, his Maeve, who looked incredible in the simple blue gown Tara had chosen for her attendants.

Except for the divine cleavage, nobody would suspect Maeve had recently given birth, because she'd returned to her pre-pregnancy size almost immediately.

As Rayne listened to the words of the priest the certainty inside him grew that he could answer yes to all of it.

By the time Simon and Tara were married all he wanted to do was hold Maeve in his arms and tell her he loved her.

But he would have to wait.

The reception was a huge outdoor picnic, all the speeches a success, and the ecstatically happy couple finally left for their honeymoon in Hawaii and would then fly on to Boston, where Maeve's father waited to meet his stepson's new wife.

Back at the manse after the wedding Rayne needed a beer and a bloke to drink with, because the only sane woman was Louisa, who kept feeding him.

Maeve still hadn't settled, though she seemed to stress more than anything about Connor being even a little upset, which was strange when before she'd sailed along blithely and just enjoyed him. The help from her mother wasn't doing its job.

Rayne decided he would survive until Maeve's mother left. He'd lived with worse people and his lips twitched. Could just imagine Maeve's mother's downturned mouth if she knew he was comparing her to a cellmate.

'There you are, Rayne.' The object of his thoughts appeared and he plastered a smile on his face.

'Connor is crying and Maeve asked for you. Though I can't see what you can do that I can't.'

'Thank you.' Excellent reason to escape. 'The wedding was great but I think everyone is tired now. I'd better go and see.'

When he gently opened the door to their room he found Maeve with tears trickling down her face as Connor screamed and kicked and fought the breast.

'Hey, Connor, what are you doing to your poor mum?'

Maeve looked up tragically and he crossed the room to sit beside her on the bed. He dropped a kiss on her head. 'He won't feed. And Mum keeps telling me to put him on the bottle.'

'Bless her,' Rayne said, tongue-in-cheek and Maeve's eyes flew to his, ready to hotly dispute that, until she saw his smile.

Her own smile, while still watery, gradually appeared. 'She makes me crazy.'

'Really? I hadn't noticed.' He leaned forward, kissed her, remembered again how each day he felt more blessed, and took the unsettled Connor from her. Tucked him over his shoulder and patted his bottom. 'It's been a big day. And you've been busy making sure Tara had a fabulous time so you've run yourself into the ground. Why don't I take Connor for a drive and you can have a rest before tea?'

'No, thanks.'

Maeve looked even sadder and he frowned. 'What?'

'Can't I come with you both?'

He grinned. 'You mean escape? And leave your mother here without us?'

Maeve looked guilty at the disloyal idea. 'She means well.'

'I know. Maybe we could get Louisa to look after her. Your mum's probably tired too. It's a long flight and she only got here yesterday.' He had a vision. One that he'd been building up to for days now but had wanted to leave until after the wedding. 'I'd really like to take Connor to the duck pond. Would you like to come with us for an hour until sunset?'

Maeve nodded, looked brighter already, so he left her to get ready, and sought out Louisa first, begged a favour he promised to repay, then found Maeve's mother.

Gently does it, he warned himself. 'What do you think if I take Connor for a little drive. Just to get him asleep in the car?'

A judicious nod from the dragon. 'That's an excellent idea.'

Now for the smooth part. 'Maeve wants to come but she feels bad about leaving you on your own.' Desiree opened her mouth but before she could invite herself he said, 'But I see Louisa had just made you a lovely afternoon tea and is dying to have a good chat with you. What would you like to do?' Opened his eyes wide.

Desiree slid gracefully into the trap and relief expanded in his gut. 'Oh. Poor Louisa. It would be rude not to stay for that. Of course.' She looked pleased. 'How thoughtful. She really is a lovely woman.'

'One of my favourite people.' And wasn't that true. Then he escaped to his family and bundled them into the car.

Ten minutes later Maeve sat on the bench in front of the lake, holding Connor in the crook of her arm. Their son had decided he preferred to feed alfresco and was very happily feeding. Every now and then Maeve would throw breadcrumbs to the ducks with her free hand.

Rayne stood behind her, gently rubbing her shoulders. They both had smiles on their faces.

Maeve said, 'I don't think I could bear to lose a man who rubs my shoulders like you do.'

Rayne felt the happiness expand inside him. 'Does this mean you want me to stay?'

She twisted her neck to look at him and pretended to consider it judiciously. 'Yes, I think so.'

Rayne had waited for just this opening and unfortunately in the euphoria of successful strategies he rushed it. 'Only if you'll marry me.' The words were out before he could stop them and he cursed his inability to be smooth and romantic when she deserved it all. He'd done everything the wrong way around here.

She opened her mouth to reply and quickly he moved around to face her and held up his finger. 'Wait.'

'So bossy,' she murmured, and he smiled as he went

down on one knee beside her—right there in front of the ducks.

'Please. Wait for me to do it properly.' He took her free hand in his, brushed the crumbs off it and kissed her fingers. Maeve leant back against the bench and Connor ignored them both as he continued with his afternoon tea.

Rayne drew a deep breath and let it go. Let everything go, let the past, the mistakes and the pain and uncertainty all go so they could start fresh and new and perfect. Because the three of them deserved it. 'My darling, gorgeous, sexy…' he paused, smiled at her '…impossible Maeve—'

Before he could finish she'd interrupted. 'Impossible?'

'Shh.' He frowned at her and she closed her mouth. 'Darling Maeve—' and he couldn't keep the smile off his face '—will you do me the honour, please, of becoming my wife and share with me the rest of my life?'

Her face glowed at him, a trace of pink dusting the high cheekbones that were still far too pale. 'Now, that, as a proposal of marriage, was worth waiting for.'

'An answer would be good. Come on.'

She teased him. 'My darling, strong, sexy as all get out Rayne.' Leaned forward and kissed him while he knelt before her. Connor still ignored them both. 'Yes. Please. Pretty please. I would love to be your wife and share your life.'

His relief expanded and he squeezed her hand. 'You won't regret it.'

Her face softened. 'I know I won't. But my mother wants a big wedding.'

He smiled. He could do that. It was a small price to pay for the world he now had. 'I thought she might. As long as Connor is pageboy and you are my bride, I will agree to anything.' He stood up and hugged her gently again and smiled into her hair. 'It's not going to be dull.'

A month later Maeve woke on the morning of her wedding in her parents' house huge in Boston. Down the hall Tara was sleeping without her new husband because Simon had gone to support Rayne on the night before his wedding. She wished she'd been able to stay with Rayne but they would never have got that past her mother.

Connor stirred beside her and she sat up with a warm feeling of relief in her stomach and reached for him. Rayne would be missing Connor and her as much as they missed him.

How could life change so dramatically in just two months? The answer was simple. Rayne loved her. Which was lucky because her mother had put them all through hoops as she married the first of her daughters off in the grand fashion.

There had been family dinners at exclusive restaurants, wedding breakfasts under the marquee in the back garden, and bridal teas with all the local ladies, as well as bridal showers and multiple rehearsals and today, finally, the wedding of the year.

Maeve had always wanted a big wedding, the chance to be the big star, but funnily enough now that it was here she knew she would have been happy with a two-line agreement in front of a celebrant as long as she was married to Rayne.

Her mother wouldn't have been happy, though, and it was good to see Desiree finally pleased with her. But today she would marry Rayne, they would pack up and leave on their honeymoon then head back to Lyrebird Lake, and Maeve couldn't wait.

Her husband-to-be had been amazing. Patient. Comforting when she'd become stressed, loving when she'd least expected it but had secretly needed that reassurance, and always so brilliantly patient and capable with Connor—and her mother.

When she thought about it, Rayne had learnt to be patient with mothers very early in his life and he was showing his skills now.

Her over-achieving sisters were here and she realised she'd finally grown out of worrying that about a hundred relatives were scattered in nearby hotels. She and Rayne and Connor were united in the birth of their family and their future and she couldn't wait.

Eight hours later Rayne stood beside Simon, this time as the groom and Simon the best man, and Rayne's hands were just slightly shaking.

In Boston, their bigger than *Ben Hur* wedding that Maeve's mother had organised had seemed to never get any closer.

But finally, today, it would happen. Their family would officially be joined forever. Maeve was putting so much trust in him he felt humbled, and before God, and before the ceremony even started, he silently vowed he would never let her down.

The music started, the congregation stood, and then she was there. A heartbeat, a shaft of divine light, and she appeared. Standing at the end of that very long, very floral-bouqueted aisle, with her father beside her and a huge church full of people to witness them being bound together.

Maeve's next older sister, the first bridesmaid, was almost up to them, coming closer with stately precision, Connor in her arms in his tiny suit, because that was the only thing Rayne had insisted on.

Then the second sister, and then the third, and then… Maeve. Sweeping down the aisle towards him, way too fast. To hell with the slow walk, he didn't bother to look for her mother's frown at the break in protocol, just grinned at her and held out his hand. He loved this woman so much.

The mass began and he missed most of it as he stared at the vision beside him. Remembered the last two months, the joy he'd found, the deep well of love he hadn't realised he'd had to give.

'Do you take this woman…?'

Hell, yes! He remembered to let the reverend finish. More waiting until finally he could say, 'I will.'

'Do you, Maeve, take this man…?'

The words drifted as he stared again into her eyes. Those eloquent eyes that said he was her hero, always would be, that she believed in him so much and loved him. What more could a man want?

Then she said, 'I will.' That was what he wanted!

'With the power vested in me and before this congregation I now declare you man and wife…' And it was done. Rayne lifted the veil, stared into her tear-filled eyes and kissed his wife with all the love in his heart in the salute.

Maeve clutched her husband's hand and couldn't help the huge smile on her face. The cameras were flashing, she was moving and signing and smiling, and all the time Rayne was beside her. Protecting her, loving her, and finally reaching out to take Connor from her sister so that he carried their son and it was time for the three of them to walk back up the aisle as a family.

Maeve met Rayne's eyes, saw the love and knew this was the start of an incredible life with the man she had always loved. She couldn't wait.

\* \* \* \* \*

# LET'S TALK
## *Romance*

For exclusive extracts, competitions
and special offers, find us online:

 facebook.com/millsandboon

@MillsandBoon

 @MillsandBoonUK

**Get in touch on 01413 063232**

For all the latest titles coming soon, visit
**millsandboon.co.uk/nextmonth**

# MILLS & BOON
## A ROMANCE FOR EVERY READER

- **FREE** delivery direct to your door
- **EXCLUSIVE** offers every month
- **SAVE** up to 25% on pre-paid subscriptions

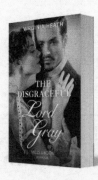  

## SUBSCRIBE AND SAVE

# JOIN THE
# MILLS & BOON
# BOOKCLUB

* **FREE** delivery direct to your door

* **EXCLUSIVE** offers every month

* **EXCITING** rewards programme

50% OFF
YOUR FIRST
PARCEL

# Join today at
### Millsandboon.co.uk/Bookclub

# MILLS & BOON

## THE HEART OF ROMANCE

---

## A ROMANCE FOR EVERY READER

---

### MODERN

Prepare to be swept off your feet by sophisticated, sexy and seductive heroes, in some of the world's most glamourous and romantic locations, where power and passion collide.

### HISTORICAL

Escape with historical heroes from time gone by. Whether your passion is for wicked Regency Rakes, muscled Vikings or rugged Highlanders, awaken the romance of the past.

### MEDICAL

Set your pulse racing with dedicated, delectable doctors in the high-pressure world of medicine, where emotions run high and passion, comfort and love are the best medicine.

### True Love

Celebrate true love with tender stories of heartfelt romance, from the rush of falling in love to the joy a new baby can bring, and a focus on the emotional heart of a relationship.

### Desire

Indulge in secrets and scandal, intense drama and plenty of sizzling hot action with powerful and passionate heroes who have it all: wealth, status, good looks…everything but the right woman.

### HEROES

Experience all the excitement of a gripping thriller, with an intense romance at its heart. Resourceful, true-to-life women and strong, fearless men face danger and desire - a killer combination!

---

To see which titles are coming soon, please visit

## millsandboon.co.uk/nextmonth

# JOIN US ON SOCIAL MEDIA!

Stay up to date with our latest releases, author news and gossip, special offers and discounts, and all the behind-the-scenes action from Mills & Boon...

 @millsandboon

 @millsandboonuk

 facebook.com/millsandboon

 @millsandboonuk

*It might just be true love...*

# GET YOUR ROMANCE FIX!

Get the latest romance news, exclusive author interviews, story extracts and much more!

# MILLS & BOON

## MODERN

# Power and Passion

Prepare to be swept off your feet by sophisticated, sexy and seductive heroes, in some of the world's most glamourous and romantic locations, where power and passion collide.